IN BEDS OF FLOWERS

IN BEDS OF FLOWERS

The Canviant Trilogy
Book One

by Jess Layne

Editing: Copy - Hannah Sol Marie (IG: hannahsolmarie)
Proof - Sam Celentano (IG: samcelentano)
Cover art and chapter headers: Valerie Jain (IG: aethrasticdesigns)

ISBN 979-8-9918960-0-9 (paperback)
ISBN 979-8-9918960-2-3 (hardback)

To Mike, who has been my biggest supporter.
To my friends, who encouraged me to run with this story.
To my family, who should not read past Chapter 32.
And to you, the reader. Cheers.

In Beds of Flowers contains certain content that a reader may wish to avoid. This includes sexual desires and actions, explicit sexual content, kidnapping, suicidal ideation, murder/death, loss of a child, prejudice to disability, verbal and physical abuse, sexual harassment, off-page sexual abuse and assault, and off-page rape.

Your mental health is first, always.

Spice Rack

If you are a fan of spice in your books, please skip this section to avoid spoilers.

For anyone who does not want to read the spice (referring to items which surpass kissing, thoughts of arousal, and the recognition of physical attraction) in this book, please note that the following chapters will contain such scenes: 31, 33, 35, 39

Please know that skipping these scenes may result in a subsequent loss of understanding of the emotional growth and change in certain characters.

PRONUNCIATIONS

Pronunciations listed as spoken in the Ceraschen dialect.

People:

Althea / Thea Cardenia: Al-th-ay-uh / Thea: Th-ay-uh Car-den-ee-ah

    Dion Evestre: Dee-on Eh-ves-tray

    Ciaragen / Ari Vey: Kyā-ruh-gen / Aa-ree Vey

    Atlas Malik: At-lass Mal-eek

    Amedeo Monserre: Ah-meh-day-oh Mon-seh-ř-eh

    Oleander Gervan: Olee-an-der Jeh-r-vah-n

    Melisan: Meh-lis-ah-n

    Oksana Mikhyala: Ox-ah-nah Mik-yah-lah

    Olin Evestre: Ah-lin Eh-ves-tray

    Amahd: Uh-mah-d

    Kya: K-eye-uh

    Bayani: By-ah-nee

    Nuria Bentashi: Noo-ree-uh Ben-tah-shee

Jolie: Jo-lee
Adathan / Adan: A-duh-than / Ad-an
Acacia: Uh-kay-shuh
Javi Kahale: Ha-vee Ka-ha-ley
Talia Kahale: Tah-lee-uh Ka-ha-ley
Sione Natia: See-oh-ney Nah-tee-ah
Deimos: Day-m-oh-s
Ymeda: Ih-meh-da
Evelyn / Evie: Eh-veh-lin / Ee-vee
Emelina: Em-eh-lee-nuh
Tychea: Tie-kay-uh

Places:

* signifies a capital country, or city

Weaschte: Way-ah-sh-teh
    *Cerasche: Seh-rah-sheh
    *Ebenet: Eh-ben-et
    Jasiira: Jah-see-rah
    Vait: Vah-eet
    Dahlih: Dah-lee
    Brenik: Breh-nik
    Heranelle: Heh-rah-ney-eh

Eshelle: Eh-shay-yeh
    Sabrian: Say-bree-ehn
    *Colina: Coh-lee-nah
    *Oschverre: Osh-veh-řeh
    *Matriel: Mah-tree-el
    Dremerre: Dreh-meh-řeh
    Grevosch: Greh-voh-sh
    Estrella: Eh-stray-ah

Planici: Plah-nee-chee
Obala: Oh-bah-lah
Parvata: Par-vah-tah
Ardhavi: Ar-dah-vee

Evredis: Eh-vreh-dees

HIERARCHIES

Eshelle - Fae and faeries

High King : 1
    Queen : 1
    High Lord / High Lady : 1 per country
    Lord / Lady : children of High Lords / Ladies
    *The mortal status of the parents impacts the title of the children. I.E. An heir (of any gender), once parents are deceased, will take their place as High Lord / Lady (Last Name).

    *Lord / Lady may also apply to those with titles granted to them by the High Lords / Ladies of the country in which they reside.

    Duke / Duchess : rank beneath both High Lords / Ladies, and Lords / Ladies.

Weaschte - Humans / Mages (humans with magic)

King / Queen: 1 of each
    Prince / Princess : children of the King / Queen

Duke / Duchess : 1 per country

Lord / Lady : children of a Duke / Duchess

Lord / Lady : may also be granted title by the Duke / Duchess of the country in which they reside

Earl / Countess : beneath both Dukes / Duchesses and Lords / Ladies

MAP

Weaschte:

Cerasche is slightly inland, its closest coast composed of cliffs. Dahlih is northeast of Cerasche.

Evredis Sea:

The ocean that separates Weaschte from Eshelle.

Eshelle:

Oschverre is the northernmost country in Eshelle. Its capital, Matriel, is a fortified city. Sabrian is coastal, and hundreds of miles southwest of Oschverre. Its capital, Colina, is slightly inland.

PLAYLIST

Scotland - The Lumineers (ch1)

Achilles - Gang of Youths (ch2 & 7)

I'll Be Good - Jaymes Young (ch9)

Navigate - Band of Skulls (ch17)

Safe & Sound - Taylor Swift ft. The Civil Wars (ch20)

How Villains Are Made - Madalen Duke (ch22)

Beautiful Day - Joshua Radin ft. Sheryl Crow (ch25 pt. 2)

Never Let Me Go - Florence + The Machine (ch31)

Carry You - Ruelle (ch36)

The Loved Ones - Sanders Bohlke (ch42)

A Storm is Coming - Tommee Profitt & Liv Ash (ch44)

General Vibes:

Daylight - David Kushner

Something in the Orange - Zach Bryan

Girl With One Eye - Florence + The Machine

Shadow - Livingston

Are You With Me - nilu

PROLOGUE
CONTEMPLATION

THEA - AFTER

THE BREEZE OFF THE EVREDIS WINDS THE LOCKS OF MY HAIR through its fingers. They catch the tears that threaten to spill as I contemplate how much my life has changed in less than a week.

Just six days ago, I knew what my future held. I may not have been glad of it, but it was known. Safe. Not easy, but two out of three isn't bad. It's great, actually, in comparison to the zero I have now.

Now, I have no idea what my future has in store. All I can be certain of is that, whatever it is, it will have been by my own doing.

Well, perhaps I can be certain of one more thing–one *person*. Though even that thought feels dangerous, after all that has occurred this past week. Where betrayal and secrets have been just as constant of companions as he has been.

I can feel many eyes on me, while his remain on the sea before us, as mine do. Last week, their stares might have daunted me. Now, I have faced far worse than judgment; that precursor to sentencing. To fate. To destiny, or whatever other bloody word one wishes to call it.

And so, I turn from the sea and its breeze to face the future which my actions have brought me.

PART I

IN BEDS OF FLOWERS

PRETENDERS

1

THE GATHERING

EACH FIBER OF SHREDDED ROPE I PICKED FROM MY SKIN STUNG the circles of raw flesh around my wrists. Focusing on this pain, on the detail of the task, was the only thing keeping me from falling into a panic. I made myself breathe slow, deep breaths in an attempt to convince my nervous system that everything was alright. I couldn't afford to succumb to the lingering fear. Instead, I held onto my tenuous control as tightly as those ropes had been knotted around me.

I wasn't sure that I would be able to pull myself back together if I gave in. At least not with the timeliness necessary.

I squeezed the last fibril between the nails of my forefinger and my thumb, and pulled it out. Nothing but torn skin left on that wrist, I moved on to the other.

No, it wouldn't be helpful at all to allow my terror to overcome my will. I took another deep breath that only slightly shook, continuing to pick the small beige strands out of my stinging flesh. Seven seconds in, seven seconds out. The timing was just another factor to keep my mind occupied.

I tried to convince myself that I was overreacting. I escaped, after all. I had only minor injuries. A split lip and a swollen cheek, already healed. The rope burns on my arms would be next, and there were no marks on my ankles from the ties that bound them. The sleeves of the summer leathers I wore went just past my elbows, leaving my forearms bare to the bite of the ropes. On my legs they extended the full length, the fabric thinning as it went beneath my foot, hooking under my arch. The design kept them in place inside the shoe. Usually, I would have worn my boots, but when I dressed this morning it was so gods-damned hot out–unusually so, for the early summer–that I hadn't been able to force myself to wear them instead of my laced flats.

Those flats were in a garbage bin about six miles away from where I was now. I would've ditched my entire ensemble there, but I'd ventured that a barefoot woman was less noticeable than a completely naked one. After all, the blood had been most visible on the shoes. The splatters on my leathers were practically invisible, no doubt a purposeful design of the fabric, albeit one that I never noticed before today. Two miles from where I'd deserted my shoes, I washed away the blood on my hands, face, and neck in a birdbath. I'd had enough presence of mind to make sure that it was the kind that refilled via waterline, so that the pinkened water would not sit stagnantly, awaiting keen eyes. Such as those which had meant to keep watch of me in that cell.

Those who took me might be dead, just outside of that dark, damp room, but whoever requested that they do so wasn't. Hence, the barefoot woman covered in blood sneaking her way through neighborhoods and wooded areas, taking the most convoluted route possible back to the castle.

It had still been light out, which made it ten times harder to be as invisible as I needed to be in my state. Out of some blessing from Tychea, goddess of fate, I'd come across no one during my escape, despite the balmy weather. Regardless of how many might or might not have known my face, it would have been reported that a bruised woman in all-black had scampered through so many iron-fenced backyards. I didn't need those reports somehow making their way to the male whom those who held me had been waiting for.

Trekking all the way home with nothing covering my feet but a strip of fabric under my arches had left my heels and toes filled with splinters and covered with dirt, grass, and broken leaves. It had been easy enough to brush the surface debris off before striding through the gates, but much harder to keep my gait smooth and steady as I'd walked inside and down the halls. Past the staff who shook their heads and either smirked or sneered at my bare feet.

Typical Althea, they thought. My lack of decorum either charming or disappointing, depending on who you asked. But as those steps had pushed splinters further into my feet, I'd barely been able to bring one corner of my mouth up in acknowledgement to the former. And I'd scarcely hidden my grimaces for those who looked down upon me.

That pain, combined with the burning of my wrists that I'd kept behind my back as I walked, had blended together to form a deep annoyance. That feeling and my will alone kept me from giving in to the panic that had started to creep in the moment I'd passed the castle gates. *Not yet*, I told myself as my body began to recognize its safety and prepared to lose itself in it. I'd kept myself together until I entered my chambers, and closed my doors with a soft *click*.

My trembling knees had faltered, and I'd sunk down the adjacent wall, to the floor. I'd kept my control, even though my body begged me to let go. Instead, I healed my stinging feet. Though my gifts would still be manifesting to their full strength for another year or so, the one that had made itself known the earliest was healing. That magic had warmed my skin as it worked, and seconds later, the splinters lay scattered on the floor, the holes they left behind sealed over, no pain remaining to tell me where they'd once been.

From the time that I'd woken, bound to a chair, and throughout my escape, the adrenaline had been so all-consuming that it left no room for anything else. Everything happened so quickly that I hadn't the opportunity to think about anything but the next step. I might have felt pride in knowing that I'd expertly utilized my training in the midst of an unexpected fight, in which I'd been outnumbered. But there was no room for that emotion among the chaos that otherwise whirled within me.

However valid it might be, I knew my being kidnapped wasn't what truly pushed the panic up against the walls of my heart and mind.

No, the thing that continued to threaten to send me over the edge was the memory of how it had felt to make my first kill. Then my second, and my third. The way the knife had caught on things they didn't put inside training dummies. Or how, when I pulled the blade out, blood didn't just spill cleanly out of the wound, but rather splattered all over me. I could still taste the copper from my second victim, before I realized I should be keeping my mouth closed.

Victim. That's what he was, right? What all of them were. Though I was sure that they'd been prepared to harm me, I still struggled with labeling myself as the only victim of the situation. I, after all, was alive. I was still breathing, my heart still beating; I would see my friends and family again.

A lump rose to my throat, and tears seared my eyes. I

wanted to pretend that those males who took me were loners; that they never took partners, or fathered children. But instead, my mind summoned images of kids and spouses they held with gentle arms.

As I pictured those children and partners forever waiting to be embraced just once more, the tears fell at last. It was a strange thing, grieving for the deaths which were only a result of defending my own life. But another part of me *wanted* to feel this. It was what separated me from them; an offender versus a defender.

That part of me also believed that if I didn't feel this strange form of remorse, then it'd be as though I killed them for spite, not for salvation. If I didn't feel this, then their loved ones would be alone in their grief. I needed to feel this, if only for a moment, because a moment was all I had now. So I gave that to myself before I did what I must.

I closed my eyes and allowed my magic to work its way into my arms. I no longer needed to direct it as much as I once did; particularly when tending to myself, it seemed to find its way on its own. It healed my still raw, though fiber-free, wrists, and warmed my clammy skin. Another fourteen-second breath, and I opened them at the last second of my exhale. No more tears— at least until later. After.

From my place on the floor, I saw a lilac-colored gown hanging on the front of the walnut armoire. Kya, my favorite lady's maid, had likely hung it there for me before she went to the staff living quarters for the evening. All the other staff that were normally on shift—guards, doormen, maids, servers— would be in attendance for the gathering this evening. But my lady's maids wouldn't be needed tonight. For this occasion, the one which would bring a permanent change to my life as I knew it, my mom was to be the one to help me get ready.

And she would be here any minute.

I'd debated, on that harrowing journey back home, whether I should tell her, tell *anyone*, about all that had happened. About all that I'd done, and had been done to me. Through all that crazed thinking, though, I came to the decision: *no*. At least not yet. Perhaps I shouldn't trust my stress-ridden mind to make this decision soundly, but I wasn't likely to be stress-*free* until after the final gathering in two nights. And so that mind conjured my reasons for remaining silent.

I hadn't been truly free at any point in my life. As a result, the rebellious streak that hit when I was fifteen never really went away. I snuck out often; I practiced throwing daggers at night, with no training master to instruct me. I was loud and irreverent whenever judging eyes wouldn't see–a limitation which I already bore too often.

If my mother and father learned of what had happened, all of that *freedom* would go away. I would be watched constantly. There would be no space for irreverence, never mind sneaking out at varying hours of the day. I only had a couple days left of that freedom as it was.

And that was the second reason, in a way. I had wondered if, if I did tell somebody what had happened, these gatherings would be postponed. Part of me had actually considered speaking up as soon as I had the thought. But there were two problems with that: first, how that glee could only make that which I considered the rational part of my mind *irrational*. And second: that "postpone" was the operative word; I would never be free of my duty. Best to get through it now. *Now*, because there was no time left.

I had to lock down the anguish, fear, and despair that remained heavy in my heart and mind. To push them deep within myself, where they wouldn't bubble up when it would be...inconvenient–and any time within the next few hours would be *very* inconvenient. I had to stamp those emotions down into the depths of myself before my mom got here, because if I was still in their throes when she arrived, she'd notice. And, because of the importance of this evening, she wouldn't ask. Both of us would simply *know*, and I couldn't deal with the anxiety that would come with that on top of the rest.

As I took one more fourteen-second breath, I imagined packing those emotions and memories into a chest in my mind. Once they were in, I shut the lid, and locked it. The visualization was done with just two seconds to spare, and it was like my mind was blank. All those thoughts and feelings had been taking up such a significant amount of my headspace these past hours that, without them, my mind felt almost *too* quiet.

I sighed, filling the silence with the sound of it, and finally stood from my place on the floor. I walked on only slightly shaking legs to the vanity set between two windows on the other side of my bedchamber. I plopped down on the emerald velvet cushioned stool before it, and faced the oblong mirror framed in intricately wrought gold.

My hair was in disarray, half of the black locks pulled back into what was once a full braid, the other half strewn about my face and shoulders. My face was wan, the usual warm beige tone seeming leeched, and even the freckles across my cheeks and nose appeared dull. The only color came in the form of the post-cry pink splotches on my skin.

I allowed my magic to tend to that inflammation, which helped. I undid the rest of my hair from its plait, and ran a brush through it, trying to quickly get all the knots out. Another look in the mirror showed smoother-looking hair, a slightly pale complexion, and–damn. Lines around my wrists that were just a bit lighter in color than the skin around them. Hopefully only noticeable to my eyes because I knew to look for them.

I picked up the sound of heels clicking down the hallway

towards my door. I remained at my vanity, lowering and straightening my shoulders, and fixing my expression into a mask of calm contemplation. I lifted my brush back to my hair, pulling it through the strands as though I hadn't just done so. A few seconds later, there was a knock on my door; two raps, quick and quiet.

"Yes?" I called softly, hoping my tone sounded as I meant it to–peaceful, if a little excited, with no concerns on my mind at all. The doors opened, and I saw in the reflection in the mirror that my mom stood at the threshold, a small smile on her gently lined face.

"Nearly ready, Aly?" she asked as she entered, using the nickname only my family and closest friends called me. Her brows raised once she turned from closing the door, her blue eyes taking in my utter lack of ornamentation. Well, with the exception of the small amethyst stud that I never took out of my left ear, pierced through a small point at the top. When I was twelve, believing that I was no longer little and should not be treated as such, I'd taken a needle to that point one night, and stuck the stud through the hole I'd created.

I fiddled with that earring absentmindedly now. As my mom looked at me from her place in the doorway, her head tilted. I knew just from the angle of her neck that she could tell that something was off. I cursed internally, but gave her a sheepish smile.

"I could be, with a little help." A grin of her own was her only response, though her blue eyes remained a bit wary as she walked over to me, scanning me from head to toe.

I put my brush back on the vanity, and tried not to stare at my wrists. Hoping that the difference in skin tone was too small a detail for even her to notice, I stood and faced her, my arms at my sides. I closed my eyes, not wanting her to somehow see the shadows in them. I'd done so in the past when she'd gotten me ready for other occasions, so it was nothing out of the ordinary. Indeed, she posed no questions to me as she worked her magic. Warmth touched my face, tickled my earlobes, brushed my hips. Knowing it was done, I opened my eyes, and quarter-turned towards the large mirror that sat in the corner of my bedroom.

My mom came to stand behind me, and adjusted my hair, which now hung in large curls to my waist. She twisted the thin band of gold that sat just above my brow so that the small point in the circlet was centered. My lids were dusted with a shade of lavender that made the green of my eyes even brighter, my cheeks were glowing and pink, my lips stained as though I just ate blackberries. The evening sunshine streaming through the windows cast a glow on my newly iridescent skin.

The pristine gown that had been hanging on the armoire now covered me in place of my bloody leathers. The bodice was fitted, the gossamer fabric cowled straight across my shoulders, into sleeves that didn't stop at my wrists, but rather continued in a point on the back of my hands, looping around my middle fingers. Conveniently, this covered the damning new skin, and that took some of the tension out of my neck. When I looked at my mom's reflection, her summer sky eyes were filled with what she called her *my daughter is my sunshine* look.

"Beautiful," she said. I turned from the mirror to smile at her, and she touched my cheek in a gentle caress before dropping her hand. "How are you feeling?" she asked, the question innocent enough considering the gathering we were holding, and about to attend. But I knew that she chose her words with care; even with no time to listen, she would keep our guests waiting to do so.

"As ready as I'll ever be," I responded, shrugging with more nonchalance than I felt. She smirked, but the concern was still there in her eyes. Even so, she held her arm out for me, and I linked my own through it. As we walked to the chamber doors, she waved a hand, and they opened before us: a small magic that most Mages could do.

We strode down the hallway, the silence between us strained as we made our way towards the enormous room where tonight's gathering was to be held. The anxiety I'd known would come if this happened was compounded as I heard the many voices emitting from the Hall. Otherwise, the only sounds were our heels clicking down the white marble floors. But our steps were swift, and we reached the last hallway before either of us could break.

My father stood at the end of it, a few feet from the doors we would walk through in a moment. A grand golden crown sat on his blond head, and he was speaking with the doorman, Noah. As he heard us approach, he excused himself from the conversation before turning to us. Brown eyes met mine, and he grinned, inclining his head, both of which I returned.

Then his gaze slid to my mom, and his smile widened as we reached his side. Wordlessly, he bowed low to his wife. She dropped into a curtsey before him, which I mimicked. From behind his back he pulled out her crown, and placed it gently on the brunette-and-white curls she had pulled into a chignon, before pressing his lips to her cheek. The skin beneath that kiss flushed pink, and as I looked at the color, I could only wish that whoever I was determined to spend my life with made me feel like that after over twenty-seven years of marriage.

"It seems that even after nearly twenty-one years, our daughter still doesn't have the ability to get ready on time," my dad said, one brow lifted as he looked at me, a teasing edge in his gaze.

"Indeed," my mom agreed. "Not sure where she gets it from, seeing as both you and I were ready an hour ago." She squeezed my hand before stepping away to stand beside my father.

I gaped at them, even as some relief at the normalcy settled in my chest. "Well, I *would* have been ready if you thought training leathers were appropriate court attire." However invisibly bloody they might have been...

"I have a feeling you would have found a way to be late regardless," my mom countered, humor sparkling in her eyes.

"Though the looks on the courtiers faces would have been a sight to see," my dad added with a barely concealed grin. My mom shrugged, acknowledging that, and then the Queen straightened her shoulders. As one, the three of us turned to the solid walnut doors, their golden handles gleaming in the window-lit hallway. Noting our readiness, Noah knocked on the doors with three quick raps, then stepped aside as those doors were pulled open from the inside to reveal the room beyond, and the people within.

My least favorite doorman, Artur, announced, "Their Majesties Aron and Lydia Cardenia, King and Queen of all Weaschte, and their daughter, Her Highness Princess Althea Maria Cardenia."

The Hall–formally known as the Great Hall, but who had time for all that–stretched out before us. The apex of the domed ceiling was made of glass, and through it now streamed the deep golden light of sunset. Around that glass was a painting, artwork which I believed was too frequently ignored, despite its intricacy.

Such color and beauty. Soft blushes and blues around the edges, starting at the crown molding, blended together in a heavenly display of clouds. The colors grew more saturated, and more variable, as the painting continued on to the center, where it outlined the domed glass in the ceiling in brilliant lavenders, oranges, and deep blues. As frequently happened in the evenings, those colors almost exactly matched the sunset now showing through the glass.

I liked to imagine that whoever painted it managed to get a mattress to balance on the top of the ladder they surely had to use. The only other thing I could imagine was the neck pain that person must have had for the rest of their life due to looking up for all those hours.

White marble pillars lined a seven-foot wide pathway to the center of the Hall before fanning out in bilateral waves, supporting the frame of the circularly structured ceiling. Great crystal chandeliers of forever-burn candles–which would not sputter out until the magic in them was extinguished–hung at varying heights. In the center of the room was an empty wooden floor for dancing, much better than the slippery marble that surrounded it. And at the end of that space was a dais, where two thrones and four chairs sat. But between that dais, and us, were our guests.

My parents walked forward, and I fell into step behind them. As we entered, all those in the room either bowed or curtsied, and heat flooded my cheeks as I felt so many eyes rest on me. I'd long been accustomed to being watched, but tonight felt different. Tonight was about me, and they all knew it–and they were not being shy about it.

My heart hammered as we continued, and I felt dozens of stares on my back. Whereas usually they watched me with interest, perhaps a bit of curiosity, or attraction, tonight their gazes felt...*hungry*. Tonight, their eyes and their hearts were driven by the possibility of the shift in power that I could provide for them after these gatherings ended.

Will alone kept my hands from shaking as we turned to face them atop the dais. Their bodies remained bowed, but their faces were not. Wolves and sheep alike stared up at me, and I knew then that the dangers of the day had not ended when I killed those Fae males.

2

FALSE INDIFFERENCE

DION - 21 YEARS EARLIER

IF I HAD TO SPEND ONE MORE MOMENT LISTENING TO THIS simpering fool, I was going to need to find a quick way to a long rope.

The female before me was attractive, and, based on the gleam in her eyes and the flush across her face and chest, she thought the same of me. I'd learned at a young age that females enjoyed what I often dismissed. Whether it was the dark hair and broad build I got from my father, or the tan skin and hazel eyes I got from my mother, I didn't care to know.

To be perfectly honest, I had never cared whether they–*they* being the dozens of citizens I met each day–were good-looking or not either. A plain face was, actually, more welcome. They, at least, didn't conjure the image of the gravestone burned into my memory.

In any case, the wine that was never far from my desk helped as I met with every one of them.

Being charged with taking these supplicants off of my king's shoulders was a privilege. I told myself that every time I accidentally contemplated the tediousness and monotony of my life. That he trusted me enough to represent him in these matters–to conduct myself with the dignity and grace a leader should have–was an honor not many could say they'd attained.

Really, I knew it was just because he didn't feel like doing it, and he knew that I wouldn't, or couldn't, refuse him. Whenever that knowledge reared its ugly head, I would shove it down into the corner of my soul for safe keeping. When I left the world I knew for the Void, it would be there with the rest of my sinful deeds and thoughts.

The female in front of me was the thirty-fourth person I'd had to speak with so far this evening. By the tenth, I'd started drinking the wine kept under my desk. By the twentieth, I'd stopped listening to anything any of them said. And by the thirtieth, I'd stopped speaking to them, as my words had become slurred. Still, they blathered on, needing only a nod from me to continue the endless spew of complaints or hardships. If they smiled, I smiled. If they cried, I arranged my face into what I hoped was a remorseful and sympathetic expression. And each time, when they finally finished talking, I would say the same thing:

"Thank you for bringing this matter to my attention. I will present it to the High King immediately, and we will work to find a solution."

I'd said the line so many times over the years that I didn't even need to be sober to speak it without slurring or stuttering. Granted, the sincerity in it had gone from genuine to forced in that time frame as well. It was bound to happen, as each time I did bring a matter to the king, I was either falsely assured that it would be looked into, or simply ignored.

Thus: a complacent drunkard, and master of horse shit. Otherwise known as–

"Lord Dion?" the female asked, leaning forward slightly.

I cursed myself internally, forcing my gaze and mind to focus on her. At some point, my eyes had left her face, and stared instead at the desk in front of me. She must have finished her statement, and I was too preoccupied to notice.

I pasted an apologetic half-smile on my face, and said, "Apologies, miss. I fear I became absorbed in thinking of solutions to your concerns, and neglected to hear your last sentence or two in my haste to provide an answer to you," I lied, as smooth and elegant as any courtier should be, even a drunk one. I managed to keep my voice steady and asked, "Would you be so kind as to repeat just those last few words?" I leaned towards her and folded my hands on the desk, holding her gaze in a way that made most women flustered.

Indeed, she glanced away quickly, her cheeks flushing, and I ignored the gravestone flashing in my mind's eye. The second it took her to regain her composure was long enough for me to relax my jaw, and store the image for my usual nightmares. Then she looked back up at me through her lashes, and said, "I was only saying, if you could send word to me when the issue has been addressed, I would greatly appreciate it." Her eyes glittered, and she left her lips slightly parted.

Once, that look might have had me asking her if she would like to stay. Offering a cup of wine, and telling her that I could take her to parts of this city that she'd never seen before. Once, I would have been filled with a sense of satisfaction that one look could make this female so enamored. Now, I could barely stand to see the lust building in her gaze without wanting to be sick.

"Of course, miss. Thank you for bringing this matter to my

attention. I will present it to the High King immediately, and we will work to find a solution."

And maybe it was the wine, or maybe it was having to say that Void-damned sentence another time, but after the female smiled and left, I actually did get sick into a vase that sat behind my desk.

⇹

Later that evening, I sat at a long, black marble table in my usual spot halfway down, with no one beside me. At one end of the table sat the king, the queen at the other. Across from me was Lord Olin, my twin brother, and the counterpart to my services to the crown. Where I was supposed to be there for the people, listen to them, and at least pretend to help them, Olin was the one who...*disposed* of them. Not all of them; just the ones who came to *'complain'* too frequently. It wasn't information that I gathered for him, but he learned it nonetheless.

He would also attend to anyone who *stopped* coming to me about their king or his realm, but rather turned to their friends, or family. Because why not silence people for continuing to voice problems that were never resolved, or for speaking their frustrations to those they believed they could trust? That might have been the saddest part; that these people hoped, were failed, and then punished for *our* failing.

Might have, but couldn't be. Nothing could be sad, or frustrating, or upsetting, if you stopped caring.

That was the trick, I learned. When I cared, that was when I went to bed each night searching for solutions, keeping myself awake to figure out ways to help, only to be told that none of them would be done. When I cared, that was when I was shown by the small number of people around me why that was a mistake. So, I didn't–care, that was. Instead, I drank, kept none but my own company, and counted the days of my life as if that would make the amount of them remaining any fewer. As if it would make those days any less devoid of meaning.

The only sound in the dining room was the scraping of knives on plates, soft chewing, and the occasional sigh from the queen. Usually, by the third sigh, the king would ask her what was bothering her. She was now on her fifth, and he only seemed more irritated with each one. Which could only mean that they both knew that the issue had to do with him. No doubt an argument that occurred before dinner.

I was sure I'd hear the specifics from someone by the end of the night; I was honestly surprised that I hadn't already. Whispers flew around this castle faster than an arrow from a bow. I could thank my utter lack of a social life, and any interest in one, for the absence of whispers about me. The only words that were spoken of me were usually along the lines of *grumpy* and *asshole*. And, I'd gotten used to them long ago.

The queen sighed again, and again the king ignored her. Clearly, he would not be the one to end the childish behavior—and I couldn't help but be, however horribly, glad that they hadn't had any luck conceiving when they tried in the past. I feared that otherwise, I would have never lived another day without putting a stop to whining, crying, or general displeasure. As I was about to do now. As if that wasn't already my full-time job.

I cleared my throat. "My Queen, I fear that either myself or Lord Olin have upset you in some way. How ever can I remedy your discontent?" I asked, eyeing her with a sincerity and consideration that I didn't feel. Olin grimaced at me, and, by the look in his eyes, was cursing me for bringing him into the conversation. I had to fight the smirk I wanted to throw back at him.

Melisan looked at me and blinked, her cheeks flushing in

both embarrassment and attraction, the latter as usual with her. I'd never reciprocated past a kindly-meant smile, and she never acted on it. In my darkest moments, I wished she would, if only because I knew the king would kill me for it.

She cleared her throat lightly, tucking her auburn hair behind an arched ear, and said, "Lord Dion, you have done nothing of the sort. I apologize for making you think as such. No, I simply have many thoughts on my mind, and I'm afraid I wasn't able to keep as quiet about them as I'd have liked."

Bullshit. When she wanted to be quiet, she could be. And when she wanted the world to know her mind, she could do that, too. But the dining table was not the place to air her and her husband's business. Not because she couldn't–she had done so in the past, to the amusement of Olin and the wait staff. But because to speak ill of him before us was unbecoming of his queen and wife. To be fair to her, that she had only lost control enough to confront him at the table twice over the decades was a testament to her respect for her marriage, and her husband. Especially knowing how inattentive her husband was to his people–

I stopped myself before I could continue on how that thought would relate to her.

Everyone knew that, while they had a happy marriage on the outside, there was something festering on the inside. It was well-known that Oleander, High King of the Fae, had loved another before the queen–Oksana, her name had been. Supposedly a great beauty, albeit with little power to be spoken of. One would think that would make her a bad match for the king, but it was obvious to me that he wanted his wife to be meek; subservient to him.

Melisan was certainly that. Kind, and lovely, but with scant power to make her a threat to his masculinity. It made sense for a small male to believe a female's own possession of power could diminish his own. Whatever was claimed to have changed about him over the decades between Oksana, and Melisan, clearly that had not.

It was the common belief that after Oksana ended her relationship with him, she was killed. Not from any jealousy on Melisan's part, as the pair had gotten together twenty years after the king's so-called heartbreak. After knowing him these past eighty-odd years, I believed Oleander killed her from spite. Of course, the general population couldn't be allowed to think that.

The story was that Oksana had known international secrets that would have been disastrous if shared outside court. I always held to the belief that it wasn't *international* secrets, but rather secrets about *him*. Ones which only Melisan, Olin, and myself were privy to now.

But that couldn't be true about the sovereign of Eshelle. No, no. It had broken his tender heart to take her life. So much so that, even one hundred years later, he still neglected his realm. And his wife.

After all, here I was, playing marriage counselor for him.

Now that I'd brought to the queen's attention that she wasn't being as docile as she perhaps should have been in the presence of others–people who could bring whatever awkwardness from this meal to listening ears–at least she would stop with the damned sighing.

"Well, Your Grace, please know," I started with my gaze on her. Oleander's reasoning for choosing her out of all those presented to him years ago was apparent. Not that the king was an unattractive male–even if he'd been born a peasant and a bastard, he would have had no trouble courting females. It was just that what I knew of his personality, and what I knew of hers, made their outward appearances starkly different.

Regardless, as I continued my sentence, I moved my eyes

towards the king, "that I am always grateful to be invited to dine with the High King and yourself." Oleander's eyes met mine, and while I wouldn't say there was kindness in them, there was enough to tell me that I had done my duty. I nodded shallowly to him, which he returned with a slight lowering of his eyes before turning them to the queen. I took the opportunity to glance at Olin, who was now grinding his teeth as he stared at me. He knew it was no accident that I had brought attention to him to ask who had offended Melisan, and left him out when offering thanks for the meal and the company.

I had to admit, pissing him off was one of the few joys I had, or allowed myself these days. When we were young, our mother went to lengths to help us get along. Whether it was forced proximity, friendship under the guise of mutual enjoyment of childish things, or the use of positive and negative reinforcement. Nothing worked. Not because we were stubborn–at least, not *completely* because of that.

Rather, it was much more so because of something I'd realized when we were seven, and had stuck ever since: Olin was an ass. And there was nothing that anybody could do to make him decent enough to be friendly with.

After all, how decent could a person be if their power was torment? As Olin and I had grown, I found my grounding through loyalty. And while a fat lot of good that was doing me now, I was still owning that.

Meanwhile, Olin had found his purpose in pain. Causing it, increasing it, reveling in it. I wasn't sure if he was a complete psychopath, or just evil. I supposed the verbiage mattered little, when he killed nearly as often as he slept.

The rest of the meal passed without incident, or any more sighing. Only at the end did the king speak, to remind me and Olin of our individual meetings tomorrow morning. He held his arm out to the queen, bowing his head as he only ever did for her. And, Void take me, the female blushed at the small symbols of service. After nearly an entire dinner spent trying to get her husband to pay attention to her, pink flooded the apples of her cheeks as she smiled softly, taking his arm.

It used to touch me that even after arguments, the pair could be found grinning at each other, holding hands, or just looking at one another without a trace of anger. Now, I could never see it as anything but an act.

I knew there was a defining moment that had made me this way. An event that caused me to detach myself from my life, and the people in it; passing, or permanent. Something that made me this person who couldn't listen to complaints from his people without getting obliterated with drink. Who couldn't address someone with sincere concern or care. Who couldn't stand the sight of love–even if it was fake.

But there were also years of individual moments that had torn at me, and made me a bit less each time, until *that* day, when I was him; he was me. And my hatred for that person, for myself, only grew the longer that I existed. Possibly the worst I felt, though, was when I thought about changing. Because it was too late for all that. I didn't exist in a world where that could happen. And the work that it would take if I did would probably only wreck me more. And so, I figured I would stay this way for the rest of my life.

Forever.

3

MAGIC & MASKS

My parents and I sat in our places on the dais. They, of course, occupied the two thrones in the center. I was in a slightly less ornate chair beside my mother. The other three seats were identical to mine, but unoccupied; waiting for my siblings, who would arrive tomorrow. These gatherings were a bit dull without them here to join me in quietly making fun of the snooty lords, and generally driving our parents up the wall together. But, being the last unwed sibling, I was the only one who still lived at home with mom and dad.

Though Nik, my oldest brother, would be moving back home soon. Since he was the heir, eventually this place, and this kingdom, would be his. But, being the good man our parents raised him to be, he'd granted his wife, Izabel, her wish to live near her family in Jasiira for the first five years of their marriage. An amount of time that our mother had thoroughly objected to, but that even she had to agree was fair, considering they would have the rest of their lives to reside here. It tortured her, though, to have her very first grandchildren live so far away.

Then there was Iris, the second oldest, and my only sister. She married three years ago, and had not made the same bargain with her husband as Izabel had with Nik. They did, however, only live a week's travel away, in northern Vait. They had a two-year-old named Cleo, who had everyone she'd ever met wrapped around her incredibly little finger. Not a surprise, considering her mother was just a grown version of that. Beautiful, sweet, and talented–things I'd hated her for, until one undefined day when we started bonding instead of fighting.

Lastly, Ben, still older than me, but only by just over a year. Ben wed Lorraine, one of my best friends, a couple of months ago. He'd taken her away to live outside Ebenet–Cerasche's capital city, and home to our castle–therefore not only removing himself, but her from my day-to-day life. He was still not forgiven. He pointed out that Lorraine was stuck with me as a sister now, too. "So, you're welcome," he'd say whenever the topic came up. In response, I told him that fact didn't counteract his crime, right before I stuck my tongue out at him.

Luckily, all of them–my siblings, their spouses, and their children–would be here tomorrow. The thought made my heart flutter, and my lips pulled up slightly at the corners. It'd been over a month since I'd seen any of them, and nearly six since I last saw Nik and his family.

Through my wandering thoughts, I picked up the sound of my name being whispered. An inconspicuous glance towards my parents showed me that they'd turned slightly in their thrones, speaking quietly. About me. My mother's back was to me, but it was with her voice that I heard my name. From the concerned set of my father's brow, and the way he met my glance, I knew that she was telling him about my upset from earlier–regardless of how little she knew about it.

But, for the heartbeat that my eyes were on them, my father held my gaze. In my periphery, I saw him shake his head. Whether that meant the topic wasn't to be broached now, or not ever, I couldn't be sure. But, I did know that not once in my nearly twenty-one years had my mother been able to mind her business, and I didn't expect her to start today.

Not for the first time, I thanked the gods that mind-reading wasn't on her roster of gifts. Still incredibly powerful, hence her match with my father, who was heir to the crown of Weaschte, and a skilled verdanti–a gift which allowed its bearer to discern truth from lies. For my mother, the ability to shift physical appearance wasn't only for the parlor trick of changing clothes and adding makeup to a bare face in an instant. If she wished to, she could shift here and now to look exactly like me. Just as my first gift had been healing, hers had been shifting.

As Mages, we needed only our hands, minds, and hearts to guide our magic. With our hands, it could be physically directed, particularly if one's gift was controlled with touch. But strength of mind, and presence of heart–that vital part which told us how to use our magic for good– were the real indicators of a powerful Mage. I couldn't yet heal a person without placing my hands on them, and when I was young I could only heal small injuries. Now, as long as my hands made contact with a person, I could heal skin and muscle; bone and nerves.

It wasn't unusual for a child's gifts to vary so greatly from the parents'. We'd known since our beginning that magic was given by the gods. No human questioned why they gifted what they did–or didn't.

Not all humans had magic. My sister did, but Lorraine didn't; nor did the last of our triad of insanity and girlhood, Hanna. In fact, Mages, the wielders of magic, were the minority.

My great-grandparents had none of it in their blood, but delivered a son that did. And, even with both of my parents being gifted with magic, only Iris and myself had any, while Nik and Ben were born without.

As was the case with many throughout the continent. It had enabled a people who might have otherwise oppressed one another, to instead work together to establish equitability for all citizens. Nobody wanted to see their brother, or daughter, or grandfather subjugated, and so most strived to provide not only safety, but prosperity to all peoples. Personal interest, I realized long ago, was key to ensuring peace.

My dad stood from his throne, interrupting the thoughts running away from me–something my parents said happened much too often–and I quickly focused my gaze on him. Posture was drilled into me as soon as I was old enough to understand the words *chin up*, so even during daydreams I sat up straight. I lifted my chin just a bit higher, though, as my dad stepped forward on the dais, and addressed the court.

"Thank you all for coming this evening," he said as the crowd hushed, his deep voice echoing slightly in the domed space. As I looked out at the faces, all turned towards him, I recognized some.

Lord Boseman and his Lady, whom I could never remember the first names of, to my mother's significant distress. A general who'd been at our court for a few days now named Ciaragen Vey. Duchess Hanna Mayfeld, as gorgeous and bright as a field of dahlias, and her husband, Duke Gregor Mayfeld–whom I'd told on their wedding day not to hurt her or I'd cut off his member with a butter knife. They both smiled at me as my eyes landed on them, and I forced my responding grin to be demure, my teeth hidden behind my lips.

"You all know why we are gathered today," my father continued. "On the day of Princess Althea's twenty-first birthday, she shall choose a suitor from those of you gathered here tonight. That suitor will have the honor to continue his courtship of her until her twenty-second birthday."

A round of applause from the court at that, celebrating this tradition. When a human born with magic turned twenty-two, their gifts reached a sort of accumulation point that we referred to as their Apotheos. After that time, no additional gifts were gained. One could only continue to increase skill in whatever magic they already had.

Because of this, the royal family always, since the time it was recorded, required the magic-gifted women to have a husband by that age. It was determined that would be the only possible way to keep her safe, and within her primary responsibilities of continuing the family line. And, in return for heirs, the man would be responsible for her protection–since clearly she was weaker and frightened and girlish and needed him, *even though* they reached their Apotheos at the same time. I stopped myself from sucking on a tooth, and forced my expression back into one of serenity.

I was raised to take part in this custom; grew up knowing it to be my fate. Knew it, and accepted it as best I could, because I cared about my family and our people more than I dreaded an arranged marriage. So, as the familiar feeling that I had refused to acknowledge in the weeks leading up to today curled in my gut once again, I ignored it.

"This tradition has been in place for generations, and carried on with our three children before." Yes, my mother and father, at least, had included the male heirs in this tradition as well–the first in royal history to do so. I never could decide if I was happy about that equality, or sad that my brothers had to do it, too.

"It will now hold true with our fourth and final child: Althea Maria Cardenia, Princess of Weaschte." My father turned halfway and gestured grandly to me. I took my cue to stand and step forward, heart pounding as the crowd applauded politely.

I employed that impeccably trained posture, keeping my shoulders back, and my chin up, and stared down the center of the room, meeting no one's eyes. Until I found a familiar face towards the back of the Hall, holding a tray of champagne. He smiled at me, and I found myself able to take a steadying breath.

My father went on, "Just as it was with Prince Nikolas, Princess Iris, and Prince Benjamin, the decision on who will have the *privilege* of marrying her is hers, and hers alone." Then he stepped back, allowing me to take the foreground. I gave him a warm smile, and kept the happy tilt to my lips as I faced the crowd, and began.

"My choice will be made by the evening of my birthday celebration." All of my rehearsals seemed to have paid off, the words coming to my lips with little thought. "As your King has said, tonight will be an opportunity for all of us. If you are chosen, you will spend tomorrow and the following day here at the castle. On the former, the princes and princess will be here to meet each of you and give me their thoughts. On the latter, my decision will be made.

"But, before any of that, I need some food in my stomach, or else I fear I would be terrible company indeed." A scattered laugh from the crowd at that, though mostly from the women present. The men, it seemed, had become a bit nervous. *Oh no*, I thought sarcastically.

My mom and dad came to stand on either side of me, and Nina, our head chef, took her cue to work her magic. In a blink, the tables throughout the Hall filled with platters of food. A long table appeared a few feet from the dais, set with ivory linen, bouquets of roses ranging in color from sunset orange to blush pink, and a pale blue runner beneath them all. Full dishes of meats, vegetables, potatoes, and more scattered across its length, golden chargers gleaming under white plates.

The smells hit me, and I realized then that I hadn't eaten since breakfast, nearly twelve hours ago. My stomach rumbled so loudly that my parents heard it, causing my dad to clamp his lips shut to keep from smiling. My mom turned her head towards me, laughter in her eyes. She frequently said that she didn't know how my *"scattered brain"* could forget something as primal as the need to eat.

I only smirked back at them, letting them believe what they would of the cause behind my noisy stomach. Then, we descended the three steps to the main floor, and servers in white coats pulled out our chairs for us.

We didn't immediately sit. Instead, we stood before our chairs, everyone gathered doing the same in front of theirs. My mom took both my dad's and my hands, her palms warm and soft. Everyone in the room joined hands as well, and as one we closed our eyes, and my father began tonight's prayer:

"Gods, hear our thanks for the food before us, and for the people around us. We thank Kami for our feast, Hestian for our friends and family gathered. We thank Tychea for keeping war from our lands for another year. By your will, we have been blessed, and by your will we remain so."

Once he finished, a collective inhale sounded through the room, everyone opening their eyes as they exhaled. The breath was our way of accepting blessings; by breathing in after the prayer, one took them into themselves, and by opening one's eyes as they breathed out, one saw clearly what they were already blessed with.

And maybe it was the events of today, or maybe it was just because I needed to feel a bit lighter, but I felt the gods' presence even more heavily than usual upon that breath. I allowed the feeling to settle in my chest, granting it the ability to bring me peace, however temporary. I promised myself then that I wouldn't think of the events from earlier until I was once again alone, and could sort through what occurred and what was said while I was held captive.

Holding tight to that feeling of peace, I looked around the Hall as everyone sat down. There was a large bar area in the far right corner, temporarily erected for feasts and gatherings. Pristine crystal tumblers and flutes gleamed on shelves behind the barkeeps, and bottles of liquors ranging in color from clear to deep amber rested within and atop a grand credenza beneath the shelves. As the drinks were made, and poured, they were magically transported to the guests who ordered them.

In another corner were seven musicians. The sound of string and wind instruments floated to me, played softly enough for conversation to be conducted during the meal. As I listened to them, humming along to the tune, I saw a pair of dark, familiar hands plate a little bit of everything on the table for me. When the plate was full enough that only the rim was visible, he set it down in front of me, and I looked up.

"Thank you, Atlas," I said to him with a smile, having to crane my neck a bit to look him in the eye. Atlas joined our staff only a month ago, but had made himself well-known on his first day, when he spilled a bowl of soup onto my lap. Nina, the head chef, nearly fired him on the spot, but I'd talked her down with little difficulty.

Atlas had been my assigned server ever since. "If you're going to pour things on people," Nina had said, "it may as well be one that doesn't mind."

"You're welcome, Princess," Atlas responded now, his baritone voice kind, giving me a small smile in return. As his pretty gray eyes held mine for a bit longer than was considered proper, I shoved down the jolt of excitement I felt in response.

I'd thought the sensation would dissipate with familiarity. Surely the attraction was based off his novelty, and not his stormcloud eyes, genuine smile, and strong jaw, right?

But after over four weeks, three meals per day, plus the times I'd *conveniently* run into him grabbing a midday, or midnight snack, I couldn't help but be annoyed at my body's lack of understanding what my mind already knew. *Never going to happen.* Still, I had to force myself to drop my eyes first, and ignored the respectfully deep bow I saw him give me from the corner of my eye. *Never.*

Shaking my head, and swallowing the feeling that one word sent through my gut, I dug in, forcing the sensation down with the bite. I managed to convince myself as I did so that I had no concerns other than how I could fit all of the food into my mouth at once, and still have anyone willing to be my suitor by the end of the meal.

However, that same hunger had me forgetting the decorum so painstakingly trained into me over the years. Despite my best attempt at composure, I was apparently not as ladylike as I should be, as my mother looked over at me now, brows raised at my stuffed cheeks.

Her lips were pressed together to keep from laughing, but there was a look in her eyes that also told me that the side of her that's Queen didn't approve. Not because of the amount I was eating–no, she had personally dismissed a handful of master chefs over the years who suggested a princess should not eat as I do. She gave me this look now because of how my appearance, not my appetite, might be perceived by possible suitors. Though I didn't really care what they thought, I cared what *she* thought, and so my cheeks heated as she held my gaze with the gentleness of a mother, but the seriousness of a queen.

"You know, Nina made one of your favorite desserts for tonight," she said, instead of reprimanding me on the spot. "I'd hate to see you suffer to not eat it because you have no room remaining."

Recognizing that she'd done her part to regulate the discussion, I did her the respect of swallowing before speaking, needing water to get the bite down without choking. Once my mouth was clear I said, "There is always room for dessert. In fact, anatomists have discovered a second, little stomach, that only accepts foods with ridiculous amounts of sugar."

"Have they now?" Her blue eyes lit with amusement. "I wonder if you could also explain to me how that second, little stomach is going to cope with being filled up, when combined with dancing with courtiers?"

"Ah, yes. They've not quite determined that, but for the sake of research, I think I shall conduct that experiment for them tonight," I responded, and promptly shoved a forkful of potatoes into my mouth.

4

PARLOUS

"I've decided to promote you," Oleander said.

I looked up from the documents I was reviewing, wondering if I heard him correctly. We were sitting at the absurdly large mahogany desk within his personal quarters, working. Of course, the work for me was to sit in the most uncomfortable chair ever made, and read the most boring documents ever written, until my eyes fell out of their sockets.

I supposed the work for him was to watch me do these things, while *also* not completely finishing the bottle of wine we were '*sharing*'. Multitasking at its finest.

My own glass remained empty after its single fill at the start of our meeting. I didn't dare reach across the desk to take the bottle from its place beside the king. No matter how much reading these papers, with their details of plans and pain, made me crave the sweetness of grapes and oblivion.

"Majesty?" I asked, my brow furrowing.

"I want to promote you," he repeated, and, though his words were slightly slurred, his pale eyes remained steady.

I set down the documents, and straightened in my terrible chair. My long-slumbering emotions of hope and excitement began to rouse, sniffing the air around the proposition. I stamped them out immediately, shoving them back into their imagined caves where they'd stayed and starved for the past several decades. Not yet.

Not ever, I reminded myself.

I cleared my throat, and leaned forward in the chair. "Your Majesty, I am honored. How can I serve you in this new position?" I asked, nauseating myself with the groveling.

Though that nausea might also be a result of knowing that, regardless of any monstrosities he might ask of me, I would have to accept. Such was the plight of a male with nowhere else to go.

The king began, "Some time ago, one of the citizens that Olin and I assisted–" I nearly sneered. As if any of the nation's people that came to us had ever been *assisted*. "–was of *High Lord* Amedeo Monserre's household. A bald male...the supplicant, not Amedeo. Though his looks surely can't be spoken for...Anyway, the male became a bit of a nuisance. One of the females who came to you yesterday was from that blasted place as well, and has apparently been running her mouth throughout the city. But, Lord Olin and myself believe that it would be too conspicuous to...attend to her as we did with the others."

Of course. There was no decency, or actual concern involved at all. Just self-interest, and the desire to remain *inconspicuous*. Possibly mixed with a dash of still caring what the people thought of their current sovereigns. Or, at least caring what those who backed them thought.

I didn't ask what my role would be. I was sure he would

explain it when he was finished with his drunken ramble, and painting over atrocities with pretty words.

"Lord Amedeo is not a great supporter of my reign." *To say the least*, I thought. Amedeo walked the line of treachery and the–ever dwindling–freedom of expression with expert skill. But, I didn't fail to note how the king ignored his proper title, and had mocked it before.

"He's made no secret of it," Oleander continued, "and I'm sure he would be just as plain in his opinion of what may have happened to his people, whoever they were. Certainly dressed like commoners."

What level of amateurity were they acting with to not ascertain someone's rank before ensuring their everlasting silence? These were the actions of males who believed that they were beyond reproach. And I had to recognize that they were right. After all, who could speak openly against them without fearing for their family's safety? Who had not come forward persistently enough to create a spark of change, only to be snuffed out before the first flame?

But the king was apparently waiting for a response to his blathering, those pale eyes glassy in his inebriation. So, shoving all of that knowledge aside, I asked, "If I may, Majesty. Why not...depose the High Lord?" hating the words even as I said them. Though I'd never met Amedeo, or his wife, I heard that they were kind, generous, and fiercely protective of their people. Just a few of the reasons why they were such a threat to the man before me, who was none of those things. The only thing he was, was king. And though the fact that he had no redeeming qualities to speak of made me resent my very existence with each day spent in his service, it didn't make that any less true.

The king gave me a look dripping with disdain. "As I've said, he has made his contempt well-known. If anything were to happen to him, no matter how accidental it may seem, anyone who has paid him the slightest attention would look to us." He took another gulp of wine.

To you, I wanted to say. The man who ruled for nearly a century by only bloodright, and had done nothing within that time to gain support outside of those who'd stood with his family before him. He valued that support above others because, over the generations, those high families had become the most powerful and wealthiest houses in Eshelle. Why seek approval from peasants and lesser houses, when a few big names could keep you in power forever–as long as their stomachs were full, and their pockets happy?

Amedeo Monserre was why. Several years ago, upon a sudden influx of wealth, he branched out from his trade of agriculture, and into textiles, smithery, lumber. He even supported some of the smaller nations outside of his own. His name could now be attached to nearly every good within Eshelle, and could be heard spoken in a positive light throughout most of the continent.

"As you say, Your Majesty," I said, bowing my head in a passable act of respect and submission. "What shall my tasks be, then?"

He smacked his lips around another sip of wine. "You will establish yourself within his home as an emissary to the crown, and play the courtier. Get invited to his gatherings, dine with him and his wife. Do whatever you please outside of those socializations. You'll be sent with enough gold for food and drink, clothing, females, whatever you like.

"Make him trust you," the king went on. "Then, find a way for me to destroy him–his house, his name, his reputation–without taking their lives. Understood?" The king raised his brows, and took a long drink from his cup, eyes holding mine over the rim of the glass.

"Understood, Your Majesty," I confirmed, bowing again. "When shall I depart for High Lord Amedeo's court?"

"Tomorrow. A dispatch was sent this morning, notifying him of your visit." He took another sip of wine, then clicked his tongue at the empty glass in his hand.

Yes, why wait to send the dispatch when I couldn't refuse?

"Very well. I assume Lord Olin has further details for me?"

"You assume correctly," he said, and jerked his chin towards the door in a very kingly dismissal before picking up the bottle of wine on the desk and taking a pull from it, no longer bothering with the cup. I stood from my seat, my ass aching from being in it for so long, gathered the papers, and bowed low before taking my leave.

As the door shut behind me and I walked down the hall towards my own chambers, I imagined. My imagination took me to places with laughter, comfortable chairs, and kind rulers. But, just like my hope and excitement from moments ago, I shoved those thoughts away, cringing. No matter what High Lord Amedeo's court held, I would be there as a spy, and a deceiver.

As such, the only laughter that I could have would be forced. The chairs might as well have spikes on them for all the comfort I would feel sitting in them while feigning friendship with a decent male and his wife.

I thought, from time to time, about treason. There was no way to sugar-coat it. Or, there was, but I refused to do so. I would not call myself a deserter, an expatriate, or any other fancy word I could come up with to make myself feel better. If I left, or intentionally disobeyed orders, or allied with this other male, I would be nothing but a traitor. The little honor I had left was in my loyalty to the king. Ridiculous as it might seem, I wanted, needed, that one last shred of honor within my battered soul.

Whether this king deserved my loyalty or not remained to be seen. And whether it was best to stay faithful to this king, rather than lose my honor in favor of someone who may be more deserving of my allegiance, was another factor I did not allow myself to consider. Not because I knew what the answer would be–though I supposed it wasn't *not* that. But rather because it begged another question that I hadn't dared to answer:

Was my allegiance actually worth anything at this point, anyway?

5

DANCING WITH WOLVES

THEA - 2 DAYS EARLIER

MY HEART POUNDED AS I ROSE FROM MY CHAIR AND DESCENDED the white marble steps. I reminded myself that the men were supposed to approach me, and not the other way around, though I wondered if anyone would be brave enough to be first. Or if I was destined to stand in the middle of the dance floor like an idiot, until someone was forced onto it with me. Heat rose to my cheeks at the thought.

Though not strictly traditional, I was permitted to choose my own partners. I didn't *have* to wait for someone to step up, if it seemed that no one had the guts to do so. But, I was supposed to let them play the gentleman in coming to me. "It may seem like an outdated portion of the tradition," my mother had acknowledged when I'd asked her about it–as if the entire thing weren't outdated. "But remember, these men have come from all over the continent for the opportunity to court you. We need to give them the respect of allowing them to approach you first."

She'd looked at me from under her lashes then, and tucked a lock of black hair behind my ear. "But, if you're standing there waiting for more than sixty seconds, I think it's a safe bet that you're the bravest in the room, and should be allowed to choose the first on your own."

If she only knew who I would choose if given the chance. To dance with gray eyes and calloused hands on mine—

I took a breath. There were still fifty-two seconds left in my minute. I reached my spot in the center of the dance floor, so rehearsed that I could have found it blindfolded. Right on cue, the orchestra began to play a simple song, one that almost every boy and girl learned as soon as they could count an eight-step.

All at once, three men started towards me, and I told myself I was relieved. It seemed they'd been more nervous about not knowing the dance than they were about actually dancing with me.

One of the men reached me within a few strides, his long legs covering the distance before the others could make it three quarters of the way. He bowed his head to me, and I curtsied to him, though I kept my chin up, not lowering it demurely as an older generation would expect of a woman. After what was basically a fancy nod, he was lucky to have gotten what he did from me.

"Your Highness, may I have this dance?" he asked, holding out a gloved hand. Not an unusual fashion necessarily, but one not typically seen on younger men. For some reason, the crisp white annoyed me. Like he'd never had to work, or get his hands dirty, a day in his life.

But, in front of the entire court, I could only respond, "You may," and place my hand in his. He smirked slightly, and led me into the dance, first holding our hands high in the air and circling me around the large circumference of the floor. Parading me. Lovely.

Finally satisfied with his display, he pulled me to him, resting a hand respectfully high on my waist. This close, I realized that I'd neglected to notice how tall he was; the top of my head hardly reached the man's chin, and I was not a short woman. Despite his height, which sometimes made men falter in attempts at grace, he was a good dancer. His steps were perfectly timed, and he spun me with precision when the wind instruments lilted higher in pitch. Too bad *he* neglected to give me his name before he swept me into the movements.

"I don't think we've been properly introduced," I told him, trying to be ladylike about it. If he hadn't been so determined to show the room that he'd gotten to me first, we probably would have had time for introductions at the start.

"I suppose not. Roger Apleton; my father is the Duke of Brenick," he said. I nearly wrinkled my nose in distaste at his superior tone. Brenick was a wealthy country, sure, but it wasn't as though *Roger* brought about its prosperity. And the cocky little smirk on his face made me want to ask where Brenick was–claim I'd never heard of it before. I restrained myself only because I knew he wouldn't see the comment as a slight to him, as I would mean it, but rather as girlish stupidity. As if I never cared to learn the geography of the continent my family ruled.

In the end, I only said, "I hear it's lovely this time of year," with a forced grin, biting out the true statement.

"I would be happy to show you around sometime," he said. That grin got even more arrogant, as if the mere invitation put him in the running. I tilted my head slightly, and gave him a smile that didn't reach my eyes.

"We'll see." I held his gaze with that look, and his expression finally faltered. But oh, he'd been trained well. Even those who joined us on the dance floor weren't close enough to see that his happy expression was now forced. An entire minute passed where he said nothing at all.

"We still have another day," I reminded him. To anyone listening, it would sound reassuring, maybe even flirtatious. If one were to correctly translate the sentence, however, it would mean, "If you'd like, I can kick you out now." If he didn't start to control the way he was beginning to look at me, he would be sent home faster than one of his father's pretty stallions could run.

In the space of a blink, he seemed to assess me, contemplate his behavior, and recover. As the song came to its close, he smiled, and said, "Indeed we do." He continued to hold one of my hands as he stepped back, and bowed at the waist. That was more like it.

I got my hand back, but before Roger could fully step away, another man faced me. He was a bit younger, a bit shorter, but with happy eyes and a handsome smile. Roger walked away as the new man greeted me, "Princess Althea," he started, his charming northern accent apparent, bowing low. "I'm Lord Dalton Fera. Would you like to dance with me?" I could sense his heart, beating quickly due to his nerves.

"Yes, I would," I responded sincerely. He beamed, and held out his hand, which I took, resting my other on his shoulder.

"Are you enjoying your evening?" he asked as we danced.

I decided to answer honestly. "It's had its ups and downs."

"Well I hope that dancing with me will not later be recounted as one of the downs," he replied swiftly, not taken aback by my candidness. He braced his hands on my hips, and I placed mine on his shoulders for the small lift in the choreography for this dance.

Slightly breathless as he set me down, I said, "As long as you don't step on my toes, I don't think I'll have anything bad to say." At that, his smile widened, and there was such a genuine quality to it that I grinned back easily, no force needed.

Dalton and I danced through another song together, talking nearly the entire time. I learned that he was the young Lord of Heranelle, had one younger sister, and loved chess, and desserts with chocolate and raspberries in them. I told him that if fruits were in the dessert, then it would be considered healthy, which a dessert was not meant to be. That made him laugh, and I liked the unrestrained sound of it.

I worked up the nerve to tell him of my love of training–with bow, blade, or otherwise. Physical training for women wasn't yet widely accepted in Weaschte. I was permitted only because, when I was seven, I'd asked my parents why their sons should be capable of defending themselves if necessary, and their daughters shouldn't–and they hadn't been able to answer.

I told Dalton to see how he might react. If my suitors were too insecure in their own strength or training for me to have any of my own, it would not be a relationship worth pursuing. And it'd be best for everyone involved for that to be figured out sooner, rather than later.

But *this* suitor only expressed how he would like to spar with me one day, and hoped I wouldn't "knock him on his ass" if I could help it. Something about the way he said it, the way he joked with me, made me believe him. Made me believe that he wasn't one of those men.

Still, as the second melody approached its end, I felt anxious as I wondered how I was going to detach myself from him. It would be rude of me not to move on from him to dance with the many other courtiers in attendance. However, my anxiety proved to be unnecessary. At the song's conclusion, Dalton smiled as he stepped back, bowed, and gave me a light kiss on the back of my hand. I curtsied in return, and grinned as he departed.

I was approached by four more courtiers before I took a break. Duke Edvard Kelley, who was kind enough, but twice my age. Contrastingly, Lord Viktor Bruswik, just sixteen-years-old, tried his hand. Lord Garet Fenwe, who had *his* hand only an inch above my ass throughout the dance, regardless of how often I moved it back up to my waist. And finally, Lord Belamy Nevar, who had been nearly as charming as Dalton, albeit far more nervous.

I walked up to where my parents sat at the dais, and nearly plopped down on the ground in front of them before I remembered myself. If it were just the three of us, I would have sat on the floor between their thrones, gown and all, as I'd done since I was little. But there were about a hundred other people here tonight who would notice, and whisper about my impropriety.

Instead, I sat, as I was supposed to, in my wood and velvet chair. Immediately, I heard footsteps approaching me from the left, and turned to find Atlas with a wine glass filled with water in hand. I smiled at him. "You're gods-sent, Atlas." My fingertips brushed his as I took the glass.

He chuckled, lowering his head in acknowledgement, storm-gray eyes holding mine. "Happy to be of service, Princess," he replied, then bowed to me and my parents before taking his leave. I gulped down the water, but magic had it automatically refilling.

"I think we know," my mom said, and I realized I'd been watching Atlas travel across the Hall, stopping at tables to take drink orders. My cheeks heated as I looked at her, hoping she hadn't noticed where my gaze had been. Or rather *who* it had been on.

"But who is your favorite so far, and who is a definite no?" Her eyes were intent on me, no trace of reproach in them.

"Dalton, and Garet, respectively," I responded quickly, relieved. "I think I'll give Belamy the chance to proceed as well;

hopefully after spending a bit more time together his nerves will calm." I shrugged, and took another sip of water. "As for the other no's: Viktor, Roger, and Edvard, in no particular order."

"Well, I can understand Garet. It's a good thing nobody was looking at your father's face after the second time he let his hand wander." She sent a meaningful look in my dad's direction. I looked at him, and he shrugged as if to say *what do you expect?* before turning back to the room to glare. I knew without having to follow his gaze who that look was meant for, and *almost* felt sorry for Garet being on the receiving end of it.

"But, Aly," my mom continued, and I used nearly all of my willpower not to roll my eyes as I prepared for her to justify any of the others. "I know he's a bit on the older side, but Edvard–"

I lost the battle with my will then, and cut her off before she could explain why a man with children my age should be allowed to proceed. "A *bit*?" I asked, my brows shooting up. "Mom, he could have been my father. And dad has aged much more gracefully than he has." I raised my glass to my dad in a mock cheers, which he returned with his glass of wine, a smirk on his face.

"A third of them getting passing marks isn't bad, dear," he said to her. "We still have two hours left for Aly to make her selection tonight. And it's better that she narrows it down sooner rather than later, I think." He paused for a sip of wine, then continued, "I, for one, can't believe that Ed tried his hand. And I have half a mind to *speak* with the young Lord Fenwe." His eyes darkened at that, as he stared pointedly into the Hall. If I were to spot a Garet-shaped hole in the wall later, I wouldn't be surprised.

"I suppose you're right," mom conceded with a sigh. "I know that Ed lost his wife a year ago now, gods rest her, but honestly, a princess? As his *second* wife?" She shook her head.

"Well, we took the scenic route, but we got to the same destination in the end," I said, and patted her knee. I stood as she rolled her eyes at me, and walked back down the steps to place my water glass on the now-empty table in front of the dais. It would be set with dessert plates and cutlery shortly, but until then, I really did have to start making my way through the courtiers.

But, before I could reach the dance floor, Hanna intercepted me. Her strawberry blonde hair had been cut short since I last saw her; now in a style that brushed her shoulders, and framed her face beautifully. I squealed upon seeing her–likely to my mother's chagrin–and threw my arms around her slender shoulders. And as I did, I felt...something different.

Pulling back quickly, brows raised, I asked, "Do you have something to tell me?"

Her lips stretched into a grin, even as her silver eyes widened. "You can tell already? You hugged me for one second!"

"I felt the new life as soon as I touched you," I told her as my eyes welled with joyful tears. I'd been able to sense pregnancies for years now. It was a talent I discovered only after Nik came home with his wife, Izabel, for the first time after they married. After that, my mom had immediately brought in a prenatal healer for me to learn from.

That healer told me that it was highly unusual for someone to be able to heal themselves, others, *and* unborn babes. Typically, it was one or the other. A blessed gift born from a blessed union, she'd said.

"Oh, none of that, you'll ruin your mother's work!" Hanna exclaimed, brushing her fingers beneath my eyes.

"Tell me everything right now," I demanded, taking her hands from my face to grip them in mine. I walked us toward the outskirts of the Hall, coming to a stop between two of the pillars. After not-so-inconspicuously glancing around, Hanna told me that she was nearly three months along, and hoped it was a girl. She wanted to name the child after her late mother, Sara, which made me tear up again. She said that Gregor had no preference; he'd be happy with a boy or girl. In a world where only men might be heirs to title and land, this was good news indeed, and also informed me that this would not be their only child, if Hanna's hopes were achieved.

And, because she was one of my best friends, she also told me about the night she believed the babe was conceived, the details of which had me giggling with her. I used to get jealous when such things were discussed. Being a lady and being a princess set us with differing expectations of the level of *inno-cence* we had to maintain in order to remain *suitable*. But, some-where along the way, I became giggly and juvenile with my friends as we talked about their intimacies with men, instead of resentful for not having any stories of my own. I'd actually learned quite a bit from their depictions of...events, and one thing I looked forward to, regarding my impending betrothal, was being able to finally put that knowledge to practice.

Perhaps, as we stood in a room with dozens of watchful eyes and listening ears, we should be more demure, more proper, but I was far from caring. She was beginning to tell me how Gregor had gone the extra mile to further ensure success in conceiving, when our whispers and laughter were interrupted by the clearing of a throat behind me.

Hanna, facing the man, went almost slack-jawed, her silver eyes wide. I turned, more annoyed at being interrupted than embarrassed about being overheard, to find one of the most handsome men I'd ever seen.

6

ENTERING THE LION'S DEN

AFTER A MONTH OF TRAVEL ASTRIDE MY HORSE, I RODE THROUGH the open borders of Colina, the capital city of Sabrian. Behind me, a wagon carried my belongings. It had honestly felt pathetic as I'd packed and realized how little I owned. Not for lack of gold–the one good thing about my job was the salary– but for lack of a want or care to buy myself things.

Olin had assured me that Sabrian would have no shortage of shops for me to buy more clothes, or any other items, should I need them. A subtle way of saying that he believed I would need to be here long enough that I would run out of things to wear. That it would take me longer than expected to complete my tasks.

Prick.

As my pitiful amount of belongings and I crossed the border, I took in the city around me. My immediate impression was that it was at least better than Matriel, the capital of

Oschverre. It didn't smell like piss and wine in the streets, and there weren't broken cobblestones every few paces. Though that could be attributed to the fact that mine was the only carriage I saw on the road.

Everyone was walking. Fae and faeries alike meandered around, some clearly at work, and some clearly not. But neither seemed to feel any negativity towards the other. The workers smiled from their stalls and shops, and the shoppers grinned back, dipping their chins in acknowledgement if they passed by a store without stopping.

What kind of make-believe shit was this?

I felt like I was the only sane person in a fever dream about peace and prosperity. Where everyone but myself had some delusion that everything was pretty; rainbows and butterflies and sunshine. While I was the only one who saw the rain and ravens and darkness.

That was, until they saw me.

My horse and wagon made it obvious that I was not from here. But I didn't for a second believe that it was the reason behind the dropped smiles, or the stares. The Fae and faeries in the streets stopped in their tracks to glare at the coat of arms carved into the gleaming silver plates on my chest, as well as my horse's, and painted onto the sides of the carriage. They halted conversations, put down food and drink, and halted mid-laughter to either pointedly look away from me, or glare with ferocious dislike–even hatred. I met eyes of green, brown, and deepest black that took up the entire eye. And, even in those depthless faerie irises, the loathing was palpable.

But those glares only moved to me after they'd seen the coat of arms: the rippling snake, coiled in a figure eight around stems of oleander. The coat of arms of the Gervan family, only changing once every millennium or so when a new king in the family line was crowned. I sometimes wondered if the same ignorance for the plant extended to the serpent–a scary-looking beast, to be sure. Black and white, with bright green eyes, thick as a grown male's forearm. But the Eshellen Kingsnake–the cleverest of names, truly–was nonvenomous. Only the oleander in its grasp was poisonous.

And I thought, too frequently, of how intriguing that was.

After a long moment in which I met the eyes of a female who looked at me with a great sadness, rather than hatred, I could no longer bring myself to hold the gazes of the people of Colina. Instead, I lifted mine so I could only see above them. In the distance sat a castle at the top of a rolling green hill. As I rode toward it, with its pale stone exterior, celestite shingles, and plentiful windows of plain and stained glass, there was a distinct moment in which I recognized the beauty of this place that I was supposed to somehow bring to ruin.

⇔

After what felt like an eternity of making my way through the streets of Colina, all the while keeping my chin up to avoid the stares of those walking around me, I finally made it to the castle gates. As my horse came to a halt, I looked down towards the two guards who'd walked forward from the walls to greet me.

"State your name and business," one of them said to me, a hand already on the pommel of his sword.

I nearly sneered at the lack of propriety, and the tone. He knew who I was. I was sure that even if his High Lord had somehow not informed all guards of my impending visit–which I doubted very much–he would know based off the plate on my horse's chest alone.

Though he kept his eyes on mine, I knew that he also took note of where my blade sat on my hip. I wasn't about to test the limits of the High Lord's welcome, or this guard's impulse control. But the insult in his watchful eye, and in that readied hand, was enough that I cleared my throat, conveying both displeasure and annoyance in the two-beat sound.

"I am Lord Dion Evestre, emissary to His Majesty, Oleander Gervan, High King of Eshelle, here as a visitor to the court of High Lord Amedeo Monserre. His Majesty sent a dispatch notifying your lord of my impending arrival." My words were professional, but I kept my face set in an expression that tended to spike fear, or at least intimidation, in those it was directed towards.

"Aye, so he did," the guard replied, seeming to give less than a shit about my importance or my expression. But he looked to his companion briefly, and they shared a nod.

"Well then *Lord Dion*," the other guard said, scowling as he did so. "We shall have you taken to the High Lord right away." The first turned away from me, and looked at the gate. Though nobody pulled a lever, or spun a crank, the thick cross-hatched metal began to rise into the pocket in the upper part of the wall.

Metallurgy; a rare power, and still, I envied its simplicity. To have the majick of water, or metal, or earth could have changed the course of my life. Not the killing power that had made me so invaluable to a terrible king.

I cleared the thoughts from my head when a female walked under the still rising gate, towards me. One wouldn't exactly call her lovely, though her sienna eyes were somewhat spectacular. There was a small, polite smile on her full mouth that did not reach them.

I hid my surprise at a female being sent to escort me, particularly alone. She must either be very powerful–which I didn't sense from her–or the High Lord must know I would not be stupid enough to harm someone of his court right at his gates.

I was relieved to know he at least thought that much of me.

Both of the guards bowed to the female as she neared, so I supposed chivalry was still very much alive here. Then they turned and moved back up to their posts against the wall. When the guards spun back towards me, they both looked straight down the road to continue their watch. Like I wasn't even there, right in front of them.

If I was being honest, I knew that our king was not well-liked– particularly here. But I would be lying if I said I hadn't expected some kind of welcome party, or at the very least a *welcoming* party. These people wanted nothing to do with me, and were not afraid to show it.

I supposed this was what happened when a king was unloved by the entire continent he reigned over. When, at best, the people felt indifference towards him, and terror or hatred at worst.

Interrupting my thoughts, the female said, "Lord Dion," and bowed her head in what was essentially a large-scale wince. "High Lord Amedeo is expecting you presently. If you would leave your horse and wagon with Arthur, I will take you to him."

There was no question in her words; it was said like a command. A red-haired guard–Arthur, I assumed–walked through the gates, stood beside her, and stared up at me with unreadable blue eyes.

"I would prefer to wash and change before being presented to his High Lordship," I replied. We'd passed only two taverns with both operational pipes and vacancies on the journey, and I probably looked just about as good as I smelled.

Her smile remained, but her eyes...even I felt a chill from the look that filled them. "You will meet him now, or you will not meet him at all." Her grin widened, and dimples flashed on each terracotta cheek. Again, I had the realization that the feature was beautiful, but the thought was gone in a flash, replaced by only annoyance at how I was being treated.

I had no doubt that if I refused again, I would be quite literally turned away at the gates. Swallowing my pride and my words, I nodded once, and dismounted. I handed the reins to *Arthur*, then turned once again to the female.

"Very good," she said, setting my teeth on edge. "Follow me." Again with the damned commands. A muscle twitched in my jaw. But she turned from me with no further comment, striding through the gate.

I followed her in silence towards the castle. I knew better now than to expect any kind of small talk, or courtesies such as asking about the comfort of my travels. If she did ask, my answer would have to be that even with the saddle chafing, weather exposure, and shitting on the side of the road combined, I'd been more comfortable on the journey than in the past hour since I made it to the city.

Still, I observed my surroundings as we walked through the grounds. The area in front of the castle was pleasant, but ordinary, insofar as the foreground of a palace could be such a thing. The lawn was a well-maintained clover field, their flowers popping here and there, likely in places of low foot traffic. The cobblestone walkway from the gates to the castle was made from a stone only slightly darker than the pale beige of the walls themselves. The path reached the tall walnut wood doors, and then circled around the walls, seeming to continue around the entire castle.

But I wasn't here to admire the scenery, no matter how charming I had to begrudgingly admit it was.

As we stepped through the doors, I made note of the guards–how many, where they were posted, and if I sensed any particularly strong powers among them. While the female and each guard bowed their heads to each other as we passed, not one of them acknowledged me.

I expected it, to an extent. But I'd failed to account for the emotions *I* would feel, knowing that theirs were justified, and how it would stir up a defensiveness that wasn't deserved. They were right. I was wrong.

I'd been able to ignore it, when I was only a terrible male working for a terrible king. But these people had higher expectations, set by better leaders, and a righteous court. The repercussions of my blatant disregard for moving past my evil and indifference were surfacing now, and I was angry, therefore, at the assuredly imminent facing of the consequences of my own actions.

The power I hadn't used in over sixty years reared its ugly head in answer. I felt it start to sear its way through my blood, but I violently cut off its air, forcing the beast into its feigned docility once more.

It was only after my internal victory that I realized that the female and I were striding into a great chamber, at the end of which sat a dark-haired, brown-eyed male who could be none other than the High Lord of Sabrian. As soon as we passed through the large wooden doors, they closed behind us, and in front of them–blocking the exit–appeared two more guards. I stopped at a customary distance from the dais, and clasped my hands behind my back.

To my astonishment, rather than standing beside me to introduce me to the High Lord, the female continued on, towards him. They shared only a look before she took her seat in the throne on his right. And, as soon as she did so, it was as though a veil was lifted from her. Before, I had seen that there was beauty in her smile and noticed that her eyes were striking. Yet somehow I had not held to those recognitions, my mind directed quickly back to annoyance. Not by my own improvidence, but by majickal design.

As the glamour–those bits of majick that could hide all that a person was, if the caster was powerful enough–was removed, I saw her truly. With a face which artists would come from far and wide for the opportunity to paint. Strong cheekbones, and a nose that would have overpowered a less exquisite canvas, framed in night-dark hair. As though she knew what I was now realizing, the corners of her full lips tilted up in a mocking smirk. That she–that *they* had placed a glamour on her, not to make her look unattractive, but to make it so that even when I noticed her beautiful features, my mind would not believe them. But that beauty wasn't the most astonishing thing about her.

I was nearly taken aback by the power that radiated from the female. It was a wave of energy that crested over me, so powerful and deep that I was left drowning even in its trough.

I almost forgot myself in the face of that power, but managed–after a beat–to bow my head to the couple and say, "High Lord Amedeo. My Lady. I am Lord Dion Evestre, emissary to His Majesty Oleander Gervan, High King of Eshelle. I am very pleased to make your acquaintance."

The High Lord gave me a small smile that did not reach his dark eyes. But did not speak.

It took all of my effort not to shift on my feet. I waited another moment, while they both stared at me, no kindness to be found on their faces. Feeling perhaps the most awkward I'd ever felt, I said, "I regret that your Lady and I were not properly introduced. As such, I apologize to both of you for my lack of courtly etiquette when I arrived in your great city."

"She is my High Lady," he said, barely-concealed anger in his voice.

I blinked. High Ladies were more common in the southern

part of the continent than they were in the north, where the king's beliefs were more easily enforced. But the king had only said *his wife.* I had assumed, to my obvious detriment, she would be called Lady. I should have realized that just because the king didn't allow his own spouse to hold an equal role in his decision making–hence the restriction for Houses nearest him to do so–did not mean that those with more modern sensibilities would do the same.

"I apologize," I said again, the sincerity feeling foreign on my lips. "I must have been incorrectly informed. High Lady." I bowed to her.

"Would you like to apologize for anything else, while you're at it?" the High Lord asked as I straightened.

My brow furrowed. "High Lord?"

"Did you not think, for instance, to acknowledge our people as you paraded through our city?" he asked, gesturing to the windows on the south-facing wall before clasping his hands a few inches below his bearded chin. "Do you *apologize* for not extending the courtesy of your surely substantial purse as you passed by their many shops and kept your eyes up as though you are so much better than them?"

My face began to heat, both in chagrin, and in anger. I had kept my eyes up because I hadn't been able to bear the hate and mistrust in theirs, and to know that they were right to feel that way. I hadn't thought that look translated to *please, come into my shop so that I'd have to talk to and serve you.* "High Lord, I can assure you that–"

"And did you not think," he interrupted me, "at any point to speak with my High Lady, perhaps to ask her about our city? Was the fact that she was presented as plain, as a commoner, enough for you to disregard anything she might have to contribute? Or did the mere fact that she was a female cause your silence?"

The accusations started to set my power on edge again. A feral beast, long since fed; denied for decades the blood it so desperately craved. As I felt it start to awaken, I tried my best to clamp down on it. "High Lord, I–"

"Or do you really see yourself as Higher Than, Better Than, simply because you wear the crest of a ruler who has done nothing to benefit these people, *our people*? Do you think that your pretty face keeps us from seeing the monster within?"

My power was burning, setting my blood ablaze, even as I tried to leash it. I felt it start to emanate outwards, and I knew my skin glowed from beneath the surface like coals being fired, and the air began to smell of embers and ash.

"There he is," the High Lady breathed. And with that one sentence, I realized I was the greatest fool who ever lived. That this was their intent. The shame in being so easily tricked–and in just as easily losing control–was enough of a distraction from the roiling anger that had so quickly become rage. It gave me the strength to yank the reins on the beast of my power, urging it back into submission

"The male who once helped to bring a continent to its knees," the High Lord agreed as I struggled. "Who, even after decades, cannot control his abilities."

"Which means he either glories in the lack of control, *or*, and more likely based off of his expression, he has not used it in so long that he has not been able to practice control in the first place," the High Lady went on. Why did they build on each other's sentences like that? As though one or the other could not finish a thought alone.

My power under my command once more, I spoke through my teeth. "I suppose that was a fun little experiment for you. Did it not occur to either of you that you could have been injured, or worse?"

But my dissipating anger was quickly revealing itself to be

something far worse: fear. For those in this room who could have been hurt; whom *I* could have hurt. Solely due to a lack of control that I hadn't needed in so long, having not felt *anything*–not anger, rage, nor terror–which might have triggered it. But the last thing I needed was for them to scent that fear now. Have them know that I didn't wish to hurt them. I spent the past month of travel dealing with that knowledge myself.

I shoved the emotion down as relentlessly as I had done with my majick, schooling my expression hopefully too quickly for them to have seen that flash of feeling in my eyes.

"No," the High Lord replied easily, without examining me, and I restrained a breath of relief. "It didn't, for a few reasons, not the least of which being the shield that was put up around you the moment my mate was out of your range."

"So, what was the purpose, then?" I asked, my nails digging into my palms behind my back. I stored away the bit of information he'd given me; *mated*. Though mates were not rare by any means, some never found theirs. I'd heard of some who didn't try to find them, happy with plain and simple love. I'd even heard tales of those with more than one mate. I knew that sometimes the bond hit instantly, and sometimes, when the heart or soul were blocked, it took time. Some said that the bond could be of the deepest friendship, and did not necessarily mean romantic love. In any case, it was supposed to be infallible. A true soul bond; exquisite and everlasting.

"I'll tell you what, Lord Dion. I'll explain my purposes, when you explain yours," the High Lord said, and raised his eyebrows. He sat back in his throne, leaning a cheek on his fist, as though fixing himself for a proper story. The High Lady smirked beside him.

I gave a false chuckle as I looked down at the mosaic of tiles beneath my feet. Craftsmanship and artistry such that, in any other circumstance, I might have admired it.

I looked up at them once more. "My purpose here is to act as emissary to the king."

High Lord Amedeo pursed his lips, and looked to his mate. She, in turn, nodded toward the guards who had not moved from their posts at the doors throughout this entire encounter, not even during my...outburst. The two males immediately began striding towards me, the metal of their armor and swords clinking.

"That's it, then? Am I to be sent home, or kept as your prisoner?" I asked as the guards reached my sides, my own sword untouched.

"Neither," the High Lady–who had still not given her name–responded. "If you were sent home, His Majesty would likely send another emissary with less...restraint. And if we were to make you our prisoner, well, we don't know how much of that restraint you would keep when locked in a cell."

"You will be taken to the chambers we have readied for you," the High Lord said, continuing his mate's sentences again. "Your belongings are there already. Should you need anything else, a personal guard and attendant will be stationed outside your door."

I smirked without any real amusement. "And am I to stay within those *chambers* for the entirety of my visit?" I asked. *Guard.* Sure–but guarding the person in the room, or the people outside of it? Oh, they might not call me prisoner in name, but in practice–that was a different story.

"How would you be a sufficient emissary for His Majesty if you were unable to take part in our court?" The High Lady's own half-grin held some real humor now. "You may wander the castle, the grounds, and the city as you wish. We only ask that you be present for all court gatherings, and dine with us this evening."

"Your guard will be waiting by your chamber. She will be able to inform you of any meals, and gatherings for which you are expected. And, should you wish to take us up on the offer, she would also take you into the city." The High Lord frowned slightly.

I worked to keep my surprise from my face, after hearing both of their statements. Between the freedom to explore, and the fact that they seemed to put much more faith and opportunities in their females here than they did in Eshelle's capital country, it seemed I would have much to do and learn. As much as I liked to consider myself a modern male, I lived in a place where that term might not be adherent to the actual standards of modernity and equality in societies such as this.

The High Lady said, still with that half smile on her face, "Arthur, Sam, if you could take Lord Dion to his chambers, please. And be sure he finds the washroom." She wrinkled her nose at me, and her mate laughed.

I sucked on a tooth at the insult, but said, "Thank you High Lord, High Lady." I bowed my head to each of them. "I shall see you this evening for supper, by which time I hope to be smelling less like a horse's ass." The line was out before I could have thought to stop it, and I wondered what had come over me to lose my propriety so suddenly. I snapped my mouth shut and prepared for banishment–from the hall, or from the city.

But they laughed. Actually *laughed*.

"Best get to it, then," the High Lady said.

"You'll need all the time you can get," the High Lord added.

7

THE LIONESS

AS I THREADED SHADOWS THROUGH MY FINGERS LIKE WISPS OF black ribbon, I heard footsteps approaching from the stretch of hallways to my left. I took a deep breath through my nose to calm myself, the shadows disappearing back into the spaces between the bricks in the wall I leaned against. This was the job, I told myself, dropping my hands to my sides. If I wanted to rise through the ranks, I had to start somewhere.

I just hadn't realized that *somewhere* would be guarding the enemy.

The sources of those footsteps rounded the corner of the hall, but I kept my gaze straight, staring at the limewashed stone wall opposite me. In my periphery, I could see three males approaching. By their scents, I knew two of them—Arthur and Sam. As I registered the third scent, beneath the stench of horses and sweat, I committed it to memory; the smell of the male I hated most in the world. More than even his king, I

65

thought, as I worked to calm the rage that had been building in my heart for six months.

As they neared, I turned my head, keeping my face void of emotion. The unknown male–who could only be that *lord*– might have been handsome, if one knew nothing of him. With brown hair that curled over his forehead, and slightly uptilted hazel eyes, paired with above average height and a strong build, most would think him attractive.

And of course, he would be; the king had a talent for vanity, if nothing else. Rumor had it that, though the streets of Oschverre were piss-covered and broken, the castle itself was a sight to behold. It only made sense that he would have good-looking lackeys.

The male's eyes met mine then, but no feeling registered in them. I may as well have met the gaze of a belly-up fish. I fought the urge to shudder. I'd forgotten the most useful reason for this male to be pretty. How better to hide the rotten power within than with a pristine, sparkling shroud?

At last, the males reached the door directly to my right. The lord looked as though he was expecting me to speak first. Not likely.

Arthur broke the silence for us. "Ciaragen, this is Lord Dion." Arthur reluctantly turned to the male, "M'lord, this is Ciaragen Vey. She will be your guard and escort during your time here in Sabrian." Then he looked at me, and, though I kept my eyes on the lord's, I could feel the weight of his gaze begging me to behave.

With a tight-lipped grin that was more of a wince, I said, "My Lord, I am at your service." I was surprised I made it through the sentence without vomiting. I couldn't risk bowing, though; that might send me and my stomach over the edge.

"My Lady–" the lord started.

"I'm not a lady, my Lord. Just a guard," I lied. I certainly was a lady, but had no desire to be referred to as *his*.

He smirked, hazel eyes glittering with challenge. "Forgive me, but the Veys are the House in power in Dremerre. That would signify that your parents are the High Lord and High Lady of that country. And you, their child, would be Lady. So, *my Lady*, it's a pleasure to meet you. I'm sure we shall have the grandest of times together during my visit."

A grand time would be watching my fist connect with that pretty mouth. Better yet, putting my sword through that dense abdomen. I felt no sense of satisfaction with the images, however, knowing that they could not come to pass. So, instead of doing either of those things, I nodded in false agreement as he talked to me of my House, my *parents*–

My fists clenched at my sides, and I pulled the leash on my anger, and my power. "Well," Arthur said, much too loudly for our close proximity, snapping my attention back to the matter at hand. "We'll leave you to it, then." He gave me one last warning glance, the half-second-long look filled with reproach, and caution. Then he and Sam both inclined their heads to the lord in the most half-assed bows I'd ever seen, and walked away so quickly they might as well have run.

I turned from watching their backs to find the lord watching me. "Well," he started, his volume much more regulated than Arthur's had been. "Are you going to get my door for me, or does the fact that you're a Lady negate the *servant* part of your duties?"

"I'm not your servant," I said through my teeth.

"Escort, attendant, servant. Semantics. I suppose that the definition of your term of preference states that I am responsible for opening my own doors?"

His eyes flashed with a bit of humor, and I realized that he was messing with me. Or–and, in my opinion, more likely–he was seeing how much he could disrespect me without consequences. Either way, he was looking for a reaction, I was sure.

Not about to give him the satisfaction, regardless of his reasoning, I simply said, "I'm afraid so. But the handle is right there. You see, all you need to do is twist it, and then push a bit, and the door will open," I explained slowly, even miming the actions with my hands, as though talking to a toddler. The humor still gleamed in his gaze, and I had to force myself to say, "Though I apologize if you're used to better accommodations in Matriel."

His eyes shuttered. "I'll make do," he muttered quietly. He opened, walked through, and closed the door without another word.

I couldn't bring myself to care enough about his sudden departure to wonder what about my words had triggered it. I supposed that he was accustomed to being able to show one side of himself–chatty and annoying–then switch to another–withdrawn, still annoying–without having to hold to the pretense of politeness. How else would the king's resident executioner keep up appearances?

⇎

The lord didn't leave his chamber all day. Lunchtime came and went, and he did not emerge. And, since nobody came to relieve me, and I had no intention of speaking to him unless absolutely necessary, that meant that I also did not get to eat. Which meant that it was now early evening, and I was bloody starving.

What was he even *doing*? He must have put up a sound shield within the room, because I'd only heard movement for about thirty minutes after our encounter. The unmistakable noise of the shower running. Sounds of unpacking; chests being unlocked, the armoire doors opening and closing. Footsteps, a chair scraping against the floor. And then silence. Absolutely no sound came from the other side of the door for hours. It would have been puzzling if it weren't so unsettling.

I stood there, beside the door, all day, toying with my shadows and braiding my previously unbound curls. Eventually, I became so bored that I started counting the limewashed bricks on the wall in front of me. First, just within the scope of my immediate sight, then extended out to what I could see if I shifted my eyes in either direction. I had just finished counting down twenty feet to the left when I heard footsteps coming from inside the chamber. I realized I was slouching against the wall, and straightened just in time.

The door opened, and he emerged, looking better now that he'd had a wash. He looked down at me and frowned. Not exaggerated, just a small tilt to the corners of his mouth, but it infuriated me. I was the one who'd been deprived of lunch, the one who had sore feet from standing still all day, and *he* was displeased with *me*?

But he walked out into the hall beside me, closed the door behind him, and began walking in the direction whence he came earlier.

"That's the wrong way," I said, irritated. Did he think the *guard* portion of my job description only applied when he was in the chambers?

He turned to look at me and raised a brow. "Are we not dining in the great room?" he asked, referring, I was sure, to the reception hall, where guests were greeted before they were permitted further into the castle. The mosaic on its floor, and the grand hammerbeam ceilings could give off the impression of a *great room*, I supposed. But everything in this castle was lovely. Well, with one exception now.

"No," I answered, not bothering to soften my tone. "The

High Lord and High Lady take their supper on the balcony in fair weather."

Another frown at that. As if dining anywhere but in a hall with dozens of courtiers, and the females that surely fawned over him each evening in his home city, was abhorrent. With effort, I held back my own sneer at his arrogance. "Follow me."

I set off in the opposite direction he had, and immediately heard him catch up to me, his footsteps half a step behind me and a couple of feet to my left. I had expected–more like hoped for–a continuation of the silence that he had exhibited for those hours in his chambers, as we made our way toward the garden-front wing of the castle.

I was disappointed.

"You know, you're not a very proper lady," he said matter-of-factly.

I almost whipped my head around to glare at him, but I sensed that he gloried in evoking a reaction from his antics. So, still looking ahead, I replied, "I'm not sure what you mean. And I'm not a lady."

"Right there, for instance. Any decent servant would have added *my lord* to the end of that sentence. And would never have commanded that I follow them. Instead, it would have been something like, *would you be ever so kind as to follow me, my Lord?* Or *it would be my absolute pleasure to escort you to this evening's dining location, my Lord.*"

I exhaled in a sharp huff through my nose. "First of all, as I've said before, I am not your servant. I am your guard and escort, which means I will protect you if need be, and I will lead you to wherever you are summoned, or wish to go in your free time." A fact that had me grinding my teeth every time I thought about it. As if this male needed guarding, with his sinister power. As if he needed someone to bring him to supper and court, or deserved to explore the wonders of our city.

Nonetheless, I continued. "Secondly, I would never utter such groveling words–to you, or to anybody. And lastly, if you really want me to add your title when I speak to you, I shall start doing so, Lord Devon."

From the corner of my eye, I saw his head tilt, and felt his gaze move to my face rather than the hall ahead. I waited for him to get annoyed, or angry, or at the very least correct me. But his steps did not stutter, he did not tell me that I used the wrong name, and I did not feel the heat his power was said to produce.

"Very well then," was all he said.

I'd won. Whatever this idiotic little banter he sought was, I'd gotten the last word in it. A small feeling of triumph rose inside me, and my steps quickened, my chin lifting ever so slightly, and–

"Although, how is a lady like yourself supposed to protect me?"

And...I lost. I lost, because I couldn't control my temper. Because I couldn't hold back the words I'd been thinking over and over again in my head since his visit had been announced. I whirled on him, stopping him in his tracks, and spat, "If it weren't for my orders to do no harm to you, you would have needed protection the moment you crossed the border into our city. You would have been dead before you could have drawn your first breath within its streets. You would not be disgracing my High Lord, my High Lady, or their land with that filthy coat of arms you wear, you murderous swine."

And gods save my soul, but when hurt passed through his hazel eyes, I felt victory again. But the look was there and gone in a flash, replaced by a careful indifference. I waited for rage, for any sign of that power to rise in response to my threat, and my accusation. I waited for him to make his move so that I could make mine.

But he only turned away, and began walking down the hallway again. He must have seen the intent in my eyes. Must have known that any violence towards me would not have gone unanswered. And, no matter how powerful he was, he had to know that he would not make it out of this castle if he used his majick on anyone inside it.

I started walking as well, hastening a bit so that I was once more in front of him, careful not to look anywhere but straight ahead as I passed him.

In the following five minutes it took us to reach the entry to the balcony, he did not speak again.

8

FATED ATTRACTION

WITH DARK BROWN CURLS, GREEN-GOLD EYES, AND A STRONG build, the man before me would capture any woman's attention. Possibly in his late twenties, with small lines around the corners of his gentle eyes. His full lips were pulled up in a soft smile, showing me exactly where those lines came from.

"Princess Althea," he said, bowing low. "My name is Dion."

To my complete embarrassment, I opened my mouth to speak, and nothing came out. I felt heat rise to my cheeks, and tried again. "Lord Dion," I managed, curtseying. "This is my friend, Duchess Hanna Mayfeld." I gestured to Hanna, and she stepped up to my side with a curtsy of her own.

"A pleasure," he greeted her, giving her a small bow.

"Likewise," Hanna replied, then glanced at me significantly. "If you'll excuse me, I'm going to get a refreshment." She bowed to me and inclined her head to Dion.

When she parted, I turned back to the lord to find his eyes already on me, that soft grin still gracing his lips.

I smiled back in return. "I'm sorry, Lord Dion, but I don't believe I was made aware of your attendance tonight." The best way I could think to ask *who are you?* without alerting him—or my mother—to the fact that I'd forgotten yet another courtier's name.

"I was invited fairly last minute, and arrived even later, I'm afraid. I would have liked to be the first to ask you to dance." An unfamiliar accent lilted his words as his eyes roamed over my face.

"Well, my Lord, better late than never," I replied, bolder than I'd ever been with a man—as if I'd had the chance to be much of anything towards men in my minimal exposure to them. Even as I thought it, I forced my eyes not to seek the tall, strong figure that I somehow always knew the whereabouts of, even before I consciously looked. Instead, I kept my eyes on the lord in front of me, as he held out his hand in offering. I took it, grateful that he hadn't noticed any preoccupation on my part, and we made our way onto the dance floor.

It was apparent immediately that he was a very practiced dancer. Every movement was precise; the steps, spins, and breakaways all timed perfectly to the music. I could feel all eyes in the Hall on us, and as we danced, I glanced at the surrounding crowd. Unlike the songs I shared with my other partners this evening, nobody else joined us on the floor.

"They're watching you," Dion murmured, and I turned back to him. His eyes, I believed, hadn't left my face since he first approached me. The realization made my cheeks flare with a blush, and he gave me another one of those small smiles.

"They're not," I responded, as bashful as I was supposed to be when given a compliment by a man.

"They are," he returned. "Why wouldn't they be?"

It was a rhetorical question, meant to woo me through flattery. And, gods damn me, but it worked; I felt a pretty, mindless smile come over my face in response. When did I become such a simpering damsel? So easily flustered and flattered?

"So, Lord Dion," I said, attempting to compose myself. "Tell me about yourself."

"I'm afraid there's not much to tell." He spun me just as the wind instruments pitched into a higher octave. As he pulled me back into his arms, he continued, "I'm the son of a lord and lady, just like most of your prospective partners. I have one brother, no sisters. I was raised to love my king and country, and have served both loyally throughout my life. And, I love dogs, and chocolate. Not together, of course," he added, making a mock-serious face.

I laughed, the first time I'd done so with a dancing partner tonight since Dalton. He grinned in response, those little lines popping out once more. I realized Dion might well be older than I thought he was, but, unlike Edvard, he was interesting. Either way, it would probably be impolite to ask–at least, at this time.

"What are you thinking about?" His head tilted slightly.

The final notes of the song saved me from having to answer, and I was almost caught off-guard by the swiftness with which he tilted me into a dip so deep that my head stopped just inches from the floor, my hair forming an onyx pool on the ground. He pulled me back up to a standing position, and my hair fell around my face as people actually *applauded* us. I felt another blush fill my cheeks.

With those pretty hazel eyes on mine, Dion bowed and pressed a kiss to the back of my palm, his lips warm and soft on my skin. He straightened, his gaze never wavering from my own. "Princess."

Then, without another word, he turned and walked into the

crowd. Luckily, their eyes followed him as well–I couldn't blame them, after his show of skill, and as I saw the striking figure he set from behind–and I was granted a moment to gather myself.

I strode off of the dance floor, and Hanna, ever the loyal friend, was beaming at me from her place beside Gregor–both of them giving me a double thumbs up. *Very subtle*, I thought, rolling my eyes, but I couldn't find it in myself to feel embarrassed at their display. I could only smile in response; a smile that grew even wider when I saw that dessert had finally been served.

⇔

The evening's end approached and I wasn't ready for it. But, like all the gatherings and galas of old, this one would end at midnight.

When the sky, visible through the domed window on the ceiling of the Hall, was a blanket of black flecked with diamond-bright stars, I at last finished dancing with the final suitor. He would have been alright, I supposed, except that his mother watched us so vigilantly I could only imagine what she would be like as an in-law. I might not have experience with men, but I could understand how...interesting our marriage would be if he valued her opinions on our lives more than my own.

As Lord Momma's Boy departed, I walked towards the bar for the first time this evening. Not once, out of all the men who danced with me, had I been offered a drink, or a break to sit, or–well, do anything that I wanted to do, more than make dull conversation during dances I knew so well I could perform them in my sleep.

As if they couldn't be bothered with socializing with their

competition, or even the other visiting nobility, many of my suitors had left as soon as their dances finished. Out of all of those that I'd considered asking to stay, only Dalton, Belamy, and Dion remained. The latter had stepped away for a bit, but had since talked with many in attendance. I was charmed when he'd even taken the time to speak with Artur, the doorman, who looked a bit pale as he spoke with the nobleman. His position as my least favorite doorman held, though. Because while Artur never seemed to look me in the eye, his own always at his feet, he had no difficulty holding Dion's gaze.

As I approached, the three bartenders all puffed up a bit, each of them ready to take my order. When I reached them, I remembered myself just before leaning my elbows onto the bar, settling with placing my hands on it instead. Still, I grinned at them, and said, "Surprise me."

Hired only for these gatherings, these men were some of the best mixologists in Weaschte. Under their employer, they were supposed to remain nameless. No matter how many times I asked–at all of my siblings' courts before mine–they never told me. So, I named them myself. Peter, Piper, and Pickle, after the strange tongue-twister my brothers had taught me when I was little.

Peter placed a tumbler of amber liquid with an orange garnish in front of me. Piper, a flute that bubbled but was a sunset-pink in color. And Pickle, just a shot of something clear, with a lime wedge on the rim.

It's him that I looked up at from the drinks. "Well played." He gave me a mock bow, and I chuckled. "We clear?"

Peter and Piper, ever inconspicuous, turned from me and began to polish the spotless glasses above the credenza. Pickle gave me a subtle thumbs-up after a moment, and I took the lime wedge off the small, slender glass, and shot the clear liquid down in a gulp.

The motion so practiced you'd think we'd done it more than twelve times over the course of six years, I slid the empty glass back over the bar, right into his hand, while with my other, I stuck the flesh of the lime between my teeth. As the citrus exploded in my mouth, the small glass disappeared beneath the counter, and I picked up the pretty, princess-looking flute as if it was what I'd held the whole time.

I tossed the remnants of the lime into the nearly invisible bin behind the bar. "Thank you, gentlemen." I lifted the glass in a cheers to them. "Peter, could you save that for me? There's still an hour left."

He smirked, but nodded, and stowed the tumbler beneath the counter. I winked before turning back to the Hall, towards those in the room with expectations of me.

I felt eyes follow me as I strode back to the dais, but between the shot and the pink drink it was harder to mind as much as I did minutes ago. In the center of the dance floor, my mom and dad swayed adorably to the easy tune played by the musicians. I made sure to skirt around the floor, not wanting to interrupt their fun–or have them interrupt mine. But halfway to the dais, halfway to a gods-blessed *chair*, I was intercepted.

"Princess Althea?" a deep voice called, and, sighing internally, I turned to the man with a smile–an expression which became a bit more genuine when I saw the timidness on General Vey's face.

"General," I greeted him, and curtsied as he bowed to me.

"I was wondering if you would like to dance with me." His deep blue eyes flicked to the drink in my hand, and he grinned, true humor lighting his handsome face. "Unless you'd like to finish that first."

The kindness, and the utter lack of judgment in his voice and in his expression had me replying, "I'm a talented multitasker."

He laughed, and held his elbow out to me, blatantly showing the golden band on his ring finger. A dance without expectations, then. Even better. I took his arm with my free hand, and he snapped–and suddenly there was a drink in his fist, too. Tumbler and flute held aloft, we walked onto the floor I'd been avoiding just seconds ago.

The musicians caught the new air we were bringing to the dance, and the tempo picked up. Ciaragen put his hand on my waist, I rested mine on his shoulder, and he clinked his glass against mine before taking a drink. Giggling as he swept me into a simple dance, I did the same.

More people, who'd been slumped in their seats a moment ago, waiting for the night to be over, joined us, grinning now. The three bartenders worked swiftly in the corner as drink orders poured in, following their oh-so-proper princess's lead. A few skulked at their tables, brows lowered as they watched me dance with a man not within my standing, a drink in my hand. I took another sip and ignored them.

Ciaragen, I quickly learned, had two left feet. It was almost like he'd learned the woman's part of the dance with how often his toes just barely missed mine. But, between his easy laughter, and the nearly empty glass in my hand, I found I didn't mind getting my toes stepped on.

After a particularly clumsy spin, my face likely pink from laughing, he said, "I mean this as a compliment: you are one of the least serious princesses I've ever met."

"Well, sir, I *take* it as a compliment, and must say that you are one of the least serious generals I've ever met."

"Cheers to not living by the expectations of others," he replied, and held his glass up. I felt warmth fill my eyes at the toast, and clinked my glass against his once more. He downed the last swallow of his drink, and, not to be outdone, I followed suit. "Would you like another?"

I grinned, and handed my empty glass to him. "Yes, please."

With a bow, he headed back towards the bar. I stepped off the floor, too, and found myself moving towards the east wall of the Hall, where grand windows framed in gauzy white curtains overlooked one of the three gardens at Castle Cerasche.

I pulled aside a curtain, and tucked it behind me, the fabric a comforting weight against my back. The evening primroses had bloomed, shadowed beneath a small maple tree, whose red leaves glimmered with the light emanating through the windows.

I glanced back to the bar, and Piper was making Ciaragen our drinks. Seeming to sense my gaze, he turned, and I nudged my head towards the pinewood door adjacent to the window before leaving my place there to walk into the beckoning garden.

The early summer air was cool without the sun out to heat it–a welcome chill after being touched by and dancing with so many people. I tipped my head back, letting the weight and warmth of my hair leave my back for the first time this evening, and sighed. The breeze carried the perfume-scented strands, and rustled the many blossoms and leaves that surrounded me on the sand and stone path. I closed my eyes, my shoulders dropping, my fingers loosening at my sides–

The door handle clicked as it twisted from the other side, and I turned, expecting to see Ciaragen with my drink. Instead, I found Atlas, carrying the tumbler Peter had put aside for me. His storm gray eyes held mine as he approached, the door shutting quietly behind him.

"Princess," he said, his deep voice quiet in the serene space. "The general was pulled into a conversation with your parents. He asked me to bring this to you, and said he hopes you'll save him a dance tomorrow, as well." He held the glass out to me, his fingerprints cutting through the frost that coated it.

I took it, and blushed as my fingers brushed his, as they had earlier. "Thank you," I remembered to say, only a beat too late.

"Of course, Your Highness." He bowed to me, and then turned to leave. But, before the logical, sober part of my brain could stop me, I breathed, "Wait."

He did. Paused with his hand inches from the door, and I didn't let myself think about it too much before continuing. "Stay."

He looked through the window, into where he was probably still supposed to be serving drinks. Where the people waiting for them likely noticed that the server had left through the same door as the princess, and neither had returned.

But still, he hesitated. And that was all I, and the liquid courage in my blood, needed. I stepped up to him slowly, allowing him the chance to say something. To walk away. He only turned to face me, his gaze unreadable. I stopped when just a foot of space remained between us.

"We should get back inside," he said, but his voice was rough.

"They've been talking about me all night. What's one more whisper?" I sidestepped him, moving into the shadows on the other side of the door. His strong body seemed almost anchored to mine, his eyes never wavering from my face as he spun in place to follow my steps. I stopped, only to lean against the sandstone wall of the castle, and took a sip of the amber liquid in my glass.

He glanced down to that glass now, and his jaw tightened. But his voice was gentle when he replied, "You're not thinking clearly. I can get you some water–"

"I'm thinking that out of all the people in that room, you're the only one I couldn't stop looking at all night." Including Dalton. Including Dion. Including every gods-damned man I was *supposed* to want.

His eyes darkened, and he took a step closer to me. And it wasn't the chill in the air that made me shudder. I watched his nostrils flare as he breathed, and the next step he took seemed almost involuntary. It brought him where I wanted him: right in front of me, as solid of a barrier as the stone behind me. So close that when he took a breath, his chest brushed the knuckles of my fingers wrapped around the tumbler.

I pressed my other palm to his chest, and breathed his name. I could feel his heart thundering as his hand rose, and clasped mine. He pulled it from his chest to press his lips against it. A gesture that, so many times tonight, felt at best sweet, and at worst disgusting. But here, now, with him...I felt a lovely tightening low in my belly that I only ever felt around him. His breath caressed my knuckles, his lips warm and soft against my skin.

His mouth moved, and he said against the skin of my wrist, "I couldn't stop looking at you, either." Against my elbow, my eyes closing, "All night, all I could see was how gorgeous you are." Against my shoulder, as my breaths thinned, "But you are infinite, Althea." Against my neck, just below my ear, "And I will not be the one who limits you."

His lips left me, and I opened my eyes, feeling very much like I was emerging from a stupor. He stroked my cheek once, his eyes still dark, but certain, and then he moved too quickly for me to stop him. Walked right through the pinewood door without a second glance.

As childish or illogical as it might be, rejection washed over me. The lust went as quickly as he did, and while his words to me were noble, and caring, and lovely, I didn't feel them. What I felt was shame, embarrassment, and sadness. At wanting him and not being able to have him; at losing my control so easily; at putting myself in a situation where he had to reject me, since I wasn't strong enough to ignore him.

The rest of the emotions–otherwise known as reality–came in full swing, as their brothers and sisters rioted in my heart. Those I'd locked away hours ago hammered at my control now, forcing me to concede. To cry, or scream, and relive the memories of this afternoon.

Not caring that anybody still remained in the Hall, waiting for their guest of honor, I set the half-empty tumbler on the ground, lifted my skirts, and ran down the stone and sand pathway of the garden.

9
THORN

*DION - **21** YEARS EARLIER*

I SAT AT A ROUND WALNUT TABLE ON A BALCONY WITH THE HIGH Lord and High Lady of Sabrian, unable to even look in the direction of my guard. After declining to join us at the table, she stood against the wall across from me, staring straight out to the land before her. The couple holding power over that land sat just a couple of feet apart from each other on the opposite side of the table. I alone had my back to the city.

What that female–Ciaragen, her name was. What she had said to me, the passion, sincerity, and venom with which she'd spoken...It sat like a lead weight in my gut, and I doubted that I would be able to stomach more than a few bites of whatever was about to be served.

My long-detached emotions pulled me in two. They begged me to remember the gravestone. To avoid the same pain of my past actions, as I had been doing for so long. And yet they also asked me to do better. To use this chance, this place–this only opportunity I might ever have for the remainder of my life–to become a male who didn't need to hide behind false apathy.

I was a murderer. Perhaps not so recently as my guard believed, but I was. I supposed the timeline would matter little to her. She was someone who had clearly been raised to love her country and its people. Unlike me, who had that love ripped from me over sixty years ago.

Anyway, based on the permanent marks my deeds had left on my soul, the timeline didn't mean much to me either.

I could have tried to make excuses for my behavior. I was young and zealous; I did not question orders; I was loyal to my king. But those words meant nothing. This female was young, and already had more backbone, more righteousness, than I had now. Yes, at the time I'd believed that I was killing those people for a reason–even if they weren't outright traitors, they'd conspired against their king, against *my* king.

Until I found out that some hadn't. That, in fact, many had been silenced for little more than gossip at a pub.

And then people had stopped gossiping. Stopped talking altogether when anyone they didn't recognize was near, and were still cautious even when every face was familiar. Thus, the king had developed a new position for me within his staff. No longer a royal executioner–a title which had started to make me sick to my core after my realization.

I could no longer tell myself that I was loyal; obedient. Instead, any 'job' I carried out thereafter, no matter the justification given, had me wondering if the details of it were even true. If they–meaning the king and my brother–were just telling me the stories they knew would allow me to sleep at night. Though even that soon became impossible.

No longer a royal executioner. My duties in my new role were to host supplicants, act as though I sincerely cared about the problems they presented to me, and then report those to the king. An 'act' that had only become so after years of caring. My attempts at actually serving my country, my continent, and its people, had been put quickly to rest–along with the person who'd come to me for help. Only then had it become an *act*. Encouraged and aided by the king, and my brother.

As His Majesty's executioners, Olin and I had worked alongside each other with the same purpose and the same goal. Once I stepped away, he was doing it on his own–not that he minded. With this change, we were two pieces of a puzzle whose picture was Eshelle on its knees.

"Lord Dion?" someone said, pulling me from my withdrawn state. I blinked, and realized that both the High Lord and High Lady were staring at me, their brows raised. The subjects of my newest position.

"I apologize. I seem to have gotten lost in my thoughts," I said, hoping they wouldn't inquire as to what those thoughts were about.

"I'm sure you were thinking of something much more important than your hosts attempting to have a conversation with you." The High Lord swirled the contents in his wine cup.

My cheeks heated. These people obviously were not entertainers of the usual passive-aggressiveness employed in most courts. "Certainly not. My rudeness is inexcusable. If you wouldn't mind repeating yourself just this once, I will pay the utmost attention going forward."

Even as the words left my mouth, I wondered how long I could kiss their asses without tiring. Luckily, my significant experience in that area had built up a sort of tolerance in me over the years, like a drunk getting used to his cups.

The High Lady replied, "I think I won't." I blinked once, and a saccharine smile spread over her face. "But, do be careful, Lord Dion. I fear that your nose may become permanently discolored if you continue to talk like that." She gave me a falsely concerned pout, and then turned to her mate. "Shall we have them bring out supper, then?" she asked him, to which he smirked and nodded in response.

I had to work to keep my face composed. Whether I was offended at the lack of propriety, embarrassed by the acknowledgement of my behavior, or even amused at the charming frankness with which she'd insulted me, I couldn't be sure. I was too busy trying to show no surprise. In fact, externally, all I did was nod once, and hopefully managed to look vaguely bored.

Before us appeared several dishes, all containing the lighter fare of the season. The seafood only the wealthiest saw in the fortified capital city, seasoned with aromatic herbs and a hint of lemon–nothing so heavy as the rich food to which I was accustomed.

I waited a beat for someone to serve us, but no one did. With a more subtle glance at me than I would have thought she was capable of, the High Lady reached for a platter, and skewered a piece of fish on her own fork, then laid it on her plate. She passed the dish, not to her mate, but to me. Those bright, keen eyes held mine, seeming to challenge and examine me all at once. Though a bit taken aback, I didn't hesitate to take the platter from her and serve myself just as she had done. I looked to the High Lord, and held it out to him. He took it without a word.

So followed the rest of the items before us. Before I knew it, I had a plateful of food–white fish, roasted vegetables, rice cooked in a seasoned oil, a salad with strawberries and a dressing that smelled sweet and savory at the same time. My mouth was watering, but I waited.

"You wait to pray," the High Lady said.

Though she hadn't spoken it as a question, I answered, "I didn't wish to be discourteous if your household prays before meals." Many liked to pray before, sometimes even after meals. I was not one of them.

"You don't thank the gods in Oschverre?" the High Lord asked, his brows furrowing over eyes of steel.

"I can't speak for everybody in the capital, High Lord," I began. I didn't know if I should lie–not when they seemed so quick to see right through my hollow words. Before I thought it through enough, and the pause became too long, I continued, "But no. I don't."

I kept my eyes on his, waiting for the shaming. Or the question. *Why?* Since it seemed that I wasn't minding my tongue as much as I should have been thus far, I prepared to give a generic answer. Probably something along the lines of *my parents weren't religious.* Which was not a lie, but also not the real reason: that I had stopped believing in the gods even before I'd stopped believing in my king.

But the High Lord and High Lady merely exchanged a glance, picked up their forks, and began to eat. As I sat there dumbly for a moment, my surprise getting the better of me, I caught motion from behind them.

Since we'd arrived, no part of her had moved from her position at the wall behind her High Lord and High Lady. And, while she'd faced me, her eyes had stared over my head. Until now. Now, my guard's eyes–the deepest of blues, like the sky at dusk, or a stormy sea–were boring into mine. Her lips were pressed together slightly, and a small line had appeared between her delicately arched black brows. She didn't seem to be aware of the expression.

But then she saw my gaze on her, and I watched those eyes harden–a frozen sea, the sky after a lightning strike. I quickly looked back to the High Lord, once again feeling as though I wouldn't be able to stomach a bite of what was on my plate.

The little food I'd managed to eat shifted in my stomach as I walked back to my chambers with my guard. Her words from earlier hung in the air between us, as palpable as if she were saying them again right now.

What could I say, really? That I was different now? I wasn't sure that was true. After all, if the king had not 'promoted' me (twice) I would still be one of his executioners. Perhaps it would have eaten me alive by now, but who knew which route I would have taken to escape?

I would like to believe I'd have ended myself, or deserted, rather than continue to kill innocents for him. If I was honest, though, I believed there was a distinct possibility that, to cope with what I was doing, my mind would have eventually created an escape wherein I learned to become detached from my actions.

Was I really different beneath the surface now, or was I simply a product of my changed circumstances?

The question nagged at me as we made it to the hallway where my chambers were located. I looked at my guard from the corner of my eye, grateful that I had copied our position from before dinner–slightly behind and to her left.

She was a tall female, almost half a head shorter than myself. Her chestnut skin was nearly completely covered, between her white and gold uniform, and the large quantity of black curls spilling from her head. I couldn't see all of her face at the moment, but I caught the edge of her delicate but distinct jaw, the cut of high cheekbones, and the fringe of dark lashes that I swore would brush her cheek if she looked down. For she had not yet, at least not in front of me.

Suddenly, just feet from my door, she stopped and turned towards me. I felt very much like a mouse who hadn't realized it was walking into a trap until the metal struck. The metal in question in this case, of course, was in the form of those deep blue eyes. I could no more escape them than I could chew off my own foot. They held my gaze with a steadiness that was almost intimidating. And the almost was a lie.

"Why don't you believe in the gods?" she asked.

I blinked, and blurted the first response that came to mind: "Why should I?"

Now she was the one to blink. Those big, strange eyes stared up at me, the black brows over them once again furrowing to create that small line between them. "Because you seem like you could use it," she responded, and I could tell that she hadn't thought through her words either, by the way her full lips pressed tightly together after she spoke.

I stared at her for a moment, and, to her credit, she did not look away, even after speaking so candidly. If anything, her chin angled higher, and her brows scrunched closer together over her bottomless eyes. Instead, as I watched the hatred in those eyes grow with each passing second, I was the first to avert my gaze.

"I'll take that under advisement," I said simply.

My hand was on the knob when she replied, "Don't lie."

I stopped, and turned my face to her. Her mouth was set with anger and displeasure, and something else I couldn't place.

Lying had been a consistent partner for all of my matured life. Lying to prisoners when they asked if the king would spare them. Lying to supplicants who asked for aid from their king. Lying to the king about being honored to be in his service. Lying to myself about nearly any damned thing in between.

Yet, I couldn't find it in me to tell her that I wasn't lying now, or that I wouldn't in the future. That falsehood somehow wouldn't pass my lips, even as I opened them to speak. So I didn't respond at all. Instead, I dipped my chin slightly in a parting gesture. I opened my door, walked into the foyer, and locked it behind me when it was shut.

※

Ciaragen

I CURSED MYSELF AS I STOOD OUTSIDE OF HIS DOOR, PLAYING guard.

All evening, I'd spoken true to him. Perhaps not always–okay, not at all–in my best interests, but I'd done it. I wanted him to know that I did not consider it a privilege, or some sort of promotion, that I was the one chosen to look after an emissary to the king. I wanted him to know that I was aware of who he was and what he'd done. What I hadn't expected was for him to care about what I thought.

Because he'd clearly been affected by my words to him before supper. He cared then, and, maybe in a different way, he cared again just now when I'd asked him about his lack of belief in the gods.

Probably the worst person I could ever ask, for about a million reasons. After all, how much success could one have in a relationship with religion if murder was their profession?

Because you seem like you could use it. While true, what had overcome me to say something like that to him? And, why, for the love of all the gods, did the wording make it sound like I cared? As soon as I'd realized how my words could be interpreted, I'd snapped my mouth shut, and stared him down. There could have been no mistaking the loathing I'd let show in my eyes.

Now, I listened for any activity on the other side of the door; I heard none. What did he *do* in there?

And what was he *going* to do here? We knew his intention was to learn about my High Lord and High Lady, and supply that information to his master. We, however, were not participating in that little arrangement; we had no intention of providing him with any useful information. And that little snag would definitely keep him here longer than he intended.

My High Lord and High Lady were determined to dine with him, speak with him–*learn* about him. As his guard and escort, I would take him through the grounds, and through the city, if he was interested–and we were supposed to make him interested. I was to protect him, and make him feel as welcome as I could within our court.

Essentially, he would be very busy, and not at all in the way he was supposed to be.

I would admit that '*welcome*' bit could use a little work on my end. I'd kissed the asses of many before him. I knew how to play my part, and do what I had to for the good of my people, even if that meant ignoring my pride. And yet every time I faced him, I found myself wanting to spit every foul thought I had in my head at him. Day one, and I had already surpassed *wanting* to do so, and actually done it.

Well, that was going to have to change. *I* was going to have to change; get my act together. If we were going to have any success at all, I would have to pretend to at least tolerate him. My High Lady had said to me just this morning, "Feel about him what you will. You have all my support in doing so," her head had tilted slightly, her eyes filled with grim understanding. "But remember that our court is a rose; he mustn't see our thorns just yet."

I took a deep breath. For her, for her mate; for Sabrian, and for its people. For them, I would become a rose. For them, I would hide my thorns from the male who killed my father

10

THE MEMORY

THEA - 2 DAYS EARLIER

I SAT ON MY BED IN MY CHAMBERS, IN ONLY MY UNDERCLOTHES. As soon as I'd removed the dress I'd worn this evening, it had been like removing the self I'd been for the past hours. As I'd eaten, joked, flirted, danced. Once the gown was in a puddle around my feet, I'd felt a much different, and much heavier weight replace it.

I killed three people today.

Silent tears started running down my cheeks, though nothing else moved. My lips did not tremble, and my forehead did not crumple. My entire body was still. It was on the inside where my emotions wreaked havoc; an internal whirling tornado of anger, despair, and guilt as the memories lashed at me with their spiraling wind.

I was alone in the garden.

A place I visited frequently, without my guards', or my parents' knowledge. The only people who knew of it were my closest friends, and my sister, all of whom had accompanied me here for more than a few picnics over the years.

The late morning sunshine streamed through the branches of the great pine I laid beneath, my head cushioned on a blanket of moss covering one of the exposed roots. There was a bird's nest in one of the lower branches, and I could hear chicks tweeting softly within it. Could practically sense their littlest hearts fluttering like the wings that would soon carry them.

I sighed. I really should be getting back to the castle. I'd left training early with the excuse that I had to prepare for the gathering tonight. My training master, Amahd, being a man, thought it more than reasonable that I would require seven hours to do so.

I normally didn't like to go out in public in my leathers, but going back inside to change would have been too much of a risk. Any number of people might have stopped me, and actually made me start getting ready, or even asked that I assist with setting up. Though it was considered unusual for a woman of noble birth to participate in household chores, my parents believed that under-standing the work that our staff did every day would help us to appreciate them more. They were right, of course. And I did enjoy the fact that I knew how to bake fresh bread, put on a duvet cover, and hone my own blades.

It was just that, with the events of the evening approaching, I wasn't really in the mood to set tables, or help in the kitchens. What I wanted was to lie in my favorite garden, and not think about the gatherings that had consumed my every thought and action for weeks.

So much time, preparing for dances and speeches. There was a weight on my shoulders which got heavier and heavier as the evening approached. When I must select a few men from all of the eligible nobility, whom I could potentially see as my future husband. I had a lot of emotions about it, and very few of them were pleasant. But in all the time spent leading up to tonight, I hadn't let myself take even a moment to contemplate that silenced, scared piece of my heart.

I heaved another breath, and sat up as I exhaled. I looked out into the expanse of the garden. Brightly colored flowers bloomed in bushes, on trellises, and in small groupings in pots or in the ground. Iron chairs, not lost to rust due to the magic that protected them from the elements, were spaced about in pairs around small, matching tables. It was under this tree, though, on top of the clover that flowered in these warmer months, that my friends and I would lay our blanket, break out the food and the wine, and laugh until our stomachs hurt.

I sighed again, this breath easier than the last. I rose, brushing any moss from my hair, and any clovers or dried pine needles from my body. I stretched, pointing my toes, and bringing my arms above my head, a soft sound escaping me as I did so. With one last look around the garden, I began the walk home.

There was a dirt walkway that circumferenced and split the garden in places. I took the path which led to a trail within the trees that separated the garden from the main park. The trees were mighty things that had to have been there for at least a century, with their trunks as thick as a man, and an abundance of branches.

This stretch of the trail was short and only slightly curving. From about midway, one could see either end with clarity, even at dusk. So I was not prepared in the least for the large man that came out from between the trunks, and struck the left side of my face.

I jolted from the memory for a moment. Remembering the man, the blow. I touched my lip, my cheek, feeling only the flesh I'd healed, no tenderness or pain remaining. The man had been tall, and built like an ox–a wide chest that narrowed only slightly to an equally thick and muscled abdomen. But his face–I couldn't see his face in that part of the memory. Only in the next one.

I regained consciousness in a room that smelled of damp stone, rot, and rust, and opened my eyes only to find that the room was scarcely lighter than it had been with them closed. The only light emanated from an inch-wide gap beneath what I could make out as a door. Probably a good thing that it wasn't bright, considering the pounding headache I had. Likely either due to the blow I'd received, or from hitting the ground afterwards.

My heart started pounding, too, sending throbbing pulses through my temples. I looked down at myself, even though I could barely see anything; my night black leathers completely disappeared in the darkness. But, as my body came back to me, adrenaline erasing pain, I felt that I was sitting in a chair. My arms were bound by rope to its back; looped around the bars and then in a figure eight around my wrists. My feet hung slightly off the ground, ropes also tied around my ankles, connecting each of them to the chair legs.

No more than an animal caught in a trap, I began twisting my wrists, pulling with all my strength to try and free them from their bindings. I felt the fibers rip into my skin, but didn't register any pain.

My breath came faster and faster through my teeth, and before I could even think to leash my fear, it began to take hold of me. My mind whirled, spinning around the thoughts of never escaping, of being violated, beaten, or killed. Tears–panicked, desperate tears– stung in my eyes, and my throat became thick with them.

Stop, an internal voice commanded. My voice, but in a tenor I'd never heard, with an authority I'd never used. But I did. I stopped. My breathing was still quick, my heart still racing, but the tears that flowed were only those which had already pooled.

Think, that voice said as I calmed.

I closed my lips, and pulled a slow breath in through my nose. The stench of the room filled my lungs, but I disregarded it as much as I could. Instead, I focused on my physical surroundings.

The room had no windows. Only that door, made of what had to be metal, with the rust scent so strong. Which almost definitely meant that it would squeal like a pig for slaughter when I opened it.

But was the man even near to hear that noise? Not in this room, it seemed, but on the premises of wherever it was I was being held. It wouldn't be overly surprising if he had left. Assumed that I was just a girl, who liked to play at being trained with her black leathers. Not capable of escaping my bindings, which I had to admit had been skillfully done. But it would be foolish of me to make any assumptions, even if he had done so himself.

A plan. I needed a plan. Getting myself out of those ropes was the obvious step one. Then, assuming it wasn't locked, the door would creak when opened. I needed to be prepared if the man was out there. If he was, I would need a weapon. Most likely, he had at least one on him. If I could disarm him, I would be the one who walked away from the fight.

If the door was locked, I would have no choice but to wait in this quiet room until he came to get me. I could feign still being tied up, ascertain where his weapons were, and then the plan would follow the same way in the end.

Unbind, door, disarm, disable, escape. Hopefully.

Before any of that, though, I needed to heal my current injuries. Though adrenaline kept me from feeling them now, I could have a concussion, which would only be worsened in the fight. I sent my magic to my face and head, allowing it to find the areas that needed mending.

I felt my gift warm my lip, and the space from my cheekbone to my hairline on the left side of my face. Nothing on the back of my head, though, which meant that the headache had only come from the hit, and not from my skull smacking against the pathway.

Once healed, it was time to get out of the damned bindings. No knife, not even a sharp hairpin I could use, as I'd only done my hair in a simple braid down my back this morning. When the man was tying the ropes, my muscles would have been relaxed in my unconsciousness. Tensing only made them tighter. Which left me with just one option.

My stomach clenched as I thought it. Not because of the pain I was about to experience–inflict on myself–but because it was a part of me that I hated. My other 'gift'. My secret.

Everyone knew that I could mend.

No one knew that I could break, too.

My healing was a gift from the gods, my most cherished possession. I healed everyone from unborn babes, to century-old people near their deathbeds. I healed myself from minor scrapes, through broken bones. But I could also break those bones.

I'd hardly ever done it intentionally, and never to anyone but myself. I first discovered it when I was five, and desperately didn't want to go to a very snooty lord and lady's gathering a three-day carriage ride away. They had monstrous children; boys who pulled my hair when our parents weren't looking. The only way I could think to avoid it was if I was hurt or unwell enough that my parents would be forced to leave me at home. A broken leg or something–the instant I'd thought it, there had been blinding pain as my femur had snapped. I'd screamed so loudly from my room that my parents had heard me from outside the castle.

They'd assumed I'd fallen off my bed, crooning at me and telling me that this was why I shouldn't jump on the mattress. Even then, I'd known to keep the truth hidden. Secret.

I might have been able to heal myself, but being just five years old, my parents weren't confident enough in my abilities. They'd demanded I wait for a proper healer, to ensure that it was mended correctly. So, I stayed home, my mother electing to remain with me. She held me in her arms as the healer did her work, and for a while after that. She carried me on her hip if we needed to leave my room, practically snarling at anybody who tried to tell her that she needn't do so. She laid with me in my bed for days, reading me stories, and sharing what she claimed to be an amount of ice cream only appropriate for broken bones. And my father had taken my siblings to that gathering.

Since then, I had used the breaking—I couldn't quite call it a gift —only twice. Both times to experiment with it to make sure it hadn't been a very strange coincidence, and both times only on small areas of my body. And, of course, only when I was trained enough to heal the breaks myself.

But now, in this dark cell, I took a deep breath, and used the breaking for the fourth time in my life.

As I broke the bones in my hands, I could only be thankful for the adrenaline coursing through my veins. The pain was sharp, zapping through my body and brain. I had to clamp my lips shut to keep from screaming, and new tears welled in my eyes, but I didn't allow myself to stop, even as I bit through the flesh of my lips. I was careful to keep my tongue against the roof of my mouth.

Once the carpals above each of my thumbs were shattered, I was able to slip my hands out of their bindings, the ropes sliding agonizingly against the broken bones. Shaking, I set my hands on my lap gently, palms up. Without looking at them—it might be dark, but I didn't think my mind would react well to even part of that sight right now—I sent my power to them, as well as my lips, and both were healed in seconds. With the pain cleared, I wiped the tears from my face, and resumed.

I tore my fingernails as I untied the ropes around my ankles, and regrew them as soon as the ropes laid on the ground at my feet. My nails might be the only weapon available to me until I got a real one.

Completely unbound now, I stood, and silently stepped towards the door. I slid my hands around the sides of it without touching its surface, for fear that the man on the other side may hear the brushing of my skin against the metal. It was best to assume that he was there, so that I could prepare for the fight.

My right hand made contact with the doorknob, tapping it lightly as I stopped my motion. I paused, wrapping my hand slowly around the knob, pressing my ear against the door to listen for any sounds on the other side, hardly daring to breathe. When I heard nothing, I took a shuddering breath, and stepped to the outside of the door as I steadily twisted the knob, thanking the gods as it turned; it wasn't locked. Then, I opened the door as quickly as I could, so that any wailing of the hinges would be short-lived.

It didn't make a sound.

And neither did anything else—no footsteps, gasps, or voices. Which meant that I had to be alone, at least in whatever area I was being kept. If I wasn't so focused on not making any noises of my own, I would have let out a gasping sob of overwhelming relief. I hadn't realized, until that moment, how much I'd been hoping for more time to prepare for the fight I was sure was to come.

As I stepped around the door and through the threshold, I entered an outer room. I could see my surroundings now as the early afternoon sun poured through a single window in the cement wall of what must be a basement. The window was barred, so that was out as a means of escape. The only furniture in the room was a chair that was placed just outside and to the right of the door to my cell. The only thing occupying it at the moment was an empty mug that reeked of liquor.

About ten feet to my left, there was a staircase. Though my heart was pounding, I kept my breath quiet as I walked towards them. At the top, there was another door—wooden instead of metal. I placed a toe on the first step, to test it, and my heart lurched when just that small pressure released a squeak from the wood. I halted, and listened. And heard voices. Plural.

I closed my eyes. And this time, I took control of that voice in my head, and told myself—

You. Will. Live.

I remembered from somewhere in the depths of my memories of sneaking to Iris's room late at night when we were little, that the best way to avoid creaking floors was to stick to the edges. Walls, or in this case, the balusters. So, opening my eyes, I placed my right foot on the far right side of the first step.

Not a sound.

Exhaling, I made my way up the stairs, keeping the pattern of only stepping on the outer edges of each one. As I made it to the top step, the voices became clearer. I pressed my ear against the door.

"...be here any minute," one was saying. He sounded close, maybe a few feet from the other side of the door. One.

"You think he'll take her to them first?" another asked, further back from the other. Two.

"He will do whatever he wants," another replied, his voice flat. Three.

"He wouldn't mess her up too bad, not until after they see her. Know we've got her at our mercy," the first voice responded. I prayed that there weren't any more, staying silent as the known three spoke.

"He will do whatever he pleases, regardless of the consequences, like always," the third voice countered.

"You shut your damn mouth, Adathan," the first man snapped. "He'll be High King one day. More than anyone, you should watch your tongue."

High King? There was no such thing in Weaschte...

"He's not now, though, is he?" Adathan sounded completely indifferent to the menace in the first man's tone.

"You want me to tell him your thoughts there, hmm? If not, I suggest you shut your fucking mouth before I do it for you."

"While it would be fun to watch you attempt that, shouldn't I check on her? It's been an hour."

Shit.

Think, think, think.

There was no way I was going to be able to fight through them if one of them stood in the doorway. Even with all of my strength, I wouldn't be able to physically tackle a man of that size.

I did have another capability at my disposal...

No. I couldn't do it. Using the breaking on myself was one thing, but where was the line drawn? Somehow, it felt cleaner, less repug-

nant, that they might die by blade, than if I were to snap their necks with magic, and be done with it. More dignified—for them, and for me.

"Probably should," the second voice agreed.

Without giving myself a chance to think it through, I jumped from where I was on the top step, and somersaulted into a landing so clean that even Amahd would be proud. I ran on my toes to the metal door, and closed it. Then dashed back to the steps. Instead of climbing them, I went to the far wall beneath and behind them, and crouched. Staring through the slats, the shadows protecting me, I quieted my breath, and waited.

"...go, Marcys. We'll stay up here," the second voice was saying.

"Yeah, I think I will. Don't wait up," Marcys, the first man, responded, laughter in his voice.

My stomach churned. Though I'd never been violated, some intrinsic, womanly part of my gut knew the intent behind those words. Knew the dark humor with which he spoke and laughed. And suddenly, I wasn't so scared to kill him.

The door at the top of the stairs opened, shining light down into the basement. I deepened my crouch, and kept my breathing quiet. I listened to heavy feet walk down those steps, boards creaking all the way. From my hiding spot, as he descended, I saw his legs appear, then the daggers at his hips. Those would be my targets, I decided.

Then came his torso, and the sword strapped across his back. But I was not prepared for what I saw when his head was visible. There, poking out from his blond hair: pointed, arched ears.

Fae.

I stopped breathing altogether. I knew very little about the Fae people from across the Evredis, but I did know of their heightened senses, speed, and agility. And vastly more powerful majick.

If he didn't already scent me, it was probably because he assumed whatever scent there was only lingered in the air from *when they'd brought me in, and saturated the space through the crack beneath the door to my cell.*

My heart pounded in my chest. I had already been nervous about fighting a man so much bigger than myself, but a Fae male? Deep, true fear settled in my gut as I wondered at the power that he might possess.

Stop, that voice said once again. You will fight. You will win.

I closed my eyes as I listened to the sound of the male's footsteps cross the small room. Time seemed to slow as I steadied myself. As I adopted a complete blankness of mind, all thoughts, doubts, and fears left my head. I embodied only the word survive.

I felt nothing as I opened my eyes. I watched as the male approached my cell door, and calculated. There was no emotion, no racing of my heart, or sweat beading on my brow. I took a breath.

And I moved.

No time for thinking; no reason to think—only act.

He heard me, of course. Perhaps a fraction of a second slower than he would have been, not expecting me to be anywhere but tied to that chair, at his mercy. With how small the room was, that slight hesitation was enough for me to reach him, duck beneath the arm he haphazardly threw out towards me, and snatch one of the knives from the sheaths at his hips.

I retreated, blade clutched tight, as he sent a wicked backhand in the direction of where my face had been.

"You bitch," he spat, feral rage in his dark eyes. I didn't bother responding as I rolled over my shoulder on the ground, and, as I came up, sliced a gash in his thigh so deep that his leg gave out. I ignored the wrenching in my gut at the wet tearing sound I'd never heard before, never wanted to hear. And, as much as I knew anatomy from my studies as a healer, I was only barely prepared for the spurt of blood that came from his femoral artery, and splashed across my throat and chest.

He cried out as he hit the ground, and I knew the others would come to investigate. But with his Fae healing, I couldn't take the chance that he wouldn't bleed out before his body could seal the wound. Two was better than three. And, knowing what he'd wanted to do to me, I didn't hesitate to plunge his own dagger into his temple.

I was almost grateful as two sets of footsteps came thundering down the stairs. There wasn't time to fully recognize the sound and feel of steel scraping against bone, and tearing through flesh and brain matter.

I turned from the dead male to find his companions racing for me. Both dark-haired, both very easily over six feet tall, and both with pointed ears. Faster than I would have thought possible, my eyes and mind registered one drawn dagger, another sheathed.

I lunged for them before they could move to capture me, once again having the element of surprise on my side as they took in the sight behind me. I chose to go for the one on the right first. While the one with strange golden eyes stared at me, seeming to be in some sort of shock, the other's green gaze was shooting back and forth between myself and the bloodied body of the male I'd just defeated, and I needed to take advantage of that distraction before it was lost.

I swung upwards with the dagger, aiming for his neck, but he turned just in time to come away with only a narrow line on his chin. From the corner of my eye, I watched the other one move, and the distraction cost me. In a blink, the other male had a muscled arm wrapped around me, pinning my arms to my sides. His other hand grabbed mine, and attempted to splay my fingers open.

I stomped hard on his instep, and he barely seemed to notice. My pinky and ring finger were giving out, and I started to panic, think-ing, thinking of how I could get free, and–CRACK.

The male screamed, and released me. He stared in horror at what had once been a hand, but was now a skin-covered mess of unnatural angles. I didn't have the time to recognize my own alarm at the site. I shoved my knife into his chest, feeling it as the steel scraped bone and tore through muscle. He let out a sound halfway between a shout and a choke. Panting, I pulled the blade out, and then gasped as his blood sprayed out from the wound, and droplets of it landed on my tongue.

I couldn't afford to register that, either, even as I allowed myself to spit onto the floor. There was still one more. He'd been holding back, probably anticipating that his companion would disarm me, and he'd only be needed to tie me back up. When the second male fell, I whirled on my final opponent. I saw only that his eyes were focused on me before I threw my blade right at his heart.

Dagger glinting in his grip, he lifted his arm to block his face and turned slightly, and the knife instead lodged itself about four inches below and a few inches medially from his armpit. He grunted in pain, and I used the fact that his arm was still blocking his line of sight to run to him and yank the blade out, guessing that—

There was a soft hiss as I skipped back out of his reach, and I knew I'd been correct. I'd pierced his lung.

He coughed, and the smallest amount of blood came up. He lowered his arm, and though he wheezed each breath, I knew that alone was not going to take him down. I was sure that if I didn't end him, and only used his incapacitation to escape, this wouldn't be the last time I would see him.

I repeated the move I'd used on the first male, and rolled over my shoulder on the ground. But this time, instead of just coming to a knee to strike my blow, I brought the knife down at the bottom of my roll, stabbing into his foot. As he doubled over in agony, I pulled it out, spun it in my palm, and then I thrust the blade up into his gut.

Hot blood poured over my hand, and I released the dagger to get away from that feeling. He collapsed to the floor, blood coming out from his side, his stomach, his mouth, his foot. I looked deeper into the room, and saw the other two males lying still, their eyes unseeing. As the last took what would be some of his final breaths, that internal voice told me enough. It would be enough. Move, that voice said, not giving me even a moment to contemplate what I'd done.

I dashed up the stairs, not having to worry about being quiet anymore. When I opened the door, the amount of sunshine that streamed into the room from the two windows felt blinding. It looked like the kitchen of a house, but I didn't pause to look around. After a blink to adjust my eyes, I found the exit, and ran to it. I planted one hand on the frame as I yanked it open with the other, leaving behind a handprint of blood. I didn't bother to close the door behind me as I sprinted for the trees.

I WAS CRYING WHEN I EMERGED FROM THE MEMORY. THE emotions within me rivaled even more now, and I felt like I might burst from the pain of it. The agony of regretting something so deeply, yet feeling as though it had been deserved, all while holding the gut-wrenching anguish of having to take a life. Lives.

Thoughts of the encounter were spiraling in my mind, attempting to distract from the abyss yawning open in my chest.

The fact that they hadn't used their blades, for one. They'd had them–the first, a sword *and* a dagger, even after I'd taken the latter. So, if they hadn't used them, I could only imagine that they'd been resolute in their mission to keep me alive for the person they worked for.

Which begged the question: who *did* they work for? This male who hoped to usurp the king across the sea? The High King of Eshelle. Of the Fae. What little I'd been taught about them, that was included.

But, treason? He had to be either completely terrible, or simply weak enough that usurpers saw ripe pickings. In either case, those males had clearly been against their king and his reign. But what in gods' names did that have to do with me?

Why had they taken *me*? Put me in a position where I had no choice but to–

I could still feel the blood on my hand, taste the copper on my tongue. Hear the sounds they'd made as they died. See their eyes, wide with shock, anger...fear. They had not been ready to die.

But neither had I.

Was I still in danger? I didn't think so, and that helped me hold to my resolution to keep quiet, at least for two more days. Even the male who employed them wasn't foolish enough to try to infiltrate Castle Cerasche now. With dozens of guards for our family alone, plus those accompanying the visiting nobility here for the gathering–even a Fae male didn't stand a chance against that many skilled humans and Mages.

That thought sent a disarming sense of safety through me. The adrenaline high of reliving those events released me now, and I was suddenly exhausted. Not surprising, really. I trained with Amahd early in the morning, and took my miles-long walk to the park directly after–or, in the middle of, since I'd left early. I didn't bother giving thought to how things could have been different if I had just done what I had told him I was going to do, and went to prepare for the gathering.

And then, having to mingle and entertain and flirt for hours. All the while, pretending–even to myself–that I was unchanged from who I'd been this morning. That I cared about choosing a suitor. The only moment when I'd been truly uninhibited was in that garden, with Atlas. Its end was another thing that had me aching for sleep.

I scooted further back onto my bed and leaned to the side until my head hit a pillow. After mentally and physically feeling so much this day, my body and mind began to go numb now, at this late hour. There's a sensation of my emotions being drained from me. They left my expression, my mind, my heart.

The latter was a whirlpool–one where the end wasn't a bottom within me but rather a void that existed outside of myself. My body felt limp, and I thought that even if I tried to command myself to lift a finger, I couldn't do it.

It was therefore without really meaning to that my legs curled up to my chest, and my arms wrapped around my knees. As if my mind only had the capacity for autonomic tasks, and this was becoming one. A survival method, like breathing, like a heart beating, to somehow make my body as compressed as possible, so that it would not shatter.

Though exhausted, I couldn't seem to close my eyes. Instead, I stared at the wall across from me, not actually seeing it.

I didn't know how long it took for my eyelids to give up. All I knew was that some time later–minutes or hours; it was still dark–I briefly woke to find that my body remained curled up. And that, at some point in that indefinable timeframe, it had become wrapped in my mother's arms. My head rested beneath her chin, and her body curved around the bundle of my arms and legs. I could feel her long, soft breaths running through my hair as she slept.

I closed my eyes once more, and did not wake again until the sun was shining brightly through the windows.

11

PLAYING (PRETEND & WITH SWORDS)

THEA - 1 DAY EARLIER

AS I LOOKED INTO THE MIRROR IN THE MORNING, MY FINGERS working to braid back my hair, I tried not to notice the shadows in my eyes. Instead, I stared just past my right cheek, where I saw in the reflection the clean leathers I laid on my bed after I made it. The silence was stark, empty of my usual humming. My heart just felt too heavy for it.

The only thing that lightened my mood was the knowledge that the rest of my family would arrive today. It could be anytime now. But my soul needed the escape of training before I could face them. I needed to be able to smile, and have it feel real.

But first, I had to eat. And, for possibly the first time, I wasn't looking forward to it. Artur reliably kept his eyes from mine as he opened the doors to the dining hall for me. The long pine table, stained a rich brown, sat in the center of the white marble floor of the oblong room. Underneath it laid an intricately designed rug from Jasiira–a wedding present from Izabel's parents, to ours. A chandelier of dimly glowing forever-burn candles hung from the ceiling, with crystal strings that glimmered in the light streaming through the east-facing windows.

Only my mother was seated, my father nowhere in sight. I walked to my usual seat across from her, which would be on my dad's left if he were here. She watched me as I sat, her blue eyes seeming split between concern and parental disapproval.

She might have come last night to hold her child. Knew that something was wrong, and sought to comfort me the only way she could, without knowing what that something was. Still, I wasn't so naive to believe that her being my mom negated her being my queen. I knew what that disapproval was for without her even saying a word.

Still, the first thing she said was, "Good morning, Aly."

I managed not to sigh. "Good morning, Mom."

A slender, chestnut-hued hand placed a plateful of eggs, toast, and fruit in front of me. And while something in my chest eased at not having to face Atlas so soon after last night, something tightened in turn at what the only reason behind his absence could be.

Still, I looked up at Kya and grinned at the sweet-faced lady's maid. She smiled back at me, and I watched her dark eyes flick down to my leathers. Her brows raised slightly in question, and I knew that only my mother's unusual silence kept her from sitting beside me and voicing it aloud. I nodded once, smirking, but once she left my side and my gaze met my mother's, the expression fell.

"Kya, Elena, would you give us a moment, please?" she asked our lady's maids. They both bowed, the former shooting me a concerned glance before following her mother out into the hallway. Leaving me alone with my own mother, and the heaviness between us.

"Would you like to speak first?" she asked. I made myself meet her eyes once more, and found their blue depths to be calm.

I took a deep breath, and began speaking on the exhale. "I went out to the gardens on my own, and expected General Vey to meet me. I know he's married, and both of us intended on taking a walk as friends. But Atlas came to deliver my drink instead, saying that the general had been pulled aside to talk to you and dad. I didn't mean to end up out there alone with him."

She nodded. "We did speak to the general, yes. He's an old friend. But it was noticed when more than a moment passed, and neither you nor Atlas returned to the Hall. Some...Aly, some of your potential suitors were taken home by their parents, or left of their own accord this morning, before notice of who was selected to stay was delivered."

My heart strained, and my face heated at the news. But even as a part of me felt embarrassed for the implications of their departure, another was glad. Glad that I didn't have to deal with as many weak-minded men this evening as I had yesterday.

I realized that maybe my mom expected me to speak–to ask how many left, or who they were–but the words didn't come.

"Althea Maria." Uh oh. First and middle name together, from the time I was little, meant business. "I'm not..." She huffed a breath, and her expression softened a fraction. "You just have to be more careful."

She was being kind. Gentle, and probably going easy on me, all things considered. So I bit my tongue on my retort, and nodded, looking away from her. I didn't say that I'd been careful all my life, and finally got to experience even the smallest amount of pleasure for the first time last night. That being careful didn't mean that any of those other men could make me happy for the rest of my life.

Those thoughts that had battered at the walls of my mind and heart for so long, had become even more vocal since yesterday. Because, all cards on the table, my life on the line, I'd realized fully that I didn't want this. I'd shoved it down with the rest of the thoughts and memories and feelings from that basement, but after the numbness of last night, it came back in full force this morning.

From the corner of my eye, I saw her extend a hand to me, palm upturned. I looked up at her, and she asked, "Will you pray with me?"

In answer, I placed my hand in hers, and closed my eyes. I didn't hear the words of the prayer, or feel the blessings as I had last night. At some point, Kya, Elena, and Artur re-entered the dining hall, but even they remained quiet until my mother stood, her plate empty. It was a mark on her intuition that she didn't wait for me to finish, as she usually did, and instead left me to my thoughts and my food. Her lips lightly pressed against the top of my head, and then she departed without a word.

Elena set about clearing the dishes from the table, and I thanked her quietly. As I walked towards the doors, I felt my little shadow hesitate a few paces back. I turned halfway to her, and gave Kya a small smile before nudging my head towards the door, a gesture for her to follow. Her answering smile was bright, and I was sure only her mother's watchful eye kept her from running to my side. I tried to catch Artur's eye as we exited, to thank him for holding the door open for us properly, but his gaze was, as always, on his feet. I muttered my thanks anyway, and headed with Kya to the training yard.

⧓

Amahd was sharpening one of the many blades stored within the shed on the outskirts of the training yard when we arrived. His back was to us, dark head bent over his work. His own leathers were cut at the shoulders, revealing muscled arms which counteracted the bits of silver in his hair.

Kya and I walked across the circle of compacted dirt that we used for swordplay and hand-to-hand. I knew Amahd could hear us as we approached the shed, but he didn't look up as he said, "Good morning, Princess. Miss Kya."

"Good morning, Sir," we replied simultaneously, stopping just within the threshold. I clasped my hands behind my back, shoulders pinned, chin up. I held back my grin as Kya copied me just a beat late.

"You're early." He still sharpened the blade–a broadsword.

"I woke up early. Couldn't sleep. And Kya's up with the rooster."

His dark eyes finally lifted from his work to examine my face. I tried to keep my expression impassive, my eyes blank. Being a trained warrior, he understood how to read a person unlike anyone I'd ever seen. He was continually trying to teach me the art of inscrutability–an art which I'd only started to understand and attempt to perfect within the past year. Since my last birthday, when I realized there was just one more year until I was to be betrothed.

Still, I knew he sensed something was off with me. Though his face remained stoic, I noticed the slightest narrowing of his eyes before he said, "Best get started, then."

Amahd grabbed three broadswords, and instructed Kya to do her best against the training dummy across the yard. Having just started training a few months ago, I knew he only let her use the blade thicker than her forearm because he'd lost every battle of wills against her so far. It had proven much more effective to just let her tire herself with whatever I was doing, and *then* suggest the alternative.

I made the mistake of watching her walk over to the dummy, the sword looking even larger beside her petite frame. Without warning, Amahd brought his own blade up, and took a swift slice right for my head. There was no time to think; only act. Duck, and parry.

Thus commenced twenty minutes of chopping, slicing, and blocking. My right arm was so tired that I switched to my left for the last five minutes. Being much more accustomed to my slimmer blades and daggers, the heavy broadsword was a new challenge. I had no doubt that Amahd did this intentionally, having noticed that I was out of sorts when I arrived. I really had to focus on my moves and countermoves. Offensive and defensive. Moving to Amahd so swiftly that even he looked surprised. Deciding to lift the blade to block, and counter, instead of using simple ducking or twisting maneuvers.

By the end, sweat dripped from my brow, and down my back beneath my leathers. I was doubled over, hands on my knees as I attempted to catch my breath. "Hand to hand next?" I asked. Kya stood beside me, similarly breathless, broadsword set on its stand in the shed. Once, in the beginning, she'd rested the tip of a rapier in the sand, and leaned on it like a walking stick. We'd talked since of how we never wanted to see that look on Amahd's face again.

"Depends on if you want to do that or weighted exercises first," he responded, shrugging. I groaned, the only kind of complaint I ever allowed myself in this yard, and Kya echoed me.

We walked over to the spigot, and cool, clear water came out when I twisted the handle. Rather than retrieve cups from inside the shed, I just opened my mouth beneath the flow, took a few gulps, then put my face under it. It cooled the blood pounding through my temples, and the heat in my neck as it trickled down my jaw. As I stood, moving so Kya could get some, too, I swept the water from my face back through my hair. That the strands were black as night made them hot to the touch with the sun beating down on my head.

"If you're quite finished using up all the water in Weaschte, let's move on to weights," Amahd decided for us.

Then came forty minutes of carrying loads heavier than my body weighed, hefting things over my head, and squatting and lunging my life away. Amahd coached Kya as I ran through the familiar workout, and then we moved onto hand-to-hand.

She and I practiced punches, kicks, and blocks for a quarter of an hour, each blow landing hard on our straw-filled dummies. After that, it was strict fighting between me and the training master, while the lady's maid scurried off to clean up before she's required to prepare the Hall for the luncheon. Amahd got one kick past me, which felt like it could have broken a rib if he'd put his actual force behind it. I tried not to gloat when I got in an uppercut to his jaw, and a knee to his side, both of which he was gracious enough to pretend to need a moment to recover from.

By the end, I was covered in sweat and the light brown dust of the training circle. In the black leathers, with my possibly even darker hair, my entire body felt like it could burst into flame. It took all of my willpower to not just turn the spigot on and lay on the ground beneath it.

"That's it for today," Amahd said, and began collecting the scattered weights to put them back in their rightful places. I started walking towards him to help, but then he ordered, "You're done. Go eat."

My dad frequently said that I talked back less to Amahd than I did to him, and I couldn't disagree when my only response now was, "Thank you, Sir."

A few hours later, I was still full from the oatmeal and eggs and fruit I'd stuffed myself with after training. Before I'd gone to clean up, I gathered from Elena who remained to court me. And I couldn't find it in myself to be disappointed, or embarrassed, when she told me that only three out of the five I selected chose to stay after the *situation* last night.

Especially when, walking through the gardens in a pretty yellow dress, Dalton came to find me. I found his company to be not unpleasant. He was as sweet and charismatic as he had been last night.

Moments later, Dalton having bid me ado with a kiss to my knuckles and a kind smile, I found Kya waiting for me by the exterior door leading into the Hall. I walked along the outer path of the garden towards her, trying to ignore my last memory of this space–of being pressed up against one of the sandstone walls.

Her thick curls were tied back now with a silk wrap around her hairline, keeping them out of her pretty face. She grinned as I approached, and said, "Your sister hasn't stopped asking for you for the past hour." That had me smiling back at her, because of course, Iris would be pestering my lady's maid in the sweet-but-annoying sisterly way of hers until I arrived.

Kya knocked on the pinewood doors to the Hall. She would be in attendance for the luncheon should I need anything, but would be standing with her mother against the wall (a bit of courtly decorum which I loathed). Artur pushed the doors open, and somehow managed to avert my gaze all the way to the other side of the door, holding it for Kya and I. All the same, I thanked him, and walked with my friend into the next step of my fate.

12

HIELA

I STOOD BY THE WINDOW OF MY CHAMBER FOR HOURS, LOOKING out into the city beyond. Even when I tired, the thoughts racing through my head wouldn't allow me to rest. So instead I looked, and I pondered.

The city was beautiful. The Castle of Colina sat on the hill, but not so high that I couldn't make out the people, the movement, the life below. Light shone from countless sources; the moon, the faerie lights shining in the plentiful windows, great chandeliers of the glowing glass orbs scattered throughout the streets, hanging with bindings from one chimney to another. With all that light, I could make out that people still shopped, mingled, and even danced. I could hear the soft music of violins, and wind instruments playing multiple melodies.

None of this existed in Matriel, the capital city of Oschverre–not the light past midnight, and certainly not the dancing in the streets. Even music was regulated to be played only indoors unless there was a mandatory holiday celebration. Oleander didn't participate in many Fae traditions, but he loved any reason to drink during the day, and to kiss the asses of the many Oschverren nobility who still supported him. Aside from that, all he had to do was hold court–where Melisan did most of the legwork–wave to the people from the castle steps, and try not to get too lost in his wine before dessert was served.

As I looked at *this* city before me, I recognized why I was truly here. Why the king was threatened by the High Lord of Sabrian.

Threatened, when so many nobles supported his claim just because of his bloodright, or because they found him easy to work with when they wanted something. For some, it was even because they had revered his father, and continued that feeling towards the son without any action or affection from the king. But I thought that the real reason, the one that beat out all the rest, had to be that the Gervan line held not only the armies, the navy. They held the Might of Eshelle.

The unspoken force of the land. Once, the trees and the beasts of the realm had fought in battles, just as the Fae and faeries had. And for centuries now, they'd slumbered. The trees were decorative, and the only animals to be seen were the regular ones that could be found even with the humans of Weaschte across the Evredis.

High King Oleander Gervan was said to be the only one who could awaken that force that was rumored to dwell deep in the earth of Eshelle. His father, his grandfather, and so on, had all had this power before him. No one else could ever hope or dream to not only summon, but *control* the Might.

I believed that to be a load of horseshit.

I was sure Oleander knew that to be the case, too, and only used the threat of it to keep his people in line. And if ever there was proof to that, it was in his unspoken fear of the High Lord of Sabrian.

It wasn't just because of the whispers–that I was now convinced had been intentionally spread–of Amedeo's displeasure with the crown. It was because of this, what I saw before me. Because if word were to travel that Oschverre wasn't the height of trade, commerce, and peace, the obvious follow-up question would be *why?* And the answer would not be hard to find.

It was difficult to infiltrate the capital, and even more so to overthrow the king. But to spread gossip? To initiate a cascade of rumors that would bring into question the strength, integrity, and ability of that king? That was easy.

Oleander had fallen right into the Sabriani's trap, without even doing anything differently. But that was the point, wasn't it? All he had to do was what he'd *been* doing: nothing. The only thing that had been needed was a catalyst. A spark that would ignite the minds of the people. Sending me here had been the match. Seeing the coat of arms in their home–a symbol that threatened their peace and prosperity–would make the people quicker to act to save it before it was lost. Soon, all Eshellens would hear from the citizens of this area about the wondrousness of Sabrian, and its own capital city. Rallying surrounding nations to their cause–the cause of preserving what was good, and fixing what was not.

And, when the word finally reached the capital, those living in Oschverre would look around and question.

They would question how fit their king was to rule. Why another country within his land was a hub of success, while the one in which he resided was decaying, in every sense of the word. They would question if he was strong enough to lead his people, to fight for them, to create a better world for them. And, when he was found lacking, they would realize that perhaps someone else would be more fit to rule.

Amedeo's design, indeed. And I couldn't find it in myself to disapprove. Because they–the High Lord, High Lady, the people of this country, this continent–would be right to think those things. Oleander had never used his power for the good of his people. His political power, passed down from his father, which he had squandered for the past several decades. Not majickal power. For he had none.

My jaw tightened as soon as I thought it, and I forced my mind to clear. Though most mindworkers only had a short range they could reach with their power, I was in the proximity of many castle guards, staff, and even some townsfolk. I'd sensed power from many as I'd made my travels earlier today, but I didn't have the ability to discern the *type* of majick they possessed.

I shifted my thoughts away from the matter–It really had been just earlier today that I'd arrived in Colina, Sabrian. And yet, between my interactions with the High Lord and High Lady, the verbal sparring and lashing with and from my guard, and every feeling and thought in between, it felt like much longer. And, coming from someone with an immortal lifespan, that was saying something.

I was suddenly so, so tired. Not just from today–though it certainly didn't help. But from the understanding that I had lived so long, and had so long left to go. From the fact that within that time, I could not foresee a point in which I would get to be happy ever again. The fact that the last time I had been, was now almost seventy years ago.

And so, not only to sleep as my body wanted me to, but to escape those feelings and thoughts, I finally moved from my vigil at the window, and walked to the bed. I undressed, pulled back the sheets, and lay completely bare to the world on the cool mattress.

I closed my eyes, and did not find sleep for some time.

⧻

When bright golden sunshine streamed across my face, I knew two things: first, that I had forgotten to shut my drapes before I'd gotten into bed. And second, by the dull throbbing in my head, and the weight of my eyelids, that I had only slept for a few hours.

I groaned as I sat up, and rubbed my eyes so hard with the heels of my palms that spots of light appeared in them when I stopped. I stooped to pick up my trousers, not needing the entire staff within the gates beneath my window to get a free show through the very open glass panes. I glimpsed myself in the full-length mirror in the corner of the room, and grimaced. My hair was disheveled, there were circles under my eyes, and, after a month of travel, I was far too lean.

I sighed, but continued to get ready for the day. Once bathed and dressed, I approached my door, and took a breath before opening it.

She was there, of course, her scent of rich vanilla and bright bergamot filling my lungs as I stepped into the hallway. Those deep blue eyes flicked once over me, and just that half a second of her focus on me made my gut roil—with guilt, or nerves, or both.

But she merely said, "Good morning."

That was it. No title, no pleasantries. But no anger, either.

"Good morning," I replied, keeping the surprise out of my face and my voice. She seemed to be at a loss for what to say next. Her full mouth opened and closed twice, yet no blush of embarrassment colored her chestnut cheeks. Instead, that small line formed between her brows as she scrunched them slightly. Deciding to spare her, I asked, "Am I too early for breakfast?"

Her eyebrows straightened. "No. I'll take you to the dining room." Then, without another word, she began walking. I followed, just slightly farther from her than I had been yesterday.

Her footsteps were quiet, tempoed. Very clearly trained, so thoroughly that the walking pattern–chin up, arms at her sides, palms open to grab weapons quickly–had transferred into her everyday gait. I watched as her curls bounced with each of those steps, and I had the strangest urge to loop one of the ringlets around my finger.

I clasped my hands behind my back, and shook the peculiar notion out of my head. Thankfully, a moment later I heard the sounds of scraping forks, scooting chairs, and happy conversation coming from down the hall. Of course, that all stopped when I walked into the room.

The High Lord and High Lady were there, as well as the guards who had accompanied them yesterday. Then there was a female with black hair, and crystal blue eyes, who looked remarkably like the High Lady of Sabrian. Beside her was a female with nearly onyx skin, and eyes almost as dark. Her head and brow were bare, and a curving golden tattoo ran from above her left ear, to below her occipital, and continued beneath her white shift, visible down her back. She was so striking that it took me a moment to move my eyes to the last unfamiliar face: a male with sleek blue-black hair, and angled brown eyes. Those eyes held mine, pure challenge in them. I did not look away.

"Lord Dion, Lord Bayani," the High Lady said after a tense, silent moment. "If you're finished with your pissing contest, I would love to eat my breakfast in peace." She didn't look angry, or even annoyed, as I would have anticipated–but rather, amused. Her expression reminded me of how people looked when a child was doing something that they shouldn't be, but that something was cute. Like sitting in a puddle. To her, we were just kids fighting over a seat at the grown-ups table.

Lord Bayani instantly looked to her. Unlike me, he did not blush, or seem embarrassed in the slightest. Instead, he smiled, bowed to her, and said, "Forgive me, Hiela. I hope your eggs haven't gone cold." My brows furrowed slightly at what he'd called her. Was that her name?

"If they had, I believe I would just need to get Lord Dion a bit riled, and he'd warm them up for me in a jiffy," she said, her eyes on me. I startled at her casual mention of my power–as though it were a fun trinket used to heat up leftovers, and not the killing power that it was. That she *knew* it had been used for. And, by the looks on their faces when I'd walked in, so did everyone else in the room.

Yet they only smirked, or rolled their eyes–*rolled their eyes*– at their High Lady. Whose bright sienna gaze was still on me. Waiting.

I cleared my throat, and responded, "I think a skillet may serve you better, High Lady, but I appreciate your confidence."

"Suit yourself." She shrugged, and I felt as though I'd passed some sort of test. "And, Lord Dion, if you noticed Lord Bayani's charming nickname for me–we would like you to use it as well." She gestured between herself, and her mate, who sat at her side. "Hielo, and Hiela. All of that *High Lord* and *High Lady* nonsense can get a bit exhausting."

I restrained a blink at her allowing me the sort of familiarity that her court was being granted. Instead, I said, "Thank you, Hiela." The word was nice; rolled off the tongue. Her eyes warmed, the look in them pleased. She resumed eating, her mate beside her giving me a small nod before doing the same.

I glanced at my guard, about to ask where I should sit, but she was already sauntering over to the table, seeming more at ease than I had seen her thus far in my stay here. She took a seat right next to the female with the golden tattoo, and beamed at her, the expression open and lovely. I was slower to find my chair than she had been, partially from looking at that smile perhaps a beat too long, but also because my options were limited. Hielo was at the head, Hiela to his right, and the female who must be her sister sat beside her. The only place open was the other head of the table, or two spots on Lord Bayani's other side, Hielo to his left. And since I would not presume to take the former...

Lord Bayani gave me a half smile, and his eyes gleamed with a new challenge. I threw a falsely oblivious grin back at him as I took my seat. Then, for an awkward moment, I sat there in silence, an empty plate before me. Until Hiela used her fork to pierce a sausage from the platter on the table, and put it on her own plate. The same as last night, then. It seemed, however, that all the dishes were placed out of my arm's reach.

I cleared my throat, and looked to Hiela's sister. "Would you pass the potatoes, please?"

Those crystalline eyes stared back at me with mistrust, but also some...consideration? "Of course," she said simply, picking up the tray, and holding it out to me.

"Thank you," I said as I took it.

Slowly, conversation resumed around the table. My guard glanced once at me, then did not again throughout the remainder of the meal. Though the rest gathered finished their plates before we did, not one of them got up, or stopped chatting, or checked the time on the clock against the wall. Every one of them stayed until all plates were cleared, without fussing about meetings, or with general displeasure at having to wait.

"Lord Dion?" a rich tenor voice addressed me. I found the female with the golden tattoo looking at me expectantly.

"Yes, Lady..?" I trailed off, embarrassed yet again as I realized I had not asked for anyone's name.

"Nuria," she granted with a smile, not seeming the least off-put by my thoughtlessness. "My mate and I wondered if you might like to join us to walk the gardens after breakfast." She reached to grasp the hand of the blue-eyed female beside her.

I blinked, surprised by the invitation. "Certainly," I answered, but looked to my guard. Though these females were surely strong enough to fight me if they wished to, I didn't believe that was their intention. It was therefore with only the knowledge that she would be duty-bound to accompany me that I added, "So long as Lady Ciaragen doesn't mind?"

Her deep eyes widened slightly, but I couldn't read her expression otherwise. She looked quickly at Lady Nuria. "I would love to join you and Jolie on your walk." I couldn't help but notice that she did not include me in that enjoyment.

"Splendid," Lady Nuria said, while Lady Jolie smiled somewhat conspiratorially at my guard. The three females stood, and I followed suit.

But before I stepped away from the table, I bowed to Hielo and Hiela, and said, "Thank you for the meal."

If they were surprised by it, they didn't show it. Hiela merely dipped her chin in acknowledgement, and the High Lord's lips twitched up ever so slightly before he did the same.

13

AND HER PLANS

Ciaragen - 21 years earlier

I observed the lord closely as we walked with Nuria and Jolie through the castle's sprawling gardens. Though the brightly colored flowers, the hummingbirds flying past, and my sweet friends provided plenty of distraction, a large part of my focus was on him throughout the stroll.

Nuria was a light. Radiant in looks and in spirit, I doubted she'd ever met a person who did not come to like her in her two centuries of life. She held Jolie's hand the entirety of the walk, sometimes bringing it to her lips to press a kiss to the back of her palm. Jolie blushed each time.

The lord noticed. I watched as his hazel eyes wandered over the flora, and observed the intimacy between the two females. And not once did his face harden with the prejudices I had expected. Indeed, he seemed to soften somehow as Nuria continued talking.

She explained the different flowers, several of which were

native to Sabrian. She told him each of our favorites–I nearly glared at her when she gave him mine–and smiled widely as she told him that it wouldn't hurt his reputation here if a bouquet of each were to show up at our doors. Which made *him* smile. Not the smirk I'd seen, or the sarcastic grin he'd given Bayani; a true smile.

I shouldn't have been surprised; Nuria's joy was infectious. And, to be fair, he could be faking it. Being in the king's employ, he had to be a good liar. I wouldn't put it past him to be immune to her charms. She could only have an effect on those with hearts, after all.

"Ari?" I heard Nuria say. I realized I'd been staring at the lord, my brow creased in thought. He was looking back at me, seeming both wary and amused, probably thinking that I was watching him because of his looks. It took most of my self-control to not glare, and tell him not to flatter himself.

"Did I miss something?" I looked between Jolie and Nuria.

Jolie, the quieter of the two, grinned. "I asked Lord Dion if you worked guard duty through the night, and if that was why you were so cranky," she said softly, jokingly.

"I told her that I'm pretty sure that if you *were* cranky, it would be because you have to be at my side at all hours of the day, but that it surely wouldn't have helped if you'd been up all night," the lord added.

"To which I decided we should ask you," Nuria finished. "And now we're caught up. So, which is it?"

We continued strolling down the path, passing briefly under a latticed archway, vines of honeysuckle creeping up the sides. "First of all, I'm not cranky. But, if I was, it would have to be for the former reason, because Arthur came to relieve me last night shortly after supper."

There was a strained silence, in which the two females looked at the male, watching for any reaction. And I remembered then that they were roses. Not the kind in the garden, but the ones Hiela spoke of.

What occurred to me for the first time, though, was that they may not believe him to be as malicious as he was said to be in the reports I'd seen from Oschverre. They saw something else in him, and they were using my loose tongue to test their theories. To see if they were right, or if that infamous power would lash out when so much as a cross word was said to him. Or if it was leashed enough to only be used when needed.

Nuria, Jolie, our Hielo and Hiela...they were playing him. Perhaps not in a way that was detrimental to him–their plays being friendliness, kindness, and camaraderie. But I couldn't think of another way to describe it. They were using the loveliness of our home and its people to sway him to our cause. Our side. They wanted *him* with *us*.

And they were using me to make it happen. Knowing what he'd done to my family–to me. They weren't oblivious to who he was. I remembered back to breakfast, how our court had allowed their opinions of him to shine through. But, rather than continue to ostracize him and possibly make him further committed to his task, and his king, they'd allowed themselves to open up, like petals on a flower.

Posturing as friendly, pretty roses. And I was the thorn.

The comprehension wiped all emotion from my face. Still, by the look in their eyes, I could tell Nuria and Jolie sensed my betrayal. Jolie's majickal proclivity toward emotion, combined with the couple's already abounding empathy gave me no hope to hide it from them.

But Nuria only said, "Well, there you have it, my lord," with a shrug, and a chuckle. Then, turning back to the path, she took the lord's arm to bring him along. But before his eyes left mine, I saw a flash of what could have been sadness, if I'd cared enough to search for it.

⇔

And so the day passed. We showed the lord the gardens, the stables, the orchard. Let him smell our flowers, pet our horses, eat our apples. We ate lunch outside, beneath the shadow of a great willow. When dinner came, everyone, even Bayani, flared their pretty petals for him.

All throughout I said perhaps ten words, most of them being 'thank' and 'you'. For passing the bread, for holding the door, for sharing an apple. Everyone noticed, even him. I could see it on his face, though he didn't say anything. I would occasionally catch his eyes on me, though. Half the time I caught him, he would quickly look away. The other half, he seemed to not notice that I was looking back at him for a moment. When he would finally come to, his expression cleared as easily as frost wiped from a window.

Now, we were walking down the last hallway to his chambers after supper, where he had exchanged pleasantries with everyone at the table. Well, with one noticeable–and not at all upset about it–exception.

Last night, I made the mistake of speaking to him. I had no interest in repeating that error tonight. Unfortunately, I wasn't the only one who had sway on that choice.

In front of his doorway, he turned to me. "I recognize that you dislike me. Maybe even hate me," he said candidly. I held back a blink at his head-on approach. "But I shouldn't be here for long. I know this isn't what you want to be doing with your time. I tried to make it more bearable for you today. I figured walking through the gardens would be preferable to standing outside my door all the while between meals. I'm sure you would have enjoyed it far more if it had been just you and your friends. But, still. I hope it was better. Than yesterday, I mean."

I stared up at him for a long moment, seething, as he dared

130

to look like he meant what he said. This male thought *dislike* might have been a strong enough word for what I felt for him. Thought that any pretty little activity could make spending time with him, no matter with who else, even slightly tolerable.

The hateful words bubbled up my throat, ready to lash at him, wound him if possible. But after my realization from earlier, I wasn't keen on being the second variable of the experiment right this moment.

So, my face and voice void of any emotion, I said, "Noted."

That infuriating sadness flashed in his eyes, gone so quickly that I could convince myself that I imagined it. He stood up slightly straighter, inclined his head to me, and said, "Good night, then," before walking through his door, and closing it softly behind him.

I ground my teeth, damning his expression, at the dejected way he'd spoken, at the day in general—and leaned against the wall and waited for my replacement.

I wondered, as I absently wreathed my fingers in shadows, if he was contemplating killing me yet. I'd certainly given him enough reason to do so already, but maybe he had his anger under better control than it was rumored he used to. I almost wanted to burst into that chamber and goad him into it. To learn just what that power of his looked like, and how it would fare against mine.

Though, that was what they wanted. What I was being used for. My teeth clenched together again, and a muscle ticked in my jaw.

The sound of footsteps from my side of the door interrupted my thoughts. I let my shadows dissipate, and a moment later, Arthur appeared, face as stoic as it had been since he'd started here almost half a year ago.

"Thank the gods," I said as he approached, pushing off the wall.

"Hope today wasn't too bad," he replied.

"Save your hopes for something with a chance." I crossed my arms. "Are they still up?"

He knew who I meant. His brow furrowed slightly, but all he said was, "Yes. In the library."

"Thanks. See you in the morning." I patted his shoulder once as I started in the direction of the castle's library. Unfortunate, that I was to release my anger there of all places; it was one of my favorite spots in the castle. Filled with the comforting aromas of paper, ink, and wood. Well lit throughout the day for reading, no need for a candle or any majickal light. Soft couches and chairs, worn perfectly from use.

And, of course, the books. Thousands of them, stacked up on three floors of walnut shelves. The High Lord and High Lady gave full access to anyone within the grounds to take and read any tomes they wanted, so long as they brought them back once finished.

Thoughts of the library were calming me, dulling the razor-sharp edge my anger had taken since that walk in the gardens. I was reluctant to let it happen. I wanted to be mad; I wanted them to know how their secrets had affected me. So, I gripped that anger tight as a vice as I walked down the hall in which the library was located.

As I rounded the threshold of the open double-doors, I set a resolve to focus only on them. If my eyes wandered around the circular, high-ceilinged room, and all that it contained, I knew my icy rage would thaw–at least a little bit.

They looked up as I approached. My High Lord seemed surprised by my arrival, but pleasantly so. My High Lady, on the other hand, had a bleak set to her lips, and had closed the book in her lap the moment she saw me. Once I was about ten feet from them, I stopped, and clenched my fists behind my back. I opened my mouth to speak–

"Would you like to sit down, Ciaragen?" my High Lady asked. I couldn't decide whether the gentleness in her voice made me more angry, or calmed me down. She had a way about her–a genuine quality of being utterly who and what she presented herself to be at all times. Now, that quality made it difficult for me to maintain the same steeliness of my expression, and my mind.

I huffed a breath. "No, thank you."

She nodded once, and placed her book on the small table between herself and my High Lord. "Then, please, say what you need to say." Folding her hands in her lap, she looked at me with an openness that made me hesitate for a beat.

I restrained myself from saying the possibly–definitely, now that I was facing them and could see their concern–not appropriate thoughts I'd had in the gardens. My brows scrunched, and I simply said instead, "You assigned me to him as a test." It wasn't a question, but she nodded again, while her mate looked on, his own book now resting atop hers. "A test for me, or for him?" I asked.

It was she who responded. "Both."

I felt my eyebrows pull closer to each other. "Why?"

"I'll start with the easier: him. He has a power that has not been seen in centuries, over which it seems he does not have enough control. If we are going to sway him, as I'm sure you've already realized we intend to do, we first need to know if that power will raze this castle before we get the chance. And we figured placing him in frequent proximity with a female who may lose her temper with him, therefore causing him to do the same, was as good a way as any to test that." She raised her brows slightly, and my cheeks flushed.

But she went on, "It wasn't so much a test for you, as an opportunity to confront the male who caused your father's death. Whether you did or did not, or even choose to after today, is entirely up to you. You will not lose face or station either way."

At this point, my brows were nearly touching. "So, you thought that I might attack him, verbally, and physically, and that would either lead him to lose control enough for his power to surge–or not?" I clarified.

"Yes."

I looked at my High Lord. "And what did you both think would happen if the former occurred?"

"You would have been able to defeat him if he'd attacked. And, if he'd fought you with such ferocity that you needed to take his life, we were prepared for it. Ciaragen, your father was a member of our guard, not to mention a general of our armies, long before you were born. We were heartbroken at his death." Truth. Both of them had come to my father's funeral, and stood in the crowd of mourners as we sent him down the river behind my family's estate, tears streaming down their faces all the while. "We trust you as we trusted him."

There was such earnestness in his gaze, in his voice. After a long, tense moment, I nodded once, my brow finally relaxing.

Hielo stood, straightening his jacket. "For the matter at hand: are you willing to continue to serve as guard to Dion Evestre?"

I glanced up at him, then at Hiela, who was still seated, her hands folded patiently in her lap.

"Do I have to be nice to him?"

Hielo chuckled. "No. Though, do forgive Nuria and Jolie for their part. They were just doing what we asked them to do."

I sighed, rolling my eyes a little. "I will." Then another thought came to me, and I raised a brow. "Will everyone else keep pretending that he's one of us? I just want to prepare myself for tomorrow. All of those discolored noses, you know."

They both laughed then, Hiela standing to join her mate.

"I'm afraid so. Our goal can only be accomplished if everyone continues to play the role they've been given," Hielo responded, and his mate picked up, as she often did: "So, if you can do the part we put upon you to play, just for a little while longer, Ciaragen, we would be grateful.

"And, if you find that you can't bear it," Hiela said, those incredible eyes holding mine, "please come to us."

Chin high and eyes shrewd, I chose my words carefully. "No more hiding things. Perhaps I should have grasped, when you asked this of me, that you did it for more than one reason. That I didn't is on me. But, when you didn't make it clear to me when I very obviously didn't understand–however unintentional it might have been, you hid that from me. And though it didn't now, in the future that miscomprehension could mean the difference between our success, and our failure."

It had been my father who'd taught me to command a conversation like this. Who had shown me that our High Lord and High Lady appreciated that rank was typically highly regarded–but that here, in their court, lack of communication was worse than insubordination. *Respectful* communication, I should say. The kind where each person in the conversation was regarded with integrity, with the goal of understanding one another a bit better by the end.

"Absolutely," Hielo agreed, Hiela holding my gaze as she gave a dip of her chin. I nodded once more, stepped back, and bowed low before turning on my heel and walking out of the library. I hoped I would find the time to return soon.

14

CHANGELINGS & CHANCES

THEA - 1 DAY EARLIER

THE FIRST HOUR AFTER GREETING MY FAMILY WAS A WHIRLWIND of kisses and hugs, catching up, and smiling until my cheeks hurt. For just that hour, I lost myself in them.

Nik and Izabel, towing their three children, all under the age of five. Ben, and a hugely pregnant Lorraine. Iris and her husband, Zakary with their daughter, Cleo–who hadn't allowed me to put her down since I first picked her up fifty minutes ago.

It was a pleasant distraction. An amazing one, even. My siblings and their families were some of my favorite people in this world. Yet, even among them, the weight in my gut didn't lighten.

I had not and could not process all that had happened yesterday while in this perpetual stress. All I'd allowed myself to recognize was that, in the nearness of losing my life, I had come to fully resent my current position. And still, knowing that it would not change, I remained silent on all counts.

Because, if I started shouting my fears, I didn't know how or when I would stop. I couldn't do that to the mother who found her love this same way, and held the result of such love in her arms last night.

So, pushing aside the experience that was harder, that was *too much* while I sat bouncing a toddler in my arms, I focused on what was to come. On what I *knew*, and what that would lead to, as opposed to what I did not. For that...*that* would have to wait until *this* was done.

I thought about what would happen when I chose–in possibly the loosest form of the word–a man to marry. I couldn't help but wonder if I'd be happy in that life. The life of marriage, of bearing and raising children. Seeking fulfillment only in those specific areas.

I looked at Ben and Lorraine, at Iris and Zak, and wondered if I'd manage to pick the person who suited me like they suited each other.

Lor and Iris seemed happy; fulfilled. But their dreams had always been to become wives, and mothers. I enjoyed the idea of loving a man, and having him love me back–of raising children who were a bit of me and a bit of him. But it wasn't my dream.

I didn't know what my dream would be if I didn't have to marry. Kind of pointless to even ponder it. Instead, I tried to think only of what I wanted within the single option open to me.

Though not my dream, it was my hope to have a husband who loved all aspects of me. Who would make me *happy*, not simply content. I couldn't know what to hope for in other, more intimate areas of our relationship, since my virtue had been so gods-damned guarded all of my matured life.

From the moment of my first bleeding, men wouldn't come near me with a five-foot pole, knowing what the consequences would be. The first time I'd ever been alone with a man was last night–when I'd finally been able to feel what was so forbidden. At least for a moment.

"Aly?" I heard Iris say, having apparently zoned out as I thought about all of this. And of course–*of course* as I'd been daydreaming, my gaze had been on Atlas. I wouldn't know that he'd noticed my stare if it weren't for the way he glanced back at me. Only once, quickly enough that anyone else could write it off as a general scan of the room. But when those storm-gray eyes landed on me for half a heartbeat, I couldn't help but imagine that I saw longing in them.

My cheeks flushing, I focused on my sister. "Sorry, what?"

"Do you want me to take Cleo?" she repeated, her eyes flashing between Atlas and I as she held her hands out for her daughter.

"No, no, no, no, no!" Cleo shouted, nearly bursting my ear drum. And I couldn't help but be grateful for the gift of a screaming child to distract my sister from catching me staring at the handsome server. "Staying wif Auntie." Cleo clutched me so hard with her toddler strength that even if I unwound my arms from her, she wouldn't budge.

"I haven't seen this duckling in months," I told Iris, pressing my cheek against her daughter's. "She's fine where she is."

She crossed her arms over her chest, the stern movement counteracted by the way her summer sky eyes lit up as she looked at Cleo. The toddler was playing with the pearls on my necklace, her tiny fingers twirling and pinching them as she observed the light gleaming off their surface. Her blonde ringlets, just like her mother's, shone in the gentle sunlight streaming through the window. I tugged gently on one of them, and watched it spring back into its original form.

"They are little miracles, aren't they?" I looked back at Iris, and she looked at her daughter, eyes shining with love. And I thought that if the sun burnt out, Iris wouldn't notice, so long as she had Cleo.

"Though I don't envy Nik right now," Lor chuckled from my other side. We all looked over to where Nik was, in the center of the dining hall, trying to wrangle the two of his children that were able to walk, while Izabel cradled the third. "I have to agree with Iris. I can't wait to meet this one." She looked down in adoration at her swollen belly, and ran a palm down the length of it. "I just pray that he or she is born healthy."

"I'm sure they will be," Iris told her, and I nodded in agreement. I could feel it without even touching her; the perfect health of her baby.

She looked up, the gleam of gossip in her eye, but a bit of worry as well. "Did you hear about the Dimaski's baby?"

Iris and I sat forward a bit in our chairs. "No," we said together.

"When the physic presented the babe, he gave her the news," she whispered, and I knew it couldn't be good if the physic was involved, rather than just the midwife. Despite how I longed to have both her and Lor here, I was glad in that moment that Hanna could not attend this particular gathering. With how new her pregnancy was, she didn't need to hear whatever horror our friend was about to share.

Lor glanced around, making sure that no one was close enough to overhear as she breathed, "A changeling."

"No," Iris gasped while my brow crumpled in sorrow. Nothing that I could heal, then. A changeling wasn't a human baby at all–it was a faerie. Not a Fae; we believed only their distant heritage could be linked to the creatures which terrified impending parents of Weaschte. Though no one knew whether that was true, or if faeries were entirely their own–created by whichever god sought to incite chaos at the time.

For a changeling wasn't hurt, or ill in some way, though

there were always physical markers that made it easy to distinguish. A changeling was a child of the faeries, switched out with the real baby, who was stolen away to live amongst the faeries forever. They *could* choose to return the human baby and take back their own offspring, during a ceremony we referred to as the 'Ritual'. Unfortunately, only the faeries could decide whether or not the humans ever saw their baby again, Ritual or no.

The barbarism that I could never quite understand was, if the faeries did not retrieve their child, and give the human babe back in return, the faerie was left to die. Still a *baby* by all accounts–but what did I know of the fury of a parent who lost their child?

"I didn't ask for details," Lorraine continued, still keeping her voice low. Her dark brown brows furrowed over her similarly hued eyes, and her voice broke as she continued. "All I know is that, when they performed the Ritual, the faeries didn't come. They let their own perish, rather than give the babe back to its parents. They don't even know if they had a son or a daughter," she concluded, her eyes glassy with tears. My own were full of them as well, grieving for two little lives, but I blinked them back. I watched as a drop trailed down Iris's cheek.

"Is sad, Momma?" Cleo blurted, dropping my pearls, and pointing to the tear running to my sister's jawline.

Iris quickly wiped it away, and opened her arms. I immediately moved to pass Cleo over, and thankfully the child didn't object this time. Once she had her, Iris folded her daughter to her chest, pressed her nose to the top of her head, and breathed in deeply.

"No, my love. Not sad," she said.

⸪

The skirts of the jade green gown she'd created for me swished along the floor as I turned from the mirror to my mom, a smile on my face. "Thank you," I said, feeling the smooth fabric over my waist.

She waved a hand, far more nonchalant than the emotion shining in her eyes. No words came when she opened her mouth at first to speak. She tried again, and got out, "Oh, it's nothing. I'm glad you like it."

I walked over to her with my arms out, and she pulled me into a tight embrace. Though she was a couple of inches shorter than me, I felt like a child when one of her hands stroked my newly curling hair, and she pressed a kiss to my cheek. A soft inhale sounded against my skin.

Then she pulled away, sliding her hands down my arms until her fingers wrapped around mine. Her eyes held mine, and she smiled. "I am so proud of you," she said, and a lump gathered in my throat. "You are everything that I dreamed of, and more. And, one day, if you have a daughter of your own, I hope that you will get to look at her when she's all grown up and understand just how deeply I love you." Her thumbs stroked the backs of my palms.

"Now." She sniffled, and gave me another grin. "I know you have a lot to think about this evening. Your friends, your sister, and your father and I are all here if you need us..." Her fingers tightened around mine. "But this is *your* decision. *You* decide who will be by your side this time tomorrow, and for all tomorrows after that."

My heart stuttered a beat, and then picked up in tempo, though I managed to give my mom a small smile, and a nod. Interpreting my hesitation as nerves she raised her brows. "Are you ready?"

No. "Yes."

⪥

The music being played in the Hall was bright and cheery, and strangers and loved ones alike danced to it with smiles on their faces. Yet I hadn't been able to help but feel separate from them. My dances were dull, my smiles forced. When Dalton had cared enough to ask if I was alright, I'd lied, of course.

I'd been taking breaks between dances for drinks of water, or using them as opportunities to sit with Ben. He, out of all of my friends and family here, was the only one who allowed me to just...*be*. He didn't talk, or shoot me glances from the corner of his eye. He only put his arm on the back of my chair as he watched Lor dance with Hanna and Iris. Simply *there*, if I should wish to lean back into him for familiar contact after so many hands on me.

I wasn't able to even pretend to enjoy this evening, as I had the last. The only person I'd been able to hold even close to a happy conversation with tonight was Atlas. I'd expected awkwardness from him at best, silence at worst. But he'd come to offer me a glass of champagne, and noticed when my smile was less than genuine. After a heartbeat of staring into my eyes, he'd looked up at the painted ceiling, and asked me what my favorite part of it was.

"The colors closest to the window," I'd told him, admiring the vibrant sunset tones, and the way the late evening sky visible through the window seemed to bleed into them. "What about you?" I'd asked.

"The colors of the middle–that in-between of the beginning and the end. I find them to be especially lovely," he'd said, but his eyes had fallen on me as he'd finished. I pretended not to notice the feeling in them, or the way the expression made my heart thump hard in my chest.

Then Nina had called him back to the kitchens, saving me

from having to change the subject. As he'd walked away, he gave only a reminder to meet him in the kitchens tomorrow to taste test my birthday dessert. After bowing deeply to me, he then turned to follow the head chef to the kitchens.

Aside from that, holding conversations, smiling, dancing... it'd all been so gods-damned exhausting. And maybe I wouldn't feel so bad if not for the violence, and the subsequent awakening I'd experienced yesterday. But now, I didn't know how to shove the anxiety, the nausea, the *disappointment* down to a part of me so deep I could forget that they were there.

"Princess?" I heard a voice say. I looked up from where I sat beside Ben, to find hazel eyes gazing gently at me, the full lips beneath them tilted up at the corners.

"Lord Dion," I greeted him, my small smile only half-forced. "Ben, this is Lord Dion. My Lord, this is my brother, Prince Benjamin."

"A pleasure," the lord said, bowing to Ben. Ben dipped his chin, his dark curls falling slightly over his brow, but said nothing as he examined Dion. "I was hoping to ask your lovely sister for a dance."

Ben looked to me, a question in his eyes. I answered with a slight raise of my brows, and he returned his gaze to the lord. "Certainly." And then he pasted on a ridiculously wide, sarcastic smile. Only the strangely low feeling of my heart in my chest kept me from laughing, but it was probably a good thing in this case. Even a lord as seemingly kind as Dion wouldn't do well with being laughed at.

Dion bowed once more, and held out his hand to me. I took it, rising from my seat, and followed him to the dance floor. He spun me as soon as we reached its edge, and then I was in his arms, one of his hands in mine, the other on the small of my back.

"You look beautiful tonight," he said.

I felt my cheeks heat. "Thank you. You look very handsome yourself." Something warmed in his eyes as he thanked me in return.

We were silent for a moment then, and I felt an immense pressure to figure out what to talk about next. The quiet that I'd found comfort in beside my brother made me nervous now, and I only hoped that Dion didn't feel as uncomfortable as I did.

But then he said, "Can I ask you something, Your Highness?"

I blinked, my shoulders relaxing. "Of course."

"You haven't seemed very happy this evening."

"That's not a question," I whispered, my heart straining.

"You're right. I suppose my question is, why is that?" His brows furrowed, the golden-brown skin between them forming an eleven.

I should deny it. I should say that he was mistaken, and that I was having a wonderful time. My mouth opened to speak the words, but none came out as those hazel eyes held my own. Instead, I heard myself say, "Because come tomorrow, my fate for my life is sealed, and I don't even get to choose it for myself."

I snapped my lips shut as soon as the words were out, and looked around wildly to see if anyone overheard. No one stared in disbelief in our direction, nor had anyone fainted in horror, but the confession felt as though it echoed around the room, resonating in my soul. So many times I'd thought these things, but never said them out loud. Now that I had, the swiftness with which they took root in my heart left me breathless as hot, humiliating tears gathered in my eyes. I blinked furiously, trying to figure out a way to escape that wouldn't draw every eye in the room.

"I'm sorry," Dion said. His voice sounded concerned, but

even if I'd been trying to look at him–and not anywhere else imaginable–my vision was too cloudy to see his face. "I didn't mean to upset you."

"Don't be silly," I responded, my voice mortifyingly thick. "You've done nothing."

But our dance was somehow moving us to the edge of the floor, and then off of it. It was done so quickly, and with an unprecedented grace, that I didn't even have a chance to try to control my emotions enough to protest. Not before Dion seamlessly transferred me to his arm, and led us through the same door to the gardens that I'd used last night. I glanced behind me as we passed the threshold, and no one followed–but many watched. Including a set of storm-gray eyes that pulled me with equal strength as the arm holding mine.

But then we were outside. Just the two of us. There was a stone bench a few feet ahead, and, without a word, he sat, gently pulling me down with him. He remained silent as I dabbed at my face with the back of my hand. His own hand was wrapped lightly around my other, long fingers warm and comforting. I took several deep breaths, and finally met his gaze, forcing the corners of my lips up in a shaky smile. "I'm so sorry," I said, my voice equally as trembling as my mouth.

"What for?" he asked, his brows pulling together slightly.

I nearly rolled my eyes, but the response had more to do with how I felt than with his sweetly-intended question. "For the scene I just made, which will surely stir rumors about us. About you."

His mouth pulled up one one side. "Is it bad if I say that I don't care?"

I didn't respond right away, too surprised by his indifference. But I answered honestly, "No. No, it's not."

He gave me a full smile then, and his thumb stroked a soft line on the back of my palm. "Well, then, I don't care. What I do care about is what you said back there." He repeated the gesture as his expression sobered. "Did you mean it?"

No point in lying now. "Yes. I did." My eyes started to move to my lap, ashamed, but I stopped them. I might've wished that I didn't feel this way, but I did. Being bashful about it wouldn't do me any favors, as much as my teachings as a lady internally shouted at me to be more demure. I brought my gaze back up to his, and lifted my chin. "I do."

His eyes lit with surprise, and some other emotion. I almost thought I misheard him when he breathed, "Beautiful."

My heart thumped a hard beat in my chest. "What?"

And then it was *his* cheeks that were flushed with color. But his eyes held mine as he said, "You're beautiful. Your honesty, your confidence. The way you hold yourself before a room full of men who some would have you believe you should be subservient to. You, who were made to rule them. You, my Princess, are beautiful."

If I weren't already speechless, I would have been rendered so now as his eyes searched mine, a question in them. And I didn't force myself to consider the propriety of it. I allowed myself instead to only feel the desire for it, after quite literally a lifetime of denying myself such things. Breathless, I dipped my chin in an almost imperceptible nod. *Yes.* My heart raced in my chest as I leaned in to meet him, and I didn't remember any thought, any feeling from earlier today or tonight. I didn't hear the music from inside, or the chirping of the cicadas in the garden.

And when his lips pressed against mine, somehow both firm and soft at the same time, I didn't tell my body to move closer. I didn't command the fingers of my free hand to touch the hard edge of his jaw. And I certainly didn't tell my lungs to release a soft, breathy sigh. All of these were reactions my body had to my very first kiss, and I nearly worried if I was doing it right, or further embarrassing myself.

But I felt his mouth tilt up at the corners, and his free hand moved to the back of my neck, his fingers twining with my hair. His lips moved in unfamiliar patterns, but slowly, so that mine learned to follow without me guiding them. My heart pounded as I contemplated things I heard ladies said could happen during–and following–a kiss, but I didn't have the opportunity to think about whether I wanted any of that or not before Dion pulled back, still cupping the back of my head.

His face, just a couple of inches from mine, broke into a wide, breathtaking grin. Without having to think about it, and with all of the girlish joy I could have ever expected, I gave a huge, uninhibited smile right back to him.

15

THE LIBRARY

THE DAYS FOLLOWING MY ATTEMPT TO BE FRIENDLY TOWARDS MY guard passed without incident. She was there when I woke each morning, and when I retired each night. And during those times, and all the times in between, I thought she might have said twenty words to me. When I'd realized how much she must hate talking with me, I had stopped speaking to her at all, so that she would not feel obligated to reply.

Her friends, on the other hand, talked constantly. I hadn't made any huge strides with Lord Bayani, but ever since I'd started exercising in the training yard at the same time as him, he no longer looked annoyed everytime I walked into a room. Nuria and Jolie, the mated females who had walked me through the gardens that second day, proved to be the most involved in providing me with tasks and distractions. Though both very lovely, and kind, I had no doubt that they had been ordered to act pleasantly towards me. I had tried to convince myself to be bothered by it, but Nuria was so intriguing, and Jolie so kind, that I frequently found myself forgetting that they may not be completely genuine.

I only saw the High Lord and High Lady at mealtimes. Try as I might to inquire about scheduling a meeting to discuss our mutual interests–or, at least that was how I worded it when I asked–they'd simply smiled slightly, and said they would have to take a rain-check.

I ended up asking Jolie later that day what 'rain-check' meant. Given that there had been no clouds in the sky, I hadn't been able to even begin to imagine what they were telling me. When I learned that it was just a polite way to say 'not today', as Jolie attempted to hide her giggle behind a hand, I couldn't help but notice that one corner of my guard's lips had turned upwards. And somehow, rather than making me feel more embarrassed, her smirk, combined with Jolie's laughter, had made a chuckle of my own burst through my lips.

I'd nearly gone into shock hearing the sound. I hadn't laughed in years–possibly over a decade. Not a real laugh anyway; only those I'd forced to either please the king, queen, or supplicants.

That evening, the High Lady–whose name I had still been unable to learn–informed me that she and her mate would be holding court here on Saturday next.

It was now the Friday before, also known as my eighteenth day in Colina, Sabrian.

On day nine, I had realized that I might indeed be here for longer than I'd originally anticipated. Though part of me was chagrined for Olin being proven right, most of what I felt leaned more towards the indifferent. What did it matter how long it took me to complete my task? It would get done; time was the best way to assure that.

I'd managed to convince myself that 'indifferent' was the

most I felt. Because being anything more positive-leaning would only end in disappointment.

Still, I'd unpacked all of my belongings that day. On the first day, it'd just been a couple of outfits, and a book; what I thought I would need before I found out all that I needed to, and could head back to Oschverre. Now, everything was in a drawer or the armoire, that book lying on the nightstand on the far side of my bed. The rest–I'd brought five of my favorite novels in preparation for nights in–were lined up on a single shelf in the small study within my chambers.

Now, I stood in the bathing room with a towel around my hips as I brushed my teeth, preparing for the day. I'd woken up later than usual, from a restful sleep. As I looked in the mirror, I noticed the thinness I'd begun to acquire while traveling was gone. Where a human might have taken months to put back on weight and muscle, it had taken my Fae body less than the three weeks that I'd been in Colina. Surely due in part to the quick-healing nature of the Fae, but I knew that the protein and nutrient-rich fare we consumed daily helped as well.

Whether there were other factors that attributed to my increased appetite, I didn't let myself consider. I only allowed myself to see the softness that had returned to the edges of my muscles, and made the hard lines of my face less stark, and felt glad of it, regardless of the cause.

As I rinsed my mouth out at the sink, I heard a soft knock on my door. "Yes?" I called from where I was in the bathing room.

I listened as the door opened, and a strong, annoyed voice asked, "Are you ready?"

The impropriety that earlier this month had tweaked my nerves, now made my lips twitch up. Though I didn't necessarily *enjoy* annoying my guard, I did prefer her speaking, compared to her silence. And since I'd deprived myself of even pleasantries in an effort to spare her, hearing her voice, however irritated, was...

"Nearly," I responded, not allowing myself to finish the thought.

I heard her footsteps get closer and closer as she spoke. "Hielo and Hiela are expecting us for breakfast. We're already–"

I turned to find her standing just beyond the open bathroom door. Her eyes were slightly wide, which I didn't think she was aware of, and I watched as those depthless irises began to travel south from my face before she stopped herself. The fact that she'd even started, though, made me stand up straighter without thinking about it, and my heart gave the smallest of jolts in my chest.

What was *that*?

She sat back on one hip, and sucked her teeth. "You couldn't warn me that you're basically naked?"

My lips tilted up at one corner, and I crossed my arms– finding perhaps more enjoyment than I should in the way her gaze *almost* slipped from my own as the muscles in my chest and arms moved. "You didn't ask. Besides, I'm not the one who came barging into my bathroom."

Her cheeks flushed, the chestnut skin turning a lovely wine-red, but her chin came up in that confident, take-no-shit way of hers. "I'd hardly call knocking and being admitted *barging*. Regardless, the High Lord and High Lady expected us ten minutes ago. Put some clothes on, and let's go." Then she turned on her heel and stormed out, the door closing not so softly behind her. And, for the second time in a week, a brief, unbelievable chuckle came through my lips.

⚎

Breakfast was as delicious as all the meals here seemed to

be; a table full of eggs, bacon, toast, and a huge platter of in-season fruit. I ate until I was fit to burst, and was therefore grateful that Nuria asked not if I would like to walk through the gardens, but rather if I had seen the library yet.

I almost thought I felt tension radiate from my guard at the question, but when I looked at her where she sat on the other side of Jolie, her face remained impassive. Mentally shaking off the strange sensation, I turned back to Nuria. "I have not."

"We must show you, then. It's looking very well like rain anyway; a perfect day for a read-in." She smiled, her mate following suit.

"As long as Lady Ciaragen doesn't mind, I would very much enjoy that." It wasn't a lie. Aside from the fact that I genuinely enjoyed the company of Nuria and Jolie, I was even more delighted to finally have the time and the will to read again. I'd read each night of my stay in Colina after those first couple of evenings, and found that I had forgotten how much I enjoyed it. The smell of the paper and ink, the quiet rustling of pages–and diving into a world wholly outside of my own.

"Oh, I'm sure *Lady Ciaragen* doesn't mind at all," Nuria said, putting a teasing inflection on the formal way I'd referred to my guard. "It's her favorite place in the castle."

My brows went up a bit at that, and I looked again at her. She was staring at Nuria, her eyes widened, nostrils slightly flared. The emotion in her eyes looked...betrayed?

"Perhaps another day," I found myself saying.

Those deep eyes shot to me, confusion sparking in them briefly before she put on her favorite mask of indifference. A mask that fell off much more than she'd like, I was sure, given how often it seemed I got under her skin.

"Nonsense," Jolie chimed in. "As Nuria said, it's the perfect day for a read-in. Ari will end up enjoying herself after a moment, if she lets herself." She gave her friend a pointed look, raising a brow in challenge.

After a pause that was *just* slightly too long, the female gave Jolie a tight-lipped smile. "Of course."

I wanted to say something to persuade them I'd changed my mind. Excuses rose to my lips: that I was feeling ill after breakfast. That I couldn't actually read, and just liked to look at the pictures. Anything to keep from doing something that clearly made her so uncomfortable. That she should be forced to do something just because she had to be where I was–per her orders, and not her will–didn't feel right.

But before I could come up with a convincing argument, Nuria said, "It's settled then." Then I was being swept off my chair and out of the dining hall by the audacious female.

Moments later, I was walking down a bright, spacious hallway, Nuria practically tugging me along, her mate on her other arm. I could hear the soft footsteps of my guard behind me. She walked with the same precision I had noticed on my first day here, but somehow her steps seemed reluctant. As if her training was the only thing that kept her from literally dragging her feet. Again, I felt like I could sense something from her–the discomfort, betrayal, and anger rolling off her.

I almost–*almost*–forgot about what she might be feeling when we stopped before a set of beautifully carved walnut double doors. A doorman was there, and he pushed them wide for us to enter–and see.

The domed space was glorious. Truly, that was the word that came to mind. With its glass ceiling, framed in colored panes along the edges in sunburst designs. Wooden beams arched within and from that artistry, and then formed the vertical frames of the uppermost bookshelves. Including that smaller top tier, there were three floors of books. The staircase that led to the upper levels was made of the same rich wood as the rest of the room, with wrought brass balusters and banisters that accentuated the elegance of the curling mass of steps.

Then, the books. Everywhere, books. Lining every shelf, to the point where some had tomes lying on their sides atop those placed right-side-up. Placed on the sills and seats of the three bay windows; on the plush dark teal chairs and couches; and on the side and center tables that accompanied them. The space managed to be cozy and elegant all at once, and I immediately felt more relaxed within its walls.

"What do you think?" Jolie, close beside me, asked.

"It's spectacular," I replied, slightly breathless.

When I looked down at her, Jolie smiled hugely at me, her ice-blue eyes alight with happiness. I felt my lips pull up at the corners of their own volition in response, and asked her, "Would you like to help me pick a book?"

Her grin shifted, somehow. I'd almost say she was surprised for a second. But then it gave way into something...softer. "I would," she answered. With a courtly grace I thought I'd lost from so many years of disuse, I held my arm out to her. And, after a blown kiss to her mate, Jolie took it.

We walked to the curling stairs, and up to the second floor. With the amount of books that were here, there had to be some kind of organization, because she clearly knew where she was going. That, or she'd simply been here enough to have memorized the locations of the titles she sought. She stopped before one of the shelves, then rose up onto her toes, her delicate neck craning as she reached to pull down a book whose binding was more worn than those around it.

"This is one of my favorites," she told me, staring lovingly at the cover. A deep navy, it read *Guardian of the River* in silver lettering. Then she looked up at me, and held the book out.

For some reason, the gesture and the kindness in her eyes

had my throat thickening as I took the novel from her hand. "Thank you."

She smiled again. "You're welcome." The words seemed intentionally sweet–spoken how a friend might say it. I hadn't realized how much I missed having one of those.

⎌

After over an hour of strolling through the library, arm in arm, while Jolie picked up her favorites and handed them to me, I had accumulated a small stack of volumes in my free arm. We still had not left the second floor–hadn't even looked at a third of the books on this tier alone.

"Lord Dion?" Jolie said suddenly, after several moments of silence we'd spent roaming slowly down a section of shelves.

I looked down at her. "Yes?" Though my arm was just starting to tire from holding the ever-increasing pile of books, I couldn't bring myself to shift anything about our current setup. Nuria was a bright, open, charming presence; a female who could make a friend of anyone, I was sure. And where Nuria was audacious and irreverent, her mate was her counterpart.

Jolie was quiet, a bit reserved, but seemed utterly settled in that quiet. She bore it calmly, content to communicate only with smiles and nods, not finding words to be completely necessary. In her presence, not once as we'd walked in silence had I felt the need to create conversation. And that ease, that calm...it had settled something in me, this past hour.

"You like to read." Not a question, more so a statement of what she'd learned about me as I pointed out the dozens of books I knew as we walked.

I answered nonetheless, "I do, my Lady."

"Is it something you've always enjoyed?"

I had to think about it, and then think some more on

whether I should be honest or not. I decided on the former. "Yes, and no."

Her head tilted as she looked up at me. "Will you explain that?"

I drew in a breath as our stroll slowed to a crawl. "My mother liked to read, but my father did not. He didn't think it was something that was supposed to be done for pleasure; only for education. He believed it to be a waste of his sons' time, when there was combat training to be done. He also believed that it was quite a female thing to do, if it wasn't being done to broaden the mind."

I thought she'd interrupt, outraged at my father's misogyny. But when I glanced down at her, though there was a slight scrunch in her brow, she only squeezed my arm, urging me to continue.

As I breathed in again, I smelled a lovely combination of vanilla and bergamot that steadied me, and went on. "My father sat on many councils. When he was away from home—which was often—my mother would read to us. Stories of fantasy, mystery, even comedy. And when she would bid us good night, she would leave the books in my room. She would say *'Go to sleep now, Dion,'* but she always forgot to take the books, and her faerie light, when she left."

I smiled fondly at the memory that I hadn't thought of in so long—too long. From the corner of my eye, I saw Jolie's lips mirror mine.

My grin faded as the rest of the story came to my mind. "Well, eventually my father found out," I said, my voice quieter than before. Olin had told him one day when our father returned from a trip. He'd done it to get me in trouble, as he always liked to do. Of course, my father's wrath at learning the truth hadn't stopped with me. Because my mother had kept a secret from her lawful husband, from her *master.*

Not even one hundred years later had I forgotten the sounds of that night, or what she'd looked like the next morning. Nor had I ever forgiven Olin for betraying her. For not thinking past the end result of me losing something that I loved–not the reading alone, but the time and the connection it gave me with my mother. I never allowed myself to consider that he had known very well what the result of his revelation would be in its entirety. If only for the memory of our mother, I never did, because I knew she wouldn't want me to kill him.

I cleared my throat, but still, when I spoke again, my voice was rough. "I didn't read for quite some time after that."

Jolie was silent for a moment, and I realized we'd stopped. Standing by the railing overlooking the circle of the first floor, she turned to me, releasing my arm. Instead, she moved her hand to my own, and her delicate fingers circled mine.

"Your mother sounds lovely," she said softly.

I looked away from her bright eyes, my own moving instead to the shelves to my left. "She was." I cleared my throat once more, and brought my gaze back to hers. "She died almost seventy years ago."

Her fingers tightened around mine, but she did not say anything. Once again, favoring the use of her actions and countenance over words. And I thought, as I looked into her sorrow-filled eyes, that it was the most sincere expression of sympathy I'd ever received. And, in the silence she granted me, I didn't force myself to verbally acknowledge her sentiment. I responded only by returning the squeeze of her hand.

Her head tilted after a moment, her brows furrowing slightly as she considered something. "You said *us*. You have siblings?"

I nodded curtly. "Just one. A brother named Olin–my twin, in fact." I chucked without humor. Twins were incredibly rare in the Fae, and of course I would be one of the lucky winners who got one.

Those vivid eyes widened slightly, and I saw questions burn within them, but her lips stayed together. It was my turn to angle my head then, as it occurred to me what her question revealed. "You haven't heard of him?" I released her hand, and leaned that arm instead on the railing between us.

She bent a hip against the baluster. "I haven't," she confessed, dark brown brows pulling together. "Strange."

Strange, indeed. I'd thought Olin's name would be even more infamous than my own, given his acts of brutality. But, to be completely honest, Olin was one of the last things I wanted to think about right now. No, I wanted to read in one of those comfortable-looking velvet chairs, and sit in silence with my–friend.

"Lady Jolie?" I said, brightening my voice as I cleared my mind of the thoughts that would serve no purpose other than to ruin a perfectly good day. Jolie's gaze refocused on me, and lightened.

"Instead of pondering the complexities of my family, would you instead like to join me in reading one of these many books I've been carrying for over an hour, before my arm falls off?"

She laughed–not a giggle, or something forced, but an actual laugh that brightened her already vivid blue eyes. The sound was cheerful, and surprised, and it kept going as she talked through the final chuckles. "Yes, Lord Dion, I would like that very much."

As I smiled at her, and offered her my arm once more, I didn't allow my propriety or my inhibitions to get in the way as I said, "Call me Dion."

16

DAGGERS & DESSERTS

THEA - EARLIER, THIS DAY

TODAY WAS MY BIRTHDAY. BY THE END OF THE DAY, I WOULD BE essentially betrothed. I might as well have the ring soldered onto my finger now. Might as well speak my vows right after cake tonight.

After my confession to Dion last night, I couldn't find it in myself to even pretend to be excited. I supposed that at last having someone who knew the truth of my mind, and agreed with it, had added kindling to a flame whose only destiny was to be doused this evening.

Despite having had my first kiss–a very good kiss, at that–with Dion, I knew little to nothing about him. I'd been so embarrassed not to know off the top of my head what his surname was, and where he hailed from, that I still hadn't asked. All I knew about him was as follows: he was handsome, seemingly kind, and a wonderful kisser.

Was I supposed to base my decision off of who I had the

most physical chemistry with? Or who I felt I connected with as a person? Given my emotional state for most of last evening, I hadn't even gotten to hold a proper conversation with Belamy or Dalton. The latter had been kind enough to note my lack of enthusiasm, and, rather than making me feel badly about it, had instead told me that *he* was feeling under the weather. He'd kissed the back of my palm gently, and told me that he hoped to see me in the morning.

Did I want to marry him, though? Was the fact that he was emotionally intelligent enough to tie myself to him for life?

Not to mention, I had so little experience to push me in either direction. My virtue had been strictly guarded by others– or was, until I could prove that I would protect it myself. As such, I'd never been able to be physical with a man. Or even get close enough to one to have it be a possibility. When I turned an age to be interested in such things, I somehow only ever found myself in the company of women.

Since I had none of my own experience, over the years I'd done what I could to be as prepared as possible for this time in my life. I listened to stories from trusted tellers. From my tables of women, I observed how men acted, and what they said and did when they didn't think anyone paid attention. I learned that some men could be gentlemen to your face, and diminish you the moment your back was turned.

Dion and Dalton didn't seem like they would do that. But how in gods' names should I know? They could be bloody serial killers, and I would be none the wiser.

Staring up at the canopy over my bed, I heaved a sigh. Lying there thinking wasn't going to change the fact that I knew nothing about these men, but getting up and going to see them might.

As I brushed my teeth, and sifted through my closet for a day dress, I realized that I'd been able to do all of this thinking uninterrupted. No one had come to rouse me, or wish me a happy birthday, or shame me for sleeping so late. Knowing my family, the most likely reason for this was that Ben, Iris, and Nik were keeping our mother occupied. One perk of being the youngest: the oldest knew how to look out for you.

Still, half an hour later, I walked down the halls in a pale yellow A-line frock that floated to just above my ankles. I took the lowest traffic route possible, only passing a few staff members—all of whom wished me a happy birthday with a smile—before I reached the training yard.

Amahd saw me approach, and arched a dark brow. "Interesting combat gear," he said.

I smiled a bit sadly at him. "I'm not sure I'll be able to train today after all."

He set down the blade and whetstone, and considered me for a moment. Rather than making me feel uncomfortable, or self-conscious, I was immediately in my apprentice mindset. My hands clasped behind my back, chin lifting without any thought as I weathered his gaze.

Amahd came to stand in front of me. His near-black eyes, just a few inches above my own, stared into mine with unwavering intensity. "Why is that?" he asked.

I felt heat rise to my cheeks, but kept my chin up and my voice steady as I replied, "I woke late, and have much to do, and think about, before this evening."

"Indeed you do. You don't think that a few minutes in the yard would help to clear your head?" He raised his brows. My lips twisted to the side, because he was right. It probably would. But, should I be training on the day that my life might change forever? As if he read my thoughts, Amahd continued, "It is when life is most chaotic that these moments of clarity are needed. How are you to make this decision, when your mind is stuck?" He used his summoning magic, and a short but wicked dagger appeared in his open palm. He extended it to me, and my fingers wrapped around the hilt without a second thought. Amahd gave me a rare grin, and we walked to the target pitch.

My strides stuttered a bit with surprise when I saw Artur hurriedly putting weights away in the section of the yard adjacent to the pitch. As he passed us on the path back to the castle, he gave me a low bow, quietly thanked Amahd, and practically ran away.

"Strange man," Amahd said. "Kind, but skittish. And lifts far more than a man of his stature should be able to."

I agreed with him on the first bit, but only smirked before responding. "Is someone a bit envious?"

"Is someone a bit cocky because she knows I can't put her through the wringer today for asking such a thing?"

I shrugged. "Dresses can be cleaned. Your ego on the other hand…"

Amahd halted, and I fell in beside him. "Hit the bullseye," he commanded, jutting his salt-and-pepper bearded chin towards the center target, about fifteen yards away.

I sighed, but took my stance. I dropped my shoulders, loosened the tense set of my jaw. The teasing conversation, the weird run-in with Artur, the events that would happen later today–they all fell away. I breathed in the dust-and-grass scent of the yard, and on my exhale, I whipped the blade over my shoulder, flicking my wrist just so.

With a *thunk*, the dagger sank into the red at the target's center.

"You won't get all that time to prepare in a fight. Again." He summoned the dagger back to me with a snap, and I caught it a foot from my face. Without pause, I twisted and threw. *Thunk*: an inch to the right of center.

"You aimed for his brain, and instead he's missing part of an ear. Again." Summoned, and caught inches from my belly.

Thrown, and this time buried just above the red mark. "Oh, good. You hit his shoulder instead of his heart. Don't forget, he's moving, Princess."

With that, the dagger wound up back in my palm, while the target jumped to different places in the yard. Staying for only a second each time, the only indication of its move being Amahd's snaps. My heart hammered as I tried to track its pattern, but, of course, there was none. A worthy opponent wouldn't give any, either.

With that thought, I quickly snatched the dagger hanging at Amahd's hip, and threw it. A second later, I tossed the other with my non-dominant hand. When the target at last stood still, two blades stuck out of it, a hair's breadth from each other within the red of the bullseye.

Amahd whistled, and I beamed. When I turned my head to him, his dark eyes were crinkled at the corners with his own small grin. My smile softened, and I resisted the urge to give the training master a grateful embrace. Feeling much lighter than I had just moments ago, I said, without the reluctance I might have had then, "As much as I'd love to throw daggers all morning, I have princess-y duties to attend to."

Amahd dipped his chin, and started towards the target. "Best get on with being *princess-y*, then." A gruff dismissal, gentled by his next words, spoken kindly over his shoulder. "Happy birthday, Princess."

⹏

My breakfast was a brownie I took to the staff wing to share with Kya. Afterwards, the time for relaxation at an end, I took a walk in the gardens, where Dalton and Belamy reliably approached me. Pleasant conversation, promises of seeing each other later. Etcetera.

I didn't see Dion at all. Not in the gardens, or the halls, or the common spaces like the library, cards room, or gallery. Did he think our kiss last night sealed the deal or something? That poor little virgin me would be so head-over-heels for the first press of a man's lips against mine that I'd choose him regardless of anything else?

It had been a good–maybe even a great–kiss. But it only stirred more questions. Dion seemed kind enough, but Dalton made me laugh, and was even sweeter than Dion. But what if I kissed Dalton, and felt... nothing?

The fact of the matter was that I didn't know either of them well enough to want to spend the rest of my life with them, and that feeling carried me to the kitchens, where both my comfort food and comfort company awaited.

I found Atlas easily, his tall, muscular frame seeming at odds with the grace with which he moved around counters, carts, and cooks. None of the clumsiness that had made him spill soup on me on his first day, and his ease with his environment settled something in my chest.

In the back of the kitchens, countless sweets were piled, most yet to be baked; just sitting and rising, some cooling on trays. "Do you think we have enough?" I asked with mock-concern.

He laughed, and turned his face to grin at me. "If your heart had rule over your stomach, Highness, I wouldn't be so sure."

Now it was my turn to chuckle. "Fair enough. Which one am I here to try?" They all looked delicious. I popped an unbaked glob of dough into my mouth as Atlas reached a broad, long-fingered hand across the counter to grab a square of something.

"This one." He handed it to me, along with a napkin. "It has pumpkin in it." I looked up at him dubiously, a brow raised, and he smirked. "Ah, yes. I'd heard that you don't like when health and dessert mix. Fear not, Princess, for there is nothing healthy about this." Still, I looked between him, and the square. "If you don't try it, I'll tell everyone that you're a picky eater."

I gasped. "You wouldn't dare." The openness of my palate was a point of pride for me. This was far from the first time I'd been called to the kitchens to try something for the cooks, or the bakers, and I didn't want that privilege to end.

"Either try this, or try me." He crossed his arms and leaned a hip against the counter. I tried not to watch the muscles in his dark brown forearms flicker as he did so. For a moment, I imagined what those arms might feel like wrapped around me–

A blush creeped up my cheeks, and his teasing grin didn't waver. I quickly took a bite of the square in my hand–and was distracted from my imagination as the bread and the icing spread over my tongue. "Oh my gods," I whispered, not caring about the food in my mouth.

Atlas laughed again. "See? I told you."

I was too busy taking another bite, so I just nodded to say that, yes, he had. He chuckled again, and poured a small cup of milk, setting it on the counter beside me. I garbled what was supposed to be a thank you but sounded nothing like it. I licked my fingers after the last bite, not caring if it was unladylike. When I looked up at Atlas, I caught the movement of his head as he turned it away, seeming a little darker in the cheeks than he had a moment ago.

"That was delicious," I said when my mouth was empty. "Who made them?" He didn't answer, and so I knew: "You?" He shrugged, and I smacked his arm, unable to keep from noticing just how solid it was beneath my hand. "I didn't know you could bake!"

He only shrugged again, smirking. "Have another, if you want." He jerked his chin to the tray, and did his arm-cross-hip-lean thing again. Gods, he was even more handsome than

Dion. I shoved aside that thought at the same time that I shoved another pumpkin square in my face.

"So," he started. Some emotion passed through his eyes, but was gone before I could put a name to it. "Would it be too bold to ask who you plan on making yours tonight?"

I balked. Slightly because, yes, it was a bit bold for a server to ask a princess about her love life. But mostly because I'd somehow forgotten about that, what with the life-altering bread, and the company that served it. My mom always said that I couldn't keep my attention on one thing for more than five minutes, and I proved her right daily.

"If it is, then please accept my apology, and pretend I didn't ask," he said quickly, running a hand over the thin locs he had pulled into a bundle at his nape.

"No," I responded. "It's alright." I looked around the kitchen. No one seemed to be listening; too busy with preparations for the evening. Still, one could never know who might overhear, and report to whomever they would. I looked back to Atlas, and tilted my head in the direction of the back door of the kitchen, which led to a substantial pantry. Once we were shut inside, I took a deep breath. "Truthfully, I haven't decided."

I thought relief flashed in his eyes, but that couldn't be right. "What's keeping you?" he asked, stepping closer as he lowered his voice.

I slapped my hands to my sides, and smiled without humor. "That I don't know what the fuck I'm doing," I whisper-screamed, and began pacing between the shelves. "I want passion and fun, and humor and kindness, and I don't know these men well enough to know that they'll give me any of that, never mind all of it. Someone who can make me happy, make me laugh, even when I'm having the worst day. Who will see the dark parts of me, and love them anyway. You know?"

His eyes were soft. "I do."

My pacing stalled, and my anger subsided as I looked into his gentle eyes. Something about them had desolation stirring instead, thickening my throat and lining my eyes. I looked away quickly, mortified, and heard him shuffle–watched a hand lift and then drop. I didn't allow myself to think it through, as he so clearly was, before walking forward until I was pressed against him, and wrapping my arms around his waist, my face against his chest. He smelled of thyme and salt, and I breathed them— *him*—in greedily.

After a heartbeat of hesitation, his arms wound around me, and his cheek rested on top of my head. He sighed, and I let myself feel him, his body touching mine, and his heartbeat in my ear. My very soul seemed to calm, and in that calm, I remembered myself.

I stepped back from him. "I'm sorry," I said, a blush heating all the way up my neck, to my cheeks and nose.

"Don't be." I lifted my eyes to look at him, and found his roiling once more, differently than they had been before. Gods, having no experience with men was such a buzzkill. Just a *teeny* bit of knowledge, of knowing what a woman should do at this point would be great.

What a princess *would do is walk away*, my mother's voice said in my head. And maybe I wouldn't listen to it. Maybe I'd stay right here in this pantry, and figure out for myself what a woman might do. Maybe I'd finally let myself remember how I'd been happy to have soup spilled all over me, because his assignment had made it possible for him to be close to me each day. Maybe I'd put myself in a not-so innocent situation right here, in a pantry that had a lock on its door from the inside.

Maybe I would do all of those things. Risk my virtue, and my reputation.

I took another step back, and cleared my throat. "I, um, should go," I said, and reached for the door handle.

"Wait," he stopped me, and my heart leapt as I looked back at him. Would he ask me to stay? Would I be able to say no?

But he only murmured, "We should leave together. People love to talk." And I understood that, at least–we were alone together in a pantry that no one else had come into since we entered. And we were alone together in the gardens two days ago. It didn't take a genius to make the connection to what anyone on the other side of this door would think was happening on our side of it.

I worked to hide my disappointment–or should I be relieved?–and just half-spoke, half-sighed, "Right."

He walked over, and reached across me to grab the handle, his arm brushing mine as he did so. And if I hadn't raised my eyes to his as it happened, if I had kept them down as I hid my chagrin, I wouldn't have seen those gray eyes fixed on me, gazing at me as if he was having thoughts very similar to my own.

I didn't look away as he stepped into me, holding the handle just at forearm-length. This close, I could feel the warmth of his body, and his gaze grew even more heated. If each of us took a deep breath, my chest would touch his stom-ach. From here, I could see that his eyes were gray, yes, but with a ring of silver around the pupil. Like lightning flashing on a storm-ridden ocean.

My heart was thudding, and I felt more–far more–than I did as Dion had leaned in to kiss me last night. Even more than during the kiss itself. And Atlas and I weren't even touching. Only our breath mingled in the air between us.

Forbidden, my mother's voice in my head said. And he must have seen it as the smallest glimmer of doubt passed through my eyes, because not a second later, he was half a step away from me, opening the door.

17

THE ENDING OF FATE

THEA - PRESENT

I'M STILL TRYING TO CALM MY RACING HEART AS I STRIDE DOWN the hall to my next, and final, order of business before the gathering.

No matter what my body–I refuse to consider my heart– might want, a romance with Atlas is impossible. The hurt of that knowledge is part of what drives my feet so quickly. Because, if I'm honest with myself, the reason I'm rushing to tell someone who I've chosen is that, if I don't give someone else the accountability to hold me to that choice, I might not make it at all. Not out of those I'm meant to choose from.

When I walk into my sister's chambers, Iris and Hanna are sprawled out on the four-poster bed, its canopy pulled open to reveal the former taking a file to her nails, and the latter perching a book on her slightly rounded belly. Lor is lounging in the plush armchair by the window, her feet resting on the matching blush pink ottoman. When they hear me enter, all three look up, but say nothing. Waiting.

I look around again to make sure Cleo isn't sleeping somewhere, then take a breath. On the exhale, I say, "Dalton." Since Dion never did show his face today, that, at least, is an easy decision.

Chaos ensues. All three of them jump up from where they are–Lor a bit more slowly–squealing, and come to grapple me into a group hug, with me at its center. Their excitement, the silliness of them bouncing around, squishing me between them, is enough to lift just a bit of the weight from my shoulders, and I end up giggling with them.

After a moment, we separate, all of them wiping tears from their faces. "Have you told mom and dad?" Iris asks, her eyes bright.

I shake my head. "I wanted to tell you all first." I don't need to say why. That I'd wanted the giddy, girlish joy, rather than hearing that I'm doing the right thing for our continent, our people. I hadn't wanted to hear that yet, as the most selfish parts of me still yearn to not have this responsibility. Parts that care little of the benefits of alliance, and much more for the wellness of my own heart.

I know that Iris understands–as much as she can as a happily married and mothered woman–and she gives me a small smile, running her thumb over my cheekbone before dropping her hand.

"Well," Lor says, her hands braced on her lower back, "we'll have all the time in the world tomorrow to talk about him. But it's about time for you to get ready, isn't it?"

"It is," I reply, giving my best shameful grimace.

"Better get a move on, beautiful," Hanna joins in, throwing an arm over Lor's shoulders. "You've got a date." She winks a sparkling silver eye at me, which makes me grin. My friend through so much of my life; I feel a bit more of the weight leave my shoulders, knowing that she is here with me, as she always has been.

"Oh, and happy birthday!" she exclaims with a giggle as I reach the door. Lorraine and Iris echo her, and I thank them through a laugh.

Iris will be informing both our parents, and Dalton, of my choice. As I leave, she and our friends chorus a goodbye to me, huge smiles on all of their faces. When I close the door behind me, I hear more squealing and laughter on the other side, and my lips curl up a little at the sound. I *should* feel happy and excited. This is a day that, when I was Kya's age, I couldn't wait to arrive. I couldn't count the nights that I had sat with Hanna and Lor in my chambers, talking of the men that we might marry. What dresses we'd wear for the ceremonies. How many children we'd have with them, in our large estates that would be complete with gardens and libraries.

I don't know when exactly I stopped feeling excited about this day. Maybe when I turned twenty, and realized how close it was. Or maybe it had been when Hanna, and Lor married, and I had no thoughts of my own wedding. When I'd recognized that I perhaps should wish that I was in the same place as them, and instead was happy that I wasn't.

Whenever it had been, it makes no difference now. This has always been my fate. How I feel about it is also a choice I can make.

As I walk down the spacious halls towards my chambers, I work at locking away the emotions and thoughts that I don't have the time or space for right now, just as I had the other night. I leave room only for the ones that bring me peace. Those feelings alone have me humming to myself for the first time in two days. My voice lilts and echoes slightly in the halls, casting a calming music all around me.

This evening, I may be happy enough dancing and laughing with Dalton to forget I had felt anything else. Perhaps in the days after that, when we're settled with each other, and talking about our lives outside of what we've each come to know over two evenings, I won't be so afraid. Maybe it's enough of a commendation to his character that thinking about being with him for the rest of my life doesn't scare me *too* much.

Moments later, I'm in my room, staring at the deep maroon dress hanging on my armoire. A color which has never been available to me before. Too womanly–intended for someone who is already taken. Provocative, as much as a color can be in itself.

I hear the sound of heels coming down the hall, and I know it's my mom before she can even knock. Instead of waiting for her to do so, I open my door to find her two paces from it, her hand already raised. She looks beautiful, her gently lined face adorned with only rouge that matches her lip stain, and kohl on her lashes. Her brown and white curls are gathered into a sleek chignon on the back of her head, clipped in place with golden pins, and a gold-and-pearl crown.

As she drops her hand, her sky blue eyes fill with tears, and gleam with her *my daughter is my sunshine* look.

"Mom, you're going to ruin your makeup," I say in greeting.

She waves a hand, and scoffs, which I know means that she's too choked up to speak. With the same hand, she gestures for me to get back into the room. I do as I'm nonverbally told, and she follows, closing my door behind her. She clears her throat, and snatches a tissue from the holder on my nightstand. After dabbing it under her eyes, she says, "Sorry, Aly. I know it's your day, in more ways than one."

"I would have been very naive indeed to expect you not to cry today. I'm sure that this isn't even the first time."

"You'd be right," she says, and we both chuckle. She walks

toward me, and reaches to brush through the front of my hair with her fingers, which then move to caress my cheek. "Are you ready?"

I take a deep breath, and as I blow it out, I nod and say, "Yes." Then, "Or, I will be, once you help me." I gesture behind me to the dress, and then to my bare face.

She grins. "I think I can do that." She brings her arms up to hold my face between her palms. "Now, close your eyes, my dear girl."

I do as she requested, and the familiar warmth envelops me as her magic works. There's a slight rustling, and I feel the weight of the gown replace the lighter day dress I'd been wearing. I feel it when she's done, but she doesn't release my face for another moment. When she does, she sighs, the sound shaky.

I open my eyes to see her standing before me, her hands folded over her heart as she looks at me. Without speaking, she twirls one finger in the air, asking me to turn to look in the mirror. I heed her instruction, and I am not disappointed.

The woman in the mirror is just that—a woman. She is not the girl who wears pastels, and has to pretend to be meek before men. She is fierce in the deep red gown that hugs her curves like no other has been allowed to do before, the voluminous skirt somehow adding to the effect. The neckline cuts just barely below where cleavage begins, the first that will be seen of it outside of this chamber.

My lips and cheeks are the same color as the gown, the severity of which is lightened by the simplicity of just a slight shimmer on my lids, and kohl on my lashes. All of which makes the green of my eyes look like sea glass being lit from behind by the sun. My hair hangs in loose waves of midnight black to my waist, my only jewelry resting on top of my head in the form of a circlet tiara. My neck, ears, and fingers are all unadorned, and the reason is clear: the dress is the star.

Behind me, my mom has her hands folded beneath her chin, and tears flow uninterrupted down her cheeks. I turn to her, and she moves forward to clasp my hands in hers. I brace myself for the speech, for her to tell me that she's proud of me, and that I'm doing the right thing by following the tradition.

"Dalton is the luckiest man alive," she says instead. "And I cannot wait to see how he proves that he deserves the gift that is you." Tears burn behind my eyes at that, and I can't speak for a moment. Her hands squeeze mine, and she tells me quietly, one last tear trailing down her cheek: "I love you, my girl."

"I love you too, Mom," I reply, my voice thick. Her fingers squeeze mine once more, her final reassurance before we leave.

And the knowledge that my life will never be the same after tonight rests on my shoulders like a physical weight as we walk hand-in-hand to the Hall, and towards my fate.

⇔

Sitting between my mother and Iris on the dais, I can feel the many eyes on me. Have been able to since Artur announced our arrival, and I'd walked through the double doors beside Ben, in my red gown. I don't think it's my imagination that many who had only dipped their chins to me two nights ago now gave me full, sweeping bows. As though their respect hinged on me upholding this tradition, and naming a husband.

The thought has made me quiet for the past ten minutes, only interacting with Iris or my mother when they speak to me. I hope they contribute it all to nerves, and not to the annoyance that it is.

I look up at the painted ceiling in an attempt to distract myself. Beautiful. Every time, it's so beautiful, and I wish that I could be up there, an observer to the sealing of my fate–rather than the executor of it.

My mind drifts to Dalton, waiting in the antechamber to be announced. He knows he's been chosen, of course, but I'm not to see him until he enters the Hall. I've made my decision. The next one is up to him: whether he prefers to propose to me now, or wait until we've been together longer. Neither is frowned upon. Engagement is inevitable, which he knew when he'd come here.

My choice is final. It's done. There's no changing my mind, which I'm convincing myself is a calming fact. Dion had been notified by Hanna of my choice at the same time that Iris had told Dalton. It's probably for the best that I haven't seen him yet tonight.

Otherwise, everyone is here. All of my siblings, their spouses, and children. Ciaragen is chatting with Lorraine and Izabel, his handsome face animated as he speaks. Dalton's parents are here, as well as his younger sister, but I'm not supposed to speak with them until after the announcement is made, when everything's official. Dalton looks very much like his father–happy eyes, strong jaw, a straight nose–and I suppose it's a good sign that the man is still dashing in his advanced age. His mother and his sister are lovely–both with darker complexions than the men, and black hair instead of brown. My future in-laws. The thought makes my heart stutter, and I tell myself that the reason for the reaction is that I'm nervous about meeting them, and hoping they'll like me.

Hanna sits with Gregor at a table just across from the dais. She meets my eyes, and gives me a small, reassuring smile, lifting her chin slightly. I take the cue, and lift my own face, straightening in my chair. She nods once, but does not look away; she keeps her lovely eyes on me, calm as a summer breeze. After a moment, an easy breath finally fills my lungs, and I'm able to dip my chin once to her in thanks before turning away.

And I suppose I'm as ready as I'll ever be. As I look away from Hanna, I swivel my gaze to my right. Catching the motion, my parents turn to me. I give them a small nod, and then face forward, unable to watch the pride fill their eyes.

My father stands, and steps forward on the dais. All at once, the chatter in the room ceases. I feel the eyes of everybody in the Hall shift between my father and myself. I stare straight ahead, not meeting any of their gazes–low enough that it could appear that I'm looking at somebody, but high enough that I don't accidentally do just that.

"Thank you all for coming here tonight," my father starts. "Each of you are vitally important to Weaschte and her prosperity. We are perpetually grateful that you put your trust in us to rule this great continent, and we can only hope that we continue to earn, and deserve, that trust."

There's a round of applause at that, but no hollering, or cheering. Not yet. For now, only a show of respect to our King and Queen, and the heirs to the throne, is warranted. "We cannot forget to thank the gods. We are not they, but we know that it is only by their will and their blessings that both my family, and Weaschte, remain in such good health."

My father turns to my mother, and offers his hand. The King is the ruler, his reign and his family strengthened by his Queen at his side. She comes to stand by him now, and he twines their fingers together. They share a smile before my father continues, "Queen Lydia and I are immensely honored to be here with you to celebrate our daughter, Princess Althea Maria Cardenia, on the night of her twenty-first birthday."

He gestures his other hand towards me, and I rise on surprisingly steady legs. I move to stand beside them, but do not take my mother's other hand. I must stand alone in this moment, because when my hand is joined with another's tonight, it will be my future husband's.

Another round of applause sounds through the room, a bit louder than the last. I keep my chin high, and my shoulders back, and put on a grateful smile until it quiets.

"On this day, a year before Princess Althea turns twenty-two, and her Apotheos is complete," my father says, referring to that final culmination of my power as a Mage, "she will continue the royal family tradition of betrothal. The Princess has made her choice as to who will have the honor of becoming her intended, and, in a year, her husband."

He and my mother take a step back, and I a step forward. I clasp my hands lightly at my waist, careful to make the position relaxed. I paste a serene smile onto my face; the smile of a woman content in her role, and her duty here. Then I say, "We are truly blessed to have you all here tonight. Know that even if you have not been chosen, it is not a reflection on you, or your House. And I sincerely pray that each and every one of you finds someone whom you can cherish for a lifetime, just as I have found that person for myself."

The words have a bad taste as they leave my mouth. Though everything I said first is true, it's the last bit that has the sourness of dishonesty. Cherish is a strong word to use–almost as strong as 'lifetime'.

My heart pounds, but I manage to keep my voice steady, and tears from rising to my eyes, as I seal my fate. "That person is Lord Dalton Fera, son of Heranelle, the Horizon of Weaschte." I look to the door leading to the antechamber. Soft gasps and squeals are quickly suppressed as everyone follows my gaze to wait for Dalton to enter.

But he doesn't.

My heart squeezes painfully in my chest for a new reason. Embarrassment. I cannot turn back to my parents, not without looking like a little girl who needs her mom and dad to help her, rather than a woman about to be betrothed. A woman who, after this moment, will be not just an heir to the throne, but a Lady to another great House. So instead, I look down to where Iris sits in the chair beside my vacant one. In my eyeline already, it's not noticeable to anyone but her. Her eyes hold confusion, but nothing else—no pity, or fear. She's the one who gave Dalton the news; she would know if he had been anything other than sincere in his joy at being chosen.

But it's been a few seconds too long now, and the whispers have already begun. My heart pounds, heat flooding my face, but I say, "Lord Dalton, everyone is anxious to cheer you on." Playfully, as though I know him and his nerves.

Finally, the door opens—a bit slowly, but it opens. I sigh in relief, and my heart begins to calm. Truly just nerves, then. He'd probably either heard me, and needed a moment, or hadn't heard at all at first, with the thoughts whirling in his head. I can absolutely understand that.

A booted foot crosses the threshold, and catches slightly on the lip of the entrance.

The rest of Dalton appears all at once, as he falls forward into the room, blood pouring from his face.

Screams and gasps rent the air, and I think I produce one of them, my hand flying over my mouth. The reaction lasts only a second before I remember myself, and run down the steps of the dais. I can heal him—whatever has happened to him, I can heal him.

But I freeze just feet from him as another figure walks through that threshold, stepping over Dalton's too-still legs. The man holds a dagger that drips red, and he bends to wipe it on the back of Dalton's jacket before he sheathes it at his hip.

The man looks up, and smiles directly at me.

"Hello, beautiful," Dion says.

18

TALES & TRUTHS

CIARAGEN - 21 YEARS EARLIER

I SAT IN ONE OF THE PLUSH VELVET CHAIRS IN THE LIBRARY, MY back against one of the arms and my legs hanging over the other. A book laid open in my hands, and Nuria sat silently reading in the chair beside me. The usual scent of the library, as well as an intriguing addition of white oak and amber, had me feeling more relaxed than I'd been in nearly three weeks.

Absorbed in my book, I barely heard the conversation Jolie was having with the lord up on the second floor. Of course, as soon as the two enemies in my book had finally realized that there was something romantic between them, Nuria, sitting the same way as I was, kicked my foot. I looked up, annoyed at being pulled from the anticipated scene of affection, but her expression halted my ire. Her eyes widened slightly, and she gestured with a jut of her chin to the balcony of the second floor. I rolled my eyes, not really caring to hear that male talk.

Still, I returned my gaze to my book, but did not read the pages; instead, I listened.

Jolie had been talking and strolling with him for over an *hour*. I doubted Nuria had been paying attention to them that whole time; Jolie must have sent her a mate-bond-communication or something. I wasn't sure how it worked, not being mated myself. I just knew that mates were very...connected. Jolie must have *communicated* that an important topic of conversation was about to be broached, because all that was being said at the moment was, "Thank you."

But then Jolie said, "You said *us*. You have siblings?"

That piqued my interest. No one, not even our High Lord and High Lady, had been able to find any information on his family. We'd been meticulous in our search to ensure that if *measures* had to be taken, there would be no one but the king that would need a cover story. It seemed we were wrong. Or misinformed.

"Just one," he replied. "A brother named Olin–my twin, in fact." He chuckled, but the sound held no humor.

A *twin*? In Fae, twins were extremely rare; probably something about the balance of life since we were immortal beings. Though I kept my head down, I lifted my gaze to look at Nuria under my lashes. Her dark eyes held the same surprise and confusion I was sure mine did.

"You haven't heard of him?" the lord asked, sounding equally bewildered. I didn't listen for Jolie's response.

I had never heard the name Olin Evestre in my life, while I'd heard *his* many times, even before he'd altered my life forever by killing my father. If this unknown male was as monstrous as his brother–which I doubted was possible–his name should be infamous, even outside of the capital. This information had to be brought to the High Lord and High Lady at once.

Of course, I would not be the one to do it. Stuck in my favorite place, because of my least favorite person. Suppressing a groan, I closed my book, but tucked it under my arm so that I could bring it with me and finish later on, once I was off-duty. I stretched as I stood, pulling my arms over my head, and going up on my toes. I heard the sound of footsteps coming down the stairs, and watched from the corner of my eye as the lord walked arm-in-arm with Jolie.

"Are we leaving already, my Lady?" he asked, brows furrowing.

"I was wondering the same," Nuria said, and I whirled to her.

"I thought you had to get going." I widened my eyes at her, and flicked them in the direction of where the lord stood behind me.

"Oh, Ari, you must have been mistaken. You see, my ass is very comfortable right here in this chair, reading a sapphic romance." She took a sip of her tea, and gazed at me over the rim of the cup. Behind me, Jolie giggled, and I heard a small huff of a breath from beside her.

I turned to them, and the lord was indeed smiling. It half left when he saw my expression, but Jolie interrupted my glaring. "Come on, Ari. It's raining, so it's not as if we could do anything else. We have tea, and we can get snacks for when we get hungry. Honestly, the only thing that could make it better would be comfortable clothes."

She was right. This would normally be my favorite kind of day. If it weren't for one extremely unwelcome addition.

That addition said, "If you wouldn't mind too much, my Lady, I really would like to stay." His eyes weren't pleading–that was too strong of a word. More like, he was asking a question to which he very much cared about the answer. His cheeks flushed as he said it, and I wasn't sure if he'd meant to be so vulnerable, in expressing this want–

Of course he had. Everything he did was intentional. He'd lived too long not to master playing on people's hearts and minds. But, I thought reluctantly, regardless of what he may or may not feel, Nuria and Jolie absolutely did want to stay.

So, I sighed through my nose, and said, "Fine. We'll stay."

Jolie smiled hugely, squeezing the lord's arm–an act of affection that would have had my eyes bugging if I hadn't been working on leashing my expressions.

After grinning at my friend, the lord said to her, "If I may–I could resolve that last issue you posed." She raised her brows while I scrunched mine. His eyes flashed between the two of us, and a half-smile settled on his lips as he snapped his fingers.

A pile of clothing landed on the chair I had vacated. He walked to it, passing within a foot of me to do so, and I realized then that the new, pleasant scent in the library had been coming from *him*. Somehow, in this place that I adored, I hadn't connected the smell that I usually forced myself to hate with the male. I had let it soothe me instead, breathing deep, greedy breaths of it.

He held up two of the garments, providing a much needed distraction before I could be sick at the realization. A warm mauve set that consisted of loose, flowing pants and a hooded shirt dangled from his hands. Both of which looked like they would feel softer than satin on the skin. He held them out to Jolie, and she took them, her blue eyes filled with delight. "You have a pocket realm?" she asked, holding them up in front of the day dress she currently wore.

He smiled, a softer smile than I'd seen him give before. "A gift from my mother." At that, her own eyes filled with genuine emotion, and I resisted the urge to shake her, or shout at her *what are you doing?*

"That goes wonderfully with your eyes, my love," Nuria said, grinning at her mate. Jolie blushed a bit, but beamed at Nuria in return.

"I'm going to go behind one of the shelves to change." And Jolie actually *ran* in her excitement to go do so.

The lord grinned as she went, and then picked up a champagne colored set and handed it to Nuria. I could already tell that the tone would make her golden tattoo and her dark skin even brighter. She followed, practically skipping in the direction Jolie went.

Finally, he picked up a set of a topaz hue. I would have called the way he approached me *shy*. His eyes darted from the set to my face, and then he held the clothing out towards me. In those eyes, I saw yet another one of those questions to which he cared significantly for the answer. And, while I didn't want to give him the one he desired, I also didn't want to stay in my uniform.

So, still hesitantly, I reached out, and closed my hands over the items. As he released them, he smiled slightly. I felt my brows pull together in response, but went to change in a different area than where my friends had ventured. They had been intimate in the library before, and if they were doing so again—well, at least someone was having fun.

I walked out from the shelves moments later, wearing the set—that did indeed feel so soft on my skin I might have been content to wear it forever—with my uniform folded in my arms. The lord was also in the main room, wearing drawstring pants that cinched at the waist and ankles, and a long sleeved shirt, both in light gray.

He heard me as I approached the sitting area, and he cleared his throat before turning to me. "I got us all fresh tea, but I can make it cocoa if you'd like." He gestured to the table, centered between the two chairs on one side, and the couch on the other. The table was laden with treats and teacups, and underneath it he'd stored his other clothing. I moved to put mine there as well.

I realized he was waiting for me to say something as the silence continued. Still looking at the table, I said, "The chocolate pastries are my favorite. May I have one?" It felt abhorrent to ask him permission for anything, but there were only a few on the tray.

"Please," he responded, and gestured to them. "I don't like chocolate, anyway. Never have, really."

I looked at him, my eyebrows coming together. "Then why serve them?" I reached, and used one of the napkins to pick up a pastry.

"I noticed you favored them, when dessert is served after supper."

I blinked, the chocolate halting just inches from my mouth. I lowered it, holding it in my palm, and asked, "Why?"

He looked away, his tan cheeks coloring, but brought his eyes back up to mine before speaking. It all came out in a rush, like he wouldn't say it at all if he didn't say it fast. "I know you don't like me. Honestly, I don't blame you. But I find you to be kind, and strong, and, well, everything I'd like to have in a friend. Which I know you aren't–my friend, I mean. But I'd still like to treat you as one, even if you can never return it."

I was torn. Half of me wanted to rage at him, as usual, while the other half was so bewildered, I could barely think of anything to say in response. I was sure those emotions were flitting across my face, and he watched it all, waiting for a response.

"Why?" was all that came out, again.

His brow creased. "Why, what?"

"Why do you think I don't like you?"

He paused. "If you're asking why I would believe that, it's

because it's obvious. If you're asking what reasons I think you have for disliking me, well, I believe we all know what I used to do for the king." Was that...*shame* on his face?

I laughed once, without humor, and set the pastry on the table on top of my napkin. "Used to? You mean up until the very recent point of you being sent here to act as his spy instead?" I clamped my lips shut as soon as the words were out. Shit, shit, *shit*. He was *not* supposed to know that we knew about the reason for his being here.

There was no reaction, though, except for the indents between his brows becoming a bit deeper. "Used to, as in decades ago, if you're speaking of my active participation. Though, I cannot say I'm innocent of any harm that has befallen the citizens of Eshelle since then. My inaction has still caused loss of life." Though that shame was even more pronounced in his gaze now, he did not move it from mine.

I was suddenly just a foot from him, staring up into his hazel eyes as they widened slightly in surprise at my abrupt proximity. "Do not play with me, or my knowledge. I *know* that you execute innocents."

He managed to look confused, and even a little hurt. "How?"

"You know," I said, a cruel, acidic smile spreading over my lips, "when you first got here, I thought I might have killed you when you acted as though you didn't know my name outside of the existence of my House. But I told myself that I couldn't be surprised. You are the king's executioner. How would you remember one of the dozens, maybe hundreds, of names you'd crossed off his list for him recently?"

I listened with vicious delight as his heart pounded. "My Lady–"

"Gabriel Vey. Ring a bell?" When his expression only grew more confused, I went on. "I didn't think so. You see, he went to Oschverre about half a year ago. He had a notion that he would speak with the king himself, and make him understand that things in Eshelle could not continue as they were." He'd been adamant, had *insisted* that he would talk with the king, and nobody else; that he would either get through to him, or not, but either way the peoples' voices would be heard.

My grin turned so bitter I could almost taste it. "I told him not to go; Hielo told him it was unwise. But he went. And he did not return. You know what did?" I stepped even closer, so near to him now that I felt his breaths glide across my brow. "His bones. Charred, with a note nailed through his skull. It read *'The fate of those who contest their High King.'*"

He was silent, but his heart still pounded. "Nothing to say?" I asked, my brow furrowing in mock confoundment.

His gold-green eyes bored into mine. "My Lady. I would swear to you on my life, but as it is not something that I seriously value, it would not suffice. I do not believe in the gods. I have no family living that I cherish. But I swear to you on any shred of honor or dignity that I have left, that I was not the one who did that to your father, or to your family."

I took a step back then, and stared at him. There was such earnestness in his eyes–compounded with significant distress. But, even as part of me worked to disbelieve him, a larger, more logical part of my brain began to turn. A part that had rusted and halted after my father's murder, the gear set only to determination, and anger. I began to think on what my Hiela likely already suspected; why she had convinced her mate to allow the king's emissary to come uncontested, and remain unchained. In the time that I'd known her, her knowledge and instincts had never once faltered or failed us.

And, after hearing his conversation with Jolie, I thought that there could only be a malicious reason behind hiding the existence of another servant to the king. I didn't care if he knew I'd been eavesdropping as I asked, "Olin?"

He nodded once. And my body was not ready for the shift that confirmation caused. I must have swayed, because the lord's arms shot out and formed a barrier around me, though they didn't actually touch me. Still without contact, he somehow got me to the couch, and sat as far as he could away from me once we were there. "My Lady?"

"I'm alright. I'm..." I trailed off. I was not alright. I had been so angry, for so long, holding onto it as though it was the air I needed to breathe. What I hadn't realized was that the rope linking myself and my rage was tied not just to me, but to the male in front of me. Its severance had me floating in the unknown, and I was desperate now for something else to hold onto. And I did not want that something to be Olin Evestre.

Having lost my anger to incredulity so quickly, I now had nothing to keep the tears of sorrow, of pain, from flowing. Hot, fast, and mortifying, they ran down my cheeks. Without a word, the lord grabbed a napkin from the table, and handed it to me. I dabbed under my eyes with it, trying to compose myself. I had cried after I lost my father, so this was not the unleashing of seven months' worth of grief. These tears were only for that strange feeling of being adrift.

I managed to quell them, with a promise to myself that if I needed to continue later, I would.

"Can I ask you a question?" he said quietly, when my tears had slowed to a stop. As the final droplets rolled down my cheeks, I nodded. "Do you look like your father?"

My heart ached as I pictured his face. "Very much so." Both my sister and I took after him. Our brother was the only one who even looked a bit like our mother. But the lord nodded, as if I'd answered another question for him. "Why do you ask?"

He paused again. "I have not been a royal executioner for a

long time. For the past few decades, I have been the receiver of supplicants. There is a long history within that position, but within it all, I remember the face of every one of them that came to me. I won't lie and say that I remember what they came to me for, or their names. But, I suspect that your father somehow got what he wanted–a conversation with the king himself. Because I have never met anyone like you."

My eyes flashed to his at the double meaning I thought I heard in those words. But he went on, "I never met your father. I am glad of it, only because I know that I played no part in the pain that was brought to your family. But, that is not the case for many families in Eshelle. Regardless of whether I struck the killing blow or not, I share the guilt of their deaths; of the agony with which their families now live.

"So, please, continue to hate me if you'd like. I deserve it. I'm sorry that you now have no way to exact the revenge that you and your family would justly seek. And if you would like to never see my face again...I will go back to Oschverre. I would not continue to force you, nor anyone else, to be in my presence if they don't wish to be. My failure to serve the king would not be something that disgraces me–only the ways that I've already done so can do that."

I heard him. And, more importantly, I believed him. And as I did both of those things, I noted bits and pieces of his heart and mind that he gave me. Had *been* giving me: *the* king, he always said. Not *my* king.

Perhaps he was nothing more than a male who had seen no way out of his position. Not an excuse for what he'd done for the king by any means, but...perhaps he was changing; changed. Because our court–our people, our friends, our Hielo and Hiela–had shown him a different life.

And he liked it better.

I thought now that he might have always been this transformed male, might not have even had to *be* transformed in the first place, if he'd never been a part of that poisonous court.

A product of his habitat. I could understand that. Even as I felt sickened by what he'd done in his past, I could understand it.

I wiped my eyes one last time, and swept the napkin quickly below my nose with a sniffle. Then I straightened, pulling my shoulders back, and said to him, "You should stay. We have much to discuss." His own broad shoulders adjusted at that, while an eleven formed between his brows once more.

And I just...didn't want to. I was utterly drained from all of the emotions that had coursed through me in a matter of minutes, and from all of the knowledge that I'd gleaned, and would have to sort through. And I didn't want to. I didn't want to argue, or debate, or ask questions. Our Hielo and Hiela would hear all that we'd learned soon enough–if they hadn't already. And it would be discussed later. Not now.

So, rain tapping against the ceiling and cascading beautifully down the many windows, I grabbed my pastry and my book, leaned back against the couch cushions, and said, "But first, I was promised cocoa."

⇹

Dion

I SAT WITH MY GUARD ON THE PLUSH VELVET COUCH, AND TRIED to ignore her proximity. From where I lounged against the pillow, trying to focus on reading one of Jolie's recommendations, she was just a couple of feet away. Her legs were folded under her, her knees pointing towards me, and she seemed completely absorbed in her book.

I had learned so much in such a short time. That Olin's existence was not known, that he had murdered her *father*. I didn't know how she'd been able to stand being with me all day, every day, when she'd thought I'd done such a thing to her; to her family. It just further proved what I already knew: that she was a far better person than I. All of the things I'd said–about her kindness, her strength. I was glad she knew I thought those things of her. Even if she didn't care what my opinion of her was–and I had no misgivings that she did–I was still glad of it.

I was also relieved to have shared with her the details of my work for the king. Though I wished that none of it were true, I didn't want her to have any misgivings about who I'd been, and what I'd done. Maybe someday we would be close enough for me to share how the decades had drained me, and had made me unwilling to think of a different sort of life. Maybe she would be willing to hear that I hadn't realized that I'd needed a way out until Sabrian had given me a map. One that directed me to friends, and to *life*. To Nuria, and Jolie, and...her.

I tried not to be conspicuous as I glanced at her from the corner of my eye. Nuria and Jolie had returned a few moments after our conversation had ended, both of them looking flushed, and smelling of lust. They'd simply picked up their books, a pastry and a cup of cocoa each, and sat down in the armchairs across from us.

Ciaragen's eyes were darting over the pages splayed in her lap, and a small smile was pulling up the corners of her full lips as she read. For the first time in my presence, she looked... happy. My heart stuttered when she looked up, and I quickly brought my eyes back to my book. But she was only reaching for another pastry. She took a bite, and–

A huge glob of melted chocolate fell, and landed on the open pages of her book. She gasped, Nuria and Jolie looking up at the sound. As my own gaze moved back to hers, I watched her brows come together to form that line between them, her mouth slightly open in disbelief that was giving way to devastation. I snapped my fingers.

She stared at the now pristine book for a moment, and then her eyes moved to mine. And while the smile she gave me was small, and polite, my heart thumped an uneven beat at the sight of it.

Well, fuck.

19

A CHANGING HEART

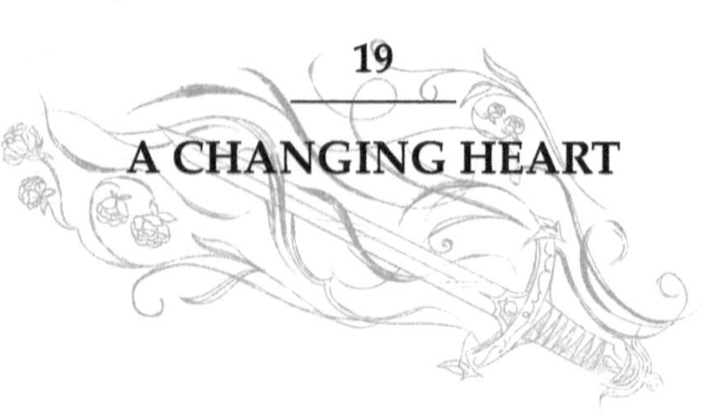

CIARAGEN - 21 YEARS EARLIER

YESTERDAY, SOMETHING SETTLED WITHIN ME.

I still felt the rage and the disorientation that had been constant companions since the moment I was told my father had been killed. But, rather than ruling me to the point that I got angry over even the smallest slights, they now felt... manageable.

I hadn't had a day off since that moment, either. I had refused, with the single exception being the day of my father's funeral. I needed the work to keep my mind occupied. I never let myself consider what might happen if I allowed myself to sit still. Then, when the lord had arrived, I had been able to occupy myself even further with my hatred of him, and my duty to my country, and to my High Lord and High Lady.

For nineteen days, I had put considerable effort into hating him. Only that sense of duty had kept me from avenging my father. Then to find out, as I stood inches from him in the library, that my vengeance would have been misplaced.

When that veil of hatred was removed, all that remained was a cobweb of dislike; a filament so thin that it could be broken by a breath. I realized that the male who only accepted invitations to activities when he thought I'd be interested in them, who confronted my rudeness with silence or politeness, who consistently challenged the picture I had of him in my head–perhaps wasn't as evil as he used to be. He had done atrocious, hideous things decades ago–things that could not be forgotten, maybe not ever forgiven. But over half a century spanned between that male, and the one who read beside me yesterday.

I wasn't sure if I could like him. I knew that Nuria and Jolie did, but I also knew that they had known and noticed these things about him days, maybe weeks, before I did. And I believed they thought of his crimes as too far in the past to consider when interacting with him now.

Maybe they were right; many learned over their years of life, having been worse in their youth than they were when they grew. Maybe I should forgive, even if I couldn't forget. But there were a couple of things wrong with that. The first being that they weren't my crimes to forgive–I'd thought that one of them was, but knew now that was false. And second, that I did not know him well enough to decide that he was in fact a different male than the killer he had once been.

I recognized that the reason I didn't feel that I knew him, even after nineteen days of being with him through nearly all of his waking hours, was that I had ignored him. As he walked through the gardens with Nuria and Jolie; as he dined with my Hielo and Hiela; as he followed me through the halls. I'd done my best to disregard anything about him, believing that if I paid too much attention, I would end up snapping, and ruining the plans my Hielo and Hiela had for him.

I was angered further by the fact that their plans did not end with a rope or a blade. That there was no intention of forcing him, body or mind, to commit to our cause rather than his king's. But rather, to simply show him what life was like here, where the rulers were just, and kind, and loyal to their people.

When our High Lord and High Lady had conspired to provide enough of a threat to the king that he would be forced to send an emissary to 'smooth things over', we hadn't been sure who they would send. When we'd received word that it was to be Lord Dion Evestre, a male infamous for his loyalty to the king and his cause, we knew two things. That our work may be cut out for us; and that if that work proved fruitful, it might have the power to turn all of Eshelle. After all, if someone so close with the king chose another party to support over him, why should the people who had experienced poverty, sickness, and starvation during his reign choose any different?

Nineteen days in, and even I'd seen him become less somber, and more social. Of course, whenever I'd noticed it, I had convinced myself that he was faking. Pretending to be changed so that our High Lord and High Lady would trust him with their secrets. Nuria and Jolie had reminded me a few days in that he couldn't pretend successfully here. That we would know. Still, I'd convinced myself that he was evil, and nothing was changing my mind on it.

Until yesterday. When I learned that he hadn't taken my father from me. And when that knowledge had settled, my mind finally opened to seeing the things I had so carefully ignored for nearly three weeks.

The way he sometimes smiled softly when Nuria and Jolie were caught in their many moments of romance. That he consistently used only respectful terms when addressing anybody, even those pointedly rude towards him. And it made me remember some things, too. The way he'd looked when I'd accosted him that first time. How, when I proved with action and silence that his talking to me upset me, he had stopped. I knew it wasn't because he wasn't conversational–he talked plenty with Nuria and Jolie, even Bayani. It was because he didn't want me to have to do something with him, even as simple as talking, if I didn't want to.

None of these things erased his past actions. They did, however, support the notion that he was not that male any longer.

Right now, Arthur was guarding at his door, while I was finishing getting ready for court this evening. The first since the lord's arrival, and, to be honest, I was a little excited for it. I expected to see some friends there, and was looking forward to the opportunity to mingle, and drink, and dance, without all that rage weighing me down.

Before I left my chamber to fetch him and escort him to the Great Hall, I checked the mirror one last time. I smoothed my hands over the vibrant blue pleats of my gown, the silk fabric smooth beneath my palms. I had my hair pulled up and away from my face, the curls piled on top of my head. On my face, I wore only a bit of blush which matched the stain on my lips. Gold earrings trailed from my lobes up to the points of my ears. The deep neckline of my dress displayed the golden lines of the tattoo on my chest that so rarely got to be seen outside of my bedroom. The petals of freesia and peonies swooped around my slight breasts, and below my sternum.

Satisfied with what I saw, I turned from the mirror, and left my chamber, striding quickly down the halls leading to the lord's room. When I saw Arthur down the final hall, he heard me coming, of course. His ginger head turned, and he said, "You look nice."

Not a glowing compliment, but I still replied, "Thanks, Arthur." I reached his side. "I'll take it from here. Wouldn't want you to be late."

"What a travesty that would be," he said sarcastically, but bowed his head, and walked away all the same.

I sighed, and leaned against the wall beside the lord's door. I raised my arm and lightly knocked three times.

"Yes?" he called from inside, sounding agitated.

My brow furrowed at his tone, but I asked, "Are you ready?"

"Nearly," he responded, then I heard a grunt, and a muttered, "Damned ridiculous piece of..."

I bursted into his chambers. "I'm sorry, what did you call–?" I began, before I saw him and realized that he wasn't talking about me at all. His hair, grown out a bit since he'd arrived, was mussed. A contorted knot of fabric circled his collar.

A short chuckle scratched my throat, but I caught it before it passed my lips. "Having trouble?" I asked.

"What in all of your gods' names is this *thing* I was asked to wear to court tonight?" he asked, throwing his hands up in a gesture to his neck, and slapping them against his thighs as they came back down.

Not ignorant to the way he'd worded that, I still had to hold back another chuckle. I'd never seen him this ruffled. "It's called a tie."

"Why name it something so simplistic when if I *tie* it, it looks like *this*?" His brows raised, leaning forward slightly as though eagerly awaiting an explanation.

At that, a laugh did escape me–it was just so ridiculous. This male–a century old, more or less–did not know what a tie was, or what to do with one. Adding that to his frankly reasonable question, stated with such an unusual abandon for decorum, and I wasn't able to help myself.

His eyes widened, just a bit, as he looked at me. As if suddenly realizing how frenzied he'd been, he straightened. With a smirk, he rubbed the back of his head with a hand, but lowered it before saying, "I should have remarked the moment you came in. I hope you don't mind me saying you look...very beautiful." His cheeks flushed, and though it seemed like he wanted to avert his eyes, his gaze held on mine.

I felt my own cheeks heat, and looked down at my dress, flattening my palms over it. "Well...thank you." That was the proper way to respond, even if it felt odd to say those words to him. I cleared my throat, and lifted my eyes back to his. "Do you need assistance?" I asked, and gestured to the tangled knot around his neck.

"Oh." He looked surprised, but managed to clear that emotion from his face quickly. "Um, yes, if you wouldn't mind."

I took a deep breath, and began to close the ten-pace distance between us, cursing myself for not just telling him he could wear his usual cravat. While I'd gotten reasonably comfortable being in proximity to him during our time reading beside each other on the couch yesterday, I was going to have to actually *touch* him to be of any help here.

But I was already standing before him, and my hands reached up to the knot he'd made. With my Fae ears, I heard it as he held his breath, and his heart began to beat more quickly. "You don't have to be nervous, you know," I said, putting a smirk on my lips to try to ease his tension; show him that I wasn't angry. "I won't bite."

He chuckled, but it sounded breathless. When I finally sorted out the knot he'd created, the rest was quick work, even if I couldn't help but notice some things. Like how, when I made the loops, my knuckles brushed against his chest. Or how, when I tucked it into his collar, my fingers ran over his throat, and I felt his racing pulse against my skin.

Finally, seeing the gleam of gold he'd arranged on his lapel, I took the tie clip, and affixed it to hold the ends together, the backs of my knuckles brushing against his abdomen. I'd seen that it was well-muscled that time I'd accidentally walked in on him changing. Now, as my fingers skimmed his stomach, I found that it felt nice; hard with muscle, but with a slight softness that was pleasing.

Why was I thinking about his body?

I quickly stepped back, putting a couple of feet between us. "There you are," I said, with a close-lipped smile.

He cleared his throat. "Yes. Thank you very much." His eyes focused on something behind me, and his brows shot up. "Correct me if I'm wrong, but I believe we're running late." I turned to follow his line of vision, and found the grandfather clock against the wall of the study chamber on the opposite side of the bedroom.

When I saw the time, I gasped. "Damn! Yes, let's get a move on." I turned, the skirt of my dress brushing against his shins as it fanned around me. I didn't wait to see if he followed, but I heard him do so.

We walked quickly down the halls, my heels clicking softly against the tile in my hurried steps. The sound of many voices emanating from the Great Hall could be heard from even hallways away. Still, he did not speak, and I knew my realization remained true. That he was only silent so that I would not have to speak to him, not because he wanted to be. Even with our short talk in his chambers, it seemed that he was still following the rules of our relationship as they'd been set these past weeks. It would be up to me if I wanted that to change.

I saw my opening when I heard his heart pick up in pace. I turned my head to him, and took a shot in the dark. "Why are you nervous?" I asked. He'd had to have been to many court gatherings before, working so closely with Oleander.

"For one, because the king doesn't particularly care for court," he answered, immediately refuting my thought. "He hosts as frequently as expected, which is about five times a year. Now, you may do the math and say, *well, Lord Dion, that would be nearly four hundred times, you old prick*, and I would have to admit to that."

He glanced at me, and I realized that I had smiled a bit at his imitation of me. But he went on, "So comes my second, final, and most important reason." He took a deep breath. "Regardless of how many courtly affairs I've attended, I've never once been to one in which I both cared what the people there thought of me, and wanted them to think better things of me than what they did know already."

We had stopped walking. I now stood facing him, and he looked at me, his hands clasped behind his back. I tilted my head as I examined him, boldly; from head to toe, and back up again. To his credit, he didn't so much as shift on his feet under my gaze.

When my eyes were once more on his, I said, "They will think whatever they will when you walk through the doors. It's up to you to make them think better of you before the night is done. And since you were honest with me, I will be honest with you." I took one step closer to him. "Three weeks ago, I thought you to be descended from Deimos, the god of Death himself. Come to destroy my home, and its people. It is well-known that your powers can bring both pain and destruction. How much of that is you, and how much your brother, you may tell me when and if you would like to. But, we both know, and so do they, that you have brought death upon Eshellens."

As he began to look ashamed, I went on, "But that is not how you seem to me any longer. Or to Nuria, and Jolie. Bayani.

Anyone who has taken the time to get to know you as you are now–and doesn't have a vendetta against you–" I added with a smirk. His lips barely twitched up at one corner. "Knows that you may have done those things, but that you are changed. And while it doesn't erase those deeds, you have shown that you are a person with kindness, compassion, and strength."

He blinked, his lips slightly parted. I expected myself to feel embarrassed by my words, but all that came was a sense of rightness. While I'd only opened myself to seeing them just yesterday, I remembered that these truths had been exemplified even as I'd constantly disrespected him. And, a male who would not react to that...perhaps it was because he thought those things about himself as well.

And maybe that helped. Maybe it made it just a bit easier to be anything better than indifferent towards him; made it possible to be...friends. He saw the faults in himself, and did not pretend they weren't there, or blame them on another–but rather, loathed those things, and actively worked to be better than he once was.

I was not foolish enough to believe I was without faults. Yet, while they weren't so grievous as his, I never tried to change them. And while I didn't want to wholly lose those parts of me, I thought that I could be better than I was now. I knew I had lost some of my good after my father was taken from me. And since then, I'd pretended that my much increased stubbornness, snark, and anger made me stronger. Less likely to be so taken off guard, so *hurt* ever again.

Really, all it did was throw a blanket over a mess, pretending that it didn't exist. The mess was still there, and I only needed to pull back the covers to reveal it, to begin to sort through it.

And I could start tonight. I could start with him.

I continued, "And while you have about three hours, not

nineteen days, to make these people see you as the male you are now, and not the one you once were, I believe that who you've become since arriving in Sabrian–perhaps even before then–is someone worth getting to know."

A *lot* of honesty. Standing in silence for a moment, our gazes unbreaking, I watched many thoughts and emotions flit through his eyes, none sticking long enough for me to identify. And then humor came–and held. With a smirk, he asked, "And, if any of them should attack me because the male I am now makes fun of their ties?"

It couldn't be helped; that coaxed a true smile from me. "Well, then, it's a good thing you have me as your guard."

⸙

An hour later, Lord Dion had met and spoken with every person in attendance at court. Luckily, most had heeded our High Lord and High Lady's request to treat him with decency. Only a few were unable to hide their sneers, or say more than two words to him. To his credit, Lord Dion treated them with the same level of politeness they were expected to have offered him, if not more. He consistently bowed his head in greeting, and spoke to them all with respect, even if they did not return the favor.

I didn't know how he did it. As I watched them treat him as I had for days, *weeks*, I saw how ugly it was. Though they didn't know him further than the deeds of his past, as I had come to, I couldn't watch as he weathered their discourtesy with such grace. I couldn't change how I'd treated him–I could only work to be better now than I had been before– but I could impact how they were behaving. So, as they sneered, I glared. And most of them started behaving at least a little bit better after that.

Our Hielo and Hiela were at the foot of the dais, talking with Lord Nathan, and his mate, Lord Sebastian. Their adoptive son ran with chunky little legs across the tiled floors, a huge smile on his chubby, dark brown face. As he neared one of the tall candelabras near the edge of the hall, one of his fathers scooped the boy up, doing so with a flourish that set him giggling like mad. "Down, back down!" he squealed, struggling with that ridiculous toddler strength.

"If I let you down, will you nearly set yourself on fire again?" Nathan asked, as our High Lord and High Lady looked on with smiles.

"Down, back down, Dada! Down, back down!" he repeated instead of answering his father's question. Nate just sighed, and then held the boy upside down by his ankles, which made him laugh so hard that no sound came out, only breaths like hiccups of happiness.

"*Ohh*, down? I thought you said *upside* down!" Nate exclaimed, Sebastian laughing nearly as hard as his son. He wasn't the only one; over half the room was fixated on the boy, smiles lighting their faces.

"I have an idea, Nate," Bash said through his chuckles.

"What's that?" Nate asked.

"Why don't we sic him on his godmother?" Bash lifted mischief- filled eyes to me.

Nate followed his gaze, and grinned. "I think that's a great idea." He turned the still-giggling child over, and set him on his feet, holding on for a moment until he found his balance. "Go to Aunt Ari, Atlas!" he exclaimed, pointing to me so that his son could follow his finger to find me amidst the many kneecaps in his eyeline.

Atlas spotted me, and then his little legs were moving as fast as they could to where I was. An enormous smile spread across my face as my godson approached, small feet stomping against the tile with none of the Fae grace he would have when he grew up. I crouched down as he neared, and when he was a foot away, he jumped into my waiting hands. They clasped just below his armpits, and I stood, swinging him up to my hip in one smooth motion. I gave him several tiny kisses all across his little face, making him giggle, as his fathers and everyone else in the room resumed their respective conversations.

"Godmother, huh?" Lord Dion asked from beside me.

"Yes," I replied. "I've been very close with Bash since we were nearly as young as this one here." When he'd asked me over two years ago, that was the first and only time I'd ever cried tears of joy.

"I imagine he couldn't have picked a better person," Lord Dion responded. I looked at him, slightly flushed, and found that he was smiling gently. Half to avoid the look that stirred something unfamiliar in my chest, I turned my gaze to Bash. A benefit of knowing each other since we were Atlas's age was that we had an uncanny knack for sensing the other. His eyes were on mine not a second after mine landed on him. They darted to the male beside me, then back, and he gave me the subtlest of nods. I turned back to Lord Dion, and asked, "Would you like to hold him?"

His brows raised, and he blinked, his hazel eyes going to Atlas, and then back to me. "Hold him?"

"Those are two of the words I used, yes." I rolled my eyes. "Come on, he won't bite, either—or, if he does, his teeth are cute and little."

A strange sort of sadness flashed through his eyes, replaced almost instantly with humor at my statement. When he looked back at Atlas, he nodded. "Yes, alright." He fumbled with his wine glass for a moment before I took it from him, tilting my right side toward him so he could more easily grab Atlas. He reached, only a bit hesitantly, and closed his hands around

Atlas's torso, his knuckles brushing my arm and my ribs as he did so. He hardly seemed to notice as he pulled Atlas onto his own hip, seeming unsure of where to rest him.

"Like this," I said, and took hold of his arms and hands, arranging them to cradle the toddler more comfortably. Once finished, I leaned back, and Lord Dion turned his face to Atlas.

"Hello there," he said softly, swaying slightly from side to side. Atlas met his gaze, and stared at him with more intensity than I'd ever seen on his little face. Then he rested his head against Lord Dion's shoulder, stuck his thumb in his mouth, and promptly closed his eyes.

"Am I that boring?" Lord Dion half-spoke, half-whispered. Meanwhile, I couldn't believe what I was seeing.

"How did you do that?" I asked, stepping closer to them, and reaching to softly brush Atlas's brow. His eyelids barely even fluttered at the touch. Out like a lantern.

"You saw me in the library; I'm guessing I could have put you to sleep too, if you hadn't been so wrapped up in your book."

I scoffed, and swatted his arm–the one that wasn't holding Atlas–lightly. And I didn't quite register that my hand remained on his arm as I pressed a kiss to Atlas's cheek.

20

CHOICE & ITS CONSEQUENCES

THE SHOCK LASTS A LONG SECOND. AN INFINITE SPAN OF ONE TICK of the clock during which I stare at the face of the man whose lips had been on mine just last night. And as I watch, the teeth behind those grinning lips morph; the canines sharpen and elongate slightly. His ears arch, forming points at the tops. And as the majick fully fades, the same face that I had thought so handsome the first time we met, becomes even more so as the beauty of immortality settles over his features.

"Fae," I gasp quietly, not having meant to say it out loud.

The guards react quickly, their training overruling any fear or surprise they may be feeling. In half a breath, a dozen surround the dais–but my brother isn't having any of that.

Ben doesn't spare a second glance to the scene unfolding before he dashes through a gap in their ranks. He picks up Lorraine from where she sits just feet from the steps, her eyes wide with horror, and runs her out the door. A human with no magic of her own to protect herself or their child, I can only be grateful that his quick thinking just saved himself and one of my best friends.

Many move to follow them, but Dion clicks his tongue, and suddenly all doors slam shut. Forever-burn candles on the tables and chandeliers are extinguished, the little light remaining coming from the dusky sky above the window in the painted ceiling.

And I realize, in the instant that screams rent the air rather than magic, how weak we are in comparison to the power before us. A room full of humans, more than half without magic, and the rest with gifts such as mine. Healing, summoning, tracking–none so strong as the killing power this Fae male likely possesses.

Yet I watch, in that same instant, Izabel usher her three children and Cleo under a table, and stand in front of them with fire in her eyes. A small gift of water in her blood, which she hadn't been able to hone into something stronger as a woman, and still she stands prepared to fight this enemy.

I am so far from all of them, and so close to that enemy. Only seconds have passed since Dalton fell through the door. Dalton, who is still lying on the floor, unmoving, a dangerously large pool of blood growing beneath his head.

My eyes on my would-be betrothed, I barely catch the blur of motion that is Dion as he moves to me. Broad, violent hands spin me so that I face the room, my back pressed against his front. One hand wraps around my neck, and the other arm goes around my waist, locking my arms to my sides.

"Now, now," Dion says as the guards caught up to the whirl of motion that had just occurred. The sound of his voice, loud enough for everybody in the Hall to hear, combined with the hold he has on me stops them dead in their tracks. "We wouldn't want our princess's pretty neck to accidentally snap in the fight, now would we?"

There's a whimper that I know comes from my mom, though I can't turn my head to look. Their guards must be holding her and my dad where they are, keeping them from moving to me. Even though she is out of my eyeline, I can feel my mom's desperate gaze on me.

My own eyes fall on Hanna, her strawberry blonde head peeking out from behind Gregor's shoulder, terror in her silver eyes. Her fear, from someone usually so bright, settles insidiously in my gut–not for myself, but for her, for her unborn child.

"That's what I thought," Dion continues, as not one person in the Hall moves, only soft cries and heavy pants to be heard. He begins to walk us backward towards the door from whence he came.

And it's not fear of being taken from this Hall, but the way he slides his nose down my neck, inhaling, and the predatory intent I feel in the gesture that snaps the leash on my control. Before I can stop myself, before I can grab hold of the leash once more, and put into practice all that Amahd has taught me, a single word slips through my lips, my voice high and scared: "Momma."

And she erupts. "Stop! *STOP!*" my mom screams, her voice like nothing I've ever heard come out of her before. Rage, terror, and something feral combine and then shift. I hear the sounds of several men struggling to hold her, and I know what's happening. She's transforming; using her gift so often used for simple tricks like adding makeup to a bare face, or changing a dress. Using it to become something stronger than herself–stronger than a human. I hear my father shouting her name, but her screams are replaced with roars, and he cannot reach her where she has gone. The place where a mother goes when her child is in danger.

"You'll want to stop her now, beautiful, or I will," Dion whispers in my ear, and turns me to see her at last.

She is fur, and claws, and fangs. I watch as she throws the last two guards from her, and lowers herself to all fours. She charges, her paws thudding so heavily that the glassware throughout the Hall shakes. I open my mouth to tell her to stop, but then Dion makes the mistake of removing the arm from my waist, freeing my hands. He is too tall for me to bash his nose in with the back of my head, but he's made the same mistake as the Fae who held me two days ago. A dagger within easy reach, and underestimating me.

I stomp on his instep in the same moment that I unsheathe the dagger at his hip. As I drive the blade into his thigh, and pull it out, I hear a great, resounding *CRACK* that echoes through the Hall, and through my very soul.

I don't hear her thumping paws, or roars. And as Dion falls, releasing me, blood streaming from the wound in his leg, I look up to find my mom.

Her fur, and claws, and fangs are gone. Human once more, her bare body lies on the marble floor, her neck at a *wrong* angle. My father falls to his knees over her, his cape covering her as he pulls her into his lap with violently shaking hands.

I see my sister faint and hit her head on the steps of the dais. I watch Nik, who must have started running to Izabel as our mother distracted the Fae, stand utterly still halfway between the two of them, his eyes on his mom. But I hear nothing except a ringing in my ears as my feet slowly carry me to my parents of their own volition. As if my body knows that, no matter how quickly I get there, there will be nothing I can heal, even if my mind has not let that sink in.

When I reach them, I lower to my knees, not feeling the

impact when they hit the floor. My mother's body shakes–no, that's my father, his sobs wracking through him. I stare down at her face. The brunette-and-white hair that my fingers brush off her brow of their own accord. The summer sky blue eyes that had looked at me like I was her sunshine. They don't hold anything now. They gaze, unseeing, towards the sky visible through the domed glass ceiling, no stars there yet to keep her company. I watch my palm run over her lids, feel her lashes brush it as I close those eyes so that she may sleep. The backs of my knuckles skim her still-warm cheek in a caress, as she did to me so many times.

The ringing in my ears begins to subside, but I wish it wouldn't. I can hear my father wailing, sobbing her name. I can hear Zak shouting Iris's, begging her to wake from her place on the steps. He's saying mine, too, I think, but I can't be sure. Everything outside of this circle of my father, my mother, and myself feels fuzzy. Other. They are not here, and we are not there.

Then there's a hand on my shoulder. I don't move my eyes from my mom to see who it is.

"We need to leave now, Althea," Ciaragen's voice says. I don't remember how to move, even if I wanted to. So I ignore him. "Princess, we must go–"

A terrible, psychotic laugh bellows from behind me, the sound so contrary to the scene before me that it jolts me out of my mindless state. I turn from my mom, and find Dion to be the source of the noise; his stomach shakes with it as he sits up, the wound in his thigh visibly healing through the hole in his trousers carved by the dagger on the floor beside me.

As he stands, so does Ciaragen, shielding me with his body.

Dion sobers slightly, though a wide smile remains on his face. He looks down at where I am, crouched behind Ciaragen's legs. "I did warn you to stop her." Then he tilts his head, and gives Ciaragen an assessing look. "I've seen you around here. Apologies, I didn't take the time to learn anyone's names–but the one," he admits, his eyes darting to me. Then he winks–*winks* at me before moving them back to the general.

"You don't know me, but I know you," Ciaragen replies. And then *shadows* erupt from him, lashing out at Dion like whips of darkness, sharp enough to remove a head. Though they are faster than I can even blink, they dissipate into nothing just as quickly.

Dion laughs again. "Ahh, I think I know you now," he says. "It's been a while, Lady Vey."

Though my mind is still in shambles, something in it recognizes the strangeness of what he's said. My brow furrows, and my body rises without me telling it to do so as I stare between the male and the man.

"Not long enough, Lord Olin," he replies, and sends another wave of shadows at him, this time in the shape of a dozen daggers. Once again, though, they vanish just before they can reach the male.

Another figure, with a familiar scent of thyme and salt, moves close to me. While Ciaragen remains guarding in front, Atlas stands beside me, his arm close enough that it nearly brushes mine. I want to ask him just what he thinks he's doing–a server facing a Fae–but speaking feels too hard while my mind darts between the different kinds of violence in front of and behind me. Ciaragen tenses as well, but his focus remains on his foe.

"You I don't know," Dion–or did Ciaragen use a different name?—directs at Atlas. "Care to make introductions, Lady Vey?"

"Not really," Ciaragen responds, and an arc of shadows rounds quickly for the male's neck before once again disappearing. What begins to register with me is that the male isn't making any countermoves. He seems to be entirely unbothered by the deadly shadows being thrown at him, more intent on carrying his conversation.

"Well, fret not, this little imbalance will be evened out. I have backup, too." He curls two fingers towards himself invitingly, and my head spins as two men move from opposite corners of the room to stand behind the male. One, I do not recognize. But another is Artur–the doorman who has never looked me in the eyes before. He does so at last in this moment where he stands beside the enemy who just destroyed the family he once pledged service to.

"Recognize one of them, Princess?" Dion asks. I feel the eyes of the dozens of courtiers in the room land on me. Some terrified, and hidden under tables; others standing near them in protective stances. "Sorry to break it to you, Cardenias, but I've had a spy among you for some time now." He looks between me, Nik, and my father as he gestures to Artur at his side.

And in an instant, the blond hair that I've known for a year shortens, and turns brown. The pale skin darkens to a deep tan, and chocolate eyes turn citrine. He grows over a foot in height, and wide with muscle. Then, I recognize him for a whole new reason: he was one of the males I'd killed two days ago.

Or thought I had.

"Though, seeing your current company, I can understand now how that slipped your notice." His eyes level on Ciaragen, who had gone rigid as the new male's true face was revealed. "Why don't you shed that false skin for our princess, Lady Vey?"

I almost step back from the general that stands between Dion and me. But *she* is directly behind me, still cradled in my father's arms. My body settles for swaying where I stand, and Atlas quickly places a steadying arm on my back. He drops it as soon as I right myself, and I feel its loss as my mind and heart race and Dion's words start to sink in. Artur has been a spy, a Fae implanted into our home–that much is clear, or becoming so. I have more difficulty grasping the other part as I stare at Ciaragen's back.

"Yes, *quite* the scandal–not one, not three, but *five* Fae right under the noses of the royal Mages," Dion continues. "I'd thought it was only *my* talent that kept them from seeing the glamour I had on myself so that none but our lovely princess– and my companions here–could see my true face. Pity. I do enjoy being better than others, but I suppose I have to concede that it was their ignorance more than anything else that kept them from seeing any of the *five*–" he stares past me, at my father and brother, his brows raised in incredulity, "–of us as we truly are."

Without warning, another wave of shadows lashes out, followed immediately by a second and third, but all dissipate in half a heartbeat.

Dion sighs. "Do stop interrupting me, my Lady. I haven't even gotten to properly introduce all of you to my friends here. *Artur*, who you know as well, dear Lady Vey..." His grin is utterly wicked as he gestures to the male behind him, then shrugs with a chuckle. Then his hazel gaze moves past Ciaragen, to me once more.

"Artur, Arthur–whatever you know him as, it doesn't matter; I picked the names for simplicity's sake. He's been mine for *decades*. Blood oaths are fun like that. Anyway, we tried to take her a couple of days ago, to avoid this whole *thing*, but that didn't end up working out for us. Actually, she is *quite* skilled in combat. Our pretty little princess murdered two Fae males with nothing but a dagger." I feel all eyes in the room move to me again. What had been a frenzy to escape–yanking on doors, banging on windows–has turned into one of the most typical pastimes in court: gossip. Though I'm sure they still fear the male before me, they are also intrigued by his story. By the person so obviously protecting me, with his power of shadows that does not occur in Mages. Perhaps they think him strong enough to defeat Dion; maybe they just want to hear the rest of the story. If they survive long enough to share it.

"Not their fault." Dion shrugs. "How could they know she would escape her bindings? And I had ordered them not to harm her. Tut, tut. Blood oaths are fun, yes, but so *literal*. So, Marcys and David are dead. *Artur* got a few holes poked in him, but he's good as new now." He reaches back to pat the male on the chest, which he takes with a straight face, those golden eyes now holding Atlas's beside me. "He had to be, in order to arrive in time to open the doors for you all on that first night. Anyway..." He gestures for the male to come forward to stand at his side.

"This is Adathan." The male's broad face remains hard as Dion goes on, "You know, I had hoped all of...*this* might not be necessary," he says, gesturing to me–no, to my *mother*. "And we would have made introductions on the way to Eshelle. I suppose I'll save the last one for later, so we have something to talk about." He dares to turn his head from us to look at the males behind him.

Another wave of shadows whips out towards him, and I almost think it will strike true–but the third one steps forward. He holds up a hand, and the shadows turn to mist.

And Dion, who seconds ago spoke amicably with all of us, whirls on Ciaragen, and screams, "*ENOUGH!*" His skin pales as veins and capillaries in his temples and eyes turn black. He raises a hand once more, and flicks his wrist.

As power explodes through the Hall, Atlas curls me to him, and then throws me to the ground, his body a living shield above me. I can see through the space between his arm and the floor that anyone within thirty feet of us is blown back–including some brave souls who had started to make their way towards us by skirting the edges of the Hall. It blasts apart the windows, along with the great skylight above us.

And I can't stand the thought of Atlas being pierced by that glass, of another person dying for me tonight. He's strong, and probably has more than fifty pounds on me, but he doesn't expect me to fight his protection. So when I shove against his chest, I free my arm and the right side of my face before he can stop me, trying to roll us. Shards rain down, and people rush to get under tables, or copy Atlas, throwing themselves over loved ones. I only manage to get us onto our sides before the glass strikes.

I listen to cries of pain, and of death sound through the Hall, only able to see Atlas's chest now. A couple of smaller pieces catch me before he manages to tuck me against him once more, and I feel blood trickle down my face, and my bare shoulder. But I don't feel the pain.

And then, in a whirl of motion, I'm standing once more, Atlas shoving me behind him. But not before I see.

I see the bodies of strangers. Blood leaking from their throats, their heads, their hearts. Some managed to take cover, or were lucky enough to only catch smaller pieces of glass in non-vital areas. I see them weep from their pain.

I see the bodies of friends. Hanna lies just twenty feet from me, Gregor behind her. Her silver eyes stare unseeingly at me, her hand reaching for me even in death. Her husband, with his human reflexes, had not been fast enough to catch her when she ran for me.

I see a woman rise from the ground in front of us, her tightly curled black hair matted with blood on one side. And on that side, I see an arched ear peeking out. And I notice how the uniform that she wears is familiar–and is now much too big on her in her true form.

Ciaragen Vey. *Lady* Vey.

"There she is," Dion says, a huge smile spreading across his face. "Allow me to properly introduce you, Princess, to Ciaragen Vey, a general of the armed forces of Sabrian, Eshelle."

Ciaragen half-turns to face me where I stand behind Atlas, keeping her other eye on Dion. Her–*her* deep blue eyes are wary, but even with the blood that has stopped flowing on her head, matting her hair and covering the left side of her face and neck, she is profoundly stunning. Immortal beauty graces her chestnut skin, and lengthens her canines.

"I'm sorry, Althea," she says, and holds my gaze for only another breath. Then it flicks up to Atlas, and I think I see something flash in those eyes, but can't be sure what before she turns back to Dion.

He sighs exaggeratedly, groaning as he lets out the breath. "This was fun before, but I've made all the big reveals. I'm bored now. Either stand down and give me the princess, or I will kill the remaining souls in this room, and take her anyway."

Atlas speaks his first words since he approached me. "You're not taking her *anywhere*." I look up at him, my battered heart with barely anything left in it to race further as Atlas begins to change, too. Not even the sparks like lightning that dance between his fingers are enough to truly shock me. The only thing I have the strength to recognize is that the two Fae with their backs to me are trying to protect me from the three that face us. I don't–*can't* wonder why.

"Gods, I *still* don't know you," Dion says, fingering his chin as though this is all just an interesting puzzle for him. "I would have said that you seem young, but don't we all? Oh, speaking of young–surrender the princess now or I'll kill the four children under that table." He points to the table my nieces and nephews are under, Izabel a slim, delicate wall before it. Still, she does not balk, only plants her feet more sturdily in the ground as she summons the water from the glasses behind her to her hands. The sight breaks what's left of my heart.

I press a hand to Atlas's back, and feel a muscle contract beneath my touch. I focus on the connection from muscle to nerves, nerves to brain. Only when I am sure of the hold I have do I speak.

"If I go with you, will you leave the rest of my people in peace?" I ask softly, knowing they will hear–but that my family might not. Not until it's too late for them to stop me.

Atlas's back tightens further under my hand, but he doesn't dare turn from the predator before us.

"You have my word," Dion answers. But his eyes meet Ciaragen's, and his veins blacken in warning as I'm sure he sees the resolution to fight in those deep blue depths. For her, for the dozens of people still breathing in this room. For the man–male who won't stand down in front of me. For my father, my siblings, my nieces and nephews.

For all of them, I focus on the connection I've made to Atlas's brain, and render him unconscious with half a thought. He drops to the ground in front of me, and the general spins toward us at the sound of his body hitting the ground, her eyes wide with shock.

"Ha*ha!*" Dion laughs, clapping his hands once, a sound of true delight. "Excellent! Such fight, such abilities this one has. You know, I–"

Ciaragen whirls on him now, and I watch shadows appear at her fingertips. But I believe Dion–one more strike and there will be no one but me left living in this Hall.

Two loud *pops* sound through the room as I separate her shoulders from their sockets, and Ciaragen screams in pain as her arms fall limp to her sides. I walk forward, grateful that the men of my family are too occupied with protecting their wives and children to stop me. Only my father is a risk, if he is able to clear his grief and shock long enough to think to fight.

"Take me," I say to Dion, again too quietly for human ears to hear. "Spare them all, and take me."

"Althea, no–" Ciaragen gasps, trying to pop one of her arms back into its socket. Fae healing must take too long for her to wait for it to do its work. Halfway between her and Dion, I stop.

"Thank you for your protection, General," I tell her, my voice gentle, but not weak. "But I won't be needing it any longer." She manages to fix one arm, but I send a flare of magic to her, and her right leg goes out from under her as I send a fissure through her fibula. Not a bad break, but it will keep her from following us.

"This is what you were talking about?" Dion asks Adathan with raised brows, and the male only nods in response. "I like it. Well, come now, Princess, no time to waste." He closes the distance between us and grabs my arm. Just in time, too, because the doors begin shaking from the other side as more guards from the castle grounds, who must have been roused by Ben, try to open them. I see people pushing their hands against the gaping windows, only to encounter solid majick.

With me so close to him, I know that Ciaragen won't risk using her power to strike at the last minute. Dion tugs me through the same exit that Dalton tumbled out of those minutes, weeks, decades ago. I step over him carefully, hoping that he somehow still lives, even as my skirts trail through the pool of blood beneath his body.

There is only enough time for me to hear my father, breaking from his stupor of grief, scream my name. Then that door seals shut, too, and I'm walking through the antechamber in only the company of the three males who killed and betrayed my family. Dion's hold on my arm is painfully tight, and he uses it to drag me quickly through the castle, Adathan leading the way. We encounter no one as we go.

"I'm quite pleased you decided to come with us, Princess," Dion says. "I'm sure it was for all the noble reasons, but, regardless of that, I'm glad." His thumb moves slightly in a stroking motion against my arm, and I have to work to restrain my shudder. "I was disappointed that you hadn't chosen me to be your husband. Afraid I took my anger out on the Fera boy. But, you chose me in the end, eh?"

We exit the halls, and quickly make our way to the training yard–which makes sense, since behind it lies the overgrown pathway I take for my trips to the city gardens. My vision blurs as I consider all that has changed, all that I have *caused* since I last walked that path. My step stumbles, and Dion jerks me along, and then–

"*STOP!*" a familiar voice commands. "Release the Princess at once." Amahd emerges from the dark of the shed, twin swords in his hands.

Dion laughs, and does not so much as loosen a finger on my arm. "Very valiant of you, training master, but I'm afraid I don't have the time to play with you just now. Adathan, Gadsby, see to that, would you?" He jerks his chin at Amahd, and the two males move to attack him as soon as the command is past his lips. They unsheathe their blades, and begin to circle, clearly planning to come at him from two sides.

"No!" A shout bursts through my lips, and I wrestle to leave Dion's grip. As one, all of his fingers break. He hisses, and drops my arm at last. I think he expects me to run straight out to Amahd, but I roll in a somersault instead, only slightly hindered by the skirts of my gown. His other hand misses a grab of my hair by inches. "Amahd!" I yell.

"Ground, three yards," he commands as he continues to

face off the two males, who seem torn between not turning their backs on the armed man, and catching me for their master. I hit the earth in another roll, and over my shoulders I see Adathan let the other male lead the attack on Amahd, while he rushes to catch me. Two daggers sit on a whetstone just a foot from where I come up from my somersault, and I grab them, spinning on a knee, rising to my feet as smoothly as I have in training sessions. I feel no fear as I face off with the male double my size.

"Calm, Princess. You will win," Amahd says. And then, without a battle cry, or a warning, he strikes out at his opponent. Even with his Fae speed, Amahd's blade only barely misses. That is all I see before they move out of my line of sight, and I must keep my eyes on my own adversary.

Adathan stares right back at me, but does not make a move. Following Amahd's lead, I take care of the first for him without so much as a sharp intake of breath to prepare. Though I use a pattern with the blades that would slice up anybody in three vital arteries, the male avoids every blow, and stands behind me a second later.

I whirl, and throw a different combination of cuts and jabs. He dodges them all. My breath hisses through barred teeth when I attack again, and I almost get him twice. I don't even have time to take pride in that before, in a burst of speed only possible for a Fae, he is inches from me. Rather than striking, as I expect, he sheathes his blades as he moves, and each of his hands wrap tightly around my own. A little pressure on twin points in my wrists, and my fingers splay, releasing the daggers.

He pulls me flush to him, and says, so low I can hardly hear, "Olin may have believed you wouldn't use that fun little power against him, but I am not so naive. I have a shield up, so don't strain yourself trying to break my fingers, sweetheart. Call off your man."

"Fuck you," I spit at him, trying to wield the breaking despite his claim. When nothing happens, I still hold his golden gaze. "Amahd will win."

"Amahd is a Mage. Gadsby is a Fae. He will lose. Call. Him. Off." His eyes widen as he speaks. And though I don't want to concede, I realize that even if Amahd beats Gadsby, Adathan will only be ordered to fight him next. When I fought him–both times, now–he was under an order not to harm me. That is not the case for Amahd.

"Amahd, stand down," I command, unable to look at him, still pressed against Adathan.

"I will have to disobey you, Princess," he replies. I hear a slice, and a grunt of pain from the Fae, and my heart clenches in my chest.

"Oh for the love of–" Dion starts, having finished with his hand.

"*Amahd, stand down,*" I repeat loudly, my voice shaking.

"Again, I must respectfully decline," he responds, and there's another slice and grunt.

"Why do I even bring you, Gadsby?" Dion asks, and then he lifts his hand–

"NO!" I shout, the sound desperate and heartbroken.
CRACK.

I know it's done when Adathan releases my hands.

Blackness greets me as my brain shuts down, and the last thing I feel is a pair of arms catching me before I hit the ground.

PART II

IN BEDS OF FLOWERS

REALITIES

21

VULNERABLE

*D*ION - *21 YEARS EARLIER*

IF ANYONE HAD ASKED ME WHAT I THOUGHT I WOULD BE DOING while acting as emissary to the crown in Sabrian, holding a two-year-old would not have been one of the things that came to mind.

Yet, here I was, doing just that. And the female before me, wearing a blue dress that had made my heart and body react in a way that they hadn't in a long time, still had her hand on my arm.

I didn't think she was aware of it; she seemed entirely focused on her godson. The flushed side of his little face that was not pressed against my shoulder in his sleep had been kissed by those full lips at least a dozen times. She brushed his cheek now with the fingers of her free hand, trailing them over his closely cropped black hair. I was putting far too much focus on *not* looking at her other hand, where it rested on the space above my elbow. If she didn't notice that she was touching me for the first time, I didn't want to make her uncomfortable by showing her just how aware I was of the fact.

"Lord Dion?" she asked, her voice soft as she continued to look at the boy in my arms. Hearing my name on her lips was also new, and my heart reacted to it by thumping once, hard, in my chest.

"Yes, my Lady?" A term I had used to tease her, once. Now I did so because saying her name would be far too much to handle when it had, seemingly from nowhere, started to mean so much to me.

"Have you ever thought about having children?" Her cheeks flushed as she spoke, but her navy eyes moved to mine, steady as ever.

My heart squeezed painfully in my chest, but I replied honestly: "Yes. Not for a while now, though."

"Would you mind telling me why that is?" Her quietness reminded me that there were, in fact, other well-attuned ears in the room with us. I had forgotten anyone outside of the small circle of me, her, and the boy the moment she had placed her hands on mine to help me hold the child.

"I would not, my Lady. But could I tell you when only our ears might hear?" I glanced around, not so subtly.

A small, but genuine smile graced her lips. "Yes, that would be alright." She looked back to Atlas. "You want me to take him?"

"Actually, Ari, it's way past Atlas's bedtime," Sebastian–Bash, they'd called him–said, coming up to us. "Though I'm sure your shoulder is very comfortable, Lord Dion."

I grinned at him, but it faltered just slightly. "I–I'm not sure how to hand him over without waking him."

Both he and Lady Ciaragen chuckled softly, but the lady said, "Here, let me." For a beat, I was confused why she was doing it, and not him, but then she pressed her body to mine, so that her belly was against the arm that held Atlas. She wrapped her hands around his waist, and nudged her shoulder into the crook of his neck. "Now, just slowly pull your arm out," she said.

I did as she commanded, trying not to think about how it felt for my arm, then my hand, to brush against her stomach as I did so. As my support was removed, she moved one of her arms to cradle Atlas's legs, the other still secure around his torso, creating a seat for him against her. His little head lolled back against her shoulder, and he did not wake.

"I'll be right back, I'm just going to walk Bash and Nate out," she told me, and I nodded.

I tried not to make it obvious that I watched her as she went–*tried* being the operative word. I picked my wine glass up from the windowsill where she'd placed it, and sipped while she escorted the two males and their son from the Hall.

"Watching anybody in particular, Lord Dion?" a familiar voice asked from behind me. I turned to find Nuria standing there, a glass of sparkling wine in her own hand, and a knowing half-smile on her face.

"Now, why would you think that, my Lady?" I asked. Part of me hoped she'd drop it, but another part luxuriated in having someone close enough to me to notice my looks, and cared enough to ask about them.

"No reason." She shrugged. "Say, have you noticed how lovely our friend Ciaragen looks tonight? That blue looks stunning on her."

My eyes moved once more to the object of her compliment without thought or hesitation. She was chatting with Bash and Nate, who now held Atlas, while Bash laid a hand on his mate's waist. The satin of her dress shone and swished as she swayed to the music playing softly in the Hall.

"Yes. It does," I agreed. When I looked back at Nuria, her eyes darted to my lips, and only then did I realize I was smiling.

She took a step closer to me, and lowered her voice. "I am saying this as her friend, but also as yours. You are both on the edge of something here, and *you* need to be sure of where your loyalties lie before you jump." For possibly the first time, her usual irreverence was absent from her face, replaced with caution.

My heart stuttered as I realized what she was implying with the first part of her warning, and again when I processed what was insinuated in the second. She raised her brow at me, and I nodded, holding her gaze as those bright black eyes bored into mine, scanning for any hesitation, or deceit. When she found none, she dipped her chin the smallest bit.

Half a beat later, her sober expression was replaced with a smile. "She comes now. The night is not over, Lord Dion." She gave me a significant look, patted my arm, then departed to rejoin Jolie at a table on the other side of the Hall.

"What was that about?" Lady Ciaragen asked as she approached.

"Nothing." I knew this answer would not suffice, but I was not able to come up with anything clever as the skirt of her dress danced around her hips while she walked. She opened her mouth to respond, a line forming between her brows. "Can I get you a drink?"

She stopped before me. "Now, Lord Dion, you wouldn't be trying to ply me with alcohol so that I stop asking you so many questions tonight, would you?" A brow raised.

"Of course not." But then a server passed with a tray full of flutes of sparkling wine. I took one with a thank you to the male, and held it out to her, my own glass still half-full.

She laughed. Her fingers brushed mine as she took the glass, and the combination of the sound and her touch had my heart reacting again, and for what I suspected would not be the last time tonight.

"That's good, because you know that wouldn't work. In fact, I think I only get more inquisitive the more that I drink." She took a long sip, and then it was my turn to chuckle.

"I would answer your questions all day." And that time, I didn't mind the thoughtless honesty this place had brought out in me.

Not when it made her blush a lovely wine-red I had to force my eyes away from, though her gaze on mine remained as steady as ever. "Well, good," she replied, and I thought she sounded a bit breathless as she did. "Because you already promised to answer one, and we still have an hour of drinking and mingling to do."

⊞

We spent the next hour talking amongst ourselves, and with others. By the end of the evening, any negativity towards me had dimmed from murderous looks to annoyed glares. For the most part, though, I thought that by the time everybody was departing, I was no longer hated by those close to the High Lord and High Lady of Sabrian.

Unlike my initial expectations of the evening, the entire night had not been spent schmoozing the nobility of their land. Instead, most of the time had been spent with those I considered friends, even if I believed I was not deserving of being that to them.

I had talked with them, and even danced with Jolie for a song. My feet had been almost as clumsy as she was kind, not losing any patience as she talked me through the steps.

"I knew them once," I'd assured her, as my right foot moved

when my left foot should have. "But it's been a while since I've wanted to dance."

Her gaze had softened. And, with her instructions, by the end of the song I could follow the steps with more ease, and even concluded the dance with a small dip, which elicited a giggle from her.

The smile from that had stayed on my face for minutes as we'd gone back to the tables to talk with our other...friends. And as I'd bid good night to those remaining in the Hall, a few interactions stood out. Nuria and Jolie had both kissed me on the cheek, with smiles spread across theirs. Bayani had shaken my hand, and the grin on his own lips looked genuine. Hielo and Hiela had told me that they hoped I'd had a wonderful time, and that they would see me for breakfast in the morning. The familiarity with which they spoke the second part had made me feel vulnerable in a way I couldn't explain.

And, now, though I'd told her that I could find my way back to my chambers on my own, my guard accompanied me as we walked through the halls. She'd removed her heels, and was padding softly beside me, her shoes in her hands.

"Admirable though it may be that you are committed to my protection even when inebriated, I know what truly led you here," I said, angling my gaze down to her.

"You do, do you? And I am not inebriated."

"I do—and alright, perhaps that wasn't the right word. I believe the kids call it *buzzed*?"

She laughed at that, swaying slightly into my arm before she righted herself. "That didn't make you sound a million years old."

"Only ninety-nine thousand, give or take a decade," I replied, that arm feeling warmer than the other.

"I'm twenty-nine," she said, divulging information about herself without being asked for the first time. Another thing I doubted she realized, but I did. "Reached my maturity about seven years ago."

"I don't know about maturity, but whatever you say."

She chuckled again, and this time the back of her hand brushed my arm in a delicate swat. "No, no, I'm very mature. Sophisticated. The epitome of class and demurity." She raised her chin, and altered her voice as she spoke, elongating vowels in the way the ladies in the capital did. She even batted her lashes.

"You've convinced me," I told her through my own laughter.

"And you're trying to distract me." She pointed at me with an overdone glare, and prodded me with the tip of her finger before dropping her hand. "I still have questions, Lord Dion, and while that's not the only reason I'm escorting you to your chambers, it is one of them." Some of the humor left her face, but a small smile was still on her lips, and her eyes remained soft.

"Ask away, my Lady." I was filled with the disconcerting knowledge that, no matter what she asked, I would give her the answer. I wasn't sure exactly when her power over me had come to fruition, but I had a feeling that it had started before our time in the library. Possibly on my first day here.

"Well, there's my question from the Hall. On whether you've ever thought about having children. You said you had, but not for a while. Why is that?" I could see in my periphery that she was looking up at me as she spoke.

I sighed, and started talking on the exhale, not quite able to return her gaze. And, for the first time, I vetted my words for her, omitting the true beginning of it. "Over time, both my position, and the demeanor I'd adopted to remain sane within that position, rendered it highly unlikely that I should ever have them. And before you can ask it, that was partly because I didn't want...the company of females. Another, possibly larger part was that I did not want to have that vulnerability."

"You...I'm sorry. You do not prefer females?"

"I do," I answered, and her brow furrowed. "It's just that, after closing myself off for so long to maintain my sanity, I lost the desire to be close to...anybody." For the first time since arriving in Sabrian, the gravestone flashed in my mind. I hadn't allowed myself to ponder its absence since my arrival here, too horribly content to be free of it.

I therefore did not question why it disappeared again as I looked into her gentle eyes. "And what of the vulnerability?"

We'd reached my door. She leaned on it, preventing me from going inside–as if I'd want to do that when I could talk to her instead. "As a person closely associated with the king, I knew no child of mine would be safe. And, in order to have one, I would have to be vulnerable enough to accept and give love, and I haven't been. Not for a long time."

She stared up at me silently for a moment. I would have felt more self-conscious if she hadn't been seeing into my very soul for almost three weeks. But as it was, I only felt myself weather it, not quite like a storm; it was too gentle for that, now. More like a breeze on a hilltop from where one could see the maelstrom forming miles out into the ocean.

When she did speak, it was with the quietness of that breeze, and the boldness and strength of the storm-ridden sea. "How long did you resent your work for the king? What was the point at which you needed to start desensitizing yourself in order to survive?"

I did not miss that she used the word *survive* and not *live*.

"November the eighth, sixty-one years ago."

Rather than ask how I knew that date so specifically, how I didn't even have to give it a second's thought, she stared at me again. Her head tilted, and her eyebrows pressed together, that little line forming between them. I had the strangest urge to reach, and brush my thumb along that line, smoothing the concern from her face.

Then, without a word, she closed the distance between us, and wrapped her arms around my waist, her face pressed to my shoulder. I tensed for a beat–I couldn't remember the last time I'd been hugged. Maybe by my mother, when she had been alive all those years ago.

But then my arms acted of their own accord, and wound over Lady Ciaragen's shoulders, one of my hands resting on the base of her neck. And I thought that perhaps the one thing better than the feeling of being held, might be getting to hold her back.

Her scent of vanilla and bergamot filled the air I breathed. It was on her skin, which was softer than I'd imagined it might be. It wound through her hair as tightly as her curls were spiraled; the strands of which were pressed against my cheek. And her body was almost flush with mine. Warm, supple, and lovely.

She pulled away, and my breath halted, hoping I hadn't overstepped in some way. Praying that my scent had not changed. But she kept her hands on my waist as she said, "After breakfast tomorrow, we're not going to go off with our friends. We are going to stay with Hielo and Hiela. And we are going to talk."

My heart straining in my chest, I said, "Alright."

"Good."

And I didn't know what made me bold enough to do it, but as she slid her hands from me, I caught one of them in one of mine. I bowed just a little bit at the waist–I knew she wasn't a fan of the formality–and brought the back of her palm to my lips, holding her eyes all the while so I would see if she was doubtful, or disgusted. But it almost seemed like she held her breath as my mouth brushed the smooth skin over her knuckles. And I felt her fingers squeeze mine as I did so.

"Good night, my Lady," I said as I rose, my voice rough.

"Good night, Lord Dion," she replied as I released her hand. Her words were a bit breathless, but her eyes, as always, were steady. As I turned and opened my door, I thought I heard a slight intake of breath, as though she wanted to speak. But even as I crossed the threshold just a touch more slowly than I normally would have, no further words came.

I closed the door behind me, and walked into the bedchamber. And stood there.

I didn't allow myself to think through my feelings, because they were impossible. I'd known her for three weeks–not even! And even if it were possible that I felt...whatever it was for her, I wasn't deluded enough to believe she could feel the same.

Except...three weeks ago, I didn't think we would ever have a normal conversation. And two nights ago, I never would have imagined she would willingly touch me–hold me.

No. *That* was impossible. Allowing myself to believe otherwise would not be intelligent, which I liked to believe myself to be.

Yet what was improbable, but clearly happening, was how my body was reacting to her, in a way it hadn't to anybody in a very long time. She was exquisite, in both appearance and personality. Strong, kind, and likely far more intelligent than I. Stunning, whether she was in her uniform, or in a dress as lovely as she'd been in tonight.

A dress that plunged down to her sternum; a fact that I'd been very purposefully not acknowledging, which had become increasingly difficult as the night went on. The partial view of her golden tattoo had made me wonder what else she hid beneath that uniform each day. Those things, together with the way the dress had moved around her hips, and the lovely glow of her skin in the bright fabric and the flickering lights, had me unable to resist.

I couldn't do anything about the *reaction* growing more and more insistent as I thought about her. She was right outside my door. And, even if I put up a sound shield and bit down on a bloody pillow–I would still feel strange knowing that she was *just* beginning to tolerate me, and my repayment to even the smallest show of friendship was to pleasure myself at the memory of it.

No. There would be none of that.

I sighed, perhaps the heaviest sigh I'd ever expressed, and picked up my book from my nightstand to settle in for a very long night.

22

FOREST & FURY

THEA - PRESENT

THE AIR AROUND ME SMELLS LIKE DIRT, AND PINE. THE SCENT, and the brisk morning air that caresses my face are unfamiliar to my rousing body. I haven't fallen asleep in the gardens since I was small. Whatever I laid my head on last night to sleep is hard, and my neck and head ache fiercely. My nose wrinkles at the discomfort, and my lashes flutter as I force myself to wake fully. My mother will be wondering where I am.

A voice that both is and is not familiar says, "Ah, our Princess wakes." And I remember that I had not–could not have, in fact, fallen asleep in the castle gardens.

I'm on my feet faster than I have ever moved, but the motion makes the ache of my head progress to a pounding that blinds me for a short moment. I blink rapidly, swaying as my body rights itself, until my vision finally sharpens to view my surroundings. The pre-dawn light tints everything a dark gray-ish-blue. I'm standing on a bedroll that must have been my mattress for the night, the cushion thin enough that I can feel the rocks under my feet. I'm in a clearing in a wooded area, surrounded by pine trees, and three Fae males.

I reach to my thigh on instinct, and feel only the fabric of my gown beneath my palm.

"You're unarmed, which is nice. We couldn't have you poking more holes in our friends, could we? Poor Adathan only barely survived last time." Dion moves to stand in front of me, just feet away. Here, in the middle of the woods, he wears only breeches, boots, and a coat buttoned over a plain cotton shirt. My own garment is torn, and covered in so much blood, visible even in the darkness.

The sight of those stains, deeper in color than even the red of the dress, brings everything from last night roaring back, tearing my heart apart as if it were happening here and now, all over again. Before despair can take hold, putting me in danger with its vulnerability, I find the rage. I hold so tightly to it, to my only hope of not falling apart. If I allow myself to feel anything else, I will crumble. If I allow myself to remember–

A scream, the likes of which I've never made, erupts from the depths of my soul, and I launch myself at him.

And, against all odds, my fist connects with his face before my arms are pinned by large hands behind my back. I pull with all of my strength, more animal than human, snarling and screaming. But the hands that bind me may as well be a bear trap for all the slack they give. I am the beast, and I fight with such fervor that I would willingly tear off my own limb before giving up.

Dion rubs his cheek. And then he says, in a language I only know from my studies: "You couldn't have done that before she hit me?"

"She's fast," the male behind me responds simply in the same tongue, his rough bass voice not even sounding strained for all the struggle I'm giving. In my rage, I don't have the ability to sort through the fact that they're speaking in a dialect which has not been used in this continent in centuries.

"LET. ME. GO." I command him in the Old Language. I shove with all my might and body weight backwards, instead of pulling, hoping to knock him off balance. He does me the justice of budging half an inch before righting himself.

Dion's eyes widen in surprise, then fill with terrible delight. "Well, that makes things easier." He dares to walk towards me. "Don't take your anger out on Adathan, Princess." I bare my teeth at him, pulling on the hands that hold me once more. Midnight hair falls in front of my face as I thrash.

"Tell him to let me go, and I'll be happy to take it out on you," I tell him, my voice low and gravelly.

"I don't think I will. A face like this needs to be protected, and you've already made my left side all swollen." He pouts exaggeratedly.

"Big, tough male needs his *lackeys* to hold back the little girl. How's your leg?" I seethe, showing a grin that's mostly just a flash of teeth, and I stop pulling for a moment. I breathe heavily to make it seem like I've tired.

He takes a half step closer, just two feet away now. "It healed completely while still at your birthday party. All better now. I appreciate your concern."

"My only concern is that I didn't kill you like I did your friends in that basement you had them keep me in. That was you, wasn't it?" I think he confessed to it yesterday, but the memory is fuzzy. Adathan, the one I had *poked* a few times with his friend's blade, stands behind me after all. Just as he stood behind Dion yesterday, as my father sobbed, and my brothers shouted my name.

I shut down the memories, focusing on the rage once more.

Dion smiles, as if my question thrills him. "It was! I

instructed my *lackeys*, as you called them, to take you and hold you there until I arrived. Unfortunately, they failed." He throws a disgruntled look at Adathan behind me. "But, after some...re-education, I forgave him." His eyes flash with contempt as he continues to look over my head, at the male holding me back. And if the implication weren't enough, the way Adathan's hands tighten just slightly on my wrists tells me what that *re-education* entailed.

Dion continues, and those hands loosen by a fraction. "After all, they were instructed not to harm you. You wouldn't be much good to me injured–or worse. But, as *you* were so intent on harming *them*, I suppose they didn't stand much of a chance. Not when we didn't know you'd been trained to the extent that you have." He glares once more at the male behind me, but this time, there is no reaction that I can feel.

"The definition you all hold for harm is much different from my own." I feel disgusted, remembering the predatory intent with which the blond male had spoken about violating me. "I'm not sorry I didn't let them live long enough to so much as lay a finger on me." While my taking his life had haunted me, in hindsight, he'd deserved his end.

Dion takes another step, now just six inches away. "They were instructed not to," he repeats, as if that is enough. As if that covers any possible infraction on his part. His expression is almost bored; utterly uncaring that someone in his employ would have assaulted me.

"But, males will be males, I suppose." He shrugs, like that's a reasonable thing to say; a legitimate excuse for anyone who so much as considers rape. "I can't blame him." His eyes roam my face and body, and darken with a desire that makes my stomach roil. He lifts a hand, and moves to brush his finger along my bottom lip.

I strike, first closing my teeth hard around his finger. Still with it in my mouth, I thrust my head up, and forward into his. He shouts, and then his other palm hits the side of my face so hard that my jaw releases, and I see stars. As I fall back against the hard chest of the male still holding me, I taste blood, both Dion's and mine, and spit it onto the ground. I feel another warm trickle of it down the cheek he slapped.

"Gods DAMN IT!" he yells, and though my head spins, I can see him clutching both hands to his nose, the one that I'd bitten on top. I feel my pulse thudding in my head, the initial ache from waking nearly blinding now.

Then I realize–my senses. Healing, and breaking. Why have they not come to me these past minutes? My healing is typically easy as breathing; fixing something like a headache, or a simple laceration, took next to no concentration at this point. And I'd used the breaking so readily last night, even–even against friends. So, where are they now?

I can feel the heartbeat of the male behind me pounding against the back of my head, but can establish no further connection to it, as my ability typically allows me to. Usually, if I had concentrated, I would have been able to sense the heartbeats of everyone here, even several feet away.

Dion storms to me then, breaking me from my cognizance, blood covering his hands. He stops just inches away once more, and I think he might hit me again. I brace everything, from my face to my abdomen. But instead he wraps a bloody hand around my throat, squeezing with enough force that my pulse pounds in my temples, and my eyes feel heavy.

"*Never*–" he hisses, his eyes just inches from mine, the fury in them terrifying, "–do that again. I will recreate *every* injury you inflict unto me tenfold. I allowed you to hit me without reciprocation once already. That will *not* happen again. You are emotional, and because you are bleeding as well, I'll call us even. But if you so much as look at me wrong, I promise that the next pain upon you will be the worst you have ever known. Understand?"

I don't move, not so much as a blink. I show no fear, even as I feel my lungs start to struggle, though I have no misgivings about the truth of his words. I don't allow myself to gasp; I know that no air would come. I will not give him the satisfaction of me seeking that comfort. I only stare him down while my body tries to take over my mind.

"*Understand?*" he repeats, squeezing harder. Still, I don't move. I never trained for torture, but a huge part of training is ignoring fear, and pushing through when your body tries to convince you to give up. I've experienced extreme pain and discomfort before; I didn't back down then, and I will not back down now, even with my life in danger. I will not allow him to win. For Amahd, who would never back down either.

So, I hold my stare as my vision clouds, and I know capillaries in my eyes have burst. The hands around my wrists squeeze, but I can hardly feel it over the agony in my chest. After another long moment, Adathan says from behind me, his tone detached: "My Lord, she's turning blue."

Dion looks like he might not care, might let me lose consciousness. But then he sighs angrily, and releases my throat. I can't help my body's reaction then. My lungs try to pull in a huge breath, but my trachea feels thinner than a piece of straw, and I end up coughing before I can get hardly any oxygen down. Loud and hard, until my diaphragm aches with the spasms.

As my body has these reactions, I fold over, and only the hands holding my arms keep me semi-upright. Rather than holding them straight back, which would strain my joints in this position, my wrists are released. Instead, a forearm reaches across the space just below my collar bone. Not close enough to my neck that it feels like being choked all over again, and not so far down that I feel even more disrespected, but supporting my upper body until I can regain my composure.

When I can finally breathe a semi-normal breath, I stand straight, my eyes watering, and the male behind me removes his arm. I turn only halfway to look at him, while still keeping Dion in my periphery. I don't thank him for not letting me fall. As if that would be the crowning moment that could make me think he wasn't a spineless piece of shit after he held my arms back as I was suffocated by his master. As I hold those golden eyes, I let the male see the revulsion in mine; if my stare could burn, he would be ash on the ground.

"Clean her up," Dion orders, waving a hand at me and the aforementioned piece of shit. Though I want to respond, my throat aches when I so much as exhale loudly. So I just continue to glare, not about to be the one who follows the order first.

The male turns from me, and starts towards a large canvas tent a few yards from us. He stops halfway when he realizes–or hears–that I haven't followed. Rather than look at me expectantly, and wait for me to play the compliant princess, he looks past me. Further into the small clearing, where Dion still paces. When his gaze is once again on mine, he only holds it, his expression unchanging.

The meaning is clear. If I don't follow, I'll be out here with *him* and forced to go in that tent with much more violent methods than a follow-the-leader situation. My jaw tightens, and I clench my fists at my sides before walking towards the lackey, opening the entrance flap of the tent myself.

The inside is nothing special. The canvas hides only a couple of bedrolls, some food, a few short stools, and a small case that the male walks towards. He picks it up and places it on one of the stools. As he opens it, I can see that it's full of general medical supplies–bandages, cotton pads, alcohol.

"Do you want to clean your own face, or shall I do it?" he asks in Ceraschen, folding his arms over his chest, looking like he already knows my answer. I glare up at him, and his citrine eyes are almost bored. I have no doubt, though, that if I refuse to clean myself, he will either use majick or might to do it himself. Because his *master* has commanded it.

Preferring my own hand to his, I take one of the cotton pads, pour some of the alcohol over it, and begin to dab at the blood on my cheek. Since he watches me, I don't allow myself to wince, even though it stings like mad. But his piercing stare, along with his stupid alpha-male stance, is getting on my nerves.

I raise my eyebrows, and say with a voice like rough stones scratching against each other, "Are you going to watch me the whole time, or can I have some fucking privacy?"

His own brows raise, just barely. "She curses. What happened to the proper little princess?"

"She died with her mother," I tell him bluntly, not allowing myself to feel the grief, and his face goes blank–surprised, maybe, with my candidness. "Now turn that look somewhere else, before I make your master come in here just to put me out of the misery of seeing it. All I'd have to do is hit him, and I'd probably be out for a day."

Without so much as a shift in his expression, he turns, and lays down on one of the bedrolls, staring straight up at the ceiling of the tent. I hadn't been foolish enough to believe he'd leave me alone in here.

I get to work on the places on my face and body where I can feel blood, both dried and running. The blood from the cut on my shoulder is dark and dry, as is a trickle from a strange wound in the crook of my elbow, but my cheek must have reopened when Dion slapped me. I take the swabs to my neck, too, just to rid myself of some of his touch.

When I'm done, there's a small hill of pink and red cotton on the ground. I look down at my dress, torn in a few different places, the skirts covered in Dalton's blood, from when I'd walked through it last night. A small part of me registers that it is the last gown my mom will ever dress me in, but I shut that thought down before it has the chance to take root.

As if he read my mind, the male says, still without looking at me, "He'll want you to be changed before you go out."

"Is what he wants supposed to matter to me?" I ask, pain lancing down my throat as I speak.

He turns his head to look at me. "If you're not a masochist, yes," he replies, his tone bored. I cross my arms over my chest.

"And what am I supposed to wear, even if I wanted to change?" I look down my nose at him, where he lays on the ground. I don't want him to know that I want this, too; that the longer I wear this dress, the more likely I am to break. And I must not break.

"He bought clothes for you once he realized he wanted to keep you with us on the journey. There's another case in the corner full of them."

But I barely hear his second sentence. "What do you mean *realized he wanted to keep me*?" I seethe, wishing my voice wasn't so raspy and small.

Large, long arms move to fold his hands behind his head, and he turns his gaze back to the ceiling of the tent. "Two nights ago, Olin came to us and told us the plan changed. Before then, you were supposed to be a prisoner in every sense of the word."

Olin...I remember that being said at some point during the chaos of last evening, but my mind had apparently blocked out the information. I don't know who Dion is, or if he even exists; maybe the name was just a cover.

But...two nights ago. The night that...

I feel nauseous when I remember. Worse than that–I want to crawl out of my own skin, and then burn it. And to know that because of that *incident*, I am now somehow desirable enough that I'm being cleaned and changed, instead of sitting in my blood and filth? I would prefer the latter, would rather my hands be in chains, than to have the knowledge that my lips had touched his. That I had *wanted* it. That it had been my first kiss.

I actually might have vomited, if I weren't so committed to showing no weakness. Instead, I take a deep breath through my nose, wincing as it expands the muscles in my neck and chest. I hate that it makes it look like I'm succumbing to his will, but I can't wear this gown any longer. I spy the chest he referred to in the back right corner of the tent, and go to it. The metal clasps keeping it closed are intricately carved, the leather finer even than some in the castle. In a tent with only the bare minimum otherwise, it's incredibly out of place.

As I open it, the first things I see are lacy underclothes. Items that barely look like they would cover what they're meant to cover. No drawers or shifts to wear instead. I feel the urge to throw up again, but swallow the bile building in my throat. I pick up the fabric between two fingers, as delicately and with as much disgust as I would a worm.

Placing them to the side, I see the clothes underneath are widely varied. There are dresses, but also pants, cotton shirts, socks, and leather boots that look just my size. I pick one of the shirts, and a pair of trousers out of the case, ignoring the lacy things on the ground.

I turn, and find the male still lying on the bedroll in the center of the tent. Though he doesn't face me, I still have no plans to disrobe with him just feet away. "Do you expect me to change with you in here?"

He tilts his head back, and looks at me upside down. "Since I'm not supposed to leave you by yourself, yes."

I cross my arms again. "You would hear me if I tried to leave. There is nothing in this tent that could be used as a weapon, except for the two daggers you have on you. And, it's three Fae against one Mage. I think you can let me change in peace."

He rolls onto his side, not moving his gaze from me as he does. "You've proven you can take on three before."

"As one of those three, you know that's not true. If it were, you wouldn't be here," I remind him, because being silent about my failure, my weakness, won't get him out of here any faster. Won't change the fact that I stand in a camp of enemies, the one nearest me having pretended to be a friend to my family for a year. Somehow–probably the trauma–it's hard to remember that the dark-haired, golden-eyed male before me is the same as the blond doorman who introduced me before each court gathering for months. But I feel the hatred simmer in my eyes as I remember that fact now.

He sits up, leaning back on his hands, seeming at ease even in the face of that loathing. "Nevertheless, you've been far too observant for me to leave you on your own. One of my daggers is sheathed under my clothes, and yet you knew about it. I think you'll try to escape, regardless of what the outcome might be. So, no, I will not be leaving this tent while you are still in it."

In a fit of temper I haven't experienced since childhood, I throw one of my boots at his face. He catches it swiftly, even sitting down, which only infuriates me more. I move, the rest of the new garments falling to the ground, and he's standing before I complete a single step. Despite his agility, I take a swing at him, my teeth barred–and he easily blocks me. Again, this only fuels my anger. My training, all of that *fucking training* with Amahd–

I am not him, and the proof of that is in how I couldn't save him. So much time spent on that stupid patch of sand, and for what? For *what*?

With a feral noise from deep in my soul that tears up my injured throat, a hit finally lands on the male's jaw. My knuckles scream in pain at the contact against bone, and it's so sweet, so welcome compared to the agony in my heart. I'm about to go for another one–

But, apparently, he's had enough. Broad, golden-brown hands wrap around my wrists, and then twist me so that my arms are crossed over my torso, and my back is to his front. He is solid, and utterly massive–taller even than Olin, my head against his chest. Nevertheless, I growl and thrash against his hold.

"Are you done?" he asks, the timbre of his voice rumbling through his chest and the back of my skull.

"Let go of me, and find out," I snarl, thrashing again.

"I put a sound shield up, so he can't hear us. But if we don't exit soon, he will come to see what's taking so long. And he will not turn away while you change. So, I'm going to let you go, and turn my back to you. Do not make me regret it."

He releases me, and I elbow him hard in the gut. He barely even grunts, and while that fact has me gritting my teeth, I don't doubt his words. I pick up the thrown and discarded clothes from the ground, and move to the opposite side of the tent. I look to find his back already to me, but I face his direction anyway. If he turns he will see much more this way, but I want to catch him if he does so. I'd find my way to one of those daggers if that were to happen.

I reach behind myself to the buttons of the dress, ignoring the pain in my right shoulder as I do so. I get to undoing them, detaching myself as much as possible from the feeling of the gown–the final gown–falling from my body when I get through all of them.

I step out of the skirts, and pull the shirt over my head, and tug the trousers up my legs. The fabrics of both are comfortable, though wearing my old undergarments beneath feels grimy. I would feel more disgusted, though, if I were wearing the lacy things from the case.

I finish by pulling on the leather boots, tucking the slim legs of the pants into them. Somehow, they fit perfectly; the leather already molded to my feet as if they're years old.

As quickly as possible for the tangled mess it is, I braid back my hair, knotting it around itself at the bottom to tie it off. Not that I need or want my hair to look more presentable with my current company–after seeing the items in the case, and hearing Adathan's words, I would actually prefer to look unkempt. But my mane of hair would get in my way if I do happen to find a window for an escape.

"All done?" the male asks.

"Yes," I reply, trying to put as much venom as possible into the single syllable, with my whisper of a voice.

He turns back to me, looks me up and down once, then nods. "Good. Let's go." He gestures with his head towards the exit, crossing his arms. Waiting for me to go first, so that I can't have even a second to myself in this wretched tent.

I shove past him, roughly bumping his arm as I go, and walk through the flaps of the tent. I hear his footsteps crunch on the ground behind me as he follows.

Olin stands in the middle of the small clearing, and looks like he'd been in the middle of a conversation with the other male. But when I emerge, his attention zeroes in on me. And where Adathan behind me had given me a once-over that I barely even noticed or acknowledged, the look *he* gives me has so much intent behind it that I have to hold back a shudder.

"Much better," he says as his eyes finally get back to mine. "Now you're ready to go to Eshelle."

23

TWO PRISONERS

CIARAGEN - 21 YEARS EARLIER

IT WAS TIME TO TELL HIM. EVERYTHING THAT WE'D BEEN covering up since he arrived.

I'd escorted Lord Dion this morning to the balcony for breakfast, still remembering the feeling of his lips on the back of my hand. As he'd walked into his chambers last night, I almost asked him if he would like to talk some more–knowing very well that the conversation would have been moved to the seating area in his room. Only the knowledge that Arthur would come to relieve me shortly, and would undoubtedly think something far less innocent than talking was happening inside, kept me from speaking.

Now, I sat at the table with Lord Dion as we awaited our High Lord and High Lady. Usually, I remained as far as possible from him while we ate. Today, I sat at his side. I wore normal clothes instead of my uniform, and felt at ease, even with the coming conversation. And I believed that the talks I'd had with him over the past two days had everything to do with that.

I looked over at him now, and he seemed to be in a daydream–or too nervous to notice my gaze. There were no tells; no drumming of the fingers, no jumping knee to tell me what might be going on internally. I could hear that his heart rate was set at a normal pace, but still I *felt* his unease.

Knowing what I did now about what he'd had to do, who he'd had to become to survive being under Oleander's employ, I didn't let myself ruminate on when and why he might have had to adopt that stillness. What inner turmoil he must have endured so regularly that he learned to fool his heart into being calm for the listening arched ears around him. Even amongst those at court, where people were expected to be able to hide their emotions, it stood out as a meticulously learned skill. One he'd had to adopt and master, or face the consequences if he failed to do so.

I nudged his arm with my elbow, and he blinked, turning his head towards me. "You okay?"

His gaze softened, and the fingers of his right hand twitched on the table, just inches from where my own rested. "Just thinking."

I was going to ask what he was thinking about, when we both heard the sound of two sets of footsteps approaching. We looked away from each other, and towards the opening of the large wood and glass doors. Seconds later, our High Lord and High Lady were there, each of them in impeccable regalia that they hadn't donned since before Lord Dion's arrival. Having not been sure that he wouldn't report to the king on their expression of sovereignty through clothing, they hadn't dared.

But everything was going to be laid out plainly today. Hielo wore a blue velvet cape that covered one shoulder, and flowed behind him, his mate in a gown of the same hue. Both of them wore thin golden circlets atop their heads, an outright treasonous act.

Lord Dion and I stood as they approached, and I didn't think I was imagining that his bow to them was even deeper than usual.

"Please, sit," Hielo said, and we did. He and his High Lady followed suit. "Before we talk, we eat. No good conversation can be had on empty stomachs." He snapped, and dishes of eggs, bacon, fruit, and toast appeared on the round table before us.

When we finished eating, and all the plates were cleared away, I could sense his nerves once more. I didn't know if they were in anticipation of what we were going to tell him, or a fear of what he thought we expected him to tell us. I had to restrain myself from placing my hand on his arm to calm him.

I wasn't entirely sure what to do with this newfound desire to comfort and touch him. Self-consciously, I peered at my High Lady, but she was studiously looking at her mate.

"The purpose of this conversation is not to interrogate you, Lord Dion," Hielo said, and I immediately felt much of the tension beside me melt away.

Our High Lady looked at him then. "We have many things to tell you, but I'm sure the thing you're most curious about at this time is the, shall we say, *jewelry* on our heads."

"They suit you both well," Lord Dion responded in earnest. And I felt something else tug at me then, pulling a corner of my mouth up with it.

Our Hiela smiled, too. "We thank you."

Her grin remained as just a small tilt of her lips as she continued. "We have worn them among friends for some time now. And we plan to do so for many years yet. Our plans in that regard will be shared with you in time—only because it is time that is required for them to take form, not for any shortage of trust in you."

It was quiet for a short moment, before Lord Dion cleared his throat lightly, and said roughly, "Thank you, High Lady."

"Although you demonstrated to us a lack of control upon your arrival, we believed bringing your mind and body to peace would help to calm the power that may rage otherwise. This is not a slight to you," Hielo clarified, as Lord Dion's cheeks had begun to color with shame. "Actually, it is proof that you perhaps never were as monstrous as stories of you claim–but were instead simply an object of your environment. An object the king of Oschverre used for his bidding, and to his liking."

It escaped none of us that our High Lord did not say 'king of *Eshelle*', but rather only the capital in which he resided; the place he had not left in decades.

"It has been only three weeks since you arrived, and from the moment you realized that we would not be treating you as an enemy, we have found out many things about you," Hiela went on after her mate. "We have found you to be kind, even to those who may not return that kindness. We have found you to be intelligent, coming from a place where brute strength was treasured over mindfulness. We have found you to be singularly honest in a world that begs you to lie.

"And we have found shame within ourselves, for we have not been as honest with you." Our High Lady's eyes bored into Lord Dion's, their sincerity, and regret palpable. But rather than offensiveness, or anger, or fear, I felt only confusion from the male beside me.

"My name has been hidden from you. You knew it; you noticed it was never said. And yet, you didn't pry. You didn't ask around, or attempt to find out through nefarious means. You let me have my peace, my secret, because it wasn't yours to know or to tell."

She took a deep breath, and I hoped Lord Dion could sense that it wasn't out of fear of him that she needed to steady herself. I wished I could convey that she did so because less than a dozen people knew her name, even fewer her whole story.

Her shining sienna eyes held Lord Dion's as she revealed, "My name is Oksana Mikhyala Monserre."

Lord Dion's eyes widened in recognition at the name, but our High Lady went on before he could think to ask a question. "You know me as the king's former...partner." I hated this story. Hated the way it hurt her, making me want to storm out of the castle, all the way to Oschverre, and kill the king with my bare hands. This was my second time hearing it, and I wished I could turn back time and somehow prevent her from having this kind of story to tell.

"I assume you've heard the same narrative as everyone else. That I was the vixen who seduced the king into my bed, kept him there until I was sick of him, then left, breaking his heart. Or otherwise, that he had killed me before I could leave, and *that* broke his heart." She smiled without humor. "No, Lord Dion. The true story is much more grim than a seductress and a quickly-healed heart.

"When I was seventeen-years-old, before I'd even reached maturity, I was brought to Oleander's court. He was a prince then, but his father was approaching death; he would be king within a fortnight. And he needed a suitable bride.

"It was meant to be an honor. *The future queen*. I admit, even I fancied the title at the time. As the evening went on, Oleander's eyes frequently wandered to me–even when he was talking with the males, or dancing with another female. But, even as the other ladies thought and whispered hateful things about me, I felt my skin crawl with each glance of his I caught. I tried to convince myself that it was nerves. Butterflies. Because who wouldn't want attention from a prince?

"Finally, he asked me to dance. I accepted. And as we

danced, no one stopped him from holding my hand too tightly. They pretended not to notice as he pushed me against him with his other hand on my hip, forcing me to feel...him through his trousers and my skirts. He asked if I could feel how much he liked me. And I nodded, fearing that if I opened my lips, I might be sick."

A tear rolled down her cheek, which she quickly brushed away. She told me once that she hated how even just the beginning of the story affected her like this. That it made her cry, and feel nauseous, and ashamed. She tried to convince herself that, with almost a century passed, she shouldn't even have a reaction anymore. I reminded her that scars may not bleed, but are always there, and remain as a symbol of survival and strength.

"I feared so much at the time. That if I pulled away, he would hurt me more. That if I rejected him openly, the whole court would form rumors about me, instead of him. That if I turned down the most wanted bachelor in Eshelle, I would be shunned by every other male I thought might come to court me. They were the fears of a child, a girl not secure in her standing, her status, or herself. But they were real to me.

"After that night, he openly courted me. But he demanded I stay in Oschverre; he would never come to my home. Part of me was and is glad of that. That I don't have any of these memories there.

"On the day that his father died, just over a week after we met, he was distraught–or at least played at it. He asked me to join him in his chambers for a drink, and to talk. Not wanting to seem insensitive, or further hurt a male who'd just lost his father, I agreed. He poured me a drink, and we did talk. But by the time his intention was made clear, when the door was barred, and I realized my guards were not outside, it was too late."

More tears trailed down her cheeks, and she didn't stop

them this time. Her mate's expression was full of devastation and rage, but, as always, he allowed her to hold her own. He let her feel, and did not weaken her by seeking to comfort her in front of others. I felt my own throat thicken as I watched my High Lady; her strength, and the understanding her mate had of her.

"I fought him," she went on. "I shouted, and told him no, and when my words weren't enough, I struck him. But when he held my wrists, and he settled himself between my legs, he was so heavy, and I had no combat knowledge to understand how I might escape him in that position. So–so–"

She gasped quietly, her hands curling into fists on the table. Her voice shook only slightly as she continued. "When he was done, he told me that I was his now. That no other male would want me, when they found out I was no longer *pure*. I believed him. My family and guards had already been sent home, without my knowledge. And so, seeing no other choice, no way out...I stayed. He proposed to me publicly, and I accepted. And each night, regardless of what I did, he would always get his way in the end.

"It's said that I left him three months later. I suppose part of me did leave that day. I had no hope left. My family thought me happily betrothed; I had no friends at court. Those who smiled and chatted with me would have turned me over to Oleander sooner than help me, if I'd tried to flee. But there was one form of escape left open to me."

A new tear trailed down her cheek. "On that night, I attempted to take my own life. And would have succeeded, if one of my lady's maids had not heard me fall after all the blood loss, and had a guard break down the door. After I was healed, it was the opinion of his advisors that I was unfit to be his queen. You see, before Oleander had...dealt with the poor female, my lady's maid shared what she'd seen. A good bit of information, finding the king's betrothed bleeding out on her bedroom floor. And I'm sure you know that gossip flies around that castle faster than an arrow shot from a bow."

Lord Dion appeared to freeze at that, seeming to hold even his breath still. Hiela continued, "But Oleander didn't want to let me go. Not by having me executed in secret, and certainly not by sending me home. He loved me, in the horrific way that a male like him could love anything. So, I remained a prisoner, now in every sense. I was locked away, with only half a dozen people in the castle knowing I existed at any given time. Each of them knowing what I went through as they helped to heal my bruises, and assuaged my aches. They forced iron onto and into me, suppressing my powers.

"That went on for quite a while. I was there when you were hired, Lord Dion. I was there when tales spread about the brutal efficiency of the king's new executioner. You're wondering why you don't remember me, I know. Well, I wouldn't have been a very well-kept secret if you'd known, now would I?" She smirked without humor, the expression terrible, and so gut-wrenchingly sad that I had to clench my own fists to keep from reaching out to her.

"I have not been the High Lady of this court for very long, my Lord. I was kept prisoner in Oleander's castle for ninety-seven years, four months, and sixteen days. His *visits* became less frequent after he wed Melisan. I don't believe she ever knew anything about me other than the story everyone else believes. I hoped that she would learn of me. I hoped that she would become hateful in jealousy, and have me killed. And when I heard she was kind, I hoped that she would find out, and set me free. When neither of those things happened, I hoped that one day he would forget about me—there were sometimes weeks when I wouldn't see him. I hoped for a lot, and I think that was what kept me going. Because, though none of what I wished came true exactly, things started to change when he left me alone.

"For it seemed Oleander no longer favored me as much as his new wife. Thus, his servants stood to gain nothing by acting or speaking against me. Some merely pitied me; others loathed me, if only because there was at last someone lower on the scale of society than they were. But those who had always wished to help, but feared for their lives, or for their families, felt safer now. They started to 'accidentally' forget to put on my irons in the long stretches between his visits, and so I saw how their minds changed when they were around me over the decades. They stopped being angry at and afraid of my power, and instead used it to communicate with me when it was too dangerous to speak.

"And when at last those immortal hearts thawed completely, and they allowed themselves to recognize what they were permitting their king to do to somebody they had come to love, they helped to free me. They battled their fear of him, for me. Because they realized what I whispered to them in their minds was true: he is one, and they are many. So, on a night where he was busy holding court with Melisan, and only proven friends were on guard, they got me out. Throughout the following weeks of travel, they worked together to glamour me when I was too weak to do so myself. They fed and clothed me, bathed me, and helped me through my discomforts.

"They were bringing me to the closest High Lord to the capital that they knew they could trust, they said. And when I saw this palace of pale stone, with its city of hills and flowers, I wept. For the decades I'd spent in a windowless room, for all that I had endured during that time, for what I knew was coming, I wept. And they held me. *She* held me. Nuria Bentashi, servant of Oschverre turned Lady of Sabrian.

"She brought me to the gates of the palace, and requested

sanctuary for her queen. Her queen," she repeated softly. "And I understood then that those who had freed me saw in me a strength I'd forgotten about. The strength it takes to survive." She lifted her chin, shoulders straightening.

"You never knew Nuria, that's why you don't recognize her. She'd been a part of the staff for less than a year. And Bayani. The others that helped me escape, and who you may have met during your time at the castle, have made themselves scarce, or glamoured so you wouldn't recognize them. But they are here, supporting our cause. They knew, through the whispers that flit about the castle of Oschverre, that Amedeo was interested only in the wellbeing of Eshelle. That he would support the claim of another to the throne, even if it wasn't himself. And he held true to those rumors; there was no hesitation between the request being made of him, and the gates being opened.

"I asked Nuria to set me down, so that I could walk through the gates on my own. And he was waiting for me. The moment our eyes met, as withered and broken as my heart was, I felt it. The mating bond. I think my soul recognized that I was safe for the first time in nearly a century, and didn't want me to wait any longer for the love I deserved." With that, Hielo at last took her hand, his brown eyes on her.

"That...that was ten months ago." Even as she said it, I still couldn't believe it had only been that long since our Hiela came into our lives. What was even more incomprehensible was how she was not a monster; not hardened against the world, determined to make others feel the pain that she'd felt.

I remembered her being introduced to me as my High Lady. Just three months after that, my father was killed. Weeks later, when I was still filled with only anger in the day, and sadness in the night, she came. In the quiet of my chamber, she brushed my tears from my cheeks with gentle hands, and asked me if I wanted to hear her story, knowing that it might help me get my fight back. And from my nod, until she finished, I felt an ever-growing unnamable burning that consumed all else. Only her presence with me had ensured that my passion was directed towards protecting what was good, and not at destroying all–in hopes that the bad went with it.

Now, that same female–who deserved nothing but a lifetime of sunshine and rest after all she endured–sat across from me, looking at the male who could determine the success of our rebellion. A rebellion that had been flimsy at best a year ago, but, thanks to her intelligence and courage, had transformed into something much bigger. Not just an idea, but a movement. Something that might inspire hope, especially to those who suffered most under Oleander's rule.

Hiela went on, "We knew who you were when Oleander sent word of your visit. And, though we didn't know how little of the atrocities under your name were actually done by you, we did hold hope that the *grumpy, dull, angry* male–if what the castle servants said was to be believed–would sway if presented with a court where he would not have to do such things any longer.

"And so, here we sit. Two prisoners, of different sorts, of a king who does not deserve his crown. I only hope that you can forgive any deception on our part," she finished.

I waited with bated breath for Lord Dion's response, and couldn't help that my eyes turned towards him as I did so.

He said, his voice unusually rough, "Thank you for trusting me with that." Eyes of hazel and sienna met across the table, and an energy threaded between them, gravitational in nature; binding them to a shared cause as assuredly as our feet were bound to the earth.

"That is not all we have to share," Hielo said, his voice filled with lingering rage. Hiela's thumb brushed along the back of his palm. He took a breath, and when he spoke again, his tone was calmer. "You may be wondering about some of the phrases my mate used as she told you her story. About how people in the castle feared her power, and how they could communicate with her without words.

"Oksana is a conveyant. She is able to not only read the thoughts of those around her, but produce her own thoughts in their minds as well. Before you ask, or think, let me explain the particulars of her power. She cannot influence minds; cannot make someone do something not of their own will, as aepercepti can. She can hear the thoughts of anyone around her who is not currently shielding their minds, but only if she chooses to; she is not bombarded by thoughts at all times, as biblionics are. *She* decides when to listen, and who to listen to, and even then she is more respectful of privacy than I would be, if I had been denied mine as she had been for so long."

Hielo's jaw ticked in another moment of anger, but Hiela squeezed his hand, and he relaxed once more. With a sigh, he said, "Just as she can choose whose thoughts she hears, she can also choose if she wants that person to hear her thoughts or not."

Lord Dion straightened right at that moment, his eyes on our High Lady, and then they darted to me, looking surprised. My brow creased, and I looked at her as well. She must have just spoken to him, in his mind, and I wondered what she might have said that would have caused that reaction. She simply smirked a bit, and shook her head.

"We have one more secret to share, Lord Dion, and then we must plan how to keep you here without arousing suspicion. After that," Hiela paused, and the fire in her eyes grew as she met each of our gazes, ending on her mate's. "We discuss our plan to remove Oleander from the throne."

24

A CONSEQUENCE OF IGNORANCE

MY ARMS HANG AT MY SIDES, MY MOUTH SLIGHTLY OPEN AS I stare with furrowed brows at Olin. I can't have understood him correctly. That he plans on bringing *me* to Eshelle.

He stares back at me, eyebrows slightly raised, waiting for a response. When none comes, he shrugs, and looks to the male behind me. "Adathan, pack up," he commands in the Old Language.

There's a snap, and suddenly the only things in the clearing are two packs, the three males, and myself. The abruptness with which this happens, the absolute clarity that this is not an if or a maybe, but definitely happening *right now*, breaks me out of the stasis I'd been in.

I step forward, crossing my arms to hide my shaking hands. "I am *not* going to Eshelle," I tell Olin, making my voice as strong as I can when my throat still feels like it's only half open.

He smirks, rolling his eyes, half-facing me as he looks

around the camp, checking his lackey's work. "Of course you are. That's where I'm taking you, so that's where you're going." He says it slowly, like I'm stupid, and it's a lack of understanding that's causing my refusal.

I take another step, refusing to acknowledge the fear and disgust that try to take hold as I near him. "I am *not. Going. To. Eshelle*," I repeat through my teeth, enunciating as he'd done with me. But instead of annoyance, venom is spit with each word.

He turns to face me fully, and his lips curl up into a smile that does nothing to the coldness in his eyes. "Oh, you are. You only have a choice in whether you come willingly, or if you will be dragged there, unconscious the entire time, only waking when we arrive. I do not have a preference. Actually, that's a lie. I'd rather not have to wait while you walk, or listen while you say such inane things."

My heart hammering, I glare at him. I can't even focus on the degrading way he speaks to and about me, because it's setting in that, if I fail to escape, I truly will have to go to the land of the Fae. "Why are we going there?" I clench my hands into fists against my arms, forcing my voice to remain steady.

"Because it's where we will wed, of course," he replies, reaching to touch my cheek.

I jerk away–from his hand, and his words. "You will not touch me, and I will not marry you."

Faster than I can blink, his hand shoots out and grabs my braid, holding it painfully tight at the base of my skull. His face just inches from mine, Olin whispers, "You will. And I will do what I like. You are lucky that some of the things I like may not be done until our union is sanctified." He pulls me forward so that our bodies are flush together, and reaches his other hand up to touch my cheek. "Two nights ago, you wanted this," he continues, his mouth inches from mine. "You will again. But, make no mistake, what *I* want will always take precedence." He trails his finger down my jaw, and then my neck.

A reminder. That if I fight him, try to keep him from taking what *he* might want, he will hurt me again. Or worse. Part of me trembles, and begs me to back down–to just nod, and agree, and figure out an exit or a fight later. Another part tells me to drive my knee up into his groin to show him I refuse to be scared into compliance. Show him that no matter how hard he hits me, I will keep swinging, too.

But before either of those parts of me can act, Adathan says, "Perhaps we should go, my Lord."

Olin's finger lingers a half second longer on my neck, and then he releases me. "Fine. We should be on our way. We traveled quickly in the night, but since she's awake, it will take us twice as long now. And her friends can't be very far off since we just *had* to make camp." He shoots a glare at Adathan behind me. "Carried her for fifty miles, then decided you were too tired to continue. Ymeda's tits, what good are those muscles for, boy?"

My heart pounds at that distance, traveled in just hours. A distance that the friends he spoke of will have difficulty covering, even if they'd been able to escape the Hall the moment we'd left. I don't hear Adathan respond, if he does at all. I turn away from Olin, and look into the boundless wood before me. And, as I stand on the edge of the space of rock and dirt and grass, staring at the trees before me, I think. Not of an escape; with all three of them alert and already packed, *and* not knowing where I am, escape would be impossible right now. No, instead, I think about my naivety.

Though I'd never needed to learn about them before, I wish that I'd taken more of an interest in the subject of the Fae and their land now. Considering Weaschte and Eshelle don't trade, or communicate–and, until now, wage war–I'd always been told that we didn't need to learn about them. That since Fae hadn't come to our realm, nor us to theirs, in more than a millennium, it would be a waste of time to concern myself with such topics of study. I had so much to learn about my own continent, and the countries within it.

Now, too late, I realize how shortsighted that was. An ideology that I'd gone along with, despite being a person I liked to think of as intelligent. Perhaps it was because I'd known I would never become queen. As a daughter and youngest child, I would never rule Cerasche, and certainly not all of Weaschte. I would never have to command armies, engage in political communication, or promote trade.

But, as with my training, I'd gone out of my way to explain to my parents why it was unfair that my brothers should be allowed to become smarter than me, simply because I was a girl. And, again, they had not been able to give me a good reason as to why that should be.

Not only did I attend the advanced mathematics courses they did; I got better scores than Ben and even Nik in that, literature, and music. Next, I learned about our trade within Weaschte. I'd been taught about the nation's fiscal wellbeing, and how it was maintained. I'd read of how wars had been waged and won in the past.

But those wars had been within our own continent. The only war I learned about between the humans and the Fae had been the Last War, fought to end the slavery of magical and non-magical humans alike. And, with us as the victors, there was very little written in our texts about the Fae side of things.

I'd had no issue with it. No desire to learn about the people who had enslaved us, and then left behind only the wicked ones of their land to steal our own children from us. What I do know—of their senses, their strength, the way they say *majick* instead of *magic*—is all based on my readings of the Last War;

the information only taught to elaborate upon why humans should be forever proud that they'd won.

Other than that, I hadn't been able to think of a good reason to learn of the Fae, or their land. It would be one thing, I'd thought, if the War had been only a few years, maybe even decades, ago. But a thousand years? A time long enough for them to not only have gotten over their loss, but to become accustomed to life without slaves. I could see no reason or possibility for them to come back to Weaschte.

And I'd figured that, even on the off chance there ever were events of trade or otherwise with Eshelle in my lifetime, that would not be my place. I wouldn't be allowed in that room, princess or not. I'd been destined to be a wife and mother, always subservient to whichever lordling I ended up marrying.

Of course, I'd always wanted more than that–but that was the lot I'd known was mine. And, in comparison to the future I somehow landed in at dusk yesterday, that old end seems like a dream now.

I'd learned how to be a good woman, and a good wife. Outside of my extracurricular learning, much of my scholarly education had been consumed by the sciences, with the goal for me to become as learned and practiced as possible in the knowledge and art of healing. I'd never thought my path would divert from the one my bloodline built for me, no matter how much I tested its limits.

Shortsighted. We have faeries in our land; the creatures which steal our babies and replace them with their own. And yet, we never concerned ourselves with their parent land, or the males and females who call it home. People who perhaps know nothing of the actions of the faeries in Weaschte, who may simply be of the same common descent. People who probably have no idea that one of their own has likely just started a war with the land of humans and Mages.

A princess has been taken. Maybe not the heir, but the daughter of the King–and the Queen. A woman whom the male standing just feet behind me murdered for daring to try to protect her child. My heart squeezes in my chest, so painfully tight that I have to focus my attention elsewhere. I must not break.

War is coming. I have been taken. But, *why?*

Olin wants to take me, to marry me. But, why me? Adathan had confirmed that it had always been the plan for me to be their prisoner, but that Olin decided to 'keep me' only after the night we kissed. Not allowing myself to get stuck on that last bit, I wonder why he planned on taking me in the first place. Why start a war with a land that has not been in touch with yours in a thousand years? Is it as simple as Olin is just so completely unhinged that he's doing this purely to end the peace the lands have held for so long? Maybe he truly would like to watch the world burn. And he, the king of the ashes.

They had said nearly as much, in that room above the dark basement where I'd listened, and, subsequently, killed. And if it's true that he wishes to rule, then the logic can only follow that he wants me to be his queen.

I have to shove that thought aside (it's easy, since there's no possibility of me allowing that to come to pass) because the larger question still remains. There's still no answer as to *why*, outside of general madness, and evil. Though I believe him to be both of those things, he's also proven to be cold and calculated enough that I would truly have to be as stupid as he treats me to think that I'm a random choice. He picked me to be his prisoner, and then his queen, for a reason.

It might be the power that my family holds. Our magic, our wealth, the love of our people. He must want them–not willing to stop with one continent, he wants to conquer two. And I am the key to that. Otherwise, it would have taken armies for him to take Weaschte. Armies he doesn't have, if he's not anyone's king except for the males in this clearing.

My mother would have been the preferred choice, of course. Iris even more so as second in line. I don't think that their marriages would have been much of a deterrent if he had wanted them. But they would have been the more obvious targets–that's why it's me. I'm easier. I'd literally been anyone's for the taking. *Had been* taken, even, after slipping through the unguarded pathway I frequented.

Which also adds up–Olin knew all of this because of Artur. Adathan. I'd thought that just because he wouldn't look me in the eye, he must have been shy, or rude. That, if he couldn't even do that, then surely he didn't watch me elsewhere. But the male had infiltrated our home, and done just that for a whole year. Surveilled me as I'd walked the halls and the grounds with guards, and without, and probably easily learned of my trips outside of the castle walls. I have to give my family and close friends credit; the fact that he never learned of the extent of my training is proof of their silence on the matter. Otherwise, I might have been overpowered in that basement, and well on my way to Eshelle already.

But my mom would still be alive.

I suck in a quiet breath, holding back the thickness that rises in my chest. It pushes my heart against my ribs, and makes my bruised throat feel so constricted I can hardly get a breath down. I press my tongue to the roof of my mouth, pushing down the sob that wants to break free from my throat, and swallow the tears that threaten to bead around my eyes. My hands clench into fists, so tight that my fingernails dig deep into the skin of my palms. I focus on that pain, squeezing even harder to pull myself out of the agony of this grief.

When skin breaks under my nails, the sting of it grants me just enough leverage to wrest those emotions, and tether them once more to the back of my mind. They will not be locked up; will always be just a thought away. But I will keep them leashed until–if there's ever–a time where I am safe enough to release them.

A throat clears behind me, and, after schooling my features into dull annoyance, I turn. Adathan stands a few feet behind me, a pack on his back, and his face a twin of what I hope mine is.

"We're heading out now," he says, nodding back to where the other two have already started walking. Away from me...

In a blink, Adathan closes the distance between us. I have to force myself to stay in place as he appears just inches away, his face lowered closer to mine. "You wouldn't have enough time," he tells me in Ceraschen, his voice so low I can barely hear.

"I don't know what you're talking about," I lie, refusing to take a step back, even as his breath hisses over my face.

"Sure you don't, sweetheart." Too fast for me to stop, he grabs my arm, and begins to pull me along, following the rest of the group. Though my bicep is thicker with muscle than most women's, his hand loops easily around, so that his fingers touch his thumb. The band of a thin golden ring on his forefinger presses slightly into my flesh.

"You will not get away." A promise.

Daring to take my eyes off the root-thick ground surrounding the clearing that we leave behind, I look up to glare up at him, and open my mouth–

And of course–*of course*, the toe of my boot catches on a particularly high root, and I stumble. The hand on my arm quickly pulls me back, and my side collides with his as he rights me. He says nothing as the two males ahead of us turn at the noise. Olin raises his brows, and the male beside me shrugs. And that's that. They just keep on walking. It would almost be comical, almost be a relief that they don't care, don't comment, if it wasn't *them* doing it.

In silence, I keep my eyes on the ground, on my feet that move over the treacherous roots, each step bringing me closer to a future that is even more uncertain than the one I'd been facing yesterday at dusk.

25

COLINA

DION - 21 YEARS EARLIER

AFTER THE MEETING WITH THE HIGH LORD AND HIGH LADY OF Sabrian, I walked with Lady Ciaragen through the gardens. She'd ordered all attendants to vacate the grounds, and each of them had disappeared inside, leaving us alone amidst the peonies.

We strolled along the cobblestone pathway, passing the wrought brass benches, and shady trees. She kept an energy of silent support as I thought through all that I'd been told. The gallantry that my mother had raised me to have came out now in the form of my arm bending almost involuntarily to accommodate a space for her hand. I was so lost in my pondering that I hardly noticed how she didn't hesitate to wrap her hand just above my elbow, over my bicep. I waited for her to ask me what I was thinking, or to pull me to the side to sit, but she didn't. She simply held onto me, that hand curling around me more tightly as we walked, its pressure sweet and reassuring. She kept pace with me in silence, and looked around at the flowers surrounding us.

I was relieved that, based on the ease of her breaths, and the lack of hurried glances in my direction, she knew I wasn't angry that they had kept so much from me. I understood completely why they'd done so, and was truly just...honored that they had trusted me at all, regardless of the timeline. I wasn't sure when, exactly, I'd fully turned against Oleander, but there was no sense of betrayal in my heart as I recognized that I would take the secrets I'd learned today to my grave.

I'd known for a long time that he didn't deserve loyalty. But that was the thing about animals in cages. If they learned that they could only grow to be as big as it allowed, and believed that they could only have an impact within its walls, then they eventually stopped trying to become all they were meant to be. Strong, willful...free.

The first piece of the puzzle was to concede that I'd been one such animal. Worse than a big cat; at least they growled and snarled, and clawed. I, on the other hand, had allowed myself to get lost in my need to not feel, and, if I was being completely honest with myself, in my self-pity. I'd hidden behind the desire to have some kind of value: that value being loyalty. But I knew that I'd just been scared, too detached from my life and any purpose I might have made of it, because I believed that I could never have my own; I'd given up my only chance at that decades ago. Really, I had stopped trying to find one, perhaps fearing what would happen if I did.

But here, in Sabrian, I felt inspired to serve a cause greater than myself for the first time in decades. New possibilities were opening themselves up before me with each passing day. Each one promising to grant me more strength and courage–and happiness. If only I continued to be brave enough to work for those things. To become a male worthy of this city, its people, and...

I looked over to Lady Ciaragen, and, sensing my gaze, she turned to me. Those remarkable eyes held mine, a question in them. But I had one for her first.

"Will you take me into the city?" I asked.

A wide, stunning smile spread across her face.

⇹

We'd changed into casual clothing–I, wearing trousers, and a cotton shirt that I'd rolled the sleeves of. She, in a sort of one-piece outfit that tried and failed to hide her figure, and looked incredibly comfortable. We both donned something called *sneakers*, which were shaped like my shoes, but more rounded, and laced up the center. Also, very comfortable.

Since she was still technically my guard, we were walking towards the castle gates alone, no additional accompaniment needed. I considered asking if Nuria and Jolie would be joining us, but couldn't bring myself to voice the question. I was excited to have this time to spend with her. Just her. I wanted to ask her questions, learn about her, and have her voice any questions she still had of me after those she asked last night. Neither of us thinking of what others listening to us might say.

So, as the attendants opened the gates, we–just the two of us–stepped into the city of Colina.

The last time I'd traveled through these streets, I had been looked upon with mistrust; with hatred. Though I was sure that some would remember my face, I hoped that most didn't. Because I had also spent that time in these roads and avenues staring above the heads of the people, trying my best to avoid their glares. I hadn't greeted them, hadn't patronized any shops. While some might say I couldn't be blamed for not wanting to dismount in the face of all that loathing, I didn't like that their only memory of me was that of a male who portrayed himself as above them.

In truth, I hadn't wanted to meet their stares because I'd known they were right to feel how they did.

Now, I'd had time in this place to start becoming the male I might have always been, if only I'd been granted the environment to do so. I believed that my mother had planned for me to become this person, when I was a boy. She had always called me her *sweet son*, as she'd brushed my hair back from my forehead, her eyes shining with love. For so long, I'd abhorred thinking of her, unable to keep myself from wondering what she might have made of me if she were still living. Seeing her *sweet son* grown, a killer, as his father had always wanted.

But with each passing day here, with these people, my friends, I was getting farther from that person, and coming back to the one she'd known I could be. And how she would have loved it here–with its castle of pale stone, gardens of flowers, and lush green rolling hills. How she would have loved these people.

The people that had awakened me, and allowed me to realize that I wanted to face my actions. When I hadn't been reading in my room these recent nights, I'd been thinking of my past choices. Processing, and allowing the feelings that came with them–the judgment, the shame, the sadness–to pass, if I could. And, if I couldn't, I held them close to my heart until the strength, the bravery I worked to gain each day, were mighty enough to face them.

That inner work was my responsibility. But I knew I wouldn't have begun it if not for these people. Not their inspiration, necessarily, as they hadn't directly made me do anything– but the way they lived so courageously, so passionately. Maybe the real start had been me desiring that for myself.

I looked over at Lady Ciaragen now as we strolled down the less populated area of Colina. As she walked, her hair bounced, and a small smile that I didn't think she was aware of pulled at the corners of her mouth. Not wanting that expression to turn, I moved my gaze once more to the path ahead of us.

It was peaceful, walking in silence beside her. I didn't feel the need to fill that void; ask questions, or babble about the upcoming activities. I enjoyed hearing only the light crunching of our footsteps over the stones, and the chattering and music of the city that was becoming louder as we continued into its belly.

The journey on horseback to the castle, when I'd arrived, had felt like an eternity. The walk back into the city felt like minutes.

As we continued, the slightly narrow paths began to widen, cobblestone sidewalks framing them. The streets themselves had been spattered with a house or two every several acres for the first bit of our journey, but now the homes were interspersed with shops. Made of brown, white, or umber brick, with brass roofs, some of which had oxidized to a calming green. Avenues branched off the main road, and I could see more homes further down those, each with sufficient land, and space for a family.

So unlike Matriel, Oschverre. The city proper was packed with stores, and the homes that weren't squeezed between them, too small for even a couple, were far from it to avoid the stench of urine and garbage. And even those homes were packed together, their fences tall, their outer walls just feet from each other.

Colina smelled like spices, and fresh bread. The aromas from perfume shops and chandleries wafted through the air, and from the bouquets of cut flowers about a quarter mile down the road.

Music trickled out into the street from shops, and laughter and conversation accompanied it. Fae and faeries mingled, no separation of the races or species as seen in the capital. All doorways, I realized, were wide and tall enough to accommodate wings, and great heights. We passed by them slowly, and I wondered who had decreased our pace first, her, or me. I would wager the latter, since I felt as though there wasn't enough time to take everything in, and I wanted to.

"See any place you'd like to go into?" Lady Ciaragen asked me, drawing my attention from the shops, from the people, from the abundance of *life* bursting through the streets.

I looked over at her, and that small smile was still on her face, even as she gazed at me. It made me grin back.

"All of them," I told her honestly. The bookstores, patisseries, boutiques, salons. Each one teeming with a sort of joy that came with doing what you loved. The happiness was not overwhelming, or disconcerting, as it had been when I arrived. Then, I hadn't been prepared to see what life could be like when the ruler of a land cared for it, and its people. Knowing I would have to return to a country where that was not the case, had me unwilling to accept that this joy was anything other than a facade that would eventually fall into disrepair, like too many Eshellen countries had over the past century.

Now, with the prospect of being able to stay–after talking extensively about what that would entail this morning, after Hiela's confessions–I was able to look at the smiles around me, and take them as they were: genuinely happy.

Lady Ciaragen's grin widened, and she said, "Well, then, we have quite a full day ahead of us." Then she wrapped her hand around my arm as she had earlier in the gardens, and pulled me through the nearest open door.

From that point until lunch, we did not sit. We wandered into so many shops, I lost count. When our hands and arms were full of bags and boxes, she asked me if I wanted to send them back to the castle. After I'd expressed concern about someone having to lug so much, she'd snapped, and everything had disappeared. She'd sent it all to her chambers, she said, explaining that the simplicity of the majick was the same as that which I used to pull objects from my pocket realm. You needed specific majickal clearance to be able to send anything into the castle or its grounds, but from there it was just knowing the layout of the space enough to send the items to where you actually wanted them to be.

"Instead of in the toilet," she'd finished, and I'd laughed, because her face told me that wasn't an imagined example.

When our stomachs started grumbling, we made our way to a restaurant that she claimed had some of the best food she'd ever tasted. We now sat across from each other at a rectangular table, small enough that it would surely only fit our plates, and the basket of bread already in the center. So small in fact that, beneath the table, my toes had already accidentally bumped hers twice.

"You have to try the bread," she said, reaching up to loop her hair into a ribbon that she pulled until the curls were all gathered on top of her head. The muscles in her arms flexed as she tied a bow, and a few shorter spirals popped out around her ears and temples.

Trying to ignore how adorable I found those little curls, I replied "What a silly thing to say."

Her brows furrowed, that line forming between them. "Why is that?"

"As if someone could sit at a table with free bread, and *not* eat it. Ridiculous."

She laughed, and I couldn't help the grin that broke my falsely serious expression as a result. "Fair enough. But do you notice anything about that bread?" She sipped her water, still not touching the object of our conversation as she held my gaze over the rim of her glass.

I looked at the loaf, and poked it once. The crust crunched under my finger, but did not yield. Not sensing anything out of the ordinary, though, I looked back up at Ciaragen, and raised a brow. She laughed again at my expression, and took pity on me. "I don't see a knife on the table, do you?"

Of course, I examined the table at once, and realized that she was right. Not even the usual set of silverware lay on our little table. "It's because you're not supposed to cut it. Too many tourists used the regular knives to cut the bread, thinking they weren't given a serrated edge by mistake." She shrugged, and picked up one of the oblong rolls. "You *break* it," she said, and then twisted her hands so that the loaf was torn in two, a half in each palm. Steam erupted from the innards, and the *smell...*

She handed one half to me, and then dipped a corner of hers into the small dish of olive oil beside the basket. She tilted it so that no oil dripped onto the table, and then bit into it. A moan slipped up her throat as she chewed, and closed her eyes. A completely innocent reaction to clearly delicious food, but, gods–

Quickly, hoping she couldn't scent or sense any of what I felt in response to that pleasured sound from her, I copied her, dipping my half of the bread into the oil, and taking a bite. And then I groaned as the flavors of the bread, the oil, and the spices mingled on my tongue.

"Right?" she asked, and I nodded, not willing to empty my mouth enough to respond verbally. We finished both rolls, and all of the seasoned oil, in minutes.

When the bread basket was empty, the waitress arrived. A faerie female with pale purple skin, and the blackest eyes and hair. She had longer limbs than a Fae, but otherwise was similarly built–if not for the serpentine tail protruding from beneath her frock.

"Good afternoon," she greeted us with a smile. "My name is Acacia. What can I get you?"

Only then did I realize that I hadn't even looked at the menus set to the side of the table. I was about to answer apologetically, and ask if she could come back in a few minutes, but Lady Ciaragen looked at me and asked, "Do you trust me?"

"Yes," was my only–*the* only–response.

She turned back to Acacia, smiling at her. "Could we both have the fish, prepared to the chef's liking? And to drink, two glasses of the Ceraschen sparkling white?"

"Of course," Acacia said with another grin, not writing it down as I remembered waiters did in some of the restaurants I'd once been to in Oschverre.

But something caught my attention as the waitress departed. "Ceraschen?" I asked of the Lady across from me.

"Yes. It's the best wine you'll have aside from Sabriani, but I might be biased there."

I smirked. "No, I just thought that we no longer traded with Weaschte. That any trade between the continents had ended nearly a thousand years ago."

"It did."

I raised my brows, for obvious reasons, and she leaned forward in her seat, enough so that her face was nearly past the midway point of the table. Taking her cue, I pitched myself forward slightly as well, but only just so, not wanting to make her uncomfortable by being too close.

"We began trading with the eastern countries of Weaschte almost ten years ago," she whispered. "Hielo himself went to the capital, and brokered a deal with the human king. But it remains a secret in both realms. For now."

She didn't have to explain why. It was a secret because if

Oleander found out, not only would he be furious enough to kill our High Lord simply for the fact that his country had more advanced trade agreements than Oschverre. No, if he knew that Weaschte was once more open to the Fae, he would take advantage of that, just as his ancestors did, likely causing countless deaths in both continents.

And it was only for now, because we hoped Oleander would not be king of Eshelle for much longer.

⇹

I was so full after lunch that I'd needed to remain seated for half an hour afterwards to avoid getting a stitch in my side. We moved to one of the benches just a couple of doors down so as to not keep Acacia from getting new customers. Lady Ciaragen had eaten nearly as much as I, and asked Acacia for some of the bread to go, which the faerie had been more than happy to get for her.

We visited even more shops, and it occurred to me that not once had I glimpsed an angry stare, or an annoyed look from anyone during this time. All shopkeepers and owners had been pleasant at worst, delighted at best. No stranger glared, and no heavy silences pierced the endless stream of conversation throughout the city. Either they didn't remember me from my time parading through the streets three weeks ago, or–and more likely, I thought–they knew the female at my side, and had long trusted her, just as I had come to.

Finally, when the sun crested to its early evening position, we began to make our way back to the castle. Lady Ciaragen had sent our things ahead of us after we left the last shop, so we now only walked with the bread from lunch. We each picked at a roll as we strolled back up the cobbled path, not wanting to ruin our appetites for supper, but unable to keep from eating it as the delicious smell was present even after hours in the paper bag.

As we passed through the gates, I realized that, with the time it would take for us to climb the stairs and walk the halls, we would be just barely on time for dinner. We still wore our comfortable clothes, and sneakers.

"My Lady, should we go to our chambers to change?" I asked.

"Why? They know we've been out."

"Yes, but I'm not sure this is entirely appropriate evening wear." I gestured down at myself.

She snorted, and rolled her eyes before gripping my arm, and pulling me up the stairs towards the hallway that would lead us to the balcony. She seemed to be more and more comfortable with touching me, and that thrilled me, however platonically she did so. Throughout the day, I had savored every time the back of her hand had brushed mine, or her hip had nudged my thigh as we'd had to squeeze past others on the sidewalk. She'd held my arm a handful of times, and squeezed once when we'd watched a particularly skilled street performer play his violin.

The comfort with which she did all of these things gave me a feeling of warmth that I hadn't experienced in a very long time. I didn't dare touch her in return, however much I craved to hold her hand, twine my fingers through those curls, or to feel her breath against my lips as I had when she'd whispered of changing the world.

Truly, I knew that I wanted even more than that. But, I wasn't foolish enough to believe any of those things would ever be attainable. So, I quieted my body's reactions to her as severely as I had done with the power that boiled in my blood for over sixty years. I supposed the two were becoming quite the same, in that sense. Both constant companions–my want for her, and my power. Two things that I tried not to think about, because either one could be the end of me if not approached carefully. Because, regardless of the words our High Lady had whispered in my mind earlier, Lady Ciaragen certainly did not want me to feel what I was starting to feel towards her.

As we reached the wide glass doors to the balcony, we saw that the High Lord and High Lady had not yet arrived. Lady Ciaragen strode to the baluster, and leaned her elbows on it, looking out to the gardens, and the hills beyond them. I stood beside her, a respectful distance away, doing the same.

"Dion," she said softly, and I saw her head turn to me in the corner of my eye. The sound of my name on her lips, without any pleasantries or titles before it, sent a shiver down my spine that I had to suppress. I looked over at her, and was unprepared for the sight of the golden evening sun glimmering off the warm brown of her skin, and the way it made the blue of her eyes seem even deeper.

I cleared my throat, but my voice still came out a bit rough. "Yes?"

She moved two steps closer to me, and resumed her stance, seeming not to notice that her elbow touched mine as she did so.

"I had a lovely day. With you," she told me, those steady eyes holding mine. "I can't remember the last time I *really* explored the city."

I grinned. "I think you may need to reconsider your career. Perhaps you should be a professional tour guide for Colina."

She laughed, and nudged my arm with her shoulder. "Perhaps."

As she moved to look forward once more, I gathered my nerve, and said, "I had a lovely day with you as well, my Lady."

Her smile was gentle, and so was her voice. "Call me Ciaragen."

26

THE GOLD THREAD

THEA - PRESENT

THE PACE WITH WHICH I'M FORCED TO WALK THROUGH THE PINE-thick wilderness to keep up with the males ahead of us is tiresome, even to me, after a few hours. My legs burn from stepping over foot-high roots, and bracing to go up and down hills. All of which almost distracts me from the need I've been avoiding for eight-thousand, two-hundred, and-twelve steps. I'd started counting when I felt the pressure in my bladder, and refused the water Adathan offered me every thirty minutes or so since.

But that pressure isn't just uncomfortable now. It's painful, and so persistent that I know my options are down to requesting that we stop, or soiling myself. And, of the two, I know which one would be more embarrassing.

I clear my throat softly, and say at a volume just as low, "I need to...relieve myself." My cheeks flame as I look up into the face of my captor, and my companion during these hours in the woods. He looks down at me now, and nods. I think he might not say anything, might not tell the other two so that they can all just stand there and *listen* while I do my business. But, of course, he looks ahead, and whistles sharply. The males stop at once, and turn towards us.

"Rest stop," he tells them, his deep voice a regular volume, since the twenty yards between us and them mean little to Fae ears. Even from this distance, I can see that Olin's eyes shift to me, and rove over my body. Only when he's looked his fill, when the churning in my stomach is almost worse than the feeling in my belly, does he look back to Adathan, and nod.

Adathan turns back to me, and gestures with a jerk of his chin towards the woods to the right of our path. "Go on, then."

Relieved that he doesn't insist that he has to come with me, to ensure that I don't run, I spin on my heel without a word, and walk into the trees off of the path, looking for somewhere private. Or, as private as can be with Fae ears and eyes so close to me.

While the roots of the trees nearly carpet the ground, the trunks are actually a bit sparse. Even several yards in, I can still see parts of all three males. I turn back toward the trees, looking for pines with lower boughs that might offer some concealment, and a light breeze that smells of oak and embers blows escaped strands of my hair over my face. When I brush them away, I finally find a cluster of trees ten more yards to my right that will do.

It's humiliating to say the least, though, to pull my trousers down to my ankles, and squat in the middle of the forest, knowing they can hear. All I can do when I stand, pulling them back up hastily, is hope that neither sickness nor discomfort seizes me later from being so vulnerable to whatever the ground below me may have held. Without my healing, I would be left to suffer with them until they ran their course.

"Come now, Princess," Olin shouts when I'm making my way back to Adathan. Who, to my dismay, now stands with his friends. Though I don't enjoy walking with him, I prefer being alone beside him to alone beside all three of them. But, his master probably summoned him while I'd been doing my business, and, like a good dog, he'd come. A dog that had more of an ominous than companionable presence as he'd walked with me, but quiet. If it weren't for the hulking mass of him, I might have forgotten he was next to me at all sometimes.

In no rush to be another dog to Olin's call, I walk at a slow diagonal towards them, picking my way over the moss, rocks, and roots. When I'm close enough to see the exact colors of their eyes–hazel, brown, and gold–the monster housing the hazel set strides for me. His previously graceful steps crash through the last of the woods between us, and only his mask of calm keeps me from realizing that he's going to grab me before his hand is painfully tight around my wrist. I gasp in surprise before I can stop myself, and he pulls me roughly the rest of the distance.

He doesn't release me as he turns, though his face is still stoic. More frightening than his wrath in the clearing had been, in its ability to deceive me. There's no anger in his eyes, no rageful twist to his mouth. The expression of complete serenity paired with the contrastingly aggressive physicality is jarring, and I have to work to keep the fear from my face.

"Come when called, or next time it will be your hair that I grab," he warns me, and squeezes my wrist enough that I think just an ounce more of pressure would snap it.

"I'm not a dog that you can summon at your will," I reply, but my thin, pained voice shakes as I attempt to keep it steady.

He uses the grip on my wrist to drag me closer, and says, "You might not be a dog, but continue to disobey me, and I'll have you begging nonetheless." Black flashes in the veins in his temples, the capillaries in his eyes, and is gone in a blink. Another warning–a reminder that his physical strength is not the only power he can wield over me. The majick that shattered windows, that killed Hanna–

CRACK.

I think for a second that it's my wrist that has broken, that he finally squeezed hard enough, and the pain signal just hasn't yet reached my brain. But then his hand falls away, and I see that two of his fingers are bent at unnatural angles. My eyes widen as I realize what I've done, and, after the heartbeat of surprise he quickly masks, some primal, animal part of me trembles at the look in the predator's eyes before me when he raises them from his disfigured hand.

"Gadsby," he calls, bracing those bones within the fingers of his other hand. The male walks over at once–a hulking mass of muscle with blond hair, and dull brown eyes that hold only boredom and malice.

"Break her pinky, then her thumb. Ten seconds in between so she can thoroughly feel it. Sixty seconds, and then Adathan can heal her since she's refusing to do it herself." He looks at me, and his brow furrows. My stomach is turning, but I refuse to beg, if that's what he's waiting for. But he only goes on, "Do not heal yourself during that minute." He flicks his gaze to the golden-eyed male. "If she does, rebreak them, until she gets through the whole sixty seconds. That ought to make her think about her actions," Then he turns from me, quietly cursing at his mending hand.

Too fast for me to stop, run, snatch my hand back–whatever I might have done to prevent this–a huge hand grabs my aching wrist, while another pinches my little finger and bends it in a way it's not supposed to bend.

I scream. There's no adrenaline to lighten it as there had been when I'd broken my own bones in that basement. Tears spring in my eyes, and beg to be released, but I can't. I yank furiously against his hold, knowing what's next, but my cowardly magic has abandoned me once more, leaving me defenseless as–

The sound and feel of my thumb breaking makes bile burn up my throat. The male steps back, but not fast enough to avoid the water and stomach acid I spew onto his boots. He grunts in disgust, and backhands my face hard enough that my teeth cut into my cheek, and, already dizzy with pain, I fall to the ground.

Though I don't see him, I hear the male's vomit-covered boots crunch away from me over the pine needles. My face is half in the dirt, the other half covered by my hair, and I can't pick myself up just yet. Not for lack of strength, or because of the pain–but because if I move my eyes, even just a bit, I won't be able to prevent the tears from falling.

Not yet. Not for this.

"Fifty-three more seconds," is all Olin says from somewhere down the path. "Do not heal her before the minute is up, Adathan. Catch up with us when you're done."

I hear two sets of footsteps depart, but the third makes no sound, wherever he is. So I don't expect it when hands brush my arms, seeming ready to lift me–

"*Don't. Touch. Me,*" I spit with so much hatred that, against all odds, the hands leave. When I'm certain no tears will escape, I move to prop myself up on my elbows, careful not to put any pressure on my right hand. I get to my knees, and then finally I'm standing. The last male stares at me with unreadable eyes, large arms crossed over his chest, knuckles white with how tightly his hands are fisted.

The pain in my hand is nauseating, but there's nothing left in my stomach. I feel more blood running down the same cheek as earlier today, and know it will scar now, having reopened twice. All I can think is: *good.*

"Twenty more seconds," the male says.

Wordlessly, I spit a mouthful of blood and saliva on the ground in front of his boots. He doesn't even twitch in response.

What seems like an eternity later, he steps toward me, uncrossing his arms. In the silence only broken by the breeze rustling the pine branches, he holds out a broad hand. I stare at it for a long moment before shifting my eyes up, but no other part of me moves.

"Can you give me your hand?" I'm surprised to again hear the Ceraschen dialect pass his lips rather than the Old Language. His tone isn't impatient, or angry. There's no inflection at all to tell me what might be going on behind those eyes. This close, I can see that they're lighter than gold; almost champagne-like in hue, or like the sun shining off the sea. A pretty color to mask the monster within.

I don't move, but neither does he. Regardless of the agony in my hand screaming through my mind, I know that I won't be the one to lose this battle of wills.

And I'm right, because he speaks first. "In case you hadn't noticed, sweetheart, he is not a patient male. If we don't follow soon, he will come back to see what's holding us up. And the result will be less fun for you than letting me touch your hand to heal it."

I don't let the doubt, or the fear show. But, no matter how much I don't want to accommodate *any* of them, I won't be able to fight or run if I have two broken fingers in my dominant hand. At least not well.

So, I'll accept this small defeat in order to stand a chance to win later. His hand still waits before me, so I place mine within it, trying not to look at the ways my fingers are unnaturally bent, choosing to look into his eyes with a steel of my own as if to say *'I'll win next time'*. His other hand wraps around mine, more delicately than I would have expected. Large palms and long fingers swallow up my hand and wrist, and a soft yellow light glows between his hands, and warms my skin as he holds my gaze, unmoved by the malice in it.

Seconds later, when he lifts his top hand from mine, and I know it's done, I look to find my fingers all in order. I lift them quickly off of his, and while I'm grateful the pain is gone, he'll be waiting a while if he expects to hear a thank you pass my lips.

But he only drops his hand, and says, "To catch up, I will either need to carry you, and run myself, or you can run beside me."

I glare at him. "I choose option two." But, he's already turning from me, pausing mid stride. Waiting for me to go first.

Huffing an irritated breath through my nose, I set off at a brisk pace, keeping my eyes on the ground for those treacherous roots. He keeps up easily, which I have to remind myself is to be expected. Even without the difference in our species, my lack of food, combined with my body being beaten and broken, means I have every reason to be moving slowly. And yet, I find myself increasing my speed, just to prove that I can.

Only when I can once again see the other two males do I remember why I may have wanted to take it easy. My stride stutters and slows, and Adathan's responds in kind, his Fae body reacting quickly to my change in pace, rather than blowing past me.

As the two of us approach Olin and Gadsby, I ponder how much I've changed in the past three days, since I took my first life. Because all I can think, as they turn to look at us, is how good it would feel to plunge a sword into each of their guts. How lovely it would be to see their lifesblood pour out of them, and watch the light leave their eyes. To use what Amahd taught me, along with my grief-fueled rage, to kill them all.

Then my stomach rumbles, and gory visions of revenge and

satisfaction dissipate as I'm forced to remember myself, and my position. To remember that I am one human woman, surrounded by three Fae males. That I'm hungry, and exhausted, and in pain everywhere but my right hand.

"Hungry, Princess?" Olin asks, a brow raising, and an amused smirk curling his lips.

I keep my lips closed, lifting my chin–straining the bruises his hands left on my neck this morning. His eyes find them, too, and I watch in disgust as a pleased look flashes, and lingers on his face. He walks toward me, and those bruises, the cuts on my face and shoulder, and a phantom pain in my hand all beg me to curve my shoulders, to take a step back and submit. But I ignore them all, standing my ground and staring him down as he stops just a foot from me.

"I won't make you say yes," he says quietly, and lifts his hand to stroke a knuckle down the line of my throat. Only the pain from that simple touch keeps me from reacting as I watch a disturbing hunger fill his eyes. Not the kind I'm feeling, but something that forces me to lock down my body and hide the deep horror before it can show on my face. He'd said something earlier about needing sanctity, being unable to pursue his *wants* without it, but when would that resolve falter?

He runs that knuckle back up my neck, and I have to work to keep from swallowing, even as bile rises in my throat. No food, but the acid burns my esophagus all the same. His eyelids lower as he moves his gaze to my mouth, and I think he might try to kiss me–try, because I won't let him, no matter what he or his lackeys may do to me after.

"Shall we hunt, my Lord?"

Adathan's question makes Olin pause with his hand under my jaw, and his face just inches from mine. Not so much as breathing as he continues to gaze at me, my heart hammers in my chest so hard I know they can hear it.

"Yes," he finally answers, and releases me. Only after he turns, and steps away from me do I unclench my jaw and release a too-shaky breath. "There should be small game within the immediate vicinity. Gadsby and I will hunt. You stay here with her. I could use a moment to...clear my head." He throws a look over his shoulder my way, his eyes flicking once up and down my body before he reaches Gadsby, and they set off into the forest in opposite directions.

I squeeze my hands into fists to hide their trembling, and look anywhere but where the remaining male stands on the path beside me. I'm feeling too much–disgust and fear blend together inside me, and my heart rages at it all. Energy is building, and I recognize the feeling I've gotten so often before breakings. This riot of emotions comes together, and my magic expels it in the same chaos and pain from which it stems.

And beneath it I finally find the thread of my healing. Gone these past hours, as though something far darker had flowed through my veins instead. But it's there now, glowing gold in a sea of black shadows, resting. And just as I would weave a thread through a needle, so do I pick up this thread of life, of *me*, and weave it back through myself.

The moment I do so, everything comes into such focus. I almost think I can feel the roots growing beneath my feet, sense the hearts of the woodland creatures upon the ground. The heart of the male beside me thumps in a steady, even beat, and my body buzzes with the awareness of my injuries.

I halt it there, not allowing it to seek out my cuts and bruises. It's been noticed that I haven't healed myself, and I want to keep them thinking that it's been a choice, and not out of my control. Because I can't help but wonder, if they think I will heal all that they inflict on me, what will they believe is permissible then?

It's clear that the male still with me has healing abilities, but they must not be very strong if Olin has only had him heal me once. I don't think this from any delusion that he cares for me or my pain, but only because he clearly likes me pretty, and I'm willing to bet that the bruises and cuts on my face are not. And, if he's still so lecherous when I look like this, I'm sure it would be much worse if my skin were unmarked.

All of that, though, doesn't compare to the knowledge that the scar on my face is deserved. Even if it would have no impact on those around me, I still wouldn't heal it.

"We'll reach the cliffs soon," Adathan says from beside me, once again speaking Ceraschen, breaking me from the line of thought that has my heart weighing painfully in my chest. I look over at him to find his expression utterly bored; uninterested in keeping watch over the human while his friends go off and hunt for our lunch.

My brows furrow. "The cliffs are over one hundred miles from Castle Cerasche," I tell him. "You went fifty last night, and we've gone maybe ten so far today."

"He lied. We went more than seventy in the night. Twenty or so to go, now. In ten, the woods will clear, and travel will be even faster. Ten more, and we'll be at the cliffs. And make no mistake—he intends for us to reach them by midday tomorrow."

Swallowing the dread that builds within me as he speaks, I ask him quietly, "Why are you telling me this?"

His gaze moves away from mine then. "Because I knew someone once with a similar start to her story," he replies, and doesn't elaborate. In fact, he seems entirely content to leave me to stew on what possibly could have happened to this woman. To draw my own conclusions, and use this information—for what? I can't escape, and I will not die unless I can take his master with me. I'm *stuck*. I am alone, and shattered, and far more scared than I let myself believe.

To avoid feeling all of those things, I step up to Adathan

with a cruel smile twisting my lips. I have to crane my neck to look into his eyes, but I put the same energy into my glare as I would if I were looking down my nose at him. His gaze holds mine, and within it is a front of impassiveness that guards whatever impact my glare, or my words might have on him.

"Whatever happened to her was because of you. Whatever happens to me will be because of *you*. And if you can't find it in your pitiful black heart to care, well, I suppose that's my problem, and not yours. But know that when he beats me, rapes me, kills me, and you do *nothing. Again.* Know that he will not be the only one I take with me when I die."

27

LOOK AT ME, WAITING

DION - 21 YEARS EARLIER

SWEAT RAN ACROSS MY BROW AS CIARAGEN AND I WENT AT IT FOR the fourth time this hour.

She'd been trying to teach me how to shield my mind for the past five days. During that time, no court member, aside from the group I'd been introduced to on my first morning here, had been invited to the castle.

Now that I knew the truth, I had to learn how to mentally shield myself before court could be held again. I was already practiced in changing my thoughts; I'd had to be, so that none would find out about Oleander's powerlessness. It was simpler in that castle, as the king had either killed those who might have learned his secret, or ensured no mindworkers were under his roof. Except the one.

Yes, I was good at not thinking about things I shouldn't. My first slip in decades had been here, as I looked out at Colina that first night.

I valued this secret much more highly than I did that one. Cared infinitely more for the people who needed me to keep it. And where not thinking of it might fail–as much as I hoped it wouldn't–a mental shield had to be there to protect what I now knew.

As I looked at my teacher, her curls piled atop her head, those small pieces poking out adorably around her face, I rephrased my thought. I was good at not thinking about *most* things I shouldn't.

"I still can't believe they don't teach you this in the capital," Ciaragen said, sitting across from me on the velvet couch in the library, her legs folded up beneath her as she watched me try to shield my mind. Each night I was tested by our High Lady, to see what progress I'd made that day. While my mind was not as open as it had been when I'd arrived almost a month ago, she told me last night, the wall I'd been working to build was more of a fence. The gate was locked, but the fence itself wasn't whole. She could 'jump it', as they phrased it.

"If there are any mindworkers in the capital, they're either employed by Oleander, or they're dead," I told Ciaragen. She'd asked me two days ago to stop mincing my words when speaking of Oleander, or of my past. So, here I was, being point-blank about another atrocity committed by the current king.

She shrugged, acknowledging that, and reached to pluck a grape from the bunch in the bowl that sat on the center table. The late morning sun streamed in through the numerous windows, and shattered off of the crystals of the chandelier that hung high in the domed space. Facets of light shone on almost every surface, dust motes floating in the sweeping beams of golden yellow. Those facets glowed on Ciaragen, and some-times when she looked or leaned a certain way, a fragment of it would land on her eyes, illuminating the deep blue so that I could see all of the tones–from navy to flecks of aquamarine.

Another shard of light fell now onto her bare shoulder as she moved. The sweater she wore draped across her chest, and the left sleeve seemed unhappy to stay at the edge of her collar bone, where she kept tugging it back into place. The skin there looked so soft, the rich tone of it just as inviting as the scent of vanilla and bergamot that came off her every time she fixed that sleeve.

It was getting increasingly harder to pretend I wasn't attracted to her. More difficult with every day that we spent together, just the two of us, as it had been for nearly a week between breakfast and supper.

Her smiles and laughs had become more frequent. We both avoided talking about our departed parents, and the males responsible, but otherwise no topic had been off-limits. We talked about her time in the military, and mine. I learned that she'd never broken a bone–a fact of which she was very proud. But when it came to discussing her favorites, my face had heated when she realized I knew many of them. Chocolate, peonies, bread, yellow–not bright like a duckling, but rather the soft tones of the sunrise.

She asked me about my favorite things in turn, and it had been pitiful how little I'd known about myself. It had been so long since I cared to think about my favorite color, or food, or... anything. When it became clear that those were things I would have to discover about myself, she'd smiled so brightly it had outshone the daylight, and told me that she would show me every color and food and *anything* she could think of until I had a favorite of each.

And in all of that conversation, in all that time watching her talk and think and smile, not only had it become harder to pretend that I wasn't attracted to her–it became almost impossible to pretend that I wasn't falling in love with her.

"Dion?" I blinked, and realized with no small amount of

chagrin that I'd been staring at her. That sweater had been rearranged so that it rested on both shoulders once more, and those eyes looked at me under unfurrowed brows, her expression only curious.

"Sorry," I said, shaking my head slightly.

"Daydreaming won't help your shielding get any better." Smiling, she lightly shoved my knee that was on the couch, close to her, my ankle crossed over my other leg.

I smirked, trying to ignore the now-familiar feeling that coursed through me when she touched me. Days of brushing my shoulder, nudging and bumping me when I said something funny or stupid–or both. Touches that, to her, were friendly, and nothing more–things that she also did to Nuria and Jolie. I reminded myself of that every time.

"I can't seem to get past the 'fence', as it were. Every time I try to build the full wall, there seems to be either a gate opening, or a gap at the top."

"Why are you still building?" she asked.

My brow creased, and I paused for a breath before answering. "Because I need to master the shields in order to protect our people, and our High Lord and High Lady."

Something warm flashed in her eyes, but was gone before I could put a name to it. "And if the secrets you know now fell into the wrong hands, what would happen?"

"War," I answered. "Oleander would learn of everything, and his allies would march here, destroy this city, and kill from its border to the castle, until he reached us."

She leaned forward. "Who are you protecting from that?"

"Our people," I repeated. "Our High Lord, and High Lady."

"Who else?"

"Nuria and Jolie. Bayani, Nate and Bash, and Atlas. You." My heart thudded hard in my chest, thinking about these people who had become so precious to me in such a short time. About them being in danger.

"And if the only way to keep all of us safe was to build a wall around us, would you stop when it got hard?"

"No." I would rather die myself than see her fall.

"Right. Our friends aren't here, so you look at me," she told me, and took my face in her hands, just inches from her own now. "Look at me, and imagine what you're keeping me safe from."

I couldn't see around her. I saw only her eyes, the lashes tangled around them, and I imagined never seeing them again. Closed forever because an enemy saw into my mind, and brought our secrets, our quiet rebellion, back to Oleander. Never again crinkling with laughter, or shining with intuition, or glinting with strength. All because I had failed her.

And suddenly the wall I'd been envisioning coming together brick by brick in my mind was not red—no, it wasn't brick at all; wasn't red. It was a wall of navy-dark night, flecked with aquamarine stars. And it was solid—no gaps, no gates. Only impenetrable night, stretching as far around my mind as it did the evening sky. Nothing was strong enough to infiltrate it, to break it.

"It worked," I breathed, my eyes widening.

Those eyes so close to mine widened as well, and a smile spread across her face. "It worked?" she asked, still holding my cheeks.

"It worked," I confirmed again, grinning back at her.

She squealed, and suddenly her arms were around my neck. She paused only to press a kiss to my cheek that set the skin there aflame before her curls laid against the side of my face as she embraced me. Stunned, it took me only a second too long to lightly place my hands on the small of her back. As much as I wanted to wind my arms around her, feel her against me, I couldn't. Not when she hugged me as a friend. Not when I valued that ever-forming friendship more than anything.

She released me, her eyes bright when she pulled back just far enough to grasp my shoulders. "We have to tell Hiela." She stood from the couch, and grabbed my hand, pulling me up and with her as she strode out of the library and through the halls.

She led me to the same balcony where we dined when it was just the four of us. At the moment, our High Lord and High Lady sat at that round table, facing the gardens. They turned in their chairs when they heard us coming, and Hiela's eyes went straight to our locked hands. They flashed back to my face, and her brows raised ever so slightly. And against that mental shield, that wall of night, I felt a request to be let in.

I permitted my sky to open up to that single ray of dawn, just the slightest bit, and heard her voice in my head say, *I told you so.*

Then she pulled that presence back, and I once more stretched that dark sky to fully span across my mind. Hiela's lips stretched into a smile, sienna eyes alight, as she said aloud, "You did it."

⊞

Ciaragen

FOR DAYS, I SPENT NEARLY EVERY WAKING MOMENT WITH DION. I talked with him for hours, watched his kindness, laughed at his humor. So different from our first weeks together, when I hadn't allowed myself to see any good in him—and, when I did notice it, convinced myself that it was an act.

I wasn't sure when, but at some point during the time that I stopped lying to myself, and saw him for who he truly was, I started looking at him differently than I would a friend. But the tipping point had been yesterday, when he'd called the Sabriani *our* people.

I was trying very hard not to think about it as he and I sat in the gardens with Nuria and Jolie for the first time in six days. I was grateful for our friends' presences, for I had no idea at all how to handle my newfound impulses. I needed them here with me so that I had a reason not to cave into what I wanted. The constant desire to not only look at Dion while he was talking, but to see his reactions to our friends' stories as they told them. To watch his hazel eyes light as he laughed, and see the way their edges crinkled when he smiled–which he did frequently now, a dimple always popping in his right cheek.

Even the yearning to stare at that smile couldn't compare, though, to the energy it took to make myself not touch him. I'd switched so easily–gone from no contact to suddenly craving the feel of him beneath my palms. Flashes of desire I masked quickly, each time I thought of what it might be like to touch him without all of that fabric between my hand and his skin. Even the memories of the feeling of his hands on my back in a Void-damned *hug* had kept me awake for far too long last night. Their weight and warmth had been hard to forget–even harder to not think about how they would feel on other parts of me...

So, yes, I was grateful for the presence of our friends, because them being with us was a constant reminder that if I did make the choice to act on any of those impulses, it would not be private. If I acted, if I gave in...*If*. I wanted it to be between me and him.

"You okay, Ari?" Nuria asked, and I blinked to find the three of them watching me.

"Yeah," I responded, quickly picking up my stemless glass

of sparkling wine, and taking a sip before continuing. "Just zoned out, I guess."

Still, Nuria had a knowing glint in her eye that made me take another drink from my glass. But, ever the loyal friend, she changed the subject after a passably nonchalant shrug. "Did you hear Hielo and Hiela will be holding court again in a couple of days?"

I nodded, and so did Dion as he took a bite of an apple.

"Did you also hear that they have invited every courtier from every border country to attend?" she asked, raising her brows, black eyes moving between the two of us. Dion and I looked at each other, and then shook our heads. With a smile that might be considered mischievous, our friend continued. "Well, I don't know about you, but I would like to get a new gown for the occasion." She placed a hand on her mate's knee, which Jolie covered with her own without hesitation; the simple intimacy as easy and instinctual as breathing.

"Nuria, are you suggesting that we leave in the midst of court preparations to shop and eat for the day instead?" Dion asked, his tone so incredibly serious that even our lively friend seemed to hesitate before responding, "Yes...?"

And then the somberness was gone, replaced by one of those eye-crinkling, dimple-producing smiles that had, seemingly from nowhere, started to make my heart do strange things. "Sounds irresponsible. Let's do it."

"Really, you'd come with us?" Her own grin was bright with humor and excitement.

"Of course. As long as–"

"Ciaragen wants to go, yes, we know. How much longer do you have to be on guard duty?" Nuria asked me, drinking from her own glass of sparkling wine.

My brow scrunched, and I saw Dion look at me in my periphery. "I don't know if I'm actually on it anymore, to be honest. I kind of just…" I trailed off as I realized that, now that his shields were fully functional, I had spent the past day with him only because I wanted to. He knew the castle well enough to get around without an escort, had no reason to be guarded, and yet I'd walked him to his chambers last night, and waited for him, out of uniform, this morning anyway.

Before the pause got too long, I went on, "But, even if I did *have* to go wherever this one went," I tipped my head in Dion's direction, "I would want to go gown shopping with you."

Nuria squealed, and clapped her hands, and Jolie's gentle face softened even more at her mate's excitement. "Then let's say we meet at the gates in thirty minutes? I have to get some coin from our chambers."

We all agreed, and since Dion's chambers were in the same wing of the castle as my own, we walked together. No longer did he walk paces away from me; we strode down the halls side by side, his arm nearly brushing mine with every step.

We stopped at his room first, and he came out with a small purse that he put in his pocket as he shut his door. And my eyes were ridiculously drawn to the way the muscles in his neck stretched when he turned his head to look around the hallway surrounding us. The way his grown-out hair curled just slightly around his arched ear–

"I don't think I know where your chambers are," he said, interrupting my thoughts. Only will kept me from blushing at what he might have scented if those thoughts had continued. Instead, I rolled my eyes. "Of course not. I've been to yours about twenty-seven thousand times, but you've never had to come to mine."

"I think you're overexaggerating. It was closer to twenty-six thousand."

I laughed, and–gods damn me–bumped his arm with my shoulder. "All the same, we've never had to go to mine. Twenty-

six thousand to one." We reached my door a moment later, and when I opened it, I left it that way, striding into my chambers while he waited behind me. "You can come in," I called back to him as I went to my nightstand to grab the small sum of money I kept within it in a little velvet bag. "We don't have to meet them for another twenty minutes."

I heard his hesitant steps pass the threshold, and stop in the foyer before the bedroom. The sitting area was off to the side, only slightly separated by a large rounded archway in a wall. Through it were similar arrangements to the castle library; a plush dove gray couch, armchairs, and a cream-colored chaise, and shelves upon shelves of books, and trinkets from my travels. It was to that room that Dion seemed to gravitate, his eyes roaming it longer than they did the rest of the space.

"Feel free to explore. I have to use the powder room before we go, anyway," I told him. He nodded, and walked through the archway, and I went to the bathing chamber on the other side of the bedroom. It connected to my closet, and, as I closed the door to the powder room, I looked in the mirror to decide if I wanted to change, too.

Having had lunch outside, I was already dressed in appropriate attire for the weather. I would likely get warm, though, if I kept my hair down as we walked. I tied it up, the shorter spirals coming out around my ears and temples, like they always did. I fruitlessly tried to pin them back for a moment, and had to give up with a sigh before going to use the restroom, unsure of when I would get to again as we shopped for gowns.

When I came out, Dion was still in the sitting room. His back was slightly turned towards me, but I could see that he held a book open in his hands. Hearing me approach, he turned fully to me, and looked up.

"*Night's Beating Heart*," I said, recognizing it immediately by the increasingly worn and tattered binding. "I've read it so much it's coming apart at the seams."

"It's one of my favorites," he said quietly, looking down at it once more. "*And if ever I should live to be what makes you sigh as you do when gazing upon that night sky–*" he recited.

I continued, "*–then I should be happy to stare at those stars with you for the rest of my days. And live with you beside them when we fade from this world.*"

He was watching me as I spoke, hazel eyes softer than I'd ever seen them. I swallowed, and said, "It's beautiful."

He nodded, his gaze landing on the cover as he closed the book, and placed it back on the shelf behind him. I waited a bit nervously, wondering what he thought about my obsession with the love story we'd just read from. Still facing that shelf, he said, his voice a bit rough, "I agree."

I walked until I was standing beside him, and looked at the folded paper crane a young faerie had folded for me in Grevosch that sat at his eye level. I watched his eyes move to my face in my periphery, and turned my head to meet his gaze. As my stomach fluttered, I lifted my chin, hoping he couldn't see the emotions roiling within me.

"We should get going." His voice was still rough, in a way that made that fluttering in my gut feel a bit lower. "Nuria and Jolie will be waiting."

Let them wait, I wanted to say. Let them wait, while I read with him. Wait, while he made me laugh, and think, and feel. And while the shape of his mouth that I'd so suddenly come to notice beckoned for me to find out why that was. But I didn't say that. What came out instead was, "Let's go, then."

28

WHISPERING WINDS

Thea - present

I LAY IN THE CANVAS TENT, FEIGNING SLEEP. AFTER EXPERIENCING the utter lack of respect Olin and his lackeys have for me, I'm grateful to not be sharing with anybody, even if Gadsby is on watch just outside. I can pretend that the fabric walls mean I have some semblance of privacy.

I turn over to lie on my back, forcing my breathing to stutter as it would shifting positions in sleep. I see a single star through the fist-sized gap in the ceiling, and can't help but think on how similar we are. Stuck in place, surrounded by the unknown. But she, at least, burns brightly while the black night threatens to swallow her up. I feel like my light went out, and the darkness has not stopped pouring in since I heard my mother's neck snap.

I don't allow the tears to come, even as they beg to be released. Because, while the star makes me feel that we're both alone, with nothing but a void to listen to us cry, I know that I'm not. I will not allow the foes around me to hear me break. Instead, I allow more darkness to come in, and numb my heart and soul to that agony. That terribly comforting blackness makes my eyelids heavy, and tells me to sleep.

I know that soon it will be time to rise, and walk the rest of the distance to the cliffs. But closing my eyes feels too much like accepting defeat. And I haven't done that yet. Won't, until the males outside are dead. After that, perhaps I'll see myself to peace.

For now, I'll stare at that star until it's blurry. I'll watch the sky go from black to navy to gray and pretend that it doesn't remind me of the shattered ceiling of my home. I'll listen to the forest around us wake, and rise with it, yawning and stretching to indicate my good night's sleep to the people listening. I'll send my magic to heal the inflammation around my eyes. Then, I'll walk out of this tent, and pretend some more, but this time it will be of how I am not afraid.

"Sleep well?" Olin asks as soon as I walk through the tent opening. He's standing in the middle of the makeshift campground, breeches tucked into boots, cotton shirt looking like he'd just donned it. The other two look like they got hardly any more sleep than I did, their eyes heavy and lightly rimmed in purple, clothes and hair rumpled.

"Yes," I respond, if only so I don't have to deal with his wrath over something so simple as not uttering a word. After no sleep, I don't have the patience–even as much as I had yesterday–and while I'd love the excuse to bash his nose in again, I don't want to deal with whatever repercussions would follow. At least not until I walk some energy back into my body.

"Good. Hungry?" He tucks his shirt into the front of his breeches too slowly to be anything but suggestive.

Fighting a curl in my lip, I only say, "Yes," again.

He smirks, then looks at Gadsby and nods. The male

retrieves some of the rabbit they'd caught last night, and hands me a leg. I take it and eat without another word, and before I can wish for water, a skin of it is handed to me. I almost thank Adathan, but catch myself just in time. He follows it with an apple, and I have an easier time holding my thanks back when I realize that he's treating me like a pig for slaughter. Feeding me, if only to give me the energy to make it to that ship.

Once I finish, I throw the bones and the core into the woods, and wipe my hands on the canvas of the tent, way past caring about being ladylike. I step around Adathan, who'd watched me do all of this, just as I'd been watched since I had woken yesterday morning. I stand at the edge of the small clearing, combing my fingers through my braid as I stare through the pine boughs; I work through the tangles until the locks are smooth, and replait them.

I imagine what it might be like if I ran, and even my imagination doesn't have a way creative or intelligent enough for me to get more than ten feet into the wilderness before one of my overseers catches me. I have to try, though. I will not be boarding any ship, leaving Weaschten soil, without a fight. I'd rather add ten more broken bones to the list of broken things within me, than add my will to it.

"Time to go," Adathan says from behind me. I turn, and find that he's already done so as well, his back to me as he follows Gadsby through the clearing. The latter carries the backpack today, and all the former has is a thin but fierce-looking dagger, and a water skin.

The tent is gone, all items packed or majickally stored in some way. While I'd been staring out into the woods, they'd been working to shorten the time I have to make my move. And what's worse is that it's not Adathan, or Gadsby–whose presences I can only barely tolerate–but Olin who waits only feet from me while the other two continue through the trees.

I walk right past him to follow them, but don't get five steps before he's beside me. I resist the urge to cross my arms, and keep them loose at my sides, chin high as I look only straight ahead.

The one good thing is that he's silent, the only sound that of our footsteps. It gives me a chance to think, since there are now only a few miles remaining between us and open land where only tall grasses might give me any coverage. There are disadvantages to both, though. Here, the roots would slow me, and the area is unfamiliar. I've been to the cliffs once or twice a year ever since I was small, and part of my plan rests on a pitiful hope that I'll see something recognizable soon enough.

Of course, the trees that source the treacherous roots would provide better coverage than grass. There, I would have to crouch or crawl to remain unseen, and thus, even though there would be no roots to slow me, my pace would still be compromised.

Comparatively, the woods seem like the better option. Perhaps there's even a cave somewhere that could provide shelter. If we're walking at roughly four miles per hour–a speed that pushes me as I continue to lift my feet several inches high with each step, but seems easy for them–then I have only an hour or so until I'm out of time. After that, if I can't make my way out through the grasses, I'll be forced to consider other methods of escape.

My heart thuds as I consider it, and I only hope that the Fae around me attribute it to the exertion from the walk. Olin and I walk a few yards behind the other two, but even if they didn't have Fae hearing, they would have heard him say, "You know, I like it when you're quiet. By my recollection, and imagination, your mouth is better suited for other things."

I stop in my tracks, and so do the males ahead of me. Slowly, so slowly, I turn until I face Olin. The low, flat voice that comes out of me, still husky from being strangled yesterday, is more menacing than anything I've sounded like before when I say, "What did you just say to me?"

He smirks, and pointedly looks at my lips for a long second before bringing his eyes back up to mine. "I said," he begins softly, practically purring. "That your mouth would be put to much better use on things other than talking. Like kissing me. Or wrapped around my–"

I drive my knee up into his groin, and when he doubles over wheezing, his nose happens to land on my fisted hand. I feel blood gush immediately, and when I draw my fist away, it's covered in crimson.

Far quicker than he should be, Olin grabs my neck, and pulls me to him to crush his lips to mine. His blood flows over our joined mouths, and my own combines with it when he bites my lower lip hard enough to make me cry out. In the same instant, he forces my body flush with his, so that I feel *him* against *me*. Then, just as fast as he'd grabbed me, he jerks me away. Still holding my throat, his fingers agonizingly tight against the bruises, surely forming new ones, he screams:

"I will *fuck* the fight out of you!" The vessels in his face blacken, while a combination of blood and saliva spatters my face as he shouts so close to it. "Until then: *Adathan!*"

The golden-eyed male walks towards me, his expression blank, hands fisted at his sides. "My Lord," he says as he halts.

Gore plasters Olin's face, and the look in his eyes is made all the more frightening for it. But I'd known what I was risking by striking him, and chose the pain over hearing him talk about me like that. A decision that the nausea in my stomach tells me was a mistake, but to which, as I stare at Olin, my heart chants to its own beat: fuck, you, fuck, you, fuck, you.

His hand still around my neck, Olin turns to look at me once more. His voice is disturbingly calm as, for the first time since I knew him as Dion, he speaks to me in Ceraschen. "I would have liked for your first experience of someone touching your pussy to be me. I would have wanted you to enjoy it. But I suppose we don't get what we want all the time, do we? Adathan," he addresses his lackey without moving his eyes from mine. "Kick her in her virginal little cunt, and knock her out. Make it hurt. I'm done with this shit."

Then he releases me, leaving a handprint of blood around my throat, and a feeling of dread coiling in my gut. Adathan steps forward, and his master moves to make room for him, but remains close to watch. I swallow the fear, the anticipation of pain, and allow only venom and hate to show in my eyes as I glare up at him. He takes a stance, and waits, drawing out my terror.

"Do as I commanded you *now*," Olin orders, menace lacing each word.

And then a strike, much too fast for me to see, lands right down my center, and I can't help it when I fall to the ground, my knees smacking against one of the tree roots. That pain is nothing, is a kindness, compared to the pain in my groin. I lift my head to glare up at the male, my teeth gritted in rage and agony, but only catch a glimpse of a golden gaze before he lifts a fist, and my world goes black.

⬌

In the darkness, there is only one sound.
CRACK.
Over and over, I hear my mother's neck break.
I think in some strange, distant part of my brain, I'm screaming. Sound tears out of my imagined lungs in such vividity that I almost think I'm awake. But something in my mind tells me that's not right.

I should be awake...I should be, but I can't remember why. I can't think, can't hear any reasoning over the *CRACK. CRACK. CRACK.*

In someplace far away, I feel a wind against my face. Its breeze has a comforting scent–some warm mixture of oak and leather and the embers of a fire sparking in the cold of winter. Something about it calms an intrinsic part of me, and makes the haunting cracking sound soften; lighten. It's now closer to reeds of tall grass crunching under feet.

I hear other things with that sound. The crashing of the sea. Ocean birds cawing from high above. The steady breathing of exertion. The last one is interrupted every few breaths by words so quiet I could imagine the wind itself spoke them.

"Open your eyes."

The plea rouses me, some tone within it implying that something very bad will happen if I don't do as I'm told. The journey back to consciousness brings pain. Not as much as I felt in my dreams, but pain nonetheless. In my face, my neck, my groin, and my damn *head*. That aches so much that when I finally do open my eyes, I have to close them quickly to dim the way the sunshine seems to pierce my very brain.

"Open your eyes," that whispering wind demands again. I heed it, even as my head throbs so heavily that it takes a moment for my vision to clear. When it does, I see the expanse of tall grasses, swaying in the breeze coming off the ocean. I can hear the waves crashing against the cliffside, and once we crest over a hill to see it, reality crashes into me, too.

The water shines like glittering diamonds as the sunlight reflects off its surface. I have to turn my head away, dots of white flaring in my vision. My nose ends up against Adathan's chest, and I quickly jerk my head back. Wincing at the jolt of pain that causes, I look up at him. He's staring down at me, eyes tight, full lips pressed together. After a moment that's perhaps just a beat too long, he says, "She's awake."

He sets me on my feet, and as he stoops to do so, his mouth passes my ear, and I think I hear him say, "Trust me." But I can't have heard him right–because what reason do I have to trust him? He keeps one hand around my wrist as he continues walking, towing me along. No, I will not be permitted to even try to run. I'm debating whether I have enough pride to keep from kicking and screaming, and wondering if that same pride will have me wind up with a fate worse than death, when I see the white sails in the distance.

My body reacts quickly, heels digging into the ground. Adathan's hand, while not tight enough to hurt, has an iron grip on me, and it tugs me along as we get closer and closer to the cliff's edge.

"No," I whisper. He hushes me, eyes shooting a warning that I ignore. "No," I say louder, pulling harder, and sinking my weight into my haunches. The male hardly seems to notice, his thick arm not even straining at my struggle. "No!" I shout, and the other two deign to turn towards us now.

My pulling and screaming won't do me any good, though. It's a useless expenditure of energy, and I'm still moving closer to the cliff's edge, Adathan and I only several yards from it now. The others are ahead, making their way through the grasses a bit further on the forming path, probably seeking a route down to sea level.

They're far enough that if I strike against the one right beside me, I think there might be a chance for me to hide in these grasses before they can make it back to us. The wind will carry my scent in too many directions for them to pinpoint where exactly I am in the swaying mass. So I must move now, or be lost.

When I pitch forward, instead of pulling back, there's only a half of a second where Adathan is caught off guard by the shift in my weight, but it's enough. It's enough for me to rip his dagger from the scabbard at his hip, a scabbard I'd pointedly ignored ever since he remarked on how I noticed it yesterday morning. Waiting for him to forget that encounter, or to at least be arrogant enough, when so close to his goal, that he might let his attention slip.

He drops my wrist and takes a quick step back, missing the slash I make that would have eviscerated his abdomen by an inch. There will be no throwing of this dagger; even if it hits home, I would not get it back.

"For gods' sakes, Adathan!" Olin yells, charging at us while Gadsby begins to move out to circle me. Surround me.

And this time, it's me who does it.

CRACK.

As his body falls, though, I feel a hideous lurch in my stomach and the scene shifts. For a heartbeat, it's not the hulking male lying in the tall grass–his massive frame squashing it enough that I can see him–but a slim woman with a golden crown. It makes me slow, that flashback, and even though I only have two opponents left now, I feel defeated.

Olin's veins have blackened, and he bares his teeth at me, canines flashing. "You little *bitch!*" he screams, roaring like the monster he is, like the beasts his people once hailed from. He doesn't have to run at me; he walks with slow, intent steps. A predator's gait.

And then Adathan intercepts him, his back towards me, arms raised to his master. I step to the side just a bit to keep Olin in complete view. "Calm down, my Lord. You don't want to hurt her."

Olin tilts his head, a cruel smile forming on his face. "I don't? I think we can agree that the past thirty-six hours prove that is a lie."

"You need her," Adathan tries instead, backing closer to me as his master prowls towards us. I consider moving to thrust his dagger through his back–make the fight one on one–but, stupid as it might be, I can't bring myself to make such a dishonorable move. A *weak* move.

Olin laughs, a humorless, maniacal sound. "What I *need* is her cunt. She's only lucky that I also *want* it." His gaze shifts to me, and those blackened eyes shadow further with nauseating hunger. "I don't care how many of my men you kill, or how many times I have to hurt you for doing so. If it weren't for the fucking *sanctification*, I'd have had you every which way already."

"I will *die* before you have me in any way," I growl at him, taking my stance and grounding in it, dagger up.

He dares to step closer, and his smile widens. "You won't. You might not want it now. Gods know that won't make me stop. But, you'll be surprised, Princess. One taste, and you'll see."

Adathan's hands begin to shake, and I watch him fist them, dropping his arms. Giving up on protecting his master from himself.

"You can't know. You've never tasted anything before." Olin's eyes travel down to my pelvis, and linger before moving back up to my mouth. "Never had a cock in that pretty mouth. Never been fucked. I'll show you how to do all of it."

Even as bile churns in my gut, I say, "You put that thing anywhere near me, and you'll find yourself without it very quickly."

The veins around his temples flash black, and fade. "I'll rape that attitude out of you, beautiful. I'll–" And then he's not talking. He's fifteen feet in the air, blasted back by a great power.

Adathan turns to face me, eyes wide with shock, and fury.

So fast that he's a blur, he closes the small distance between us, and pulls me to his chest. It's a mix of my defensiveness and unpreparedness, and his inattention that causes his own dagger to sink a couple of inches into his hip.

But he doesn't stop moving, only hisses softly as he crushes me to him. As he moves, he bends and lifts my feet off the ground, and then cradles me to his torso like I'm no bigger than a babe. He sprints the last few yards to the edge of the cliff, and just as a roar erupts from deep in the grasses, before I can so much as scream, he jumps–taking me with him.

My face buried in Adathan's chest, I have the presence of mind to gasp in a breath and hold it. My back to the sky, and his to the sea and the rocks within it, we plummet down, down. And then we crash.

A human wouldn't have made a far enough jump–wouldn't have missed the rocks that jut out from the sea, close to the cliffside. A human wouldn't have survived the impact of the water to his ribs, his spine. But Adathan isn't human, and so as we sink, and sink, he holds me still. We pass the depth to which I've dived into the sea on family vacations, and my ears pop. We reach the seafloor, less than sixty feet deep this close to the land, and he tilts us until he's on his feet. Gently, one hand moves from the back of my head to wrap around my wrist, and pull the dagger out of his hip. I feel rather than hear a grunt of pain vibrate within the chest my face rests upon.

Then I'm being set down, but one arm stays looped around my waist, tethering me to the cushiony wet sand beneath my feet. I feel a soft tap on each of my eyelids, and, though the salt of the sea burns a bit, I open my eyes to find only deep turquoise water, and a light golden gaze. Adathan points to the surface, before shaking his head. Then makes a swimming motion with his hand.

I nod to show my understanding. That we cannot surface,

so close to where Olin likely waits for us to do so. We have to swim.

He taps his lips, and the space above his lungs, before raising his brows in question. I nod again. I have enough air. For now.

He grabs my hands, eyes filled with one more question, and I nod one last time. He can do what he must to get us out of here.

And, once we are, it will be me with the questions.

He grips my right wrist once more, not even attempting to take the dagger from my grasp, and pulls that arm around to his back, until my chest is against his shoulder blades. Then he loops both of my arms around his neck, until each of my hands clasp the other elbow, the flat of the dagger pressed against my bicep. He squeezes them there, indicating to keep them tight, and then we're moving.

I have to close my eyes, and tuck my head into the back of his neck because of the speed with which he swims. At least as fast as we'd been running; cutting through the water like a knife, even with me on his back. I only have a moment to marvel at it before my lungs provide a much more pressing concern.

Slowly, so carefully, I release two fingers from my grip, and straighten them to tap his chest, hoping he understands me as I understood him. Still kicking, one of his hands wraps around mine again, and he pats it twice in acknowledgement.

We move diagonally to the left now, closer to the coast. Even with my eyes closed, I feel the looming mass of land grow closer. And when my lungs are practically screaming, when I think that breathing in the water would be better than this, he tilts us suddenly. Crouching down, he wraps both of his hands around my arms, securing them, before jumping up.

Sixty feet fly in seconds, and when my head breaks the

water, I gasp in a huge breath. I open my eyes, blinking water out of them, and use one of my hands to shove the hair out of my face. We're nearly pressed against the cliffside, and he somehow managed to find a little alcove of lightly flowing water, waves crashing against the walls around us. There is only rock above, and sea below; no exit but down.

I release Adathan, and lightly flutter my feet to keep myself afloat as he turns to me. The morning light on the water outside brightens this space enough that I can see him. And the red blood rising in the water between us. I look down in alarm, wondering if I somehow cut myself–but the blood isn't coming from me. It's coming from him; from the wound I'd made in his hip.

Though I have many more questions to ask, the first one I voice is, "Why isn't that healing?"

His sun-gold eyes move across my face, and he answers, "Salt in the water, and a high concentration of iron in these rocks; the sediment has seeped into the ocean over time." I only nod in response, my jaw tight, and he continues, "We need to go another few miles. Get to land, create a trail and scent, and then get back in the water."

My brow furrows. "What if he finds us while we're on land? Wouldn't it make more sense to just double back to where we were? Wouldn't he have left there by now?"

"Most likely, yes. The question is how far he would have gone. There's no scent to track in the water, so he wouldn't have jumped in after us." He considers for a moment. "Where's the nearest main city, or port?"

"In Dahlih, another eighty miles or so from the cliffs. Why?"

Adathan thinks for a moment. "We do both. Up a few miles. I'll carry our scents. Then back to where we started. Okay?"

I want to think through the logistics, but I don't know my

enemy as well as I'd like to, and he does. And, even if his jumping off the cliff with me makes no sense, and I don't trust him as far as I can throw him–which, given his massive height and frame would be about negative eleven feet–I don't have any other options but to follow along. Which has kind of been the story of my life these past few days, so what's one more time?

So, I only nod, saving my questions and emotions for later.

29

WHO NEEDS THE MOON?

DION - 21 YEARS EARLIER

TODAY WAS PERHAPS THE MOST EXHAUSTING DAY YET OF MY TIME in Sabrian.

Not the shopping. Though I did try on a new tuxedo that had all three females hollering boisterously at me, and they would not allow me to leave the store without purchasing it. Otherwise, I did very little but sit on small couches or soft chairs, and watch them try on dresses. And that was not exhausting either.

What *was* exhausting was having to pretend to have the same reaction to Ciaragen as I did to Nuria or Jolie. To watch her come out of dressing rooms in gowns of all shapes and colors, and merely smile and nod, while our friends complimented her, told her how gorgeous she looked, when my lips ached to do the same. She ended up purchasing three new gowns, each one bringing out her features in different ways.

There had been one, though, that I had not been able to

318

nod and smile at. I'd been struck dumb, my mouth hanging open slightly until Nuria stepped in front of Ciaragen, blocking her view of me, with a significant look thrown over her shoulder. Still, the image stayed in my mind, and lingered there even after we finished dinner with our High Lord and High Lady.

As they had come to do more frequently since I learned the truth, our friends joined us at that dinner table. And I did not think that it was coincidence, or my imaginings, that everyone at the table seemed to be looking between Ciaragen and I throughout the meal. I only hoped that she didn't notice, or, if she did, attributed it to something other than my obviously growing affection towards her.

Because what I'd realized yesterday still held true. With one error–I wasn't just *falling* for her. I'd fallen already. I thought it might have even started after I'd first seen her outside my chamber doors a month ago, and had just been too broken, too used to desensitizing myself, to recognize it for what it was. A month. Too fast for it to be possible, or it should have been. And yet, here I was.

In love with her.

Now, I was in my chambers, reading in my bland sitting room with a collection of books that had grown since my arrival, but still did not compare in the slightest to hers. And still, though I'd long since learned my way around the castle, and surely did not need a guard, she stood outside my door. And I decided right then and there, that was unacceptable.

Maybe I should put more thought into what, exactly, I wanted to say, but I didn't much feel like doing that. For the past month–for years and decades before that, all I'd done was think. No more. I would ask her if she would like to join me to read. And whatever her response was would be...what it was.

I rose from my seat, and walked to the door. I took a deep

breath before opening it, and then pulled the handle, and peered outside–

To find Arthur.

He looked just as surprised as I probably did. The only time I'd seen him had been on my first day here, and then in passing every few days since. I'd known that he stood watch while Ciaragen slept, but had never ventured out to speak with him.

Also unacceptable.

So, instead of backing into my room and closing the door as if nothing had happened, I walked out, and said, "Hello, Arthur."

He blinked, and replied, "Lord Dion." He bowed his head slightly, a show of respect, and I restrained a cringe.

"Please, that's not necessary. And, call me Dion."

He cleared his throat. "Alright. Erm, how can I help you?"

Awkward. This conversation was awkward. "Have you seen Lady Ciaragen?" I asked.

"Yes, I relieved her about fifteen minutes ago. She's probably in her chambers."

I nodded. "Right. Thank you." He dipped his chin, and I walked off more quickly than I probably needed to in the direction of her rooms.

When I reached the fork in the hallway, though, the scent to the right was much older than the one to the left. I followed that newer trail, the vanilla and bergamot beckoning me in a direction I'd never gone before. It led me to a set of stairs that zig-zagged up to another floor. This one had wooden floors, just like the library, and the ceilings were high, with geometric molding that was artfully cut around small chandeliers that hung to varying lengths above my head.

Her scent traveled through the main space, and down a narrow hall that just...ended. There was only a window on the wall, the night sky a familiar deep blue canvas on its other side. And it was open.

I braced my hands on the lip of the window, and didn't need to breathe in to know which direction she'd gone. Again, very much *not* thinking, I twisted so that my shoulders fit diagonally through the opening, and sat backwards on the sill to find a grip.

The placement of the pale stones that jutted out from the exterior wall was too perfect to be an accident. I reached up, and thought that, while having smaller hands would definitely be helpful, I'd come this far. So, on only the first knuckles of each of my hands, I hoisted myself up and out of the window.

The climb would have been easier if I'd thought to take my shoes off. But, too late, as I pulled myself up with only my upper body, not trusting that I wouldn't somehow kick myself off the face of the castle if I used my feet.

After about twenty feet, and a couple of muffled curses, I made it to the ledge of the roof, planting my elbow to drag myself up enough to get my knee over the edge. When at last I rose to my feet, in the dim light provided by a few candles around her, I found Ciaragen staring at me.

She sat just a few steps away from me, hands braced behind her as though she'd been laying down, and had only risen at the noise I'd made on my way up. The summer night was unusually balmy for how early it was in the season. And in that warmth, I had to focus on keeping my eyes on hers, and not the long legs expanding from her cotton shorts, or the strip of her belly exposed by her slightly cropped shirt.

"Hi," she said softly.

"Hi," I replied, my voice rough. I cleared my throat, hoping she'd chalk it up to the climb. "What are you doing up here?"

She smirked. "I could ask you the same question." But she didn't. She only patted the place beside her, on a blanket that she must have brought up herself. This was a lower spot on the roof, battlements and towers on all sides around us. It seemed that mystery hallway had ended in a sort of center point within the castle grounds; floors below, I could see the same winding cobblestone pathways that meandered through the gardens leading to varying entrances and exits of the castle walls.

Here, on this outcropping of roof so different from the defensive nature of the outer walls, there was the same mosaic tile that laid on the majority of the floors inside. Moss and clover had been allowed to grow in between some of the pieces.

As I took all of this in, I did as I was bid, and sat next to her. The blanket wasn't large; the space between our shoulders was as much as I could make it, and still was only perhaps a foot wide.

She turned to me, the corners of her lips pulling up slightly. "Ready?" she asked.

I had no idea what I was supposed to be ready for, but still I answered, "Yes."

Her grin widened, full lips spreading over her teeth, and my heart stuttered. "Blow out that candle, and lie back."

I turned to my other side, where a stout yellow candle sat in its own wax, and probably that of its predecessors as well. I extinguished its flickering orange flame before easing myself down until I was lying flat on the blanket. And then I knew why she was up here.

There were so many stars. Billions of brilliant white flecks of light, some farther away from each other than others. Constellations shone bright, and in the center of the sky was a swirling mass of them. A serpentine shape of dazzling enormity that stretched for miles and miles.

"You can only see them like this during the new moon," she whispered. "Otherwise, the moonshine is too bright. She likes to steal the show. But, during the new moon, when she rests, they help. They light up the sky for her."

I'd never heard anyone describe the night sky in such a way. And now I thought I would never look at it the same way I had over the past century of my life. There was a beauty in seeing the world outside of us as in need of things like rest, and support. Being given that devotion of picking up a burden that was too heavy for someone, something else.

I felt, rather than saw, her head turn towards me. I moved to look back at her, and, with the light from the sky that I had mistaken earlier as being solely due to the candles, her eyes shone. Stars of her own in them. And then I felt a slender finger touch the back of my palm.

I stopped breathing. I only opened my hand, expecting nothing. Her decision alone, to keep the back of her hand on mine, move it away, or...or.

But then her palm was pressed against mine, and she twined her fingers through my own. My hand closed around hers, and, with all that I could dare, I stroked my thumb along the side of her hand. I heard her own breathing pause in response.

I didn't know and didn't care if she could see the emotions I wasn't trying to hide as she continued to look at me with those starshine eyes. Here, where only the sky would bear witness, I allowed myself to hold that vulnerability. And she did not turn from it.

"What are you thinking?" she asked softly.

And I didn't hesitate. Didn't pause to think, or make her wait. I said, "I'm thinking that you're the most exceptional person I've ever met. That I'm amazed by you every day."

Her smile was lovely, and gentle, and she took a shuddering breath. "I'm thinking that you're not at all what I expected. And that, around you, I've become someone I didn't expect, either."

No response was needed, and still I could have said it. That I loved her. That, in this moment, the thing that I most wanted to do was kiss her. To feel her lips against my own, to share breath with her.

But she turned back to the sky before I could gather my courage, her lips still curved upwards slightly, not a clue as to what was going on inside my head. So I turned away too, my heart slowing to an even, easy pace. And I found myself content to just lie here with her beneath the stars, holding her hand.

30

WALK & WANDERING THOUGHT

AFTER SWIMMING WITH ME ON HIS BACK FOR SEVERAL MILES—taking breaks in between for me to breathe–we finally stop to enact Adathan's plan. He turns away as I hand him my shirt, so that he can carry my scent through the fields and woods above. I sit in the shadow of an outcropped rockface, arms crossed over my chest, only a thin brassiere and shift to keep me covered, grateful that it's still summer. Between the shade, the water drying on my skin, and very little clothing, my teeth are chattering as is.

During the time he's gone, my heart doesn't stop hammering. I try to slow it a few times, using the same method and magic I would if I were treating someone with heart palpitations, but it picks back up as soon as I stop. Besides, the flowing blood is probably good for me.

When I finally hear a splash, I nearly jump out of my skin. I clutch my arms even more tightly around my breasts, but when Adathan rises from the water beside me, he keeps his eyes closed as he hands my shirt back to me. He turns his back again until my sloshing in the water ceases, my shirt soaking, but covering me nonetheless.

We don't speak. With the exception of him asking for my shirt, we haven't talked since we hashed out our pitiful plan in that alcove within the sea. It's fine by me. I'll ask my questions eventually, but for now it's already too much to be constantly touching him, looking at him–none of which compares to the self-loathing I have for the fact that I'd needed him to save me.

This *male* who betrayed my family, swimming with me on his back for miles and miles. Treating me with respect, unlike his master; his bright gold eyes serious when he looks at me, never lecherous, despite the fact that he has me alone and very, very vulnerable.

If not for him, I would be on a ship, experiencing things I don't even allow my imagination to ponder. And I *hate* it. I'd needed him, and I know that I still do. That I won't make it to Dahlih on my own. That I won't be able to accomplish the task that I've set in my mind without him to guide me.

I feel the loathing–for him, and for myself–burn in my heart and in my eyes. But still, when he turns his back to me once more, I paddle to him, and wrap my arms around his neck. I bury my face once more into the crook of his shoulder and take a deep breath before he dives under the water.

By the time we get back to where we started, I'm exhausted. The constant replenishing of oxygen, only to be deprived again. Clinging to him, fighting the current. The sting of the salt water in my wounds, in my eyes. Up my nose and scratching my throat from the time that I hadn't been prepared enough for his speed in the water.

I don't feel kind enough yet to recognize that whatever

exhaustion I feel, is likely nothing compared to what he's experiencing.

But at last, we leave that tireless sea, and climb the steep path up the cliff. He has me wait about three quarters of the way up, so that he can check that no one is up there waiting for us, and then comes to retrieve me when he finds there isn't. Still, I keep my eyes and ears alert as we ascend, ready for another betrayal by him. Preparing for Olin to be waiting for us, laughing at me for believing that Adathan had taken me from him.

I have nothing but my power and wits with which to defend myself. I'd dropped his dagger that time the water had gone up my nose, and he'd retrieved it from the seafloor. And conveniently forgot to give it back. It's strapped to his hip now, bobbing with his steps.

But when we make it to the top, with the tall, swaying grasses, there's nothing. No one.

"I moved him," Adathan says in Ceraschen. Breathing heavily from the climb, I turn to him, brows furrowed. His eyes are already on me. Rimmed in red and bloodshot, but not unkind, though the rest of his face is stoic. "I moved Gadsby. You won't have to see him, if that's what you're worried about. What you're looking for."

I lift my chin, and consider him for a second. And, not for any kindness, but for a debt being paid, I walk to where he stands a few yards ahead of me. "Close your eyes," I tell him, the onyx locks of my hair blowing this way and that as they dry in the late morning winds coming off the sea. He does as I say without question. I raise my hands to his face, cupping his cheeks lightly, and stroke my thumbs over his eyelids in a featherlight motion. His lips part as my magic does its work, and I watch as the red disappears where my fingers pass.

Still holding his face, his eyes open, and they're back to

normal; the irises shining clearly. Then, I take off one hand, the other still pressed to a stubbled cheek, pull it back, and swing a right hook at his jaw. He backs up quickly after my knuckles find their mark, broad fingers lightly touching the hurt before he drops his hand.

"That was for this morning."

He straightens, sun gold eyes taking me in. Not in the way Olin had–the way that made my skin crawl and my stomach roll in disgust. Only...considering. After a moment, he just shrugs his stupidly large shoulders, and says, "Thank you. For the eyes."

"Yeah, whatever." I look away from him, and out into the grasses around us. It's late morning now, and the sun warms me, drying my hair, and sodden clothes. Still, we have only eight hours or so of daylight left. "What now?"

"Tell me what you'd like to do," he responds. Not meanly, or nicely. Does he ever use emotion when he speaks? He's only been quiet; no anger, or sadness, or humor. He hasn't so much as raised his voice, even when I stabbed him in the damn hip.

I'm already mad for so many reasons, so I cross my arms, and add his indifference to the list. The apparent lack of caring or opinion in his tone, his words, but also in how we keep surviving. If he's going to put the decision on me, then it forces me to confront what I want most: safety, or revenge. Making the choice itself isn't one of the things that angers me, though; it's that I know which one I'll pick.

I bring my gaze back up to his, my jaw tight, and loathing in my heart. "I want to go after him."

He nods, not seeming surprised by my answer–which surprises *me*. So I take it one step further. "I want to kill him."

His eyes scan mine, probably searching for any doubt, or fear, or weakness. I know he won't find any. All I feel is anger.

But I do have two questions for him before we start down this path together–something I'd accepted as inevitable when he stood with me on the seafloor hours ago, and had grown more and more loathful of over time. Because the moment he threw Olin back with his power, our futures became entangled. And if I'm going to go on this journey with him, if we are going to be in constant danger–we need to trust each other at least enough to not stab one another in the back.

"Why did you attack Olin?" Not save me. Not defend me. Because until I know more about his blood oath–until I know who he is beneath the Fae strength and the majick that deceived my family for a year, I can't think that saving me was his intention.

"Because it was the right thing to do," he answers without hesitation, his gaze unwavering.

All right. A reasonable explanation, though not detailed. No elucidation yet as to how he went from one side to the other in the blink of an eye. It seems that we're both balancing ourselves between being truthful, and being careful.

I ask my second question, the only other one that matters enough that it needs to be addressed before we can move forward. "Do you think he will go back for my family, after what we did?" Not because I want to accomplish my goal, and need to know if that's where I'll find him. Only because, if he will, *I* will stop at nothing to protect the rest of my family. If Olin is going to exact his anger at our escape on them, I would run through these woods until my feet bled, and would not stop until I stood between him and them.

"No. He knows that we're together, and that I wouldn't bring you back there yet. His focus will be you. Not getting revenge, but getting you back. Having you," he pauses, pressing his lips together before continuing, "is all he cares about."

But I don't allow that to stick. I shove down the disgust, the terror at the thought of what Olin might do if he ever did get me back, and remain focused on what Adathan said first. I take a step closer to him, and ask quietly, "Why wouldn't you bring me back there?" tilting my head as I look up at him.

"Why, so you can blame yourself some more?" I think that might be anger I hear in his voice. It didn't come out when he was hurt, or tired, but it surfaces now, as he knocks down the front of nonchalance and annoyance I'd erected with a single sentence. "Or so you can let your family talk you into staying, and *if* you somehow manage to lie your way around that–tell them you're staying, that you're safe–you can feel guilty in a whole new way for deceiving them?"

I blink, but refrain from stepping back. Though he'd never once looked into my eyes at Castle Cerasche–which I know now must have been a reflection of cowardice, or cunning–that doesn't mean that he hadn't been observing me in other ways. I should have anticipated that he'd know me better than I'd hoped he would.

"That's what I thought," he says, but there's no more anger. No snark, or sarcasm, as I would have expected. If anything, it's more... resigned. And somehow that's worse.

"Yes, your year of watching my family, just so you could betray us, served you well," I hiss at him, my hair blowing around my face in the newly forceful winds of the cliffs. "You know everything about me, and I know *nothing* about you. All I know is that you were..." I trail off when my throat starts to thicken at what the conclusion of that sentence would be. It might have started with him, but it would have ended with her. Broken, lifeless–just like my heart has been since that moment.

"I was what?" His question is soft, his lips hardly moving.

I just shake my head, and instead look towards the water.

Away from those terribly bright eyes that have already seen too much. "If we're not going back to Castle Cerasche, where are we going?" I ask, rather than answer his question. I stare out at the ocean, as if I can see all the way to the land of the Fae.

He doesn't answer for a long moment, but I just continue to look out at the deep turquoise waters. And I know what his reply will be even before he says, "Eshelle."

I simply nod at the answer which, just yesterday, had sent me into a panic. Now, I will be going for no one's purpose but my own.

"How?" We don't have a ship. No gold, no way to buy passage across the sea. Only the clothes on our backs, a half-empty water skin, and one dagger.

"He's likely almost in Dahlih by now, and he'll scour the city for us. When he realizes you're not there, he'll swim from there to his ship, and set off right away. He will know that you'll come for him, and want to be in Oschverre before we arrive, to try and capture us." He turns as he speaks, and begins walking towards the treeline miles out from where we are.

I follow him without really thinking about the action of it. Just realizing–as he probably had–that we're very exposed out on this grassy plain, and the wood will offer us significantly more coverage. If he's to be believed, Olin won't be lurking for us in the forest, but others might. Who knows how many he truly has in his employ, or what some people might be willing to do in exchange for a few gold marks?

Adathan continues, speaking louder so I can hear him over the wind, and without him facing me. "We'll need to barter with a captain who will allow us to board if we work as crew, since we don't have the gold to buy passage. I have only enough to pay our way for food once we arrive. The captain will have to either be unaware of who you are, or persuaded into discretion." His voice darkens at the last bit, and the tone and huski-ness of it has me holding back a shudder.

But I respond, voice bored and vaguely annoyed: "That won't work. Weaschte doesn't trade with Eshelle; hasn't in centuries. There will be no captain insane enough to make the journey, especially for nothing in return."

"Weaschte has been trading with Eshelle for over thirty years."

My stride stutters, and so does my heart. I have to think past the surprise, and the betrayal at matters of my own nation being hidden from me. Past it, for now, and instead ask, "So, if we find a captain, he'll allow you on his ship?"

"Probably not. But I don't have to look like this when we scope for one." He doesn't so much as look over his shoulder as he says it, but somehow I see Artur's face, watch dark hair shift to golden.

My voice is like acid when I reply. "Yes, you've already proven how your majick can fool us. Poor, pathetic humans that we are."

At that, he does turn. Halfway, and so quickly that I would have bumped into him mid-stride if I'd been any closer as we walked. Sun gold eyes peer down at me with some of the fire of their namesake. "I did not say that. Do not put words in my mouth." Still not angry–just flat, and succinct. Then, just as quickly as he had a second ago, he turns back around and continues walking. "The majick is called a glamour. And yes, it can make me look different from how I normally do."

My brow furrows, my anger doused more quickly than I'd imagined it could be. One moment there, hot and real, and the next just a memory; cooled into nothing by the damned constant curiosity of my mind. "Then why can't you use that on me, so no captain would recognize me?"

"I didn't think you would want me to."

That gives me pause. *Do* I want to be majickally disguised? Though some part of me cringes away from the thought, another whispers how nice it might be, to be somebody else. My heart is forever changed. Perhaps the outside appearing different, as well, would end the unbearable disconnect from my soul.

But both my soul and my mind know that I don't deserve that reprieve. Thus, his statement, his assumption–it hangs in the air until we make it to the woods, where it gets caught in the many branches of the pines. Torn to shreds by thousands of needles.

I have plenty of questions remaining, but can't bring myself to voice them. Luckily, I have the focus of stepping over the tree roots to distract me for a while. I might even forget that I'm walking with anyone at all, if it weren't for the fact that his booted feet leave huge imprints on the dirt, moss, and dried-needle-strewn ground for me to step into as I follow him.

After an hour of watching my own feet, and glaring at his back as he picks his way easily through the woods that continue to betray me (I mean, seriously, how many times can one person trip?), I wonder if he feels it yet. The thirst and the hunger that nag at me to satiate them. How long can his immortal body go before feeling uncomfortable with them? I don't want to reach my senses out to him to find out–to feel the pain of his hunger or thirst on top of my own.

So, we just keep walking. The roots are less raised here than they are deeper inland–likely due to some shift in the density of the sediment, or the proximity to water. And somehow the shallowness of them has me catching my toe in what feels like every other bloody step.

After the fifth time it happens, and I catch myself before I can fully trip–again–Adathan turns to look at me. It's been embarrassing enough knowing that he can hear me each time I stumble, and watching him slow so that I can catch up afterwards, but having him look at me, judging me, is much worse.

"That keeps happening because you're paying too much attention to the ground," he says.

My eyes narrow. "That doesn't make any sense."

"You have to trust your body. Your mind. Like walking down stairs with your hands full. The more you think about the next step, rather than just trusting that your body is familiar with them, the more likely you are to fall."

I hate that I understand his analogy, immediately seeing the sense in it. My mind should process the foreground for me, and make the calculations for my body to move accordingly. The only issue then would be that I no longer have the next step, and the next, to occupy my mind. And I'm not entirely sure what else I should think about. What else might keep my brain from straying to those still-leashed thoughts and feelings in the back of my mind.

Still, I keep my eyes on his as I take my next step, and it lands steadily on the ground before me. Without another word–or even an *'I told you so'* expression–he walks forward as well. I decide to keep my gaze focused on the space between his shoulder blades, high enough that I can only see the ground in my periphery.

The muscles in his back shift beneath his cotton shirt, and I recognize that, while the Fae strength might be handed to them, that kind of bulk and definition is not. He's trained for probably longer than I've been alive. And, though I've fought him twice now, I'm under no misguidance that he'd been giving it his all. In both scenarios, he'd been under orders not to kill me. If that weren't the case, I have little doubt that I would already be dead and buried.

I wonder if Olin has the same training, or if he always lets his power do his work for him. Is there even such a thing as *dodging* majick like that? Whether there is or isn't, I'm betting that my companion would know.

Before I can ask, though, he turns his head halfway to me, and says, "We'll stop to eat soon. And maybe the beast's muzzle will tell us if there's water nearby."

So, I bottle up yet another question until later. "Alright."

We walk in silence for a while again after that. The only sounds are my soft pants of breath that I try to keep through my nose–savoring the little remaining moisture in my mouth–and the crunching dirt and pine needles beneath my feet. Over time, as I keep my eyes focused on his back, I pick up on his movements–the *way* he moves. And I try to replicate it. How his foot falls, and how his weight shifts to keep so quiet. Soon enough, my footsteps soften, and I notice how, in that silence, animals begin to scurry from their hiding places.

Squirrels leave trees, and rabbits and foxes leave their holes. When they realize that the quiet was false, they stand with preternatural stillness until we pass. When we do, I wonder when "soon" is for Adathan. My training included many things, but not having access to food wasn't one of them.

The privilege of growing up consistently fed has never been lost on me; it's one of the things we used to thank the gods for each night. Now that that privilege has ended, I find myself employing the same efforts of moving through extreme discomfort as I do when training. And, just like swordplay and weightlifting, I'll be damned before I complain about it.

We go on until the sun has long since passed its apex in the sky. It shines in transparent yellow streams through the pine boughs, turning patches of the rich green trees golden. With them, the summer heat has truly saturated the woods, heedless of the shade. Much too hot for early summer, the humidity feels so dense, I could cut through it. My hair went up in a knot at the top of my head around midday. Sweat has soaked through Adathan's shirt, turning it nearly sheer, and I'm grateful that I still have my shift beneath my clothing, no matter how dirty, otherwise my body would be just as exposed. Our few and far between stops for miniscule sips from the water skin at his hip do nothing to staunch the heat.

When finally we encounter a small flock of wild turkeys, Adathan pounces on them faster than I can blink. In seconds, one is in his arms as he walks back towards me, its neck already snapped. The rest of the flock gobbles loudly deeper in the woods, having flown off when the predator struck.

"This will be enough to keep us for today and tomorrow," he says, and uses his forearm to wipe the sweat from his hairline. "Would you rather pluck the feathers, or find us something to carry it in? The backpack Gadsby was carrying was gone before I got to him."

The last bit has the tone of an apology, and I can't really understand why. It isn't as though I'd brought it up to him. I'd forgotten that pack existed, honestly. Still, I don't have to think about his question to know my answer. "I'll look for something."

He nods, absently stroking the feathers of the bird. "Keep an eye out for a water source."

I just set off into the woods, not enough energy to glare at him–but a little left to mimic him. *Keep an eye out for a water source,* I mutter to myself in a mockery of his voice.

"What was that?" he calls to me.

"Nothing!" I shout over my shoulder, then, more softly as I step through the trees, "Stupid, good-hearing turkey murderer."

After about fifteen minutes of fruitless searching, it occurs to me: the pines. With their skinny limbs which might be malleable enough to be woven together–*and* provide the sugar, and some of the moisture we need to keep moving.

Several minutes later, my arms are full of long, thin limbs, hands sticky with sap. My nails are torn from the effort it took to part them from their branches, and I send my magic to them, if only to spare myself from how they feel when they snag on the branches, and my clothes. I walk back towards the direction I came from, making sure to keep my eyes up. My arms are full, and these are stairs, and I will not fall.

When at last I see Adathan through the trees, he's standing, the plucked bird hanging from one of his hands. Once he spots me, his broad shoulders seem to relax a bit. Or maybe slump in disappointment, that I didn't come shouting about a shining, perfect lake in the middle of the wilderness? Either way, when I get closer, he raises a dark brow at what I have in my hands.

"I'm going to weave these together," I tell him, lifting my arms slightly. "I didn't see a water source, but I figured until we find one, the sap will do. Plus, the sugar will help us when we run low on energy."

It might be my eyes deceiving me, but he looks...impressed. Then he gestures to the setup he's put together in my absence. "I've got the spit ready to go, and the bird is plucked. If you want to start weaving, I'll cook."

I nod, but first hold out one of the thicker branches to him. "If you snap it, the sap will come."

He takes it, and I wipe the pine needles that stick to my hands off on my trousers, restraining a wince as the stickiness has the fibers of the fabric snagging on my skin. The breaking is quiet, since the tree I took it from was alive and well, and light amber liquid comes from each end. He hands one to me, and I lick the bead, the musky sweetness and moisture coating my tongue in an instant. Across from me, on the other side of the small fire Adathan's made, he does the same.

I slide the dry end of my half into the waistband of my trousers, so that I don't accidentally weave it in. The fire is stifling when too close, so I take my seat several feet away from it, and get to work.

Adathan uses his dagger to slice up the animal, its thighs and wings and breasts separated for faster cooking. I hear each drop of grease that hits the flames, but otherwise, the only sounds are him turning the spit, and the scratching of the twigs as I weave them. My brow is furrowed in concentration, figuring out the thatching required for a secure bond. I have to work to curve some of the pieces as I form the base, and by the time I finish one half, I'm out of branches.

I stand to grab some from the nearest trees, licking the sap off a couple of them after breaking them from the main boughs. Utterly absorbed in my project, I then replicate the process for the other half, forgetting my hunger and the male across from me for a short while. I don't even realize that I'd begun to hum as I worked, until I'm interrupted.

Adathan says quietly, "Food's ready." I look up from my work to find him standing there, offering me a turkey leg.

I brush the pine needles off my hands, and take it. "Thank you," I say with equal quiet, but perhaps a bit more reluctance. I eat the entire leg, though, and when the bones are bare, I throw them into the fire. When I sit back, the gnawing in my stomach at last subsiding, I say with a bit more sincerity, "Thank you."

He pauses with a wing halfway to his mouth, and replies, "You're welcome. Do you want more?" He gestures with his stubbled chin towards the remaining meat kept warm by the coals. I stare, considering–and without another word, he breaks his wing in half, and hands it over to me. I press my lips together, but while my mind pretends to consider, my body leans forward, and grabs his offering.

I take a bite, then finally get around to one of the questions that has nagged at me. "Why can't we use that packing majick, like we did yesterday? For the water, the food, the backpack."

"We call them pocket realms. And we can't use one because they aren't just up for grabs." He wipes the corner of his mouth with a thumb. "One has to be located, and then it's almost like... luggage. It goes with the person who finds it. Olin has one. While we were with him, we could use it–but if we were to use it now, he would know. And he could find us by the trace that majick leaves."

"Why can't you find one?" I ask.

He doesn't look offended by my bluntness–doesn't take it as an insult to him or his power. He only answers, his rough voice calm, "If I did, he would be able to trace that, too."

I feel my brows scrunch, intrigued despite myself. "Because of the blood oath?"

"Yes. I can use ordinary majick, but anything that requires enough that I drain my energy would be noticed by him. And searching for, seizing, and making use of a pocket realm would do that. Not for long," he begins, answering my next question before I can ask it. "I would regain my strength quickly. But the risk is not worth it."

I process that, staring down at my makeshift pack. I pick at some of the pine needles, breaking them in half against the pad of my thumb with the nail of my forefinger.

"What are you thinking?" Adathan asks.

I sigh, and look back to him, and his sun gold eyes are tired, but curious. Maybe a hungry me wouldn't have responded, but a satiated me replies slowly, "Your majick...it seems so different from ours. Is it only because we're human? Where's the balance in giving a species with so much advantage, even more?"

He leans back, bracing his hands behind him on the forest ground. "Magic, or *majick* is different for everyone. It was separated by verbiage so long ago, I'm not even sure we have histories on it in Eshelle. It had to be labeled differently, because it *is* different. As for the why...you'd have to ask the gods."

"I no longer believe they're listening," I tell him flatly.

His head tilts slightly, but he doesn't ask me why. There's not even confusion in his eyes. As if he knows exactly why, and when, I stopped believing in things like blessings and prayers and gods.

"Stop looking at me like that." I don't snap, or yell it; my voice is low, and vicious. The last of the coals crackle as their embers die, and he holds my gaze, the look in his shifting from one kind of knowing to another. I watch as he sucks slightly on the inside of his cheek, then nods once. He unsheaths his dagger, and I tense–but he only holds it over the fire, cleaning it of the animal, and the layer of sea salt still coating the blade.

I get to work, too, picking up the pack, and beginning to weave the halves together. I scratch my hands up severely when knotting a few very thin branches together to make a strap, and then hold it up to inspect it with the light still shining through the trees. After ensuring the integrity of the weaving, I hang it by its strap from a protruding branch on a nearby tree, and place several pounds of rocks in it. I let it dangle there for a moment.

"I know you don't like me, but are you going to make me carry all of those?" I hear Adathan ask from behind me.

And again, it's probably only because I have a full stomach for the first time in two days, but instead of ignoring or retorting his attempt at an easy conversation, I turn my face to him and reply, "You carried me through the ocean. You're drawing the line at ten pounds of rocks?"

I think one corner of his mouth *almost* tilts up. Our–likely temporary–amends made, he says, "We should head out. We only have a few more hours until it's too dark to continue for tonight."

I nod, and unload the rocks from the obviously structurally sound pack. Not the most sanitary option for storing our food, but at least the sugar and pine might flavor the meat. I hold it out for him while he puts the rest of the bird into the pack. I'm about to swing it over my shoulders when he takes it from my hands instead, and puts it on over his own back. For all of a heartbeat, I consider thanking him, but he's already moving.

31

UNENDING NIGHT

TONIGHT'S COURT GATHERING WOULD BE THE LARGEST IN decades; all nobility from every one of Sabrian's border countries were expected to be in attendance. Not just High Lords and High Ladies, but their children, their dukes and duchesses. As such, though the Great Hall was immense, it had been decided that this gathering would be held in the even vaster gardens of the castle.

I wore a golden gown that wrapped elegantly from my waist to the floor, pooling in a train behind me. The bodice seemed of its own material, until I walked. The fabric was sheer, with an array of glitter and embroidered stars covering my chest where it needed to, and that same sheer fabric continued into the lining of the skirt. When I took a step, my entire right leg could be seen through the glimmering fabric, the gold silk of the main skirt covering everything else.

The lines of my tattoo could be seen if you knew where to

look, and focused through the glitter and stars. I'd taken a golden makeup pencil and drawn the same pattern of flowers up to my collar bone, and then to the edge of my shoulder. It continued in a thin but elaborate vine down my right arm, and ended in a flower on the back of my hand. I'd majicked the design to remain, unsmudged, until I removed it myself later on.

Maybe it was silly, because he'd already seen me in the dress when we'd gone shopping with Nuria and Jolie, but my heart pounded when I thought of Dion seeing me in it tonight. Yesterday we had been so busy with planning, and helping to set up, and all of today had been spent receiving guests as they arrived.

But ever since he'd held my hand on the roof two nights ago, every glance we exchanged felt more significant. And the heat I sometimes caught in his gaze–the longing, and, maybe, something deeper–was mirrored in mine.

I wouldn't be escorting him tonight. Our High Lord and High Lady had thought it would be a better show of trust for him to be unaccompanied when he arrived. To have him guarded, even just in appearance, would make it look like we either didn't trust him, or them. And while the latter was still being established, this small choice could help that cause.

I didn't believe anyone would harm him in a home that was not their own, but it made me feel a bit more secure knowing that he could defend himself if necessary. And, given his obvious predisposition to avoid conflict, I had no doubt that our friends would intervene if it was needed. Because, even as his self-worth was steadily growing, I still wasn't sure that he would raise a hand to someone else if he believed their attack was justified.

I was making myself more anxious thinking about it. I checked the clock, and breathed a sigh of relief. It was finally past the time he should have arrived, meaning that I could now do so as well without any whispers of mistrust resulting from it.

I practically ran out of my chambers, the heels of my shoes clicking softly on the tiled floor. I wound through the halls, and down staircases familiar as the back of my hand, until I reached the ground floor. Minimal staff were within the castle, all either serving at court, or off for the evening. I passed Arthur as I exited through the main doors to the gardens, giving him a smile to which he responded with a nod.

The space was always lovely, but tonight it was bedecked with a grandeur that took my breath away. The paths were lit on either side by glass bulbs of faerie light, which cast their soft yellow glow onto the flowers surrounding them. More bulbs hung from the branches of the central willow, bobbed in the small ponds of brightly colored fish, and floated among vines of honeysuckle and jasmine. Above, the new moon still in its phase, the stars shone brilliantly, their beauty only interrupted by bursts of tree branches, and brass trellises. Ahead, in a clearing with tables, chairs, and a space for dancing awaited, about a hundred people stood and socialized.

I kept my chin high as I strode forward, even as I looked around for familiar faces. Only strangers turned towards me, gawking. To those that smiled, I smiled back. But if they only stared, seeming to forget a person was attached to this dress, I stared right back at them until they realized their rudeness, and dropped their gazes. I slowed as I entered the crowd, scanning for my friends, and finally spotted Jolie, who stood towards the edge, quietly observing.

She sensed my approach, and when those ice-blue eyes landed on me, they widened, and her mouth popped open. She wore a sage green gown, which not only looked fantastic with her terracotta skin, but made those eyes practically luminous.

Her long, dark waves were swept behind her shoulders, silver earrings dangling from her lobes.

"You look absolutely Heavens-sent and gods-blessed stunning," she told me when I stood before her.

"Right back at you," I replied, grinning. "Where's your lovely mate?" I asked, hoping–

"She went off with Dion a few minutes ago to get us drinks." And I knew from her kind smile that she understood why I truly asked. Jolie was quieter, but just as, if not more intuitive than, Nuria. I moved to stand beside her, and leaned my shoulder against hers affectionately for a moment before straightening. Given her majick, she likely knew even more about what I was feeling than I did, but, until I voiced it, she wouldn't say a word. A true friend, she only smiled up at me before her eye was caught by something–some*one* else.

They appeared through a gap in the crowd about twenty feet away, each of them holding two stemmed glasses of sparkling wine. They were chatting animatedly about something that couldn't be heard over the cacophony of voices around us, until Nuria–resplendent in a sparkling silver gown, and a diamond and silver headpiece–looked over to see where her mate was. Following her gaze, still smiling at whatever they'd been talking about, Dion's eyes met mine.

His smile faded from his face, replaced by something like awe. My heart strained as his hazel eyes trailed all the way down my dress, and back up, and then doubled in pace as I saw not just reverence, but heat when his gaze was once again on mine.

They kept walking towards us, and as they did, I decided that I would look my fill, too. He wore a navy suit that was flawlessly tailored to him. It spread over his broad shoulders, and fit the powerful length of his legs. And–probably thanks to the female beside him–his tie had gold star accents which perfectly complimented my gown. When I got back up to his face, he was standing just a couple of feet from me, his full lips tilted up. And his eyes–they held a light brighter than the hundreds of faerie lights shining in the garden.

He handed me one of the glasses he held, and said, "You look gorgeous."

My responding smile was small, shy even–something I'd never been in my life. "Thank you. You don't look half bad yourself."

I could feel Nuria and Jolie watching us, probably what they thought to be inconspicuously. I couldn't have cared less about it, or the stares of the nobility around us. It was me, and him; thrumming heart, and ever-softening eyes.

He leaned in then, and my heart stuttered a beat as his cheek halted barely a hair's breadth from mine. "I'd like nothing more than to dance with you for the rest of the night," he said quietly, so that only I might hear, his breath caressing my ear, my neck. I arched involuntarily towards him at the sensation. "But I think we'll feel better about our service to Hielo and Hiela if we mingle a bit."

I nodded, our faces still so close, hardly breathing. And as he pulled back, I felt him hesitate a beat before he pressed a light kiss to my cheek. Heat rose to my face in response, and, before I could stop myself by thinking too much, I reached to grab his free hand with mine. He squeezed my fingers once before asking, "Who should we talk to first?" loud enough for others to hear, allowing Nuria and Jolie back into the conversation.

They stepped up, and Nuria said, "Nobility from Planici and Obala are here, and haven't been charmed yet. The Grevoschi and Estrellans have been taken care of, and are already drinking and dancing with Sabriani." She shrugged, but gave us a meaningful look before swiping her finger over her temple, under the guise of scratching an itch.

A code, meaning Hiela had information for us. Continuing to talk, and smile, Dion and I opened our mental shields by a sliver.

Her mental presence was there in an instant, and she said, *"The King and Queen of Weaschte are here. They are glamoured. You will be introduced to them tomorrow. Tell no one."* And then she was gone, and we sealed our shields once more.

Nothing changed–not facial expressions, not tone of voice–from the moment Nuria scratched her face, to now, when she said, "We'll take Planici, if you two will take Obala." She looked past the crowd, towards one of the tables, where three males, and two females could be seen talking amongst themselves, drinking sparkling wine. "Their High Lord is there–his wife passed birthing their child, the Lady on his right. Then the Duke and his mate, and their adoptive son. Got it?"

We nodded, and set off towards that table, which sat by a large hydrangea bush, its small blue flowers bobbing in the light breeze that cooled the densely packed gardens. The nobility saw our approach, and something warmed in my chest when Dion didn't snatch his hand from mine when their eyes moved to our twined fingers.

The High Lord of Obala had light golden skin, and near-black hair and brows that lowered severely over eyes that were just as dark. His daughter beside him was graced with as much beauty as he was handsomeness, but her lovely hooded eyes were a cinnamon brown. The Duke and Duchess had a similar appearance. And their son–was a faerie.

He was young, no more than five, his skin the russet hue his people were born with in the high mountains of Hart. He smiled adorably, seeming to not sense the tension emanating from his Fae parents. He might have looked Fae as well, if not for the small horns poking through his dark waving hair, and the bat-like wings that were tucked behind him.

When we reached them, Dion and I bowed, and they dipped their heads in turn. "Good evening, High Lord. My name is Ciaragen Vey, Lady of Dremerre, and this is Dion Evestre, Lord of Parvata."

"Hello, Lady Ciaragen, and Lord Dion," the High Lord responded in a deep bass. "I am Javi Kahale. This is my daughter Talia. Duke Aleki Natia and his mate, Duchess Elei. And their son, Sione."

"It's a pleasure to meet all of you. May we sit?" I asked.

"You may," he said, and then looked at Dion. "He may not."

It took all of my self-control to not react. We'd known this might happen, that some nobility might not be accepting of Dion, at least not right away. Still, I had to keep myself from showing offense, or coming to his defense. He was to stand alone, and bear the weight of disapproval on his own. Our High Lord and High Lady had pointed out that, *ferocious as you may be, he would not seem a strong ally if he needed someone else to come to his aid.'*

Hating the practically mandated betrayal, I released Dion's hand, and took one of the open seats, while Dion folded his hands behind his back, and remained standing. My hand, my breath, the very air around me felt colder when I no longer stood beside him.

"Oleander's pet spends a month in Sabrian, and I'm supposed to believe he's completely converted?" The High Lord clicked his tongue, shaking his head, and then took a sip of sparkling wine. Setting it down, and lightly clicking his tongue, he continued, "Yet, the Lady Ciaragen Vey, daughter of legendary General Gabriel Vey, holds your hand. What am I to make of it?"

"Well, High Lord, I'm sure you could make many scenarios

up in your mind to explain it. The simplest one, and the truest one, are the same. I came to Sabrian, and saw that the world outside of the capital was thriving, while the one I knew wasn't, and it wasn't hard to figure out why that was. I *converted*, as you say, within days of arriving here."

"Because of Lady Ciaragen?" Javi asked, eyeing me with unhidden judgment.

Dion's tone hardened slightly as I tensed under that look, shadows gathering around the hands I rested on my lap, beneath the table. "Because it was the right thing to do. When I arrived in Sabrian, Lady Ciaragen held as little, if not less, regard for me than you do. And if you know her, and you know her lineage, then you also know that her honor in all matters should remain unquestioned. That she has chosen to accept me is not something I take lightly, and I will work the rest of my days to be worthy of that trust. And," he added, his voice taking on a menacing softness now. "Though we may want your allegiance, High Lord...if you ever insult her again, I will show you why *our* High Lord and High Lady want my power on their side."

Shadows dissipating, I had to look down at the table to hide the smile that threatened to rise on my lips. When I raised my head once more, the High Lord's gaze was already on me. I lifted my chin and straightened my already straight shoulders, and, after a long moment, unreadable brown eyes moved from my face to Dion's.

Then, without any preamble or apologies, he said, "It seems that the High Lord and High Lady of Sabrian have taken one of Oleander's favorites from him. And now...what? You're going to ask us to join the cause?"

"Yes," Dion answered shortly–more short than he'd ever been with anyone who'd been rude to him in the past. Then, "But if you'd like me to kiss your ass to convince you, I want to point out that I'm much too far away to reach it when standing."

All faces at the table fell utterly flat as they glanced between Dion and their High Lord. Javi stared at Dion with unflinching intensity, and I readied myself for yelling, or even a burst of power from him, but–

He laughed. The High Lord cackled so loudly that people at other tables turned to stare. With a smile, his severe face brightened so significantly that he was almost a different male. The rest of the table joined in, even his daughter, and I tried to ignore the way her eyes flicked up and down Dion where he still stood behind me.

"Please sit, Lord Dion," the High Lord said through his last chuckles. Dion pulled out the chair beside me, sitting close enough that our knees brushed under the table. I pressed mine more purposefully against his, his warmth seeping through the fabric of my skirt.

We discussed with the High Lord all that we had been given leave to divulge. By the end of the conversation, even Sione seemed excited by the cause, and all of us were on a first-name basis. The faerie boy seemed particularly giddy to leave the manners I was sure his mother and father had instilled in him behind, and call me Ciaragen, like one of the adults. Indeed, his emotions got the better of him at one point when he said something adorable that we all laughed at, and his wings lifted him a couple of feet off his chair before he settled back down. I watched his Fae mother stroke the hair around his horns, and tell him he could take a nice long flight later, if he wasn't too tired.

After we'd all eaten, and shared two bottles of sparkling wine, we took to the dance floor. Right now, the band was playing a tune suitable for group dancing, and Sione gripped my hand and his mother's, jumping up and down to the music, little wings tucked tight to avoid them hitting the other dancers. Talia seemed inclined to dance close to Dion, and I realized that I wasn't bothered by it. Not because she wasn't beautiful–she was, incredibly so–but because each time Dion had laughed at the table, he'd looked at me to see if I was laughing, too.

When everyone on the dancefloor was sweating and panting from so much movement, the band at last drifted into the softer songs meant for partnered dances. Talia eyed Dion and I for a moment, then winked at me, and found a stunning Grevoschi female with bright green eyes to dance with instead. And I realized that her eyeing Dion had been to examine his relationship to *me*, not the other way around.

Flattered, I grinned at her when she looked over her partner's shoulder for a moment, which she returned. And then a strong male figure in a navy suit intercepted my view, and held out a hand. I looked up into those gold-green eyes. "May I have this dance?" he asked, and the question held the same sincerity as the questions he'd asked in the library, what felt like ages ago. And, just as he had then, he very much cared to hear my answer.

I didn't hesitate to give it to him. "Yes," I breathed, placing my hand in his. He pulled me to him, placing his other hand on my waist while I rested mine on his shoulder. I'd removed my heels about halfway into the group dancing, so he once more stood half a foot taller than me. His feet moved well, but they were the part of him I was least concerned with as his hands held me, and his body moved with mine.

After a while, when the Obalans had departed, and even the Sabriani had started to retire, my head rested on his chest as we swayed to the last honeyed notes of the final song. At some point, he'd leaned to rest his cheek on the top of my head. His hand never strayed from its place on the small of my back, but his fingers now brushed that space so softly and intimately that I sighed, the skin on my arms pebbling.

When the song finished, and the few people remaining clapped, he pulled away from me first, still holding my hand in his. His lids were slightly lowered as he looked down at me, his lips parted as if he wanted to speak, but was toeing that same line we'd both been walking.

And I knew that it was up to me to take a step over that line. That he would never, no matter how much he might want to–and the look in his eyes told me that he wanted to *very* much. Whether it was so that he wouldn't jeopardize our friendship, or because he didn't think I felt the same, or a combination of the two. He probably thought our relationship to be platonic at best and tenuous at worst, given how I'd acted around him for so long. I would be happy to show him how wrong he was.

"Dion," I breathed.

"Yes, Ciaragen?" he replied, just as quietly.

"I don't want the night to end yet."

His answering grin was soft. "I'll go wherever you take me."

I smiled at him, and led him by the hand back through the gardens. As we walked, he stooped to grab my shoes for me where I'd left them earlier in the evening, and held them as we made our way through the halls of the castle. He lagged just a bit behind me, letting me lead him, without any presumption, to where I might want to go. When we passed his chambers, still he said nothing. He was quiet all the way until we reached the door to my rooms.

There was the gentlest of tugs against my grip, and I looked back at him. His eyes flashed between the door, and my face, and he said, "Ciaragen, I don't think you want to take me in there."

I stepped toward him, leaving only a few inches of distance between us. "Why not? We've been in here together before."

"Yes, but...Ciaragen, if you take me in there now, my restraint will be–I'd want to tell you that I–" he cut himself off, and released my hand, taking a step back from me. He took a deep breath that only served to fill his lungs with my scent, and I could hear the pounding of his heart in the otherwise silent hallway.

"I want you to tell me," I said, and leaned back against the door, wrapping my hand around the handle.

My shoes clattered to the floor, and in half a second, he was in front of me, one hand holding mine still on that handle while his other braced on the wall behind my head. His pupils were wide, eyes glazed with desire, but when he spoke in a low, rasping voice, his warm breaths caressed my face with the same softness as his words.

"I'd tell you that I haven't been able to stop thinking about you since I first laid eyes on you. That I want you so badly that it's hard to concentrate on anything else. That I dream about how your lips might feel against mine, and how mine might feel on all parts of you. I'd tell you that if you ever wanted me, you'd need only ask, and I would be wholly yours. That I have been, ever since your eyes first met mine in the halls of this castle."

My breaths caught as he spoke, and my body, my heart, my soul melted at his words. And I knew that, however much I'd fought and denied it, I'd always known that he wasn't who I'd made myself believe he was. And the part of me that had always known the truth knew another now: that what I'd really been fighting was my want, my *need* for him.

"I'm asking," I breathed.

His eyes flared, shock replacing the desire for a heartbeat. But when the heat and hunger returned, he lowered his face until his mouth was just an inch away from my own. "What are you asking for?" he growled, his breath mingling with mine in the space between our lips.

"You. All of you," I whispered, voice and body trembling with anticipation.

"Then I am yours," he said, and then his lips pressed against mine. He released my hand to put his around my waist, pulling me closer to him, his other on my neck. His thumb caressed my jaw while his fingers twined through my curls, and when his tongue tentatively touched my lips, I opened them for him, a steady thrumming building in my core.

And when his tongue curled expertly around mine, showing me exactly what he might do on other parts of me, I moaned into his mouth.

I felt his lips curl up against mine in response, and that hand in my hair gently but thoroughly tightened. I made a soft, breathy sound, and then his other hand moved to help me open the door, since I'd gotten lost the moment the kiss started, not remembering where I was, or caring if anyone saw us.

I backed into the room, not breaking the kiss, our lips moving together so confidently that it felt like we'd been doing it forever. I heard the thump of his foot against the door, and then the click of it closing. I reached my hands up his chest slowly, luxuriating in the muscle, the strength under my palms. And when he shuddered beneath my touch, it was my turn to smile. My arms around his neck, he ran his fingers from my shoulders and down my nearly bare back, and back up again.

I needed him. So desperately, after weeks of denying myself, denying *him*. I needed to feel his skin against mine, to breathe his scent in for hours. I needed to have him so that I could be his, too.

I slipped my fingers into the knot of his tie, undoing it, and pulled one end until it fell to the ground. His hands stalled on my back, and I withdrew only far enough to see his face, and the question in his eyes.

"*All* of you," I repeated softly, and ran my hands into the lapels of his jacket, pushing it back and off his shoulders. He watched me, the heat in his eyes mingling with something much more powerful, and I did not break that gaze. For the first time, I let the same things shine through in my eyes for him to see.

I undid the buttons of his shirt, scrunching my fingers along the waistband of his pants to untuck it. He shuddered again with this small pleasure, and still I did not look away, even to see the evidence of how this might be affecting him. When the shirt joined the tie and jacket on the floor, I dragged my fingers down his chest, then his abdomen, until my thumbs finally hooked into his waistband.

I undid the buttons, feeling his arousal against my knuckles as I did so. When they were undone, I swiped my hands along the band to let them fall, along with his undergarment.

And when Dion stood naked before me, he put his fingers beneath my chin, and leaned in to brush soft kisses against each of my cheeks, my forehead, each fluttering eyelid. One for both corners of my mouth, and when his lips were centered on mine, hovering over them so that I almost begged him to take more, he said, "Your turn."

32

A STORY OF POWER

THEA - PRESENT

WE MAKE IT JUST OVER TEN MORE MILES BEFORE THE SUN GETS too low to see, evidence of the new moon apparent in the darkness that overcomes the forest. And with the sun also goes our warmth. My arms are folded tightly over my chest as the last dregs of its light filter through the trees around us. I've drawn my hair around my shoulders to try to keep some insulation around my neck and chest, but it does little against the chill that pierces through my thin cotton shirt.

"We can camp here," Adathan says quietly. I can't even see the whites of his eyes—just an outline of his shape. But still I keep my gaze high, trusting my feet just as I've worked to do all day before this. I hear him set the pack down. "I'll get some wood for a fire."

I consider fighting him on that, but even I know it would be out of sheer stubbornness; he has the advantage. I'd tell him I can get the wood, and his immediate rebuttal would be that he can see better in the darkness than I can. And then I would feel annoyed at his true statement, and honestly I just don't have the energy for all that.

So, I just nod, and ponder how, after spending all day with someone so quiet, I understand this much about the dynamic between the two of us. I suppose that when you're not trying to get to know someone beneath the surface–other than what he'd said to me earlier–it's easy to understand what little they show you.

And, though I still have too many thoughts and questions, the exhaustion is taking precedence over my curiosity. If I weren't so cold, I might have already laid down on the ground, and fallen asleep. And if I weren't listening so intently for footsteps, waiting as each heartbeat passed for him to come back– waiting to not be alone in the wilderness, I might have been able to calm my racing thoughts.

A lot of maybes, and too few certainties, but still I sigh when I pick up the sounds of him returning.

He sets down the wood, and I hear some arranging, then flint scratching. Sparks burst, and catch, the dried needles burning fast for immediate warmth, the thick branches carrying their flame to keep for a while. With its lumination I can see the area immediately around us; anything outside of the small circle of orange light seems ominous. Adathan sits close to the flame, poking his dagger into it to adjust some of the wood.

I move to sit across from him, and hold my hands out to the heat, flipping them back and forth to warm each side. When the cold leaves them, I place my palms against my throat to warm the blood coursing through it, wincing at the pressure against the bruises that still ring it.

I haven't healed any of the marks the past two days have left on me–not once allowing the magic that graces my blood to attend to it, as I can feel it wants to–and I wonder if he's realized why that is. I could argue that it's because, although he saved me in the end, he'd watched them hurt me, and done so himself–and he should have to look at their handiwork. But I know that the true reason is that I don't believe I deserve the absence of pain. I don't deserve to be unmarked.

Some wretched part of me is glad that he won't be either. That beneath his clothes are the scars I've left on him. That his skin is forever etched with the reminder of what he's done to my family–just like me.

"You're looking at me like you hate me again," he says suddenly, interrupting the silence previously only broken by the crackling wood. I meet his gaze over the fire between us.

"You haven't seen my face in miles. The feeling didn't stop, so neither did the look." I remove my hands from my neck to warm them before flames once more.

I wait for him to tell me that I'm lying–because even I know that I am. I'd forgotten to hate him for a little while. I'd gone full survivor-mode; my only actions had been to walk, and wait until it was time to take a single sip of water from the skin, or a bite of turkey. My thoughts had been consumed by my many unanswered questions, enough so that I might have been able to forget, for brief moments, how thirsty and tired I was.

I'd forgotten to hate him, too busy focusing on surviving with him, and on the answers he might be able to give me. And I kind of want him to call me out on my lie, if only to get me mad enough to feel past the exhaustion that dulls the loathing in my mind and in my eyes.

But he doesn't. What he says instead is, "I'm sorry."

My eyes widen in surprise, and then narrow. "For what?"

His jaw tightens. "A great number of things, but right now for hitting you earlier."

"I didn't know blood oaths were so literal," I mutter, meaning for it to come out snarky, but my temple throbs, my legs shifting under me at the memory of the pain he'd inflicted, and my tone shifts to something like mortification. Not just because of where he'd hit me, but because...I had never expected that the first touch I would feel there from a man would be harmful. My gaze drops to my knees.

"Blood oaths are so literal that if he had told me to slit your throat instead, and paint my face with your blood, I would have had to do it. My will be damned."

The way he says those last words tells me he's not just talking about this hypothetical situation. I lift my eyes back up to his, and find their golden depths earnest. "What does it mean now that you're away from him? Does it no longer apply?"

His fists clench atop his bent knees. "No. Only he can free me from it, which is to say that I will never be free."

"Even when he dies?" When. Not if.

His eyes darken in the amber glow of the fire, and his husky voice is low when he answers, "No. When you kill him, I will be free of him, too." He pauses, and I let him. I watch him think, rather than diving into my next query. But I don't expect the question he poses for me: "Does that bother you?"

"No," comes out, before I even think about it. I clear my throat. "No. That doesn't bother me." And it doesn't. That he has a mutual interest in Olin's death settles some of the uncertainty that's been weighing in my chest as we've walked through these woods. I had, after all, believed that his reasons for freeing me from Olin were not wholly altruistic. My head tilts to the side slightly. "You do as he commands, but you don't want what he wants?"

A muscle in his jaw feathers as he holds my gaze over the flames. "No, I don't. His word is my command, but only that. His will is not mine, nor are his desires my own. But if he tells me to do something, or not do something, I cannot disobey. If I do, I die. If I even hesitate for a moment, I'm in agony. So, when he commanded that I spy for him, and then that I serve him by remaining with you throughout the journey back home, that is, respectively, what I did, and will do." There's an unspoken ending to that sentence that I can see in his eyes for half a heartbeat; not nearly long enough to translate it.

His jaw tightens again, but he goes on, "He's gotten sloppy over the years. I think he believed that I was wholly loyal, so I wouldn't ever try to find loopholes in his words. But, all of yesterday, that's what I was doing. Figuring a way around his orders. I finally realized that he never put himself into the equation. He said I would remain with *you*. Not him, not 'us'. Only you."

I interrupt him before he can continue. "If you were planning the whole day, why did you say that thing about me not escaping?" I raise a brow, hoping that the fire in my eyes burns as hot as the one between us. "You seemed pretty damned confident."

"Because it was the truth. You wouldn't have escaped, not successfully. He would have caught you, and made me or Gadsby knock you out sooner, if he didn't do it himself." His voice and his eyes both darken as the coals crackle. "I needed you awake. Needed that time as we walked to think. To make sure there wasn't some underlying oath I'd made long ago that would hinder me.

"The last thing I had to sort through was the 'home' bit. And I realized, he didn't specify that it would necessarily mean *our* home–and there was no time constraint. I could take you straight back to Castle Cerasche, or I could take you to Eshelle, and back. So, once I figured out my way around his last command to me, I only had to evade one of the first he'd given: to do him no harm."

"But you blasted him back with your power at the cliffs," I remind him.

"I threw a bit of wind at him. It blew him back, yes, but the most it did to his body was perhaps dry his eyes out a bit."

I take a deep breath, thinking all of that through, and my exhale flutters the flames before me. They dance with the air, and once they resume their usual pattern, my voice holds only curiosity when I ask, "What will happen to you when he dies, then?"

"As long as I'm not the one to do it, nothing."

"So...when the time comes, I'm on my own." A stupid thought, and I damn myself for speaking it as soon as it's out. Did any part of me, even subconsciously, really believe he would do anything to help me after our journey to Eshelle is done?

But Adathan nods once in response anyway, a muscle flickering in his jaw once more, and I move my gaze back to the fire. Though my face, hands, and shins are all warmed, everything else is still cold. A combination of anticipation and chill makes me shudder.

"Will you train me?" I ask before I think it through too much. The query I had almost voiced earlier today, when this very topic of my insufficiency in the face of their power had come to mind. He doesn't answer at first, and when I look back up at him his eyes are shuttered, hands tight around his elbows.

"You know him, and his power. And Ahmad–he was *great*. He was–" I stop, and bite the inside of my cheek against the emotion that rises in my throat. Once it's mastered, I continue, hating the words as I say them: "And even he didn't win. So I–I need you. I need you to teach me how to fight Olin. Because if I can't win, I'll turn my blade on myself before I let him take me. I don't care if it makes me a coward."

"It doesn't." His voice is so quiet I almost could have

convinced myself it was the wind that spoke. He clears his throat, his hands relaxing. "Yes. I'll train you."

I almost sigh. Almost thank him. But instead, "When?"

"Tomorrow morning. We'll be up before the sun, eat something, and walk a bit so we're not in one place for too long. Then we'll train. But for now, we need to rest."

As if on cue, I yawn, my eyes going heavy as the sound escapes me. Only adrenaline and will have kept me going all day, and now the bone-deep exhaustion of being up for two days is taking control. Not even the hardness of the ground, nor the chill against my back, is enough to keep me from lying on my side, pillowing my cheek against my arm, and closing my eyes. I think I hear Adathan say something, but I'm gone already.

⇿

I've been trapped here forever.

I don't remember a time when I was not watching my mother die. When I didn't feel what agony is too gentle a word for. When my throat didn't ache from unshed tears, and my screams didn't tear me apart from the inside.

I watch her die, her neck at an unnatural angle. And then blood is spilling from too many places, and her face is Hanna's, her belly rounded with a child that will never live. And when the blood seems to pull back into her skin, and I think I might somehow be healing her, Amahd takes her place, his eyes still full of the confidence in me that I did not deserve. When his broken neck becomes my mother's, the cycle begins again.

But then, in another world, a hand touches my shoulder. The me who stares into Hanna's silver eyes stalls, her brows furrowing. Hanna's neck opens in a red smile as she lifts her head to listen with me. As her wound trickles blood onto her belly, a voice from above calls to us through the shattered ceiling, telling us to wake up, to *WAKE. UP.*

I sit up, gasping, dried pine needles sticking to my skin, still half in the nightmare. It takes a large hand gripping my chin and pointing my face towards eyes the color of the sun on deep water for me to remember where I am; *when* I am.

"Breathe," Adathan tells me. "Breathe with me." He pulls a deep breath in through his nose, and I do my best to follow, not caring that he's the only thing keeping the tears that would not come in my dream from falling now. He lets the breath out through his mouth, and I do the same, my own far shakier than his. He does this six more times, until my exhale is more steady, and my heart has calmed. And then he releases my chin.

I close my eyes, and take a few more breaths on my own. With each one, I let go of an image. I let each of them fade into the back of my mind, where the rest of my unspoken thoughts and unattended emotions await release. I suppose I should've expected that if I would not attend them in my waking hours, they would come to me in my sleep.

When I open my eyes, they find Adathan's–no judgment or pity to be found in the champagne depths. With a voice like sandpaper, I tell him, "Your breath stinks."

He sucks on the inside of a cheek before responding. "That's a lot of talk from someone with half the forest on her face."

I stick my tongue out at him before brushing the dried pine needles off my cheek.

"From the light, I'd say it's about five thirty in the morning." He hands me the water skin, and my heart sinks at the lightness of it. I take a sip only big enough to wet my tongue, and then hand it back. He cracks a thin pine branch, and extends a half to me. Not nearly as thirst-quenching as water, the sap coats my tongue, and fills my mouth with a far less stale taste than I awoke with. I recognize a throbbing that steadily builds in my head as the beginnings of dehydration.

Adathan hands me a turkey leg, for which I nod in thanks before digging in. A night in the pack has sweetened it, and given it a rosemary-like flavor. If it weren't for the small flecks of dirt that stick to it as well, it would have been a decent breakfast, even cold as it is.

I finish it all, though, chucking the bones into the simmering fire. The wood on top looks relatively fresh.

"How long have you been up?" I ask.

He shrugs. "A while."

Not very specific, but alright. I roll my eyes and stand, brushing more pine needles out of my hair. Then I reach my arms above my head and go up on my toes, stretching until joints pop. When some of the tension is released, I sigh. I straighten my dirty trousers inside the leather boots, tuck my salt-crusted shirt back in, and braid back my hair.

Moments later, Adathan stamps out the fire, puts the pack back on, and we're off again. The forest around us is already wide awake. Birds chirp high up in the trees, small creatures scurry about the forest floor. Just like before, I feel as though the life beneath my feet and throughout the woods thrums through me. It must be some part of my gift doing its best to keep me connected to the world, to life. Like it knows that I'd lost some of that feeling, and is begging for me to get it back, and hold on tight.

The trouble I'm having, of course, is that we always called them *gifts* because the gods gave them to us. And since one of the things that I'd lost connection to is the gods, I'm faced with figuring out what else to call it.

"Why do Fae call their majick 'power'?" I ask from behind Adathan.

He glances over his shoulder, annoyingly sure-footed even

without looking ahead. But he only answers when he turns back around, and speaks as though telling the tale straight from a book. "It's believed that Deimos, a god of death, saw the people of this world in a very dark time, and cried nightly for his guilt and sorrow of not being able to help; of so many souls joining the Heavens before their time. At first, his tears watered the earth, giving a fruitful season of crops. But when they did not stop, they flooded the same lands they'd brought to life.

"The people began to question if the gods existed–for what gods would give their people hope, only to take it away? And what gods would allow even those most faithful to them to suffer and starve? As a last effort, Deimos argued with his fellow gods and goddesses that some of their divine powers should be given to the people of this world. That faith in them could be restored if the people were given the ability to bend the elements; to understand minds; to be healers of the earth.

"Out of all of them, just one goddess agreed: Ymeda, who was the goddess of life. Her only request was that some of her majick be delivered to the earth on which the people lived. That the Fae might prosper, but so might the trees, the waters, and the other creatures which lived on that land. When Deimos accepted her condition, she bestowed unto him a seed of her power.

"'*Like any seed,*' she said, '*the power will grow when it is nourished. And know this, ye god of death: you will forever carry its mark within you, too, so long as you do as I ask. Bestow my majick unto person and place alike, as no people can thrive while their land suffers. And when you are struck down for disobeying the word of the majority, know that only the love you bear in your soul might keep my majick alive there in turn.*'

"What she didn't tell Deimos was that the seedling encapsulated *all* of her power; clustered into a kernel he would put no questions towards. Given freely, and taken well. As such, when their bargain was struck, and she placed it into his hand, she needed only wait until he bestowed her majick as they had agreed before she faded forever. Not into the Void, but into the very earth to which she gave so much, and so willingly to. Forever blessing it with her glory, to be brought forth by a ruler given freely, and taken well."

He sighs, the only interruption to the story I've become, however unwittingly, enraptured in. "But upon learning of her sacrifice, Deimos was enraged. That one had given all, and others none. So, as the remaining gods slept even as their people suffered below them, Deimos took from each of them a kernel of power. And with tears of grief and fury, he sprinkled them down unto the earth.

"When the gods woke, they felt that loss of power, and knew who was responsible. And so they banished Deimos to live among the creatures he loved more dearly than his own.

"We call them 'powers' because that is what they are. Majick derived from the sources themselves, not freely given."

It's an interesting story. The gods he spoke of–Deimos and Ymeda–are not ours, but are clearly still figures to the Fae. Which means that our gods are different from theirs–and perhaps they both exist, and perhaps neither of them do. The easy part to believe is that the other gods in his story would not give up even a kernel of their power to save the people who loved them so much. The rest is harder to accept, but still–it's an interesting story.

"What happened to Deimos after he was banished?"

The muscles in his back flex beneath the pack as he shrugs. "Some say he was given a mortal lifespan, and died thousands of years ago. Some believe he remains immortal, and is forced to live in exile from his home for eternity, even after this world ends. Others think that there might be reincarnation involved, and he either lives among the gods again, or down here with us, just with new lives."

"What do you believe?" I ask.

"I'm not sure I believe in any of them," he answers, and I hear the double meaning within it.

I'm not sure if it's the unexpected honesty in his words, or the way they resonate with me, but, when he looks back to assess my silence, one corner of my mouth tips up in a miniscule, tight-lipped smile. He stops in his tracks for only a moment; just long enough to return the barely-there expression before he turns back to the woods ahead of us.

33

ALL OF HIM

CIARAGEN - 21 YEARS EARLIER

My heart was racing in my chest, but not from fear, or anger. No, the steady thudding was lovely; it was from a dream coming true. It told him so much of what I hadn't yet said aloud, and I could see in his eyes that he understood the language it spoke.

Dion's hands left my face slowly, moving so that his fingers trailed down my neck, across my collar bones. I shuddered, goose flesh pebbling on my arms and legs, but his hands did not stop. They gently gripped the ends of my shoulders, and turned me so that he could see the intricate lacing up the back of the gown. As I felt him pull at the bow at the bottom, his lips pressed against the space between my neck and my shoulder. My neck arched, a sigh releasing from my throat.

I listened to the silk ribbons slip through their eyelets, and when the dress loosened, I held the bust of it to myself, wanting

"

to see him as he saw me. I turned back to him, and stared into his eyes as I lowered my arm and let the gown fall into a puddle at my feet.

"Look at me," I told him, knowing that he would not allow his eyes to leave mine otherwise. He listened, and I watched those hazel depths darken as they roved over my breasts, my belly, and lower.

Slowly, lazily, he brought them back up. "Your turn," he repeated. And I listened, too. I looked my fill at the breadth of his shoulders, the muscles in his chest and abdomen. And when I reached the vee of his hips, and what hung in its center, my mouth dried a bit at the sight, and the muscles in my core clenched tight.

When our eyes met once more, he reached up to stroke my cheek, and said, "You're beautiful." And I smiled for him, my eyes burning now. Because even a few years into my maturity I was sometimes self-conscious about my small breasts, and narrow hips. The size of everything else was more than appeasing, but in my moments of insecurity, my mind focused on those details.

I realized, though, that not once as Dion had looked at me had I felt that self-consciousness. I'd felt...beautiful. And seen. And...

I stepped towards him and rose up onto my toes to press my lips to his. He knitted the fingers of one hand into my curls, and wrapped the other around my waist, pulling me to him. I moaned as I felt him against me, and pushed myself closer as I nipped at his lower lip, and he growled low in his throat.

Then, both hands were around my waist, and he lifted me off the ground. I wrapped my legs around him, hooking my ankles against his back as he walked us to my bed, his mouth never leaving mine. When we reached it, he slid his arm up to cradle me as he bent to lower me to the mattress. I was ready for him, so gods-damned ready–

But he gently, but effectively, pulled my arms from around his neck, and unhooked my legs. I was about to protest, to ask him, beg him to take me, when I saw him kneel before me, his eyes on mine. He grabbed both of my ankles, his fingers wrapped around my heels, and set each of my feet down behind his shoulders.

As his hands traveled up to my calves, his mouth pressed against the inside of my knee. When his hands were on the backs of my knees, his lips were on the middle of my inner thigh. And when he pulled those knees wide, laying me open and bare before him, he kissed the bundle of nerves at the apex of my core. Then, just as delicately, licked it.

Even that light touch was so exquisite that I moaned loudly, not caring if there was a sound shield around the room or not. He ran his tongue down my center, and then into me, and when I felt my muscles tighten around it, he was the one who moaned. He tasted me, and the enthusiasm with which he did so made me completely abandon any thoughts of inhibition.

And I would have taken control then, but he didn't need me to. He rose once more to circle my clit, and then sucked it between his lips, with another groan at my taste. The combination of the vibration and the movement of his lips and tongue against me made my eyes roll back into my head as breathy pants came faster and faster from my body. I felt myself so close to the edge, the pleasure building so intensely as he licked and suckled me. And when he stuck his finger into me, and curled it, simultaneously growling low in his throat, I shattered.

I gripped the sheets as I came, shouting his name for even the gods to hear, and Dion did not remove his mouth from me as the throes of it wrapped around and wrecked me. And still, I needed him, needed to feel *him*, but when I moved to sit up, his broad hand pressed my belly down, and he held my gaze over it as he continued to feast on me.

I went over the edge again, and only when my cries of pleasure subsided did he move his hand, and kiss the inside of my thigh. When he at last rose from the ground, I sat up, eye-level with his navel. But when I leaned in and down, he gripped my chin, tilting my face up.

"Not yet," he said.

"But shouldn't it be your turn?" I asked.

"There are no turns for this. No expectations. If later you want to continue down that path, then that's something I would love to do with you. But not because of reciprocation–because we want to. And right now, what I want is for you to lie back on that bed, and let me give you what you asked for." His fingers tightened on my chin, and then released me. Not dropping his gaze, I did as told, scooting a bit further back from the edge of the bed.

When I laid back down, I slowly dragged my feet across the duvet, opening my knees wider by each degree. And as he appraised me, he said again, "Beautiful."

My heart straining, I reached my hands up, beckoning to him. He grinned, and then lowered himself to the bed, walking out with his arms until he was over me completely. His hand trembled as he brushed a curl back from my face, and I turned to kiss his palm. Then slowly, holding his gaze to convey my intention, I reached down between us, and wrapped my fingers around him.

He jerked slightly, and I reveled in the feel of the warm, silky skin against my palm as I ran my circled hand up and down his length. Just because I wanted to. He watched me do this, his head dipped slightly as he panted.

"All of you," I said once more, and he lifted his gaze back to mine. Heat and hunger and adoration shone in those green-gold eyes, and I held them with mine as I guided him towards my entrance.

He held there for a heartbeat when I released him, and the hand that had been in my hair moved to my hip, a calloused thumb running gently over the arch of my bone. And then he pushed in. And in. And in, until he was completely seated inside me, and I adjusted to the fullness of him. And he felt so damned good there, so utterly perfect and *right* in a way that my body and soul had never felt before, that emotion overcame me, and a tear traveled down my temple. I probably would have been embarrassed of it, if his own eyes were not shining.

He lowered his face until his lips were on mine. Then he pulled out slowly, and then thrust back in with equal speed, and I moaned as I parted my lips for him. His tongue swooped into my mouth obligingly, and he thrusted again, faster this time. I moved my hips in rhythm with his, even as his pace quickened and then held in a rolling flow that had me approaching the edge I'd already fallen off of twice.

He took his mouth from mine, and scooped his arm behind me to pull me with him as he sat up. I gasped at the even deeper fit in this position, straddling him, a pleasuring pain that became only an even deeper pleasure when I adjusted. I stared into his eyes as I began to ride him, and he gripped my ass as I did so.

"Gods, Ciaragen," he panted, his brows furrowing as I moved on him. "*Gods*," he said, and then lowered his face to my chest. He sucked my nipple into his mouth, pulling my hips down and forward, his fingers biting into the flesh of my backside, and it was my turn to speak his name to the gods. He persisted with that rhythm, that motion, as my inner muscles tightened around him, feeling him so deep with just enough friction that I–

And when I came this time, I stifled the sound by sinking my teeth into the space between his shoulder and his neck, canines piercing skin. "That's it," he said against my breast, before flicking my nipple with his tongue. I whimpered against his neck, and he chuckled, the air peaking the already sensitive bud. But when my inner muscles flexed at the sensation, he cursed, too.

He rolled us again, until I was once more on my back, and my teeth released from his neck, leaving the white oak and amber taste of him in my mouth. And if I thought that he'd already shown me all he had, I was wrong. If I thought the most pleasure I'd ever felt was not going to be topped on the same night, I was wrong. Because Dion thrust into me, over and over, fitting so perfectly inside me, his hands feeling so right on my body. And I felt it.

I felt this living thing that was like the first kiss of the sun on the sea in the morning, or the first star that came out at night. It hung there, in the sky, as it always had, just waiting to be grasped–accepted. And when I grabbed it, a warmth that was like new life being breathed into me filled my body, my mind, my soul. There was no part of me that was not bound to the male who now stared into my eyes with wonder.

And the realization of what we'd done, what we were *doing* was so beautiful, so achingly lovely and precious that I climaxed once more, and this time Dion went over the edge with me.

He called my name as he spilled himself inside me, pounding into me. I wanted all of it, luxuriated in the feeling, and in the way he held my gaze as I took what he gave me. When he stilled, I wrapped my legs gently around him, not willing to lose even an inch, of him or of space. And kissed him.

A slow, steady kiss that calmed our racing hearts. And when we separated, my mate brushed a curl back from my face, and smiled.

⇔

Dion

MATE.

The word rang in my head like a bell, over and over, its song more beautiful than any I'd ever heard. I stared into Ciaragen's deep blue eyes, still atop her, and knew she heard the same music.

And I knew that I could say it. Knew that if I told her that I loved her, she would understand. But I wouldn't do it. Not right now. Because right now, we'd just finished having sex–the best sex of my Void-damned *life*. But saying it now, for the very first time, would feel...transactional. As if she had given me her body, so only now could I give her the words I'd held onto for weeks.

No. I would tell her–in fact, I'd shout it from the rooftop of the castle, of every shop in Colina, if she wanted. I'd like to tell her I loved her every hour of every day until she told me to shut it. But not until we were no longer tangled up together. No matter how much I never wanted to have that be the case.

No, I'd like to stay here, stay inside her and fuck her, only stopping when we needed food and water, and then go right back to it afterwards. I had never felt anything so perfect, so *right*, so soul-shatteringly amazing as being with her. And the primal male part of me roared in satisfaction that this stunning female was *mine*. The rest, that was not ruled by the Fae beast, was in awe; disbelief that this kind, intelligent, brave, strong female was my mate.

And the way that she stared into my eyes told me that somehow, she thought the same. Felt the same. Her gorgeous blue eyes crinkled at the edges as an equally breathtaking smile spread across her face. In wonder at the fact that I could do so, I leaned down to press a kiss to those full lips, marveling at the feel of them against mine. My resolve to wait to tell her wavered as I felt her grin against my mouth.

Instead, when I pulled away, I said softly, "What?"

She stroked my cheek with a thumb and replied, "I'm just happy. Very happy."

My heart clenched, and I turned my face to kiss her palm. She kept her hand up, and I seized the opportunity to kiss down to her wrist, then her forearm. As my lips grazed down to her shoulder, and across her collarbone, I scented her, and her fresh arousal, and hardened again inside her. She groaned, squeezing the fingers of her other hand into my backside, pulling me deeper. I obliged her, pushing into her, into the space that felt so perfect, like it had always been meant to be *us*.

It wasn't like the first time. The build up, the exquisite tension and restraint, leading into faster, harder motions. An experience that I would cherish forever, and would serve to inspire me to give her that much pleasure whenever I could.

Flawless, and precious, but also a first time. Of learning each other, of recognizing what got the other on edge, and how to balance on it to prolong the pleasure.

This was not the first time. And I would not have her thinking that she was about to be mated for life to a bloody one-trick pony.

"You said you wanted all of me," I said as I rolled my hips in time with hers. She panted softly, and damn if I didn't want to hear those little breaths for the rest of my immortal life. Again, the awe of getting to do this with her came over me, but I shoved it down–for now. "Do you still want that?"

I pushed once, hard, into her to emphasize my meaning, and she gasped, the exhale a moan of pleasure. Then I watched her eyes gleam, as though I'd presented her with a challenge that she very much wanted to experience. "Yes," she responded, digging her fingers into my flesh for emphasis.

I grinned down at her, and growled, "That's my good girl." Her eyes glinted as she bit her lip, and then widened in unspoken protest when I pulled out of her. But I grabbed her hips and rolled her over, then pulled her perfect, round ass up in the air. I nudged her knees apart with one of mine, placed one hand on her hip and pressed the other one to her back. Like fucking puzzle pieces, when I moved forward her entrance was at the perfect height for me. Without a word, I sheathed myself fully in her, and she groaned into the down pillow against her face, her soft inner muscles clenching around me.

"Fuck, Ciaragen," I said, pumping into her. "You feel so damn good." Gods, she did. Torturously tight, and warm, and wet.

She turned her face so that I could see her smile, even as I thrusted again and again. And I quickly learned that that smile meant trouble as she started to bounce her ass against me at the same pace at which I moved. Both of us groaned then at the even deeper penetration.

"You look so good taking all of me," I growled, watching her move on me.

"Your cock feels so good deep inside me," she countered, her voice half-sigh, half-moan.

"*Fuck*, Ciara." I reached for her then, wrapping an arm around her waist to pull her up against me. I brought that hand up to grab one of her breasts, feeling the peaked nipple against my palm as I squeezed, still driving into her. I pressed my other palm against her lower belly, and reached with my first two fingers to circle her clit, eager to make her feel as good as her pussy was making me feel. She moaned, and reached behind her to grab the back of my neck, and tilted her face so that we stared into each others' eyes, and shared heavy, pleasured breaths.

My hand on her breast moved to her throat, the only pressure on the muscles at the sides of her neck. She bit a smiling lip before resting her hand on mine, and pushed my fingers tighter.

I seized her mouth with mine then, while the fingers of my other hand worked that sensitive bundle of nerves, thrusting into her all the while. She panted into my mouth, so I kept the exact rhythm and pressure, and said against hers, "Come for me."

Gods, she did. Her climax had her inner walls clenching around me, and my own name filled my lungs as she called it against my lips. The sensation in combination with the tone her ecstasy wrapped around my name had me joining her once more, filling her once more, and I thought I might die from the ecstasy of it all.

Still, even after our breaths and heartbeats began to slow, I might have stayed inside her if I could. But, as it was, this wasn't an easy position to settle down in. As my hand on her throat loosened, and I held her only so that she wouldn't tip over, she giggled. A happy, uninhibited sound that bubbled up adorably as she tried to do the same thing–keep herself from falling over.

And I laughed, too, because it was funny. After the frenzy, and the pleasure, and the indescribable things we'd likely talk about later, it was funny. So I pulled out of her, and she lowered herself before rolling onto one hip, facing me. And gods damn her and me, but when she looked down at my cock and bit her lip, I could have taken her again then and there.

And though I realized that this was part of the mating, the need for each other that surpassed rationality, I also knew that we had all the time in the world to explore each other's bodies. I could calm myself enough to let her clean up, to clean myself up. To eat, and get water. And to talk–to my best friend. Even after this, perhaps *especially* after this, she was still that to me, too.

I reached over to brush those magnificent spiral curls away from her face, and leaned forward to kiss her forehead. She smiled at me with so much joy and contentment that it made me weak in the knees, yet still I stood, and said, "I hope you don't mind if I help myself to your washroom."

"Not at all," she replied. "I need to use it, too, when you're done."

I raised my eyebrows at her, resisting the urge to look at her still-naked breasts, the strong but soft torso, and that alluring place between her long, chestnut legs. She had no such decency, watching as I hardened again as I didn't even look at those things; just thought of them.

"You're a cruel, stunning temptress," I said, and then gave her a half smile. "Lucky for me, I've had a month of resisting temptation. So when I say that nothing else will be happening until we've cleaned up, and you've gotten something to eat and drink, it would be wise not to doubt me."

"Is that so?" she asked, her voice throaty as she gazed up at me through her lashes. I swallowed, but nodded. She grinned, ever wicked, and leaned forward until she was on all fours. And then, she crawled to me, saying, "Well, my Lord Dion. You had a month of resisting me before you had a taste." She prowled closer. "Before you felt your cock inside me." Her face was just inches from my cock when she rose up to her knees before me, and my tip brushed against her belly. And then she looked up at me with only her eyes, her chin tilted down, and whispered, "Do you feel so untemptable now?"

"No," I breathed, my voice shaking slightly with restraint.

She held that pose for another heartbeat, drawing out the anticipation. And then she smiled, and hopped off the bed, her bare feet hitting the area rug with a soft thud. "Didn't think so," she said over her shoulder as she strode for the washroom.

And I smiled, too, for the clever, gorgeous vixen whose ass shook as she walked away.

34

A TENUOUS TRUST

"THAT WAS GOOD," ADATHAN SAYS AS I PANT, HANDS ON MY KNEES to catch my breath. He stands across from me in the wide space between two pine groves, his dark hair ruffling in the light breeze. While I know that tonight I'll wish for the sun's warmth, right now it's the air whistling past my sweaty face that I'm grateful for.

"You beat me in four seconds," I say, glaring up at him beneath my brows.

"That's three seconds longer than many have lasted before you."

I stand up straight and roll my eyes. "Ohh, big, bad Fae male." I deepen my voice in a *definitely* accurate imitation of his, *"I'm so tough and strong, I could fend off an entire army with my pinky finger, and flip them off with another without breaking a sweat."*

"It's not that hard to flip someone off," he responds, though his lips *almost* pull up at the corners.

"I'm also very funny, and take pride in the fact that I've never once laughed at my own joke–or anyone else's, for that matter."

"You laugh at your own jokes?"

"I'm not that smart, though, because I ask stupid questions."

He crosses his arms over his vast chest. "How long are you going to do that?"

I puff out my chest, and hold my arms out the way his sit on his body; slightly extended out, from the thick muscles in his back. Except much more exaggerated.

"I don't stand like that," he claims, though he sucks on the inside of his cheek, like it's the only thing keeping him from maybe, possibly showing a little hint of a smile.

"This is you." I widen my legs slightly, and then perform a lumbering walk in a circle, frowning deeply.

He's biting his lip now. "Is that so?"

"Wait." I walk to him until I'm standing right beside him, and then turn my head to examine him. Arms still crossed, he watches me do all of this from the corner of his eye, his expression stoic. I rise up on my tiptoes, still not nearly as tall as him, and then resume the walk, my back to him. "Now yes."

And I hear a throaty chuckle escape; one beat of laughter before he's silent again, but it's enough. I smirk, just a small twitch in the corner of my mouth, and turn around, dropping back down to my normal stance.

Adathan nods, understanding my goal, and possibly the reason behind it. That it feels like ages ago when I last laughed, or heard someone else laugh. Forever since I'd smiled without menace. The reality being that it has only been three days, and facing many more...I just wanted to feel something other than pain, or anger, or numbness. Even if it's with him. Even if I'll hate myself in a moment for needing him for that, too.

"Let's go again," he says, not delving, like he could, into the thoughts that pound against the back of my head. I nod and sink my feet into the ground. Not a stance for typical combat, but one apparently stronger for defense against majick, and for–supposedly later–attacking majick. The first twenty minutes of our training had been spent breaking down what I knew in favor of what I had to learn.

Despite everything, despite it being *him* doing the teaching, I'd stepped easily into my student role. Everything had been analytical, from mimicking his stance, down to learning how to fall when hit with a wave of unfamiliar power.

Now, he fires off a blast of power, and I have to figure out just from the positioning of his hand from which direction that power will hit me. Even from twenty feet away, I have only a fraction of a second to react. I duck left, and feel it whoosh by me, but another follows it, and this is where it gets tricky. Because unlike a blade, which whistles through the air and glints in the sun, the majick is invisible; soundless. And as soon as I miss one, another is already coming, and I have neither blade nor magic to parry it.

Still, I manage to shift slightly to my right and down before it comes over me, this time close enough to blow back my braid. But the next one comes straight for me, and I'd have to jump ten feet in the air to miss it.

He says he's using only partial strength, and I'd call horse-shit, but I've seen what even just a small blast of his power can do. It's hard to remember, though, when I'm knocked onto my ass *again*, the force of that *partial strength* enough that it takes all of my 'falling practice' to keep my neck from snapping back.

I curse, hardly recognizing the scratch of the pine needles beneath me, or the pain in my still-healing temple and throat. Before the oath is fully past my lips, I'm standing, brushing my trousers off pointlessly. "Again."

He obliges, and this time I make it past three blows before getting hit. Then two. Then four. Five. I might have felt victory over that last one, except the goal isn't just for me to dodge them. I'm supposed to be moving closer to him, too. To train not just at a shorter range, but for the end I want to give Olin.

I won't snap his neck. Poetic though it may be to kill him the same way he had... It's not intimate enough. I want to feel his blood on my hands, watch his eyes as he realizes it's over, listen to his heart stop. Only then will I trust that he's truly dead.

Unlike some people.

I make it to five again, and even close two feet of distance between Adathan and I this time. As we continue to practice, I think. Focusing on his movements and planning for them has not been working for me these past twenty minutes. The bruises on my back are proof of the number of times I've gotten up, only to be knocked down once more. Which I will do, again and again. But I shouldn't have to.

A shift in strategy. One he's probably been waiting for me to make. I need to do the same thing that he'd told me to do in the woods yesterday: trust my body.

Perhaps I should be grateful that he's not dead. Maybe I would have figured out a way of escaping Olin on my own–but maybe not. Probably not. And I haven't allowed myself to consider what I might be enduring if that were the case, but I know that a few bruises on my tailbone would be lovely in comparison.

Another five blasts of power, and I gain three feet on him this time before I get knocked down.

Perhaps I should be grateful that he saved me. I suppose that I am. If I'm being honest, the truly difficult thing is that I wish somehow that it hadn't been him. That the male who'd pretended to be loyal to my family for a year, only to sell us out, wasn't the one who stepped in for me. I've thought, over and over, about how I loathe that he is. But, I recognize, as I run at him again, that my failure to figure out a way to do it myself is only part of the issue. Something I've yet to admit, even to myself, is that I'd thought someone would have come for me by now.

Six movements, and five feet.

My brothers. My father. Even guards. I'd thought someone would have come and found me by this point. We walked these past days, while they have horses at their disposal. And, yes, this forest is vast, but are there no tracker Mages powerful enough to find me? Am I somehow cloaked from them, in a way that I cannot see nor break?

Eight, and seven.

It would explain why *they* hadn't found me yet either. Those others who had hidden in plain sight–with motives that I still know nothing about. Atlas, and Ciaragen. Fae, with the same sharp senses as the males who'd captured me.

Nine, and nine.

In our last bit of time together, they had moved to protect me. But why? Who are they to me, to my family, to have chosen to pretend to work at, and visit Castle Cerasche? And then step in against one of their own. That they, with their Fae powers, nor my own family, have yet to find me makes me think that there must be something preventing them from doing so.

Eleven, and twelve.

Unless they don't want to. I'd already considered that in regards to my family as we walked earlier, and it had made my heart ache so fiercely that now I only reflect on why that would be the case for the Fae. My actions when we parted were violent, and could be seen as a betrayal in their own right, if they truly were protectors of mine. I had put Atlas to sleep, and broken Ciaragen's bones. That I'd done it to save them might not be enough.

Ten, and fourteen.

Whether they know what my intentions had been or not, I can do nothing about it. Nor can I do anything about who did save me. I can only go on, and be perhaps glad that they haven't found me. Because they would not let me go to Eshelle. They would try to stop me from completing my task.

Eight, and seventeen.

And so it might be for the best. Maybe Adathan isn't just what I'm stuck with, but also the best chance I have. Not only at getting to Eshelle, but at actually being able to stand a chance at doing what I've set out to do once there. If an hour of training with him can teach me how to dodge invisible, immense power, what might the time of an entire voyage across the sea accomplish?

Seven, and eighteen.

And maybe I should get past the fact that he'd lied and betrayed under orders from a blood oath that I still likely know far too little about. I want to get past it–but can't.

He gets six movements in before I tackle him to the ground, disarm him of the dagger at his hip, and hold it to his throat, panting.

My knees pin his arms out to his sides, but still he could have bucked me off easily if he wasn't concerned with getting his carotid sliced with the movement. His eyes hold mine, his own breaths coming a bit quicker than usual from the expenditure of power. But there is no fear. Which means he either thinks I won't do it, or he's not afraid to die. And while the first angers me, the second almost has me pulling away the blade.

Perhaps I should recognize, at least, that Olin would have gotten to me, to my family, regardless of who helped him or not. Acknowledging this doesn't remove any betrayal or blame from

Adathan, but at least it gives me room to be able to forgive myself whenever I forget to hate him. Like when he saves my life, treats me kindly, or laughs even slightly just because I need it. An enemy still, yes–but one that I can trust will continue to have my back, if only because our fates are now entwined.

Maybe I can receive his kindness without loathing myself for it–because I'm doing that too often already; and to remove one reason...it might be worth the compromise. As long as he has my back, I can have his. Because from the moment he jumped off that cliff with me, he switched sides. For morality, as he claims, or for his own freedom–maybe it doesn't have to matter.

His chest rises and falls beneath me, and the breeze carries in a musky scent from the woods as I contemplate all of this. It clears my head, that air, but the smell clouds it in different ways as I realize just how *close* I am to him. Sitting on his chest, knees practically out all the way to my sides to pin his arms to the ground. A particularly deep breath expands his chest and throat, and beneath the dagger's edge, a droplet of blood trickles down the side of his neck.

As his exhale leaves him, my own body moving back down as his chest settles, I stare for another heartbeat into the strange, light depths of his eyes. And I realize that I have one question to ask him before I'm willing to pull back my blade.

"When Marcys came down to violate me," I start, as a bead of sweat trails down my temple, "would you have let him, if I wasn't already free and fighting?"

"No." Anger, hot and real, flares in his bright gaze. "I would have slit his throat myself before he could lay a finger on you."

I stare him down for a moment, deciphering whether I believe him or not. Some feeling in my gut is telling me that I should, even as my mind wars with it. He bears my scrutiny, face set and eyes open, in more than just the literal sense. Still no fear, not even as his blood continues to flow in a thin trickle down his throat, onto the dried pine needles beneath us.

I pull the blade from his neck, and there is no expression or exhale of relief, only a stony calm that has my whirling mind settling. Something does spark in his eyes when I brace my other hand just below his throat to stand, but it's gone before I can place it. He gazes up at me, and that blood flows for another second before stopping, only the line of drying crimson proof that anything had happened in the first place. I hold a hand out for him.

He hesitates only a heartbeat before reaching up to grab it, his broad, calloused hand wrapping around mine. The thin gold ring on his forefinger glints in the sunlight, shades darker than the eyes that hold my own. I release him quickly once he's standing, then clean the blade against my sleeve, before silently offering it back to Adathan, hilt facing him.

But he makes no move to take it from me. "Keep it. You won it," he says.

My brow furrows, but I lower the weapon. "I don't have a scabbard."

He shrugs, and then unbuckles his own belt from his hips, and holds it out to me. I sigh, and hold the blade between my teeth as I take it from him. Too big for my hips–thanks to his thick, muscular waist–only my backside would keep it in place, and I don't feel like walking however many miles with the blade smacking against my thigh. Instead, I swing the belt over my head so that the strap rests on one side of my neck, and the sheath is against my other shoulder blade.

I take the dagger from my teeth, and sheathe it behind me. Then unsheathe it, testing. As I'd hoped, it's very similar to a sword scabbard in the same position, but much quicker to draw due to its length and weight.

He frowns appreciatively, as I sheathe the blade once more,

before going into what I'd started to call *teacher-male mode*. "You did excellently in those last few rounds. Got up fast, stayed up longer. The shift from when you were thinking too much about the next step to when you let yourself simply react was noticeable. Impressive, that self-correction. Did you notice how, after a few tries, you were getting closer faster?"

I nod, and he goes on. "Good. Because it's not just dodging. That was the first step. The second, which you've now started, is to be faster than your enemy anticipates you to be. And I think that you've become–however rightfully–focused on only one enemy. But you're going to a land that hasn't seen humans in a millennium. Some–not all, perhaps not even many, but some– will expect to be able to take advantage of that. And you have to be able to catch them off guard, in a place where their speed and agility makes that rare."

A small part of me trembles at that thought, but he just continues.

"Once you're fast, the next thing you have to be is smart. Don't give me that look–I'm sure you're plenty smart. Definitely smarter than I am. I'm talking combat smart. Learning what's working, and what isn't, and then making quick adjustments, just like you did with me today. The pause between thinking and action will mean your death."

And yours, I think, but don't say. I just nod again, taking in the information and advice, as I have for years before this.

"Then there's strength. It's obvious that you've trained with weights before, and you're much stronger than the average human. But again, you're not going to be fighting humans. Fae and faeries are naturally more nimble, strong, and vicious. And I know that our current diet is not conducive towards this goal, but we're going to do our best to build your strength, regardless of resources. Any questions?"

"Not about training or tactics, no," I respond.

He leans down to pick up the pack just a couple of feet from him. It doesn't have any meat left in it currently, but I'm sure he's thinking of catching another larger animal for our last couple of days of travel, based on what he's just said.

As he swings it over a shoulder, he says, "Ask me your other questions while we walk."

35

CIARA

DION - 21 YEARS EARLIER

IN HER SITTING ROOM, SURROUNDED BY BOOKS AND TRINKETS, I sat with Ciaragen on her dove gray couch, unable to take my eyes off of her.

I'd put my pants back on, and she'd donned a shift, the light gold in stunning contrast with her skin. She had one leg up under her on the couch, the other hanging over, tantalizingly long. On the oblong oak table in front of us laid a platter of cheeses and fruits, as well as a complimentary bottle of wine. She sipped at a glass of it now, her full lips cresting on the edge of the glass.

It was difficult. Wanting her so badly that I thought the restraint might be the death of me, while also being so deeply in love with her that seeing her do so much as drink from a glass made me wonder how in the gods' names she was mine. How a wretch like me could possibly deserve this divine creature, who smiled at me with warmth and joy, like she was somehow satisfied with her lot.

That smile faltered now, and my heart jolted as I knew she must have realized it. That the sex was good–fucking *great*–but now that the high was wearing off, and she had some food in her, she regretted that she was now shackled to me for life.

If that were the case, no matter how it might shred my heart and soul, I would let her go. If she had regrets, I would not breathe a word to anybody. I would leave and return to Oschverre, so that nobody could scent us together, and she would be free of me. She could find somebody who truly deserved her–if such a person existed.

I understood that I was not that person. Had forgotten it for a short while, as she'd looked at me with those miraculous eyes, and asked for all of me. Had forgotten it, when she said it again and again. While I'd tasted her, and she'd called out my name like a prayer. For a piece of time that had felt like it stretched for a wonderful eternity, I'd stopped remembering that I wasn't worthy of her.

That naivety had ended when she'd walked into this sitting room, wearing that shift, along with a smile so bright it replaced the light absent in the slivered moon. My heart ached when I knew that I had likely just minutes left with her.

Thus, in the split second where her smile faltered now, I simply waited. For her to stand, to be horrified, to tell me to leave. My heart straining, I waited. But none of those things happened.

Instead, she placed her glass on the tea table, and then reached up, and lightly caressed my cheek. "What's wrong?" she asked, her brow scrunching, the familiar little line forming between them.

On an instinct that she was surely about to run from, I lifted my own hand to cover the one she laid on my face. I breathed in the vanilla and bergamot scent, eyes closing at the paradise it yawned open to me, and said, "I don't deserve you."

I heard it as she paused, even her heart seeming to stutter, and released her hand at once. But she did not remove hers. Instead, her free hand came up to rest on my other cheek. As she had from the dawn of my love for her, she spoke in that clear, strong, take-no-shit voice: "Look at me."

I opened my eyes to find her kneeling on the couch now, her breathtaking face just a foot from mine. "Do I not deserve someone kind?"

My brow creased. "Of course you do."

"What about brave? Smart?"

I reached up once more, but this time took her hands from my face and held them in my own. "How about what you *don't* deserve?" I asked. "A male who has killed. A male who worked for a king who did such disgusting, horrible things to our High Lady, and many others. How about a male who shut himself down so completely over the decades that he nearly stopped caring about the people he was supposed to be serving? Do you deserve that?"

Her eyes heated with a familiar fire as I spoke. The same blaze that lit when she talked of injustice. And she said, "I deserve to have who I want. I want a male who wishes to never take an innocent life again. A male who recognizes the terrible things his *once-king* has done, and is fighting to ensure he cannot continue to commit such barbarity. A male who had to shut himself off for a heart that could not endure the world he lived in. And so he found a better one, and taught a female with a broken heart and torn soul how to forgive. How to be kind, and understanding, even in adversity.

"*That* is who you are. Not a murderer. Not a tyrant. But a male who has a terrible past, but is working for a brighter future, not just for him, but for his nation. You, Dion, are who I want. And I deserve who I want," she repeated, her voice soft by the end. "I told you out there in that hall, but I've wanted to for much longer than that. I want *all* of you. And that includes the darker, dangerous parts of yourself that perhaps even you fear. But I do not. I have never."

I recognized the truth in her words. Never had she looked at me with fear in her eyes, nor had I ever scented it on her. Always, she had known who I was, and was not afraid of any of it. Not of my power, my past, my actions. Always, she had looked at me with courage in her gaze. A gaze that had softened these past weeks, giving way closer and closer to how she looked at me now.

Eyes that, like the rest of her, had never lied. It would be very foolish of me indeed to believe that now was the time that they would start. No matter how much I believed I did not deserve her, or the emotions she laid bare to me in her blue depths.

And so I leaned forward, and gently kissed her forehead, her curls tickling my nose. Then each cheek, and, light as a feather, her lips.

When I pulled back, her eyes had heated in a different way. And damn if it didn't make me immediately harden. Her eyes dipped to look at me, straining against the pants I'd put on to maintain some decorum as we ate–to not assume that anything would be happening on this couch.

That had, apparently, been a foolish thought.

Graceful as a silk ribbon slipping to the floor, she slid off of the couch, and onto her knees on the plush area rug. My heart thundered as she moved before me, and forward, so that I had to open my legs for her hips to sidle between. Her eyes held mine as she undid the buttons to my pants, and even feeling her fingers against me through the fabric had my jaw clenching.

When my trousers were undone, my cock standing hard as a fucking rock for her, she bit her lip at the sight. Her hand, which I had dreamed of wrapping around me, stroking me with perfect pressure and pace, did just that now. I hissed an oath beneath my breath at the touch, and her eyes moved back to mine, mischief and lust filling them. She pumped hard once, and a bead of moisture appeared on my tip.

Her eyes still on mine, she leaned forward, stuck her tongue out, and licked it off. The warm wetness, and the way she seemed to luxuriate in the taste was so gods-damned *hot* that I couldn't help the growl of pleasure and appreciation that rumbled in my throat.

Her grin was positively wicked before she leaned down, and slid her mouth all the way over my head. *"Fuck,"* I said as her tongue licked at the underside, along that sensitive line. Then she continued down, and down. And down, until I felt myself nudge the back of her throat. "Gods-damn, Ciara," I panted, and her chuckle around me had me clutching the couch cushions beneath me.

That gorgeous curled head moved up and down, tongue sliding, and her hand joined, adding extra pressure and friction. I moved one hand to her hair, pulling it back from her face, and knotted my fingers in it. She looked up at me again, her view cleared, and then *swallowed* my cock. The length almost completely disappeared into her mouth, and then her tongue and throat moved and contracted, jerking and stroking me without even moving her head.

I panted, the pleasure so intense, unlike any I'd ever felt. But she needed to breathe, for gods' sakes, and I didn't want her to hurt herself just to please me. I began to pull my tailbone back, to give her space, but those eyes flashed in warning. Then she grabbed my other hand from the couch, placed it into her hair, and pushed down.

Loud and clear. And so hot that I felt myself approaching my climax already.

I knitted the fingers of that other hand through the strands, pulling back as much as I could so it wouldn't bother her, and then pulled her head up, and back down. She moaned her approval, and more wetness from her mouth dripped as she licked me.

She squeezed my legs with each hand, urging me. So again, harder, faster, I moved her. Her inhales sounded as she paced her breathing around my thrusts, and her exhales were moans, so sincere and enthusiastic that I got closer and closer to that edge each second.

I felt it, too close now, and tried to pull myself from her mouth, even as my body protested. But she growled herself now, and pushed her head up and down in the same rhythm I'd been keeping, and–

"Fuck!" I shouted as I came, and still she kept that pace. "Ciara," I groaned as she let me spill and spill myself down her throat.

When at last the spasms slowed, and there was nothing left, she slid her mouth off of me, and I watched as her throat moved in a swallow. And then she smiled at me.

I grasped her face in both of my hands, and kissed her, not caring in the least if any of my seed somehow lingered. She'd kissed me heatedly after I'd tasted her, and she deserved the same respect and appreciation.

She was grinning when I pulled back. "I like what you call me," she said, her voice soft, especially considering what we'd just done.

"What's that?" I asked her, brushing a thumb along her cheek.

"Ciara," she responded. "No one's ever called me that before. It's only yours. Just like the rest of me."

My heart melted at that, throat thickening with emotion as she gazed at me with all that trust, and more. Unable to say my deepest, truest thoughts in that moment, I just leaned forward, and kissed her again. Gently, but passionately, our lips whispering together.

That quickly led to her straddling my hips and sinking down onto my cock. She came on me twice, her sounds of pleasure my favorite music, and when I climaxed inside of her she rode me softly, drawing out the sensation in a way that would have had me begging if I could have gotten to my knees. And when we were done, she remained in my lap, her head resting on my shoulder while I stroked the length of her spine. She let out a contented hum, and then kissed the tender spot in my neck where she'd bitten me, claimed me, earlier.

I should have known just from that bite that this was not simply some pent up desire that she was giving into. Claiming was an act so intimate and personal, it was only done with mates. Even those married and in love for centuries did not claim one another in this way. The primal urge to taste the mate's very essence likely went all the way back to whatever beasts we once were. I'd heard it was always the females who did it first–and was intrigued to find that held true.

I ran my fingers over the smooth skin along her spine, from her backside and up into her hair, and back. Up and down, a touch of the adoration I had for her. I would worship her entire body, her mind, her soul, for the rest of my days. I would prove to myself that, even if I would never deserve her, I would make her so happy that it would perhaps not matter.

When I felt her breath deepen and slow against my neck, I smiled softly, and turned my face into her neck, closing my eyes and breathing her in. Finding luxury in this seemingly simple moment. 'Seemingly,' because it was everything to me. *She* was everything to me.

Then, wrapping one arm around her shoulders, and palming her head, the other beneath her backside, I pitched forward, and stood, holding her. I carried her to her bed, and used a small majick to pull back the covers. Just as I had laid her down all those hours ago, I did so again now, and unhooked her arms from my neck. She mumbled sleepily, and I stroked her hair back from her face.

When I moved to pull my hand back, though, her eyes opened by a sliver, bleary with sleep.

"Stay," she said.

I squatted down in front of her, running my fingers over the curls that seemed to trap my fingers in their spirals, holding me here as much as the rest of her. "It will be noticed that I haven't returned to my chambers. It will be noticed if we leave here together in the morning."

"Stay," she repeated, and even sleep could not cloud the certainty in those eyes.

I leaned forward and kissed her soft cheek. "I will stay. Let me put the candles out, and then I'll join you."

Her brow scrunched, either in protest, or in doubt, I couldn't tell. But she nodded. I stood, and took a deep breath. And on the exhale, the candles in the sitting room and bedroom were all extinguished. The power I'd harkened to a beast a month ago purred now, content with this small expenditure. I'd done the same earlier this week, with that single candle, on the roof with her beneath the stars. My power did not have to be monstrous–when I was no longer a monster. And it gave me comfort to know that it was within my reign again. Though I knew she could defend herself, I felt better knowing I could obliterate anybody who threatened my mate, if need be.

Smiling, my heart filled with purpose, I walked to the other side of the bed, and crawled under the duvet and sheets. Ciara turned over, looked at me for a heartbeat, and then sidled closer. She pressed her face to my chest, and wrapped her arm around my waist. I did the same with her, and tangled our legs together. Within a minute, her breaths had resumed their pattern of unconsciousness.

I thought my heart would be racing. That I would feel so exhilarated by laying next to her, that sleep would evade me. But, breathing in her scent, feeling her trust and contentment, and knowing that she wanted me here even in sleep...it was the calmest I'd ever felt.

I fell asleep, holding my mate in my arms.

36

PARALLELS

AFTER A DAY OF WALKING, AND ASKING ANY QUESTION I COULD think of about the land we plan to leave for tomorrow–if a ship can be found–both my body and mind are exhausted.

Eshelle is vast; over two times the size of Weaschte. We'll be aiming to port in Ardhavi, the port closest to where we are now, while also close enough to Oschverre, where Adathan anticipates Olin to be gathering males to replace the ones he'd lost. That's as far into our plan we got before my mind had veered into thoughts of the people and creatures I might meet, possibly even before our arrival if the ship is Eshellen.

He told me about the Fae. How, as I've seen and heard, they look just like humans, but for the arched ears and sharper canines. He didn't say the accentuated beauty bit, but I know it's out of politeness and not forgetfulness.

Apparently, iron can indeed harm them. It can weaken or altogether negate their powers, depending on the amount. It

399

can (as I'd seen in the sea by the cliffs) stall the quick-healing majick in their blood. Most metalwork in Eshelle is therefore of steel or brass or copper. They use gold, silver, and bronze pieces for currency, just like us. Just no iron, which had me wondering aloud about how fences, benches, pipes–many infrastructural designs, in fact, are made of iron in Weaschte. He'd agreed with my thought on the only reason that might be, even a millennium after the Last War.

When I asked why having iron in their blood didn't impact them, he'd thought on it for a moment before bringing it back to evolution. If Fae didn't always have majick, but always had blood, then there could be the possibility that their systems were innately regulated to that bit. An answer which I'd appreciated, because that's what I would have thought as well. But when I'd asked if that meant he couldn't eat steak, he hadn't given that the dignity of a response–only looked at me, where I walked beside him, and turned back to the path ahead.

Then came the faeries. He made no comment about the ones here, those that steal human babes from their homes and do not bring them back. At that, he simply said that matters here in Weaschte are *"unfortunately out of Eshellen control."* I hadn't spoken to him for a short while after that. I only continued my questions when I could no longer hold them back, even to give him the silent treatment.

The faeries he did speak of were none of the likes that we have in Weaschte. They vary in size from inches tall–such as the sprites–to two times the size of humans, which he says more closely resemble spirits than anything else. That, like wraiths, they're not entirely corporeal, but instead of shadows, they are made of gray and white swirls of energy and being. That one had me quiet again for a moment.

The others had been easier to digest. Nymphs of the waters and dryads of the lands. Others who could appear human in stature, but have distinct differences which mark them. The rainbow colors of skin, tails and wings, horns and hooves, eyes that are wholly black or white or blue. So many different races, so much more complex than the magic and non-magic human breakdown in Weaschte.

I'd wondered aloud if the treatment of these people was as equitable as it is between the humans here. Where the humans without magic are treated with just as much respect, and are provided with the things they need in order to not just survive, but thrive, in a world where it's easier to do so with magic in your blood. Not just equality, but a step beyond it; compensation given to grant those without the same opportunities as those with.

He had responded that it was not the case between the Fae and faeries of Eshelle–at least not everywhere. That some countries are much more diversified, faeries given all the liberties of the Fae. But others keep them only as lower employees, if they allow them to work there at all, without any chance for advancement. He claimed that, compared to how it was before the Last War, this was progress. And I'd reminded him that a millennium was bound to be enough time for that.

He'd nodded, his face clouding and eyes darkening. And had been quiet ever since.

Now, it's about thirty minutes to sundown, and we're setting up camp. Based on our combined knowledge of the shoreline, we should be able to reach the docks of Dahlih by tomorrow afternoon. And finally leave these damn woods behind us.

Adathan has hung the pack on the lower branch of one of the pines, keeping it and the remaining rabbit within it off of the ground littered with dirt and dried needles. I've already moved to gather wood for the fire, picking up downed branches in the vicinity. Still silent, he holds his arms out for what I've got so far, and I pass it to him, then continue out of the little clearing for more.

After a moment, I have another armful of sticks, and hear the scratching of flint. When I turn back, intending to leave the wood beside the now sputtering fire, my brow furrows. His back to me, he doesn't see me as I squint at it, trying to make out the strange raises and indents of the shirt. I set the wood down beside him, which he acknowledges with a nod, and then move to examine what I think I'm seeing.

For the first time, I allow my senses to reach out to him. As soon as the pain he's trying not to feel registers in my body, I cross my arms, and ask tightly, "You're allergic to pine, aren't you?"

He half-turns to me. "Do I look like I'm sneezing?"

"Don't play stupid." My arms drop, and I poke a particularly raised spot in his back. He doesn't make a sound, but I feel the muscle beneath twitch in pain. And after two *days* of carrying the ridiculous pack, the shirt is probably the only thing hiding just how raw his back is from the constant irritation.

I sigh. "Take off your damn shirt." Those golden eyes move to mine, and I know that he's probably gotten plenty of people to back down with that look. But I hold his stare, an uncompromising stubbornness of my own more than ready for a battle of wills.

A muscle in his jaw ticks, but he turns away from me, and grabs the hem of his shirt–filthy like mine after days in the woods–and pulls it over his head. Only my years of training as a healer keep me from gasping at what I see.

I hardly even notice the detailed tattoo that stretches across his traps and shoulders–the skin beneath the ink strangely rippled. The entire center of his back, as well as a line that continues over one shoulder and under the other armpit, from the strap, is raised in a cross-hatched tapestry of inflammation, ranging in color from deep crimson to bright pink. But even that doesn't compare to the scars. Huge, bilateral lines beside each shoulder blade. Another set, carved on either side of his lumbar spine. I don't even know what kind of damage would have had to be inflicted for his Fae healing not to erase them.

But I don't ask. I only kneel behind him, ignoring the many other, smaller scars that pepper the skin of his back, and allow my magic to examine the severity of the damage caused by the pine.

"Why didn't you say anything? I would have carried the pack."

His broad shoulders move up and down in a shrug, the skin behind them stretching painfully. "I heal fast."

"So can I, idiot," I respond, my voice bland with annoyance.

"I'm fine," is all he says, but it sounds like it's through his teeth.

I poke that spot again, and without a barrier to the touch, his entire back contracts, though he still manages to not make a sound.

"Would you stop doing that?" he growls instead.

"Gladly. Once you stop being an idiot." I do it again, in the same place. And this time he does hiss. When he remains silent after, I move to repeat the action, but, faster than an adder, he whirls on me, his hand capturing my wrist. The movement has his face just inches from mine, sun-gold eyes bright as their namesake with anger. A snarl rumbles from deep in his chest.

Some small, human part of me trembles at the obvious predator before me. The speed, the hold on me, the way that gaze is locked on mine. But I keep the steel in my expression as I say, in a voice that purrs rather than shakes, "Looks like someone's had enough."

His eyes dip to my mouth, and then back up quickly, as if catching himself. Waiting for a lip to quiver in fear as he holds me still. Instead, I reach with my other hand, resting it on top of his shoulder, where the beginning line of pink from the strap of the pack appears. My magic tends to it, soothing the inflammation. I feel the raised skin under my palm cool, and lower, and when I can no longer sense lingering ailment in that area, I remove my hand. All the while, his eyes hold mine with that predatorial intensity.

"Are you going to let me go so I can do the rest?" I ask.

He blinks, that look clearing a bit, as though only now realizing that he still has my wrist. He drops it at once, and nods, his jaw tight. I move around to his back, my knees rustling in the dried pine needles beneath them. "It might sting at first, when I touch the skin," I warn him, and he nods in acknowledgement.

I exhale softly as I rest my hands gently on the space above each of his shoulder blades–above those horrific scars. I hadn't thought much about just how big he is until now, when even my long-fingered hands are dwarfed by the width of his back. But big men, or males, I suppose, heal just as well as anyone else. So when I feel the skin in that area regulate, my fingers trail down the muscles around his spine, and Adathan shudders beneath my touch as the magic does its work.

Saving the deepest red, the middle of his back, for last, I move my hands down his sides, and then back towards the center, until that crimson is the only hurt remaining. "This will be the worst one." Without waiting for a response this time, I trail the pointer finger of each hand around the outer edges of the irritation. I watch in familiar wonder as the healed skin takes the place of the damaged, in exactly the patterns that I draw with my fingers. His back clenches, but no hiss escapes, only a long exhale as he breathes through the stinging pain.

When at last the center of his back is nothing but tan, scarred–none so severe as those I'd noted before–skin, I say quietly, as I would with a patient, "Lift your arm, please." He does, and I see the strap has left red marks on his tricep, and the skin above his intercostals. I lay one hand on each area, soothing the irritation there. Finally, I shuffle around to his other side. His eyes are calmer now, and I don't hesitate to rest my palms on his chest, below a tattoo that stretches across his clavicle. I try and fail to ignore the raised flesh of more scars beneath my hands as I heal the last of the irritation. Finished, I drop my hands to my lap, still kneeling before him.

"Your pow–gift...it smells nice," he says.

My brows scrunch together. "What do you mean?"

"Maybe you can't scent it. But in our kind, powerful majicks usually have a smell to them. It's interesting that yours does, too."

I frown slightly. "I didn't smell anything from you when we practiced earlier."

"Wind isn't a powerful majick."

I suck on the inside of my cheek. "No. No, of course not. It's just elemental, and can knock me on my ass." I stand, brushing off my knees.

"In terms of what is considered strong in Eshelle, wind is a small majick," he says, standing as well. He picks his shirt up from the ground, and brushes some dirt off of it. "It's almost like pocket realms, in its accessibility. Except, instead of having to find one, you just have to figure out if you can wield it. Some try for decades, and can't, while others manage it on their first try."

Realizing that much of the dirt is stained, not able to be dusted off, he sighs. "Wind, in our world, is easily manipulated, if anyone in your bloodline has had the power. It's the other elements that are considered to be impressive. Water, fire. Earth, especially. For some reason, they don't pass genetically every time. Like whatever powers Deimos stole just exist, and when a Fae is born, their soul links to one at random."

I cross my arms, but consider what he's said. "Then why is wind different?"

He shrugs. "Maybe whatever god had that power was stronger, and so more got passed down to the Fae. Maybe the first person to get that power had twenty kids, and it stayed in the genetic line for some of them. Whatever the reason, over the millenia wind has become...unexceptional."

I nod, accepting that, but ask, "Then what's your power?"

He goes preternaturally still, pausing in the middle of donning his shirt, only his lips moving when he responds, "What?"

"I doubt your only trick is throwing some *unexceptional* wind at people. Olin wouldn't have some weakling in my home. Wouldn't have you help kidnap me, or be with him to take me to Eshelle if you didn't have some immense power. So, what is it?"

His lips press into a thin line, and he throws the dirty shirt over his head, the muscles of his chest and abdomen flexing as he moves. Only when he's pushing his thick arms through the sleeves does he say, "You don't want to know."

"Then why the fuck would I ask?" I snap. Because even though I know more today than I did yesterday, it's still not enough. Not when he knows so much about me after spying in my home for a year, and I know so little about him. This male who I've allowed myself to come to a tenuous trust with, and will be spending weeks with on a ship come tomorrow.

"You ask because you think I know too much about you, and you know too little about me." I blink. And wonder... "And, from your expression: no, I can't read minds. Did you ever wonder why I never looked you in the eye at Castle Cerasche?"

I don't answer, pursing my lips as my heart picks up in pace.

I don't even nod, but he seems to understand anyway. That, yes, I had wondered that. Until very recently, when I rounded it up to cowardice or cunning on his part. Yet now, in this damn clearing in the middle of a wood where no one else can hear what he might say, the earnestness in his usually carefully blank gaze has me waiting for the real reason.

"It's because I knew I was already taking too much from you, without taking advantage of reading your face. I was in your home, an enemy by all rights and reason to you and your family, and I only wanted to keep you from trying to befriend me as I knew you did with other staff. That, even before I learned Olin was coming, I only wanted to distance myself from a kindness I did not deserve."

There is plenty in all he's said that needs sorting through. But my first question is: "What do you mean 'before you learned Olin was coming'? Was he not always going to take me?"

He closes his eyes for a short moment, and as he opens them, he murmurs, "He was. I just didn't know it then. And I can't tell you more than that."

I step up to him, and damn my voice for trembling with uncertainty, and perhaps a bit of fear as to what could possibly remain to be hidden from me. "Because of the damned blood oath? Why did you even agree to that shit? Didn't you know who he was?"

He laughs once without humor. "Hard to know what you're agreeing to when you're seven years old."

My heart clenches, and I breathe, "Seven?" His jaw and eyes harden, and I know why. It's the same reason I snapped at him yesterday, when the terrible kind of knowing that was almost pity came into his expression. So, to rid both of us of that feeling, I lift my chin and narrow my eyes, and I address another part of what he'd told me a moment ago. "Even avoiding my eyes, you learned a lot. How else do you understand me so well, if you can't read minds, as you say?"

And though my tone and my words could sound accusatory, he doesn't react to them with defensiveness. I would even say that he understands why I shifted the topic so quickly, by the way some of the light comes back into his eyes. I can't help but reflect, as I watch it, how much I've somehow come to understand this stranger/enemy/male in the two days since he freed me from Olin.

His rough voice isn't gentle, only candid when he responds, "The measure of a person is easily known when they treat those who are coarse to them with kindness, and *coarse* is a kind word for how I behaved towards you. But even that is only just below the surface–visible to anyone. To go to those deeper levels...I will tell you what I alluded to yesterday: I understand your thoughts because I spent so long *not* looking at you, that instead I did something worse. I learned to listen, and pay attention past what you presented outwardly. I learned to hear what you didn't say...*wouldn't* say.

"I knew you loved training, though you never said anything about it. I knew that you hated when anyone spoke of magic as though it were the be all and end all of a person..." His jaw flexes, and he says the last piece like a confession: "I knew you did not want to marry that man."

My hammering heart stops at that, and my arms drop to my sides. I feel my cheeks heat, and hope that even his Fae vision can't make it out in the dying light of the woods. "What do you mean?" I hate that my tone is weak, rather than angry. That I don't sound enraged by his observations, but worried he might not have been the only one to make them. The things he knows about me...they rattle in my mind, bearing even more questions than I had before.

His voice is softer when he replies, "You did what you were

told. But not what you wanted. And it was obvious to anyone who looked far enough past the surface to see it."

I clear my throat of its sudden thickness, and my head of the implications of what he's telling me. Rather than address what I'm not ready to discuss, I go back to questioning him about his initial statement. "And what about the 'taking from me' part? What did you mean by that?" I ask, still more quiet than I'd like to be.

He sighs, and in the dimming light, I see his head tilt back, the column of his throat arched towards the light of the fire. When he straightens, brilliant and yet shadowed gold eyes on mine, he says, "I did what I was told. But not what I wanted."

I resist the urge to step back at the parallel he's drawn between us. Each doing what we've been ordered to, but neither finding any joy in it. Merciless, he goes on, "All that I know about you is what I could not help but learn, simply by being around you. Otherwise, I was a very poor spy, by Olin's standards."

I remember Olin saying something along those lines–about how he'd been disappointed in Adathan's spying, specifically noting how he'd had no idea about my training. Which, of course, can only beg the question of *how*? Assuming he's being honest–which my gut tells me he is–and my companion across the fire knew of my training, was it possible he'd hidden it from Olin intentionally?

It had later been implied that Adathan had suffered for that inattentiveness. Tortured, for not knowing that information–or not revealing it?

I let out a shaky breath, leaving these questions for myself to digest before voicing them. With enough quietness that only his arched ears could hear, I simply say, "Alright." I move to the pack, and relieve it of the rest of the rabbit before dropping it onto the fire. The sugary sap and slightly dried needles crackle, and kindle the flame into a warmth and light that illuminates our small clearing.

Adathan stands a few feet away, just watching me, arms at his sides. His eyes are tinted amber with the fire, and they move to my hands as I hold out one of the rabbit legs to him. He takes it, careful not to touch me as his broad fingers wrap around the small limb. I turn towards the trees, angling for one with a few thinner branches. Holding the meat between my teeth, I rip two of those branches off, ignoring the stinging in my hands.

I round the fire, holding one branch under an arm, and sliding my hand down the other to rid it of its needles as I make my way to him. Then I break it into four pieces, and hand them to him, each one beading with sap. The needles and their coating likely being the source of the inflammation, I still decide I'll keep my senses open for any ailment to his mouth and throat that I might have been missing from the consumption of the sap. I'd consider recommending he stop having it altogether, but with only a few sips of water remaining in the skin, neither of us can afford to stop ingesting the moisture and sugar the sap provides.

Rather than move to the opposite side of the fire, as I had last night, I take a seat to his right, just over an arm's length away. I rest my own branch on my lap as I heal my hands. Then I dig into the small rabbit leg, as he settles down where he stood, facing the flames as I do. And only when we've each finished our meat and the bones are crisping in the flames does he say, "Thank you."

And I reply, "You're welcome."

37

THE NIGHT AND HER LIGHT

THIS MORNING, I WOKE UP IN DION'S ARMS, SUNSHINE STREAMING in through the large windows of my room, his chest blocking the light from my face. I woke up with his scent in my nose, calming my soul, and urging me to sleep as he still did, breaths measured and even. One hand in my hair, the other draped over my hip. I woke up the happiest I'd ever been.

And stayed that way, as I'd stirred him with kisses pressed to his chest, his neck, his jaw. When he woke with a moan, that hand on my hip tightening, it had been an easy thing for him to roll us, and make love to me thoroughly amidst our warm sheets.

He summoned clothes and a toothbrush for himself, and I'd put on my uniform, knowing the delegation from multiple countries would still be here. He watched as I did my hair, marking each way my fingers braided, and when I had to rest my arms. The next time I did so, he'd reached, and began a new braid with his own fingers.

Leaving my chambers, there had been no hesitation to grab his hand, and walk down the halls together. Eyes tracked us, and whispers followed, but I heard none of it. Only the soft sounds of our footsteps, and Dion's even breath and heartbeat beside me.

Now, as we approached the Great Hall, and the noise of many voices, Dion looked at me questioningly, halting just out of sight of the guards. I smiled softly, and leaned up on my toes to kiss his cheek. He squeezed my hand in response, gold-green eyes warm as the summer day, and led me the rest of the way to the Hall.

Perhaps a few voices stuttered or stopped when we walked through the arched walnut doors, but I kept my eyes straight ahead. There were a few tables set up around the space, white linen topping each of them. Cream-colored plates and brass utensils gleamed on the surface, napkins of palest blue folded elegantly before them. Crystal vases of wildflowers sat at the center of each table, the bouquets low enough that, when sitting, you could still see everybody at your table.

Elegance and whimsy rolled seamlessly into one. Those around us were dressed in varying attire, not seeming to know for sure the expectations for a breakfast with the High Lord and High Lady. Who each stood at the foot of the dais, speaking with a crowned blond male, and a heavily pregnant–

Not a male, or a female. But a man, and a woman. The King and Queen of Weaschte, the latter's hand resting lovingly on her hugely pregnant belly, and the King's just as tenderly on the small of her back.

Dion and I started towards them, but were intercepted halfway into the Hall by Nuria and Jolie. By the way they wrapped their arms tightly around us, I could tell that it was only the extra company that kept them from squealing.

When they pulled back, Nuria holding my shoulders, and Jolie Dion's, the former asked, "Last night?"

My cheeks heated at the memories of all that we had done last night, but a wide smile spread over my face, and my heart warmed further at the utter delight in our friends' faces. They switched places, each embracing us again, and Jolie's bright blue eyes seemed to almost glow in her happiness. I looked over to Dion to find him already watching me, his hazel eyes soft. And, just because he could, he leaned in to press his lips to my forehead.

"I knew it," Nuria declared, and we looked back to them.

"You did not," Jolie teased. "You guessed."

"But my guess was right, so I knew it!" She put an arm around her mate, her dark eyes alight with joy. Jolie chuckled, ever content to allow her mate to claim the same proclivity toward emotion that Jolie had through her majick–and predisposition–and leaned her cheek against Nuria's shoulder.

"Alright, alright, you knew," I said. I had no doubt that they'd each seen days, or even weeks ago that which I had been too stubborn to acknowledge myself.

"*Thank* you, Ari." Nuria smirked, a bit of mischief adding to the glitter of delight in her eyes. I watched them dip to my neck quickly. There and gone in an instant was a scrunch in her bare brow, as she noted what I'd recognized a couple of times since last night: that I had claimed Dion, but he had not yet claimed me.

I was certain he wanted to. There was no anxiety in my heart over his hesitation. Only a bit of the lone sorrow that could reach me in the euphoria of calling him mine, as I knew he abstained for that reason. That, even after my words to him last night, he did not yet believe he deserved to call me *his*. Not in the permanent, soul-deep way his claiming would say it.

Until it was done, we wouldn't be able to communicate mind-to-mind. But, otherwise, I honestly only wished in the interim that I would be able to love him well enough that those doubts of his would fade to nothing. That, over time, he would see himself as I did. For however long he needed, I would show him over and over again, with my actions, my words, and my body that he was...exceptional. That, if I was the night from which my shadows were birthed, he was the galaxy that held me. My moon, stars, and ether, ever there to brighten up my darkness.

And when he finally sank his teeth into me, and called me his, I would know I did it. I loved him well. And I would have a millennium and centuries more to do it again, and again. Forever.

My heart gave a hard thump, and I leaned into the strength and steadiness of my mate. I quirked my lips up, matching Nuria's mischief while Dion's lips gave a longer press to my temple, breathing me in while my heart filled to the brim. "And as much as I'm sure you both want all of the details, you'll have to wait. We have to meet the king and queen from across the sea."

And, just as Dion's had always been as he observed her with her mate, Nuria's gaze was soft as she watched that moment between he and I. She nodded, and took Jolie's arm, crooking it around her own, to lead us to the foreign rulers. We followed a couple of steps behind, and stood at a respectful distance as Nuria excused her interruption.

I watched as the sovereigns flicked their eyes down to the physical connection between the two females, and seemed to be a bit taken aback by it. Nonetheless, when Nuria introduced

Dion and myself, the King thanked her, the Queen standing beside him nodding quietly in acknowledgement.

When the two mates departed, Dion and I stepped forward, bowing deeply to our High Lord and High Lady, and turned before doing the same–perhaps not quite so deep–to the foreign king and queen.

"Your Majesties," I greeted them. King Aron was the epitome of what our histories told us of the Weaschten reigns. Golden haired and brown eyed, tall and broad, with an air of power that was reassuring, rather than intimidating. His wife, Queen Lydia, stood several inches shorter, with impeccably styled brunette hair, and eyes like the summer sky, brought out even further by the warm beige of her skin. Her hand still rested on her rounded stomach as I continued, "It is an honor to meet you."

"And you, Lady Ciaragen, Lord Dion. In fact, my Lord, we were just talking with your High Lord and Lady about your visit to this wondrous country," King Aron said, his Ceraschen accent lilting the words of what they called '*the Old Language*', otherwise known as Divani, the common tongue spoken throughout Eshelle.

"I would love to speak with you about it more, Your Majesty. But, I would be remiss to not inform you of a lapse in title. This female is our *High* Lady, and bears all that comes with the role," Dion said with the air of a concerned courtier. I suppressed a grin.

And if the measure of a man was how he reacted to being called out, then King Aron was a man indeed. His brow furrowed, and he replied to Dion, "Thank you for informing me of that." He then turned to Hiela, and said, "High Lady, I sincerely apologize for my misphrasing."

Hiela smiled at him, sienna eyes warm. "Of course, I understand, Your Majesty. The differences in our titles for nobility are an adjustment, I'm sure. Think no more of it." Her gaze shifted to the Queen and softened further. "I'm equally certain of two things: that breakfast is about to be served, and that your feet must be no fun at all to stand on right now. Please, be seated at our table, and we shall join you as soon as we finish greeting our guests." She gestured to the table atop the broad dais, bowed, and took her leave, Hielo following.

I dipped my chin slightly as the Weaschten rulers passed with polite nods, King Aron taking his queen's arm to help her ascend the few steps. Unable to see her own feet, she kept her chin high, trusting her husband to lead her to her place. Their guards moved smoothly to take their positions on each stair, before facing towards the other guests to watch for any threats to their sovereigns.

As soon as we passed the top step, there was a small gap, like the film of a soap bubble popping, where the noise of the Hall was interrupted. The sound shield allowed us in, and protected any and all conversation we might have while here, while not preventing us from hearing sounds from its other side.

The table on the dais, just like the others in the Hall, was round. Its only difference was the absence of the tall vase of wildflowers; instead, long stems hung from pale blue ribbons over the backs of each chair. The King and Queen seemed to pause, unsure of where to sit with no head of the table.

"Your Majesties, if you so please, may sit in the two chairs facing the Hall," I said, and they seemed relieved, at least, that their backs would not be to a room full of Fae. The King pulled out the chair for his Queen, and tucked it gently beneath her as she sat, before taking his own seat. Dion and I took our places, he to the King's right, and me on his other side, leaving the two remaining seats for our High Lord and High Lady.

"It seems congratulations are in order for Your Majesties," Dion said, a smile on his handsome face.

Queen Lydia smiled, and once more rested her hand atop her belly. "Yes, thank you. This will be our fourth," she said, widening her eyes to emphasize a disbelief in that fact. I controlled my own expression–I had known, of course, that it was easier for human women to conceive and successfully birth their babies. But, to see such a young woman–not yet even as old as myself–pregnant with her fourth child, while Fae females could struggle to conceive even one in their centuries-long youth...

But, I kept the surprise from my tone as I said, "How wonderful. How old are your children?"

It was King Aron who answered, "We have two sons, aged five, and one, and a daughter aged three."

"Any suspicions on this one?" Dion asked.

"His Majesty thinks it's a boy, but I feel just how I did with Iris," Queen Lydia responded, that hand stroking once, lovingly, down her abdomen.

"Forgive me, but...you seem fairly close," I said, my brows creasing slightly. I knew human babies gestated for a shorter time than Fae, and Lydia looked to be over eight months along; even if she left for Cerasche today, she might still be on a ship when her baby was born.

"Yes, well, I couldn't very well leave my Queen behind on such a historic trip, now, could I?" King Aron asked, placing his hand atop his wife's knee briefly before removing it. I couldn't help but wonder if it was custom to hide physical affection in Weaschte, or if perhaps they cared little for each other. In a land where mates did not exist, and marriages were arranged frequently, I couldn't be sure.

"Dear, it's not polite to lie to our allies." Queen Lydia smirked at her husband before turning to us with a mischievous twinkle in her blue eyes. "I threatened to name the baby without him while he was away, and that gave him no choice but to bring me along."

Dion and I chuckled, the King joining in. "All the better for it, darling. I fear I would have been dreadfully bad company without you here by my side." Lydia faced her husband then, her cheeks flushing as he stared at her with such adoration, without even laying a finger on her. And I supposed I had much to learn about romantic love, watching them, now that I had a mate who could teach me.

"Well," the Queen started, glancing at her lap shyly, face still glowing pink. She looked up at us and smiled softly. "Lady Ciaragen, of course, you are right. I am very close–due within the next two weeks, in fact. But I would rather have my husband with me during this time, than across the sea."

⊞

Dion

BREAKFAST WAS A WHIRLWIND OF CONVERSATION, AND DINING, and becoming better allies with the sovereigns of the human continent of Weaschte. By the end of it, I knew three things.

That the King and Queen were well on their way to being fast friends with the High Lord and High Lady of Sabrian.

That, even with the entire host of Sabriani nobility present, Ciaragen, Nuria, and Jolie were the most trusted advisors of our court.

And, that I was lucky to be in the company of each and every one of them.

I didn't know how I ended up here. A male who, only a month ago–a period of time that sounded absurdly short every time I considered it–contemplated ending an existence that was miserable at best. Who worked for a king who committed atrocities, and helped him to commit them. I sat in the same desk chair for decades, day after day, my life and duty having as little impact as if I were not living or serving at all.

A meaningless, empty life. That's what it had been.

And now, just over four weeks later, I found myself immensely grateful that I survived long enough to make it here. That I learned what the love of a nation was, and what the passion for its people meant. That I now worked for a male and female who deserved all of the success they had attained so far. That I was here, ready and able to help them take the throne as the just rulers I knew they would be.

I had friends. Real friends, who asked me to do simple things with them, just because they wanted my company. Who, when we shopped, thought to buy me a pastry when I was in a separate store. Laughed at my jokes, were saddened by my troubles, and asked me how I was doing each day–and actually wanted to know the answer.

I hadn't had someone like that in a very long time. By my own doing, I knew; the gravestone which had kept diligent company with me until I arrived in Sabrian making me unwilling to care for anyone again. To be so *hurt* again.

But, care I did, now that I was in a place where those I cared for would not suffer for it. I could not–could *never*–forget that day, but being here...the memory was manageable. Perhaps because I recognized the love I had borne for them, and no longer resented myself for feeling it. I could not yet forgive myself for what had happened, but there was space within me now to feel that pain, and not shy from it. I knew how to *feel* again, how to *love* again, and that was thanks to this place. These people. This female.

My mate. This stunning, intelligent, brave female who

deserved the world and then some, was somehow my soul-bonded life partner. And she wanted *me*. Did not see the mating bond as some burden, but rather, as she'd said, something that she deserved. A male who would love and cherish her, forever. And, gods, if I ever intended to do anything in my life, I intended to do that.

By the end of breakfast, she had managed to garner the trust of the King and Queen of Weaschte, as had, it seemed, the rest of our court. I could sense no nerves, nor scent any fear from them as they were surrounded by Fae. As we talked with them about their children, and their expected. As we discussed the current state of trade between our nations, and how much more expedited it would be if our peoples worked together on the ships that brought the goods to each land.

An evolution was happening, and it was not going to be for the faint of heart. Which, luckily, neither of the sovereigns of the human kingdom appeared to be.

It was determined that the best course of action would be to have Fae travel within the fleet back to Weaschte when the King and Queen took their leave–which would not be until after their child was born, so long as Lydia was well enough to travel. Those Fae would work alongside any humans who volunteered to hold a ship with them, and, upon arrival, would attempt to make a good impression on the people who ran the main northeastern port in Dahlih.

Until this point, there had been limited contact between the two peoples. Due to the humans' beliefs about faeries, those sailors would unfortunately have some time to wait before Weaschte was ready to receive them. But Fae, with only their arched ears and enhanced features to distinguish them from a human, would likely be better received in the beginning.

If they were successful in their venture, then hopefully a

bridge of trust would soon exist, not just between the rulers of each nation, but between their peoples as well. And, in a few years, perhaps the Weaschtens would not have any fear of the Fae at all.

38

THE BEARER, BEARS ALL

THEA - PRESENT

I WAKE WITH A START, FILLED WITH A SENSE THAT SOMETHING IS off. My eyes adjust quickly to the dim light of the beginnings of dawn, and I sit up on the forest floor, my arm numb from lying under my head as I slept. I shiver as the cold of the air around me registers, no sun yet to warm the day into the typical summer climate.

I hear nothing, and see only trees around me in the blue-gray light. The fire has gone out, not even a whisper of smoke left, and Adathan lays close by, still asleep. Lying down, his head had probably just been a couple of feet from mine. In sleep, the Fae predator I'd seen in him yesterday is gone completely. In its place is a dark-haired male with light purple half-moons beneath his eyes, long black lashes brushing them. His full lips are parted slightly, and even his massive frame looks gentle in this state. His chest rises and falls evenly, so it's not him that I feel this sense of...wrongness from.

I stand quietly, and he doesn't so much as stir. Upright, I see nothing in the vicinity, still hear nothing, yet I just *know* that there's something not right. My healing senses have been open ever since I reached them out to Adathan last night, and though it's not him, I can feel that *someone* is in pain. As soon as my mind makes that connection through the haze of sleep, hunger, and dehydration, my feet do not hesitate to move towards the source of that feeling.

I trust my body and my instincts to lead me to it. I wander until I can no longer see our little campsite, and pause briefly every so often to close my eyes and ensure that my senses are pulling me in the right direction. Finally, probably a mile later, I find it. A heartbeat.

Labored, racing, and erratic, but a beat nonetheless. I move quickly then, my feet more sure as I track that pulse to a copse of pines, taller than the ones by our camp, their roots thicker, and protruding so high that I nearly miss her.

A white-tailed doe, lying on her side, her long neck straining as she pulls in harsh breaths. Her chest rises and falls, stained scarlet by a wound that slowly leaks more blood onto the bed of dried needles beneath her. I move closer, rounding the space so that she sees me before I get close enough to appear harmful. Still, her brown eyes whirl when I near, and she tries to rise.

Blood pours from the space on her chest, the movement ripping apart what little clotting had occurred. Once I'm just a few paces from her, I lower to my knees, and hold out my hands, palms up. I watch her nose twitch as she smells me, a combination of salt, sweat, dirt, and pine. Whatever else she scents seems to calm her, and she lays her head back down, though the labored breaths continue.

I breathe evenly, knowing she'd sense any fear, or upset. As slowly as I dare while her blood courses over her tawny fur, I reach for her.

But when my hand touches her, she thrashes, one of her delicate hooves nearly catching my cheek, and another banging painfully against my wrist. I hiss at the immediate throbbing, and quickly heal it, not needing or wanting my attention diverted. I take a deep breath, and reach once more, but this time hover just a few inches above her skin.

I've never tried to heal a person without touch, never healed outside of my own species. But there isn't another option, since even putting her to sleep would require contact with her nervous system. And I won't walk away, even if her death might be considered the natural order of things.

Steady, keeping my focus on not just the wound, but the blood, the heart and lungs, I send my magic to my outstretched hand. And then a tendril of light, thin and ethereal as a stream of sunshine passing through fog, forms between my palm and her flesh. I've never known what occurs between my skin and another's as I heal them, only that it feels warm.

I watch in wonder as that light travels into the wound on the doe, as the flesh knits together, the internal injuries sealing. I even do the extra work of manipulating her insides, temporarily increasing blood production–

She stands so abruptly that I gasp, the connection breaking. But she doesn't run. She stares at me, thick lashes high over her lovely, alert eyes. Only the blood on her coat gives any indication that she was hurt in the first place. And then, with an intention that makes my eyes widen, she walks ten paces further into the woods, and holds my gaze before lowering her graceful neck to drink from the pool of water at her hooves.

I rise, only the desire to not scare her keeping me from running to that pool. As I reach her side, she doesn't stop drinking, likely very thirsty from the blood loss. I drop to my knees once more, the dampness of the pool's edge seeping into my trousers. Not even the dirt that seems almost permanent on my hands makes me hesitate before cupping them in the water, and bringing them to my mouth to drink.

I moan, unable to help it, and quench my thirst beside the doe until the aching in my head slightly dissipates. When it does, I look up at her, and, with trembling fingers, reach for her. And this time, she lets me gently stroke the space between her eyes. Then, just as suddenly as she'd stood, she turns, and bounds away.

The pain in my chest that has been my constant companion since my heart and world had been ripped apart, eases slightly as I watch her go. I stay kneeling beside the shallow pool, allowing myself to feel calm for the first time in days. And then, in that stillness where even the creatures of the forest seem to quiet for a minute of peace, I hear rustling from behind me.

I duck low on instinct and turn towards the sound, knees dragging quietly through the mud beneath, the ends of my hair tangling with sludge and dried needles. In the same motion, I draw the dagger from its place against my shoulder blade. I stare into the wood lit lavender by the dawn sun, my heart thudding fast, but sure. At first, I see no source of the noise, but, after a heartbeat, he appears through a gap in the densely packed trees, and my heart eases just as quickly as it had raced.

Adathan's largeness is at odds with the grace of his progression through the woods. The copse of pines I'd walked past after healing the doe hides me from his sight. But I can see him as he races through the exact path that I'd taken while trying to follow my senses to the deer. And, while he's been silent in our trek through the woods these past days, his sprint is loud–if anyone but me was lurking in these trees, I'd be drawn to him, not me.

I stand, sheathing the blade, and his gaze whips to me. If I'd thought he was running fast before, it's nothing compared to how quickly he gets to me now. He bounds to me, long legs and Fae speed covering the distance in only a couple of heartbeats.

As he gets closer, I see that his eyes are wild. Wide, darting across my face, my body, even as he runs. As soon as he stands in front of me, coming to an abrupt halt from his sprint, his hands grip my shoulders tightly, but not painfully. His breaths come quickly, passing over my cheeks as he stoops to look into my eyes. Now that he's close enough, I can make out the emotion in the golden depths: panic.

"Are you alright?" he asks, eyes still roving my face, looking for something. I nod, and he breathes out a shaky sigh. "I woke up, and you were gone, and I followed your scent and then I smelled blood, and–" he cuts himself off, closing his eyes. I feel a tremor in those broad hands as they clasp the tops of my arms.

And maybe it's that I still feel soft. I used my healing ability just because I wanted to, not out of debt or survival, and, in turn, I feel softer than I've allowed myself to be for days now. So, when my hand lifts to wrap around his wrist, I let my fingers curl around him gently, reassuringly. His own fingers around my arms tighten in response, his jaw clenching and nostrils flaring as he inhales slowly. "I'm okay." I send calming, healing magic into him. Slowing his racing heart with a gentle stroke of my thumb over his hammering pulse.

His hands rip away from my shoulders, and I'd forgotten the chill of the early morning until their warmth and weight was no longer on me. "Don't," he says. "Don't do that."

My brow furrows, and a strange emotion that might have been rejection runs through me before a default annoyance with him takes its place. "Alright," I snap, and take a step back from him. "I woke up because I felt something was wrong. The blood is from a doe. She was wounded, and I healed her." No need to tell him that I'd done it without touch for the first time. No need to ask him about the light that had come from me, and knitted her flesh back together.

Some kind of emotion passes over his face, gone too quickly for me to make it out. "What did the wound look like?" he asks.

"Like a wound. A hole, with blood coming out of it."

"Was it big, or small?"

I sigh. "The clean edges were around the circumference of a fingernail. Flesh was torn around it, out to the size of a silver mark."

"So," he says slowly, "like an arrow that had been ripped out."

I nearly shudder at the pain the poor beast had gone through if that were the case, but reply, "Yes." I almost wonder why he's grilling me about this–why he was even worried about me, why he cares what the injury looked like. But as I follow his words, his implications, my expression falls. My heart pounds as I scan the woods around us.

He lifts me so quickly that I would have missed his movement just by blinking. One second I'm standing on the ground, the terror of a new realization coursing through me–and in the next I'm cradled against his chest. I don't protest, only wrap my arms around his neck as he sprints away from the space, from the water I'd completely forgotten to tell him about, and which he'd paid no attention to.

And then I watch an arrow fly just inches from his shoulder. Unable to help it, I clench my fists around the fabric of his shirt. So low I might have thought I imagined it if his chest hadn't rumbled against me, he says, "I've got you," and his arms squeeze me as he–somehow, impossibly–picks up speed. I see them as they come out from behind the pines just feet from us, their weapons and wits not fast enough to catch the male who holds me. Two have bows, and another two have daggers–to finish the job.

One of them nocks, and as he draws, the other lets his arrow fly. It goes wide as Adathan zags. Less distance covered, but better to avoid the arrows. I watch as the man takes aim, and because I've got him, too, I warn him, "He's following your path. Duck when I say," my lips beside his arched ear. No time or need for him to answer, I see the man brace to fire, and order, "Duck."

He does, and the arrow flies just a foot above, exactly where his head had been half a second ago.

"Come on, Gene! We need this money!" Another shouts at the man who missed.

I order Adathan to veer to the left to avoid the next arrow, which follows the previous shot far too quickly.

"We have two options," he says to me, his voice two-toned; menace, laced with consideration. "We keep moving, and continue with our plan. Or we stop, and I find out if the money is for finding you, or for capturing you."

It hadn't occurred to me that they might be on our side, interpreting the Fae as a threat. Just like it hadn't occurred to me that the doe had been a trap. That they'd waited in the trees until my so-called captor revealed himself, likely knowing that he would come after them if they didn't eliminate him first. The lack of food and water has made itself apparent with these lapses in judgment, but the adrenaline has cleared my head enough to think now.

If they are not on our side, I don't believe they would live if I go with option two, and Adathan confronts them. I haven't seen him *truly* fight, or wield the dagger still strapped to my back for anything more than carving up our meals. But nothing about him makes me think he doesn't know his way around a blade– or a body.

And a part of me is alright with that. With ensuring that these traitors meet an end at the hands of the male that currently hold me. But a small, surviving part of me reminds me that their deaths would mean nothing. That perhaps they need the money for gambling and brothels–or maybe for their families and food. That maybe they have no idea who they're shooting at; of the treason they're committing.

As I think, an arrow flies–but when Adathan moves to avoid it, likely hearing the rush of air coming towards us, another comes from the opposite direction, and I watch as it sinks into his shoulder.

He grunts, and though his arm beneath me shudders, he does not drop me. His pace buckles for only a heartbeat before he recovers, and further varies his course as the humans attempt to keep up. The distance between us and them has gotten much more vast since Adathan started running, but these archers have heavy bows, and deadly aim.

Blood pools quickly through his cotton shirt, and all of those wise thoughts from a second ago clear out of my head. All I can see is the man who shot, yards ahead of the others, hollering with joy at his hit as he reaches for another arrow. Only whispered words of mercy from the back of my mind, in a voice that sounds like my mother's, have me snapping his arm instead of his neck.

He goes down, his shouts of glee turning into howls of pain as he clutches his arm, the bow and arrow dropping from his hands. His companions gather around him, seeming utterly shocked, and confused as to how their friend could have possibly been injured.

"Keep going," I finally reply, my voice low. I can do nothing to heal his wound as we move, but I flatten a hand on his spine, and focus my magic on the nerves surrounding his shoulder. Careful not to numb his arm, but just decrease the pain, the warmth–and light–radiates from my palm, into his skin. The sensation of screaming pain within him decreases, winnowing down into a dull ache, while my own shoulder jolts in agony as I take it from him.

In thanks, his strong arms squeeze me once more as he continues to run through the trees. Even with the zigzag pattern, Adathan's speed finally creates too vast a distance for the humans to leave their friend and chase us. In no time at all, both their figures and their shouts dissipate into the dawn sky, and only Adathan's breaths sound in the waking forest.

⇔

Adathan carries me, not resting, not listening to my requests to stop for me to heal him, until we're far enough away that even on horseback the men would have a bit before they could catch up. When finally we stop, we're deep in the forest, at another pool of water that shimmers in the sunshine that streams through the tree branches. The frequency of these shallow pools now has to be due to our proximity to the sea surrounding Dahlih, rather than being high on the Ceraschen cliffs.

Adathan grunts as he kneels, dropping me to his knee, and only keeping his uninjured arm behind my shoulders, supporting me until I stand. Quickly, without thinking about it, I drop to the ground, and scoop water between my hands, bringing my fingers to his lips. His eyes are closed, face pale but for the flush of exertion across his cheeks. His mouth parts around my fingertips, and I tip my hands for the water to trail down.

By the time he's swallowing, I'm turning to cup more, and I don't stop until long after my sleeves and his collar are dripping with the excess that rolls through my fingers. His eyes are open now, and he watches me scoop the next bit, resting his hands under mine as his lips part against my fingertips, his tongue brushing them as he laps up the last dregs of the water I pour into his mouth.

He rubs his wet hands over his face, then back through his dark hair. He sighs, and I ask quietly, "Will you let me take care of that now?" I can sense that his pain is substantial, but quenching his thirst took precedence. Now that it's slaked, he nods, holding my gaze steadily.

I stand, and move to his back, where the slender arrow protrudes from his shoulder. It looks like it just missed the junction of the large trapezius muscle, hitting the belly of the deltoid. Certainly not an easy injury, but it explains how he'd still been able to carry me all that way.

I place a hand over the front of his shoulder, and can feel the nerves and tissue just an inch from my palm screaming. A deep hit, then. I take a breath, and tell him, "I'll have to push it through the rest of the way. It will hurt, and it might leave a scar, but I'll be able to completely repair the muscle."

"I don't care about a scar. Do what you have to do." He adds, only a bit hesitantly, "I trust you."

Perhaps a bit gentler than I would have been with him earlier this morning, I say, "I'm going to need to cut through your shirt, so it's not in the way." He makes a sound of acknowledgement, and I unsheathe the dagger from the scabbard I hadn't removed even to sleep. I pull the collar of his shirt back, and the wicked sharpness of the blade cuts through the cotton like air. I slice the feathers off the arrow shaft, then remove my scabbard altogether, and hand it to him.

"I'll do what I can to relieve the pain, but bite down on this just in case." He takes the leather from me, and clenches his teeth around the strap. I watch, holding his gaze until he nods, and then move to his back, placing the dagger on the ground beside him.

Because he's taller than me, and the arrow is angled even higher, I stand rather than kneel, as he does. I brace my hand in an L around the wound, and with no warning, which wouldn't have done either of us any good, I use my other hand to push the arrow through. The agony of it lances through him, and I pull what I can of it into myself, even though it has me grunting in pain, my body not separating endogenous pain from that which I take from him. His breath hisses around the leather between his teeth, but he doesn't shout, even as the arrow comes through the front of his shoulder.

Another couple of inches, and I move around to his front, dropping to my knees once more. My hand doesn't leave his skin as I do so; I drag it along, ignoring the way my own shoulder horribly throbs. His eyes are closed, but he still has a flush to his cheeks, and pink in his lips, so he hasn't lost too much blood. Without a word, I grip the shaft above the arrowhead, and pull the rest of the length through.

I throw the blood-covered arrow to the ground, and send my magic quickly to the open gash in his shoulder. The muscle and skin knit back together beneath my palm, and when they are fully healed, I drop my hand. Only a scar the size of my fingernail, and the crimson staining his skin remain.

His blood already on my shirt from me cleaning the dagger with it yesterday, I wipe my hand on it now. My palm is still stained pink from gripping the arrow, and sealing his wound, but I can't do anything else before I sit on the ground, slightly winded from the effort. Not of healing, but of taking the pain, *experiencing* the pain. Adathan's eyes open, and as he removes the leather from his teeth, his expression is...considering.

"Why would you do that?" he asks after a moment.

My brows furrow. "Heal you?"

"No. Why would you take my pain, if it hurts you?"

I pause at that, not entirely sure how to answer at first. Not because of the question itself, but because of the reason he asks. Which is not a question of why I would do something for someone, even though it's painful for me, but why I would do such a thing for *him*. And, after he's saved my life twice now—after he's been hurt, and hungry, and thirsty for days, and still has chosen to continue to help me. Blood oath or not, I can only think of one response.

"Why wouldn't I?"

It comes naturally, without the familiar sense of wrong that I've felt each time I've considered being anything better than indifferent towards him. I can no longer find within me the hatred for him that I once held. And maybe that's a consequence of what we've been through and talked of these last two days, but it doesn't feel like a punishment. It feels like a reprieve. And even if I don't deserve it, maybe he does. And maybe that's enough of a reason to let it be.

He blinks at my words, and perhaps at seeing my inner thoughts conveyed on my face, but then his expression hardens. "Because I betrayed you. Betrayed your family, and helped Olin to take you. Held you back while he hurt you, and then hurt you myself. Altogether, causing you so much pain that I can't imagine why you would take any of mine."

I stare at him for a moment, still settled in all I'd just thought through, and he weathers it, the liquid color of his champagne irises at odds with the solid steel in his gaze. And it's that look that has me realizing that these things I hated him for—he hates himself for, too.

My voice is quiet as I start, "If I decided to keep hating you, it wouldn't be hard to do." A lie, when looked at one way—since, in my days of experience, it actually *has* been hard to hate him. But, in another way, a truth; if I were more persistent in my efforts, I could probably find many things to loathe him for. Even if my thoughts and realizations over those days, and these past moments, have vastly absolved him.

A muscle in his jaw feathers as he clenches it, but not in anger. It seems like a measure in control, as he prepares himself for what else I might say. "But I've decided not to. And that's all you need to know about it."

Then it's my turn to bear his gaze. If he hasn't already realized that all of my loathing is now reserved for myself, he probably will. As I discovered that I no longer wanted to hate him—that it felt good to relieve him of that burden—it became clear to me what I'd been avoiding these past days. Placing the blame for what had happened on the people who *truly* deserved it: me, and Olin.

I recognize now that any blame I'd placed on Adathan had been solely to spare myself from it. But there is no room for that anymore. Olin was the instigator, and I the executor of my own pain. My own loss. No one else.

By the slight tightening of his jaw, and crease in his brow, I think he somehow sees all of that. But, he only says, quiet and sincere: "Thank you. For taking my pain."

Terribly familiar; he had needed tending to last night as well—has needed to be healed *multiple* times, because of me. Familiar, that I should once again say, "You're welcome." And I look into the trees, rather than see the understanding in his eyes. In the silence he grants me, I find another reason which strengthens my resolve for exonerating him. My brow furrows slightly. "Adathan?"

He takes a moment to answer, and his deep voice is rougher than usual when he does. "Yes?"

I look back to him, needing to see in his eyes that I'm right. "You shielded me instead of yourself while you ran." It's not a question. Though there are certainly plenty of things I don't understand about Fae majick, I know that he wasn't bluffing three nights ago when he said he was shielding himself from my breaking. I have little doubt that same shield could have stopped that arrow–if he'd been using it for himself.

He doesn't answer. Instead, he looks to the ground, picks up the dagger, and holds both it and the scabbard out to me. "We should get going. We covered a lot of distance in a much smaller amount of time than I expected. We could reach the ports of Dahlih in less than an hour." His gaze rises back to mine, guarded, as it has been less and less over the past days. And, instead of becoming standoffish myself, I take the items from him, and raise a mocking brow.

I make a show of looking at myself, and then looking him up and down. Torn, bloody, and dirt-covered. The sheer, threatening mass of him. Arched ears poking through dark hair, and stubble that somehow makes his eyes even brighter–even less human.

"You'd pass better for a stowaway than crew. Matter of fact, if I were a captain, I'd think you'd been a stowaway for months already."

He smirks slightly, the tiniest pull of one corner of his mouth, and I see for the first time that he has a dimple. "Is that so?"

I stand, brushing off my trousers with my free hand, even though there's no hope for them now. "Okay, maybe not months."

"Thank–"

"Weeks."

This earns me another exhale of a chuckle, just like yesterday. My own lips tilted up at the corners, I hold out my hand to help haul him up, and he grabs it. On his feet, I release him, my callouses scraping his as my grip slides away.

"You're one to talk. There are so many pine needles in your hair, a porcupine could mistake you for its sister."

My eyes widen. "Was that...a joke?"

"I may not laugh at my own jokes, as you pointed out yesterday, but I still make them." I walk a circle around him, pretending to examine him. "What are you doing?"

"Just looking to see where you hid the real Adathan. The broody, no-nonsense one."

His response is off by a beat, but as some kind of emotion passes through his eyes, he buries it in amusement. "Broody?" He raises a dark brow, crossing his arms.

"Oh, there he is!"

He huffs a short chuckle again, and drops his arms, but sobers a bit before he speaks again. "Okay, you're right. We need new clothes, and to clean up a bit before we start looking for a captain. There's one thing we have to figure out before we go, though."

"What's that?" I ask. I buckle the scabbard over my chest, and sheathe the dagger as he replies, "Our story. The captain will ask for one, and we can't very well tell them the truth."

My lips purse, and his gaze flicks down to them before moving to the small pool at our feet. He crouches, and begins splashing water onto himself. He pulls off his torn, bloody shirt, and uses it like a rag, wiping his face, neck, and chest free of filth.

I move to copy him, but leave my shirt on. "We'll need you to round out those ears, obviously. I'd say dull the canines, but *I* haven't even seen you smile enough to show them, so I think we're in the clear there. We don't look alike enough to pass for family, so I'll be your wife. We're...traveling to Eshelle as passionate explorers. You're fucking massive, so that'll keep them from questioning our lack of guards for protection."

He frowns slightly, looking down at himself, but shrugs.

"Okay. But why not just say that you're the explorer, and I'm your guard?"

"Two reasons." I hold up my fingers to tick them off. "Because no human would believe that a woman would ever want to, nor have the nerve to travel across the sea. And, because a single woman has much more to fear from the men around her than a known married one."

His jaw ticks again, hands fisting around his shirt, water wringing out of it as he does so. His grip relaxes after a moment. "Alright. And our names?"

"Good point. Adathan and Althea aren't exactly inconspicuous. We need something that blends in. Maybe Adam, and Maria? Yours is close enough to a nickname. Has anyone ever called you Adan?"

The smallest of smirks pulls at his lips again, that dimple popping once more in his cheek. "No."

I shrug. "Well, anyway, Maria is easy enough for me. Middle name and all. But you knew that." I attempt to joke, as he'd been one of the most frequent doormen to announce me at any gathering. It falls a bit flat, but he still responds quietly, "Yes. I do."

After an uncomfortable beat of silence, I say, "It's settled then." And get to cleaning myself, as he has. While I'm sure a glamour could just as easily hide dirt as it can any other feature, no part of me wants to be this filthy for even a moment longer.

Once my face, neck, and chest are slightly less dirty than they had been a few minutes ago, I kneel, facing away from the water. The toes of my boots rest at the edge of the pool as I lean back until my thighs meet my calves, and my hair falls into the water, nearly to my scalp. My quadriceps both sigh and scream at the stretch after so much walking, but I pay them no mind as I run my fingers into my hair.

"Do you, uh...want help?" Adathan asks.

I open my eyes to find him standing over me, my body stretched out beneath him. "It's alright, you don't have to. I can do it."

"I know I don't have to, but I'm still offering."

I pitch myself upwards, hair dripping down my back, thin streams of water coursing down my neck and chest. I look at him for a moment, considering. "Alright," but I shift a bit as he gets to his knees beside me. To ease some of the tension, I add, "Just watch out. Don't want you getting quilled."

That small, one-sided smile comes again at the allusion to his calling me a porcupine moments ago. The expression doesn't fall when he says, "Go ahead, and sit comfortably. Otherwise my help won't be much different." I blush a bit at not having thought of that myself. As I shift to sit on my bottom, legs criss crossed, he throws his dripping shirt over a shoulder. He reaches out an arm, but pauses before touching me. "May I?" he asks, looking between his arm, and me.

I nod, and he rests his forearm across the backs of my shoulders. "Lean back. I've got you." And something about the way he says it makes more heat rush to my cheeks, but I do as he ordered. He supports me fully as my torso moves horizontally, and I feel my hair pool around me, the water carrying it into a halo around my face.

Slowly, showing his intention, he reaches his other hand over, and then runs his fingers into the soaking strands. My eyes close involuntarily, and between not having enough sleep for days, and the ridiculously calming sensation of his broad fingers running over my scalp, I find it particularly difficult to open them.

Fingertips gently scrub at my hairline and behind my ears, and massage the ache that has been so constant in my temples. His hand cups the base of my skull, and pulls through the hair there. Finally, almost reverently, that hand supports my head as his other arm lifts me back to a seated position.

As he removes his hands, I pull my hair over a shoulder, and wring out the excess water. He holds up his torn, soaking shirt, and, ascertaining wearing it would be as effective as not, he only flicks it back over his shoulder. And when I realize I'm looking at him–not just looking but *seeing*–the tattoos, the many scars, the broad, dense muscles, I have to force myself to turn away.

I healed him without his shirt twice now, and hadn't batted an eye–because it's different. It's different to see a body with the intention of healing it. Now, looking feels personal. Feels like I'm crossing a line–multiple lines. The one from my upbringing being the thickest, but a thinner, newer one too. Looking at him–*wanting* to look at him...it makes too many things confusing.

As I brush the wet locks of my hair behind my shoulders, I keep my gaze on his, and not on his body, and say, "Thank you."

And then it's his turn to respond, in a voice that's disappointingly steady, "You're welcome."

39

SMALL PAINS, GREAT PLEASURES

THE WEEKS PASSED IN A BLUR, WITH ONLY THE TIME I SPENT WITH Ciara in our chambers seeming to slow it down at all.

We'd decided to move into her rooms after the day we met the King and Queen of Weaschte. Of course, it wouldn't have happened if I were the sole person in charge of how our matehood proceeded. No, if it were up to me, I'd have been too nervous to ask her to live together, even after confessing to her that I loved her–and hearing her say it back to me.

I'd done it that night, unable to keep from saying it any longer. We'd been walking through the gardens, and the faerie lights had streamed through the windows of the castle, gilding her with their soft yellow glow. Mesmerized, as I frequently was by her, it had come out without me thinking. And perhaps that was good–since I'd clearly thought too much about it as it was.

She'd smiled that beautiful smile at me, her deep blue eyes bright, even in the dim light, and said, "I love you, too."

440

And what a wonderful thing it was, to be loved by her.

Afterwards, when trying to decide where to sleep for the night, she pitched the idea. Sweet enough to offer to sleep in my chambers this one night, if I wished, but that my sorry excuse for decor could much more easily be moved into her rooms, than hers into mine. And that was that.

It still felt surreal, to hold her each night as we fell asleep, and to wake up beside her each morning. Fourteen days had passed so quickly, and I couldn't help but be thrilled for the thousands of days we had to look forward to together.

Outside of the bond with my mate that was my soul's destiny and duty, life at court had changed as well. Nuria and Jolie were considering adopting a child. Bayani had found a lover in one of the ladies of Planici. Nate and Bash had come to stay with their son, Atlas. Who, though the faerie was years older, Sione had come to play with each day–showing the toddler how he flew with his membranous wings, and not getting angry when Atlas's little fists would wrap around his horns.

Queen Lydia was due to have her baby any day now. Though undoubtedly highly uncomfortable, she attended all meals with her husband, and smiled kindly at all who greeted her. Not once did I scent any fear from her, even when she met the few faeries–including Sione–that Hielo and Hiela invited, to further integrate them into the peoples of Eshelle.

A smart move, considering all they knew of faeries was that folklore about changelings in Weaschte. Something we had not yet dared to tell them was very likely a falsehood. After all, how could we possibly know all of our descendents over the past millennium? How could we be sure that those who had supposedly hidden away in Weaschte after the Last War, did not delight in sewing chaos within the realm they still dwelled?

Those were the questions they would ask, and were not

questions that we would be able to answer definitively. The only proof we held that their stories were false, was that no such faerie currently resided in Eshelle, nor was there any record of them in our history books. But, if I were a human, fearful of what might happen to my soon-to-be newborn, the last people I would trust would be the very people from whom they believed those faeries to be descended. We couldn't possibly understand their fears, and, even the kindest of humans–which the sovereigns seemed to be–would more than likely attribute any information given on our end to a lie made to protect our own kind.

The other reason we couldn't share our knowledge, of course, was that humans would learn babies born with deformities were not faeries, as they believed. Just human babes, unlucky enough to live in a world where their parents could not accept them as they were. Clearly, a devastating revelation. Because how could we claim that the lives of countless innocent babies were lost purely because the humans could not embrace their imperfections?

So, we did what we could to show them the truth instead. To their credit, considering their–however unfounded–beliefs about faeries, the King and Queen were very receptive to those that we brought into the castle. In an attempt to show them, rather than tell them, how their theory of changelings was inaccurate, we invited a wide array of faerie species. Ambassadors of the nymphs, dryads, and sprites. Faeries with wings, and tails, and skin in varying colors of the rainbow.

And, however unplanned, Sione's friendship with the Fae child proved to be incredibly helpful. Indeed, as the King and Queen watched the boys play–play, as all children did–small, unconscious smiles graced each of their faces.

The winged boy had actually turned out to be a hit with the

entire court. Sweet, polite, and funny in a way not many children–or even a decent amount of adults–were, he got along with everyone, from ages two to five hundred.

When his parents had introduced him to the King and Queen, their tension had been palpable. As Aleki spoke, Elei grasped her son's shoulder, her fingers tight, as though preparing to leave with him very quickly, if necessary. But, when Sione bowed to them, and said with his child's voice, "It's very nice to meet you," Lydia had smiled brilliantly at him, and returned the sentiment.

Both the Duke and Duchess had exhaled softly, and grinned for the sovereigns then, the shoulders of all around them dropping with relief. And ever since, the only person that Sione talked to nearly as much as Atlas, was the Queen of Weaschte.

He asked her questions that no adult would. Her favorite color, if she played any instruments, if she liked to sing. She answered all of them gladly, never losing patience with the boy. Blue, the pianoforte, no she had a terrible singing voice, she said. And when he had asked her if she wanted to see him fly, and the keen-eared Fae and faeries nearby all held their breath without turning to them, she only asked if he could lend her his arm to walk her outside.

The King seemed content to listen and watch as his Queen made everyone around her fall in love with her, just like he so obviously had years ago. Catering to her, even with guards and serving staff near at all times. Getting her food, and water, and taking her wherever she wished to go. They were rarely physically intimate in public, though when they thought no one was looking, I would catch him kiss her brow, and she stroke his cheek.

At court, I showed *almost* equal restraint with Ciara. Luckily, she also seemed inclined to touch me whenever the situation seemed appropriate. Holding hands, linking arms. During dances, I would gently caress her waist, or kiss the top of those incredible curls. And she would scratch her fingers softly against the back of my neck, and lean her head against my chest.

In our chambers, the only restraint was always–*always*, even though the answer had never been no yet–making sure the other was equally inclined. I had to admit, even after two weeks, including many nights of little sleep–filled with quite a lot of other things that kept us from sleeping–I still could not get enough. Of her skin against mine, the feel of her lips, the noises she made when lost in pleasure.

I only looked forward to years, decades, and centuries of continuing to make her feel that good. Of showing her just how much I craved to see her happy, or content, or utterly wrapped in ecstasy. Of dancing with her because she wanted to dance; of reading on the couch with her in silence; of being inside her, or with my mouth between her legs. In no time at all, she had become the center of my universe, and I could not be anything but elated by that fact.

Now, in the sun of the early summer, we were outside, in the moderately-sized training yard that sat at the west side of the castle grounds. Bayani had been my primary companion in this space for my first few weeks here, Ciara a watchful eye around the many blades, and heavy weights. She now watched me in a very different way as I sparred with Bayani, and pretended not to notice her staring.

The lord easily blocked my next jab, and countered with a blow to my stomach that I narrowly twisted enough to avoid. We'd been at it for over fifteen minutes now, and even though we were only running drills, not *really* combatting, sweat dripped from both of us. In the scorching heat, it had only taken five of those minutes for us to forgo our shirts, and I had a feeling that Ciara preferred it that way.

I looked at her now, and found that she'd put her back to us– likely to focus on her own exercise. And I found myself incredibly distracted as she squatted down, a heavy weight held in front of her at chest height.

A distraction that Bayani would not and did not let slide. His fist connected with my cheek before I could fully take in the picture of Ciara's round ass dipping down to the ground. Albeit at probably half the strength he could have struck with, the sound of his fist smacking against my face was loud in the otherwise quiet yard.

I turned back to the male, working my jaw, and, fists still up and ready to take on my response, he shrugged, as if to say, *What are you going to do about it?* Ciara dropped her weight, and turned, breathing hard. I saw in my periphery as she examined my cheek, and deemed it a small enough hurt to go back to her workout.

I smirked. Oh, was I going to show her what I thought about that later on. I hoped that she brought that same sass with her while I did so.

After that, I stopped pulling my punches so much with Bayani. We moved faster, breathed harder. It took another minute, but I landed a punch to his side, and from that point there was no turning back. By the time a half hour had passed, I could already see the deep purple of some bruises, the first one on my face layered with a second. Neither of us had hit hard enough to break, or even fracture anything, but they didn't tickle, either.

Bayani, though, had a few more purple splotches on him than I did, and I was having a hard time not taking pride in that.

"I want a rematch," he said, already standing with widened

legs, arms deceptively loose at his sides. His hair was slicked back from his face with sweat, and there was challenge in his eyes.

Giving a half grin I hoped made him tick, I asked, "Are you sure you want to get your ass kicked twice in one day?" I slowly walked towards him, making a show of unwrapping my hands. The fabric was tinged pink on the knuckles.

"You just don't want me to show you up in front of Ari." He mirrored my smile, and took a step closer.

"Don't bring me into this pissing contest, Bay," Ciara shot back, not even stopping in her lunges to do so.

"Don't worry, we won't get you wet," he returned, a devilish look coming over his face before he added, "Wet*ter*."

A part of me wanted to rip his head off for talking about my mate, talking about her body like that in front of me–his intention, I was sure, to get the fight started up again. But a bigger part luxuriated in letting her handle it with that trademark mouth that would have me on my knees–literally–before the day was done.

"I've never needed to worry about that with you, Bay." She finished her lunges, and dropped the weights on the ground. Her gaze flitted over Bayani, as though not worth the time of day to even recognize him, but when they landed on me, her expression alone conveyed the second part of her statement. *But I always do with you.*

Bayani clutched his chest, and staggered back a step. "Ouch, Ari." He dropped his hand. "Seriously, though, if you two don't get yourselves and your scents out of here, I'm going to throw up." He pretended to retch, puffing out his cheeks and clamping his lips before plugging his nose.

"Yeah, yeah. You're just peeved because Annalise is going back to Planici tomorrow."

"My hand won't be able to compare," Bayani returned, his

tone wistful, expression reminiscent for a heartbeat before he cracked, and the three of us laugh.

A short while later, after we'd eaten and drank enough water to fill a small tub, we walked into our chambers. I usually was a bit struck by my things blending with hers, two weeks not being enough time to get used to how good that felt. But now, I hardly noticed my books shelved with hers, the open wardrobe showing my suits hanging with her dresses. No, I was too busy doing something else that felt far better than good.

Ciara's lips were on mine, moving in patterns that had become beautifully familiar. I could taste the salt on her skin, feel the supple curves and taut muscle beneath my hands. A combination of strength and softness that was so powerfully feminine, so incredibly *her*. Gods, watching her during her exercises had been an exquisite sort of torture, and I was sure she'd known it. Hadn't even batted an eye when I'd gotten distracted enough to receive a hit.

I had a promise to myself to fulfill.

"My love," I said against her lips, slowing the frenzy that had begun as soon as our door shut behind us.

"Mmm?" she hummed in response, tilting her chin further up to get back the pressure I'd taken away.

"You distracted me earlier," I said quietly, talking against the corner of her mouth now, as I lightly trailed my fingers from her waist, down her hips.

"You let yourself get distracted," she returned, and I smirked against her cheek at the sass.

"Regardless," I whispered close to her ear, allowing the air to caress the delicate arch. I felt the gasp she restrained, finding similar victory in the way that she couldn't quite help but arch her neck in response to the sensation. "For a face you claim is handsome, you showed no distress at it being disfigured." I pressed a kiss to the tender spot just beneath her ear, and gently followed with the tip of my tongue. Her breathing hitched.

But, ever my partner in banter, she pulled back, eyes simmering with heat. She looked over my left cheek, examining it, and said, "My love, Bayani could have sliced you from temple to jaw, and still it would be a face I'd be happy to sit on."

I laughed, rough and delighted against her temple. "We needn't take such extreme measures for that. In fact, please take your seat, my Lady, because I've been dying to taste you all day." I pulled her against me, so that she could feel the evidence of what pleasuring her did to me.

Those miracle eyes widened, the cheeks beneath them flushing. "Dion, I haven't bathed, and–"

"Let this be the only time that I interrupt you, and for good reason," I said, and slowly started to move down. I kissed her neck, and against it I growled, "I don't care." I pressed my lips to her collar bone, and lifted her shirt from its hem, pulling it up to reveal her high, firm breasts. I trailed the tip of my tongue around her nipple before sucking it into my mouth. She gasped, and her fingers speared into my hair.

"I want you to come on my face. Now. No delays." I clamped my teeth down gently on the taut bud, and her breathing stuttered. Trailing kisses down the midline of her belly, until I was kneeling, stooping further until finally I was at the waistband of her shorts. I skimmed my mouth around her lower belly at the same time that I ran my hands up the backs of her thighs.

I slid my fingers under the waistband, and worked those shorts down, steadily revealing my favorite part, pastime, and meal. "Do you have a problem with that?" I asked when the shorts were at her feet, and my voice vibrated against her.

"No," she gasped, and I grinned. "Good," I responded, and parted her legs slightly with my arms, then scooped her up until she sat on my shoulders, completely exposed to me. I stood with her like that, her fingers knotted in my hair for balance. I turned my head to kiss her inner thigh, and when I looked up, I found her staring down at me, her full lips parted, and eyes positively burning with lust.

I moved to sit on the edge of our bed, and said, "Hold on tight," before leaning back until my torso was completely horizontal on the mattress. And, just as I'd intended, she landed right where I wanted her.

I felt my cock straining against my pants at the first noise she made as I licked slowly, luxuriously over her center. Gods, those sounds. If they ended up being the death of me, I would die a happy male.

I tasted her, thrusting my tongue inside of her. I groaned at the tightness there, and savored the way the vibration of my voice made her gasp. Clutching her thighs, I pulled her against me so I could get deeper, and, to my extreme satisfaction, she moaned loudly in response.

But I knew where she wanted me. Swallowing the taste of her, I moved my tongue up her center until I reached that little bud that had become one of my best friends these past weeks. I circled it with the tip of my tongue, and she moaned again, even louder this time.

I drew out the sensations, making sure that I made her feel all kinds of pleasure before completely devouring her. When her pants got breathier, and she ground herself down onto my tongue, I growled. Her pleasure got me so fucking hard, but I didn't anticipate that being needed after this. This was for her— and for me, because, gods, did I want to hear those sounds, feel her throbbing against my tongue, make her feel as good as possible, as I had vowed to do from day one.

I growled once more, and she shattered. She rode my face through the throes of it, and I couldn't help but moan as she took what she wanted from me, completely unleashing herself.

I clutched her ass as she came, and when she stilled, she settled back, sitting on my chest.

"I know we don't do turns with this," she said, her voice throaty. "But I will be getting you back for that one, mate."

I grinned up at her, and she leaned down to press her lips against mine, before licking my bottom lip.

40

SAMARITAN

THEA - PRESENT

I PICK AT A HOLE IN THE LEATHER OF THE BOOTH SEAT, THE FABRIC clicking against my nail as tiny pieces snap off. Otherwise, I make no movements, keeping my head down and staring at the stained wooden table in front of me. The pub reeks of ale, piss, and smoke, and raucous laughter sounds from all corners of the room.

It's dark in this space Adathan chose for us. The only windows are at the front, so small that they're likely only there for reasons of code or permit. And it's obvious why; because, while the ground floor serves food and drink, the two stories above it are clearly used for a different sort of pleasure.

Women peruse the pub, ample bosoms hanging out of corsets so tight that I wonder how they breathe in them. On our way in I'd seen more than a handful of them eye Adathan, and examine me to determine if we're together or not, even before we'd had a chance to clean up.

We'd paid our way with a silver piece from the small amount in Adathan's purse, and, with the hoods of our new cloaks up, had immediately gone upstairs–me doing my best not to blush at the sounds coming out of the other rooms.

Adathan had insisted I be the first to shower, only giving me an exasperated sort of side eye when I asked him if it was because his poor little Fae nose couldn't bear my stench anymore. Once in, even with him waiting in the bedroom for his turn, I hadn't been able to hold back a moan of my own as the warm, cleansing water of the shower had hit me, washing away the grime of the past few days.

Clean, and dressed in new clothes, I'd waited for him, leaning against a wall a decent distance from the bed. When he exited, I'd been grateful that the clothing I'd picked for him fit; the largest size the shopkeeper had, and yet still a bit tight in the chest and shoulders. Then, we'd only had one more item to discuss before going downstairs to eat. Me.

And when it had been him to suggest I be glamoured, it didn't feel as treacherous. When he murmured about safety, and how no captain in his right mind would board a woman who looked abused by the husband with her, I allowed it. I let him turn my raven hair golden, hide my bruises and cuts. He rounded out his ears, and dulled his eyes to amber, and then we headed downstairs.

I sat down at the stained and tattered booth, while he'd gone to the bar to order us food. When I'd asked how we were going to pay for it when we still had a captain to worry about, he'd leaned in close–putting on a good show for the watching women–and told me to play the barkeep as well as I had the shopkeeper who gave me the new clothes.

Me, a maiden called Maria, who went into the store without her husband, and in fact forgot to mention that she had one. She spoke with an accent that made her stumble over her words a bit, which helped to convey her upset. She had just arrived from Jasiira, you see–such a long journey for a young woman to make. Completely understandable that she had been swindled of all of her coin by the ship's captain for passage. She was also unlucky enough to have lost her belongings to the captain's mistress, and had no clothes but for those on her back.

By the time her story was told, voice and hands trembling, the shopkeeper had practically begged her to take whatever she needed. Hardly batted an eye when she asked for men's clothing. A nice oversized fit for sleeping, which she preferred to the silk things that hung in the back of the shop. He'd even used a leather awl to pierce the belt for her scabbard so that it would fit her thigh. And when she promised to pay him back as soon as she could, he'd waved her off, saying that it was his duty to help someone in need when he could.

And though I certainly *had* been in need of the clothes now on my back–the cursed outfit I'd been given by Olin, and worn for days trekking through the woods, now disposed of–I still feel dirty for lying to get them. But I doubt that the story of me being a kidnapped princess who'd been set free and now wishes to go with her Fae companion to Eshelle would have flown very well. So, when Adathan suggested that I repeat the process with someone else, I'd just glared at him and said nothing.

Now, I see an uncommonly large form walking towards me from the corner of my eye. I look up from the table to find that Adathan's balanced our plates on one arm, with two glasses in his other hand. I also see a couple of women nearby observe him, and do the same once-over of me as the others had when we arrived. Even though he'd dimmed himself a bit with the glamour–removing a shining Fae quality to him that I hadn't realized was there until it wasn't–

he strikes quite an imposing figure. Tall, and broad, stubble cutting his jaw. I'm sure one of them will make their move eventually.

Seeming not to notice them, he holds out the hand with the glasses to me, and I take them from him, setting one down in front of his seat, and taking a sip from the other. The ale is a bit watery, but it's cold, and cuts through the smallest amount of gnawing in my stomach. Adathan sets down my plate before sitting, his weight great enough that I hear the wood of the bench groan slightly beneath him.

I smirk at the way his brow furrows, and at how he looks down, as though to inspect the stability of his seat. He looks up at me before I can wipe the expression from my face. After half a heartbeat, one corner of his mouth tilts up in return.

I feel, rather than see, the gazes of the women shift to me. Taking a closer look at what might be between us. Not nearly alike enough in looks to pass for familial, but that still leaves plenty of options available. Friends, casual lovers, and, worst case scenario, married. The option of reluctant allies has probably not crossed their minds.

But I'm much too distracted by the presence of warm food, that's not just meat and sap, to truly care what's on their minds. I dig into the potatoes first, and once again can't help the moan that escapes me. They might not be the best I've ever tasted, but that's how it feels.

I eat with abandon, and Adathan does the same across from me. He shows less signs of strain from the lack of food and water than I do, the immortal bastard. I'm sure that, even with the glamour, I look gaunt.

It still shocks me a bit when a golden lock falls over my shoulder as I lean forward to take a bite of the shredded pork smothered in gravy. I flick it back in annoyance, but it simply happens again when I take another bite. I sigh, begrudgingly setting down my fork to arrange it in some way that will allow me to eat in peace.

"Need a hand, honey?" a husky female voice says from behind me. I turn slightly to find a corseted woman, who looks to be a few years older than me, moving to stand beside me. Her brown hair flows prettily over her generous breasts, a purple sash around her waist accentuating the curves below it. She raises a thin paper roll of tobacco to her lips, taking a pull from it as a wisp of smoke seeps out of her red-painted mouth.

"Sorry, do I need a hand with what?" I ask, as the end of her durry glows.

She turns her head to the side before blowing out the foul-smelling smoke, and that pretty mouth tilts up in a grin. "With your hair, hon. It's practically falling into your food, and you're eating like you haven't been able to in days." Her sharp brown eyes dart to Adathan, an accusing look in them, but she turns her gaze back to me just as quickly.

"Here," she says, and puts the durry back between her lips before untying the band of purple fabric from her waist. She holds it out to me, and I glance at it, not entirely sure that I should take it. Rolling her eyes, she drops the durry on the floor before stepping on it to extinguish the embers.

She moves to stand behind me, and I look at Adathan, widening my eyes slightly. He only shrugs before the woman orders, "Lean forward. You've got so much hair it's pinned between your back and the seat."

Unable to do much else, I do as she says. With gentler and softer hands than I would have expected, she reaches under my hair, collecting it all, and pulls it over the back of the booth. Then, with nimble fingers, she rakes the tresses back from my face before wrapping the thick band of fabric just behind my hairline. She ties it into a bow at the nape of my neck, and tosses each end of the fabric over my shoulders.

"There," she says, and comes back around to look at me. Her eyes flit around my face, inspecting her work, and she grins again. "Trick of the trade." She winks before adding, "That should keep your hair out of your face, and your food."

I touch the fabric, feeling the smoothness of it, and then look at her. "Thank you," I say sincerely, and smile a bit, just for her.

Her answering grin is much more enthusiastic. "Oh, you're welcome, honey. It suits you better than it does me. That plum color, with those eyes? Have you ever considered dying your hair dark?"

It's almost funny. "No, I haven't."

She shrugs. "Pity. You're already a stunner, but with black hair? You'd have men falling to their knees. What I wouldn't give for looks like that." She strokes my cheek gently, just below where the glamoured slice lays, shooting another glance at Adathan.

"You're very beautiful yourself," I respond truthfully. Curvy, pretty, and kind. A lovely combination.

She waves a hand, brushing off my compliment. "You just get back to your meal. I'm Evelyn, by the way. But you can call me Evie." She holds out a hand.

I grasp her fingers in mine. "Maria."

Releasing my hand, she lets out a huff of exasperation. "See, now that is a name for a dark-haired girl. I have to walk away, otherwise I'm just going to get more and more upset that the gods gave you blonde hair instead of black. But I hope to see you around, Maria." She turns from us, and walks towards the back of the pub before disappearing behind the stairs.

After a moment, Adathan says, "Well, that was... interesting."

I chuckle once. "You're just jealous that she approached me, and not you." I pick my fork back up, and take a bite of the pork and potatoes, and my hair doesn't float forward to nearly fall into the gravy anymore.

He shrugs. "Not my type."

I roll my eyes. "Oh, I'm sure. She's only busty and beautiful. It couldn't be that you're deflecting because it hurt your ego that she hardly seemed to notice you." I finish the meat and potatoes, and immediately move to butter the biscuit I saved for last.

"I'm not the kind of male who would let a female's rejection impact my view of her."

"Man, remember? And woman. And while that's very admirable, I still don't get how someone like *that* isn't 'for you'." I take a bite of the biscuit, and the combination of the slightly sweet dough and the salty butter makes me moan softly again.

Something in his eyes shifts, but he only says, "She's just not."

My brows scrunch, but one of the things I've learned about him over the past few days is that, if he's being vague, that's not going to change if I ask again. So, I just go back to my biscuit, and wonder if perhaps he has a lover at home that he abstains for. Not that I believe he would leave me to...release himself, regardless, but it would explain the shadows that sometimes come over his face when he looks at me, and how he hasn't even snuck a peek at the many voluptuous women around him.

Perhaps he's not interested in *women* at all. His Fae lover is probably excruciatingly gorgeous, and us humans likely pale in comparison. I would have wondered if maybe he looked for another sort of partner altogether, but I just don't get that feeling from him. He seems all too much like the kind of man– *male* who would ravage a woman. *Female.* Well, and thoroughly–

I stop the thought in its tracks as my cheeks heat, and I try to look at anything but him. In my periphery, though, I see his nostrils flare, probably reluctantly smelling the stench of the pub, or trying to scent for any dangers.

His fists clench on the table for a beat before loosening, and he asks, just loud enough for those around us to hear, "Are you ready to go, sweetheart?"

I nod, and, with no napkins present, I wipe my mouth of any biscuit crumbs with the back of my hand. Adathan holds his hand out to me, though, and I remember again the parts we have to play. I quickly rub the back of my palm off on the leather booth before reaching to twine my fingers with his. The booth couldn't get much more filthy, anyway.

Adathan's hand is so large that it swallows mine right up, but it's warm, and calloused, and reassuring, so I grip it as best as I can anyway. The thin gold band of the ring he wears on his right forefinger presses against my own as he leads me to the bar. He gently ushers me in front of him once there, putting himself between me and the rest of the patrons. He leaves a slightly less than casual distance between us, and releases my hand to place his on the small of my back.

"Hey, Ilia," he calls to the barkeep, deep voice carrying over the cacophony of the pub. The grizzled man turns to us, stubble grown over his sagging cheeks, and his dark eyes take note of me before he walks over to us. A finger taps my back, signaling for me to put on the charm for the man. I manage not to roll my eyes, and plaster a happy, if a bit bashful, smile on my face.

"You both can go," Ilia tells us, and my smile falters with confusion. "Evelyn has covered you. Said that anyone who calls her beautiful always gets something extra." And, before either of us can respond, he walks away, back to paying customers.

Adathan's hand on my back becomes guiding as he leads me to the door. I see many of the women in corsets watch us leave—not able to spot Evie amongst them to thank her—and I can't help but think that we must be putting on quite a convincing show for none of them to have approached him.

When we step through the door and into the open air, I pull in my first clean breath in over an hour. I'm sure the desensitization will wear off soon, and then I'll have to wash the fabric Evelyn gave me before I can wear it again, but wear it I will. To keep the memory of the kind gesture—one of two, apparently—from the woman I'd likely never see again.

Adathan grabs my hand once more, and we meander, as if not in a hurry at all, towards the docks. The skirt I'd gotten from the shop rustles and sways with each step, Adathan's dagger comfortably strapped to my thigh, hidden completely by the skirt's fabric. Not as easily accessible as it had been across my back, but human captains would only think to search a man for weapons before allowing him and his poor, defenseless wife onto their ship. They wouldn't dare to look in a woman's skirts. Especially with her very large husband beside her.

This means, of course, that I'd had no choice but to get a long-sleeved shirt to hide the muscle in my arms and shoulders. To maintain the damsel look, and all. The neckline of the shirt at least offers some breathability, and the fabric is thin enough, but I'm grateful for the cooler air near the water versus the heat we faced inland.

Indeed, that light breeze blows my hair back, and cools my neck, offering some relief to the slight discomfort of the still-healing bruises, only hidden by Adathan's glamour.

"Ada–Adam?" I say quietly, catching myself before I say his real name, our hands swinging between us as we walk down the bustling street of the port town.

"Yes?" He looks down at me with those false amber eyes.

"How do glamours work?"

His brow furrows. "Why do you ask?"

I raise a brow, and then pick up a lock of my waving blonde hair. "Hmm, I wonder."

"Alright, smartass," he quips back, but a corner of his mouth pushes up into a smirk, a dimple popping in that cheek. He turns back to the road ahead, scanning those who pass by us for a moment. "They're very complex, in that there are varying levels. Changing a hair color–" he shoots me a glance, "–is simple. But they can conceal and change anything about a person."

He clears his throat, but continues. "Not just that, but they're...open to interpretation, I guess you could say. For example, if I wanted to glamour myself, but have you still be able to see me as I really am, I could. They don't have to apply to everyone around you. I, for instance, can still see you as you were earlier today, but if anyone else were to ask around that pub for a raven-haired woman, they would come up empty."

"Okay," I say slowly, but think on it for a moment. "Can anyone glamour things, or is it like pocket realms? Or like wind?"

He thinks for a beat. "I guess it's more like wind. Not everyone can glamour, but many can, and it's not seen as special. Actually, it's probably even more common than wind."

I scrunch my brows. "Why?"

"I think because of that variation. Like, maybe a vast majority can do something small, like change eye color. But it takes a lot more power to, I don't know, make someone invisible."

"They can do that?" I ask, my eyes widening.

"Yes. And they're not just for people. Talented Fae, and even some faeries, can glamour places. Make them appear not as they are."

"That sounds..." I stop myself before I express my fear at that. At thinking I'm in one place, but really being in another.

Or, as I had with Adathan–seeing someone as one person, and coming to know that isn't them at all.

"Scary? Dangerous? Both? It can be. But, there are also ways to train yourself to see past most of them. It's not easy–probably even harder than learning to glamour in the first place."

"Why?"

"That's a good question. Maybe because, just like in life, it's easier to let yourself be tricked into the comforting lies, than to see through them to the truths that may frighten you."

"Alright, mister philosopher-male."

Another smirk. "Man, remember?" he imitates me, from our conversation in the pub. Then continues, his tone and expression sobering a bit. "You were never trained to do that. To see past the glamours. I'm not even sure someone in your court would have known how. Not for lack of ability–it's just such a... Fae kind of majick. And since Fae hadn't been in your realm for a millennium, it's understandable that the knowledge, if it was ever shared with humans, died off from lack of use, and need."

I think through all of that for a moment. "Do you know how to see through them?"

He nods. And while this opens questions just as it answers them, the next one I ask is, "Will you teach me?"

He looks down at me, amber eyes scanning for something. I only stare back at him. "I will."

Approaching the docks, even more densely packed than the road we've been on, we choose to end the conversation there– for now. We're strolling down the road in silence, my eyes on the white sails luffing out in the sea, when–

"Maria?" a newly familiar voice says. I turn to look over my shoulder, and find Evie striding towards us, a wide smile on her face. "Well, if that scarf doesn't look even prettier on you in the sun."

I grin a bit, and turn to fully face her, releasing Adathan's hand to do so. "You're even lovelier now that I can actually see you, too."

She laughs, a husky, and, to be honest, sexy sound. "Thank you, hon. I come down here once in a while to scope for the ships coming in. Not to give you too much of a look into my business, but those men sometimes spend weeks at sea, and well...they're usually looking for my kinds of services by the time they get in."

I feel Adathan silently observing us, but we can spare a moment. If a ship leaves during that time, it wouldn't have taken us, regardless.

"We're just heading down there ourselves now," I tell her.

"Oh, well, I'll walk with you."

I immediately start towards her, but Adathan grabs my waist quickly, pulling me back to him gently, but effectively. "You don't have to do that," he says, his voice flat, like it had been before he'd jumped off that cliff with me. And right there, I know something is up. I almost turn to look at him, but his fingers tighten on my waist, and I stay facing forward.

Evie's smile drops the slightest bit as she notes the change, too. Not in his voice, as I have, but in his demeanor. The man who'd waited patiently as she had done my hair, now facing off with her, none of that patience to be found.

"Don't be silly," she recovers. "I'm sorry if I came on too strong, but I hardly ever have girl friends who aren't trying to steal my customers." Her gaze shifts to me, and her wink is a bit strained compared to what it had been at the pub. "I bet with him in your bed, you don't need any extra attention, do you?"

"Who are you?" Adathan asks while I blush, remembering my similar thoughts from earlier. He pulls me closer to him, pressing my back against his side.

Evie's smile falls more. "What do you mean? I'm just trying–"

My heart begins to race at the menace that comes to his rumbling voice when he asks her again: "Who. Are. You?"

And Evie's smile turns, her sweet brown eyes filling with hate. She closes the distance between us, not a trace of fear on her fine-boned face, her short heels clicking on the compressed gravel. Adathan pushes me behind him, but stands his ground, and I hear him inhale, scenting for any other threats. The breeze blows, though, and if anything–or anyone–is downwind of us, we're out of luck. Still, I don't feel afraid. I just place my hand on his back, leaning around him a bit to see.

But Evie stops two feet away from us, and stares up into Adathan's face, fury lining her own. "Who am *I*? Who are *you*? A man–excuse me–*male* who gets off on hurting this girl?"

I'm the one who says, "What?"

"You don't have to cover for him, Maria. I can see past his *majick*, and I see what he's done to you. The knowledge of how to do so has been passed through the brothel, ever since his kind started coming here thirty years ago. Yeah, some can't manage it. But I can. I have. And I can see the bruises on your face and neck, and the cut on your cheek." Her gaze does not leave Adathan as she speaks to me, but her next words are for him. "I bet you feel so big and strong, beating this woman. You won't by the time they're done with you."

"Who? Evie, who did you tell?" I try to sidestep Adathan, but his thick arm is immovable around me.

"It doesn't matter. You'll stick with me, hon, and we'll let them take care of him."

I don't know who *they* are, but I'm certain that they're not whoever she thinks they are. I wait for Adathan to lash out, to hurt her for not keeping quiet. He only says, "Thank you. For caring about her."

Then he picks me up faster than I can blink, and runs back up the road with me in his arms. All too familiar, this running for our lives thing is becoming. But still, I wrap my arms around his neck, and look over his shoulder to watch his back. Evie stands still in the middle of the crowd, her lovely face angry and confused as she watches us, until too many other people obscure my view of her. The passersby, bewildered, and maybe a bit frightened, watch as Adathan darts up the hill, me in his arms, with inhuman speed.

He sprints into an alley, and leaps over bags of trash and puddles of filth. A maze of small alleys and tight corners later, he sets me down, barely panting, his hands resting lightly on my shoulders.

"Sorry," he says quietly, scanning my face.

"For what?" My back is pressed against the building wall, the alleyway so constricted that as his chest rises in a breath, it's just inches from my face.

"Dashing like that. We were so close, and..." He sighs, and releases my shoulders to run his hands over his face, and then up through his hair, keeping his eyes closed. For possibly the first time, I recognize how truly exhausted he looks. Lavender half-moons beneath his eyes, jaw and neck tight with constant strain.

"Hey," I say softly, and hesitantly begin to lift a comforting hand...

His eyes flash open, and I quickly drop that hand, remembering myself. Remembering that any contact these past hours has been for show, not for any real friendship or desire. Chagrin heats my cheeks, and I don't recognize the alarm in his gaze for what it is until I note his flared nostrils.

And then an arrow buries itself into his neck.

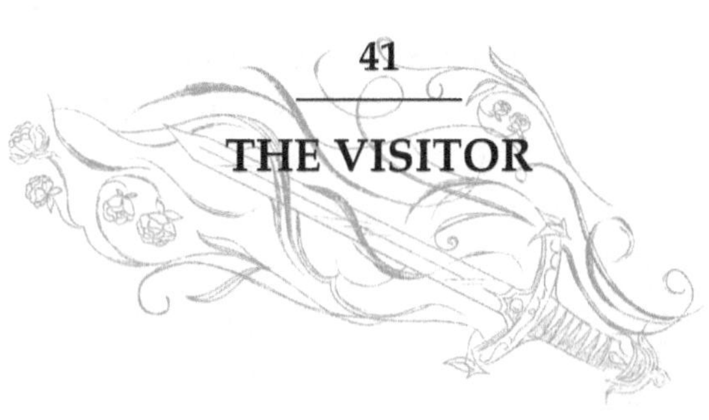

41

THE VISITOR

I SAT ON THE SUNBATHED COUCH IN THE LIBRARY, MY FEET IN Dion's lap, and a book in mine. Bayani was off with his Planician lover, since she was leaving today, but Nuria and Jolie sat across from us. The mates had opted to swap the two chairs for another couch, and Jolie lay with her head on Nuria's thighs, and looked closer to falling asleep than she seemed invested in her book.

It could be that Nuria's fingers stroked idly through her mate's hair. Indeed, as Nuria's fingers again moved gently over the strands, Jolie's eyes closed fully. She reopened them, only to fall victim to the touch again, and again, until finally she gave up. The female laid her open book over her face, folded her hands over her belly, and only a moment later, her measured breaths could be heard from beneath the book.

I grinned softly at my friend, and found Nuria doing the same, except with an exponential adoration in her gaze. She looked at her mate like she was her moon. Bright, and quiet; lovely, and constant.

And the look was familiar. It was the expression I frequently caught on Dion's face as he gazed at me. He mindlessly brushed his fingers over my calf now, absorbed in his own book. The familiarity, the lack of a need to think about the affectionate act, warmed my heart even more than the touch itself.

It also had me hiding a smile at the fact that his fingers drifted no farther than my ankle. A lesson learned, that had started with him going down to other parts of me, and ended with me accidentally kicking him in the face when he brushed the arch of my foot with a knuckle.

Well, ended for a moment, anyway. The male could not be deterred, once his nose had healed.

I grinned a bit, toes curling at the memory, but went back to my book. Since the arrival of the other courts, and the King and Queen of Weaschte, we'd hardly had the time to read with our friends. Our main interactions with them had been court gatherings, and walks in the gardens–always accompanied by some visiting nobility or other.

But this morning, Queen Lydia had begun to experience her laboring pains. Already, most courts had gone back home, but with the expected arrival of the first human child born in Eshelle in centuries, those still here had opted to stay until later in the day, when the human midwife they'd brought with them claimed the child should arrive.

Until that baby was born, no one was looking for us to show them around the castle, or bring them into the city proper. Everyone lounged in one area or another, guards of our or their own posted at various locations, and waited. We chose to do our waiting in the best room of the castle, while also neglecting to tell anyone else about it. In fact, it might have slipped our minds to share this space with anyone since they'd arrived a couple of weeks ago.

It was late morning now, and we hadn't moved since we arrived after breakfast. I was a ways into my book, and the enemies had just become reluctant allies. But, ever so interestingly, the male couldn't stop looking at his *ally* like he wanted her, and she couldn't stop herself from finding excuses to touch him. I was hoping I would make it to either an emotional or physical breakthrough before I had to put the book down.

The breeze from the open window flowed into the library, filling it with the scents of grass and flowers. I held the pages of my book down so that it wouldn't blow through to another page, and ruin the anticipation for me. But Dion straightened, his brow crinkling as he looked out the window.

"What is it?" I asked, his expression superseding even the male character putting his hand on the female's waist for the first time.

"I thought..." he trailed off, and his nostrils flared as he sniffed the breeze still coming in through the window.

But then footsteps, running footsteps, sounded from the hall. Immediately, Dion and I were up, Nuria quickly waking Jolie before following. I slung my sheathed sword–kept with me at all times these past weeks, with so many visitors in our home–across my back as we all walked to the library doors. Dion opened them before us, and stepped into the hall. In front of him, sprinting down the long hallway, was our High Lord.

We rushed to meet him, and his eyes were on me when he said, "It's time."

My heart dropped, though I'd known this day was coming. Still, I gave it no second thoughts, and neither did my mate or our friends, before we all began to race back through the halls.

"We have to stop," Dion said, his voice a whisper. "If we're seen running, everyone will know something is happening. We have to walk."

He was right, of course. Not only that, but the busybodies here visiting would no doubt go to lengths to stop us and ask what was so urgent. Still, it felt awful to slow my pace, as Amedeo and our friends did with us. Dion grabbed my hand, and squeezed my fingers between his. I knew that it was as much to tether me to the calm stroll as it was a gesture of comfort.

The walk up to the High Lord and High Lady's chambers felt longer than it ever had. I could hear Hielo's heart pounding, even with the slow pace, his fear for his mate breaking through the outward facade. When finally we reached the tower, he and Jolie strode ahead of me into the grand foyer that usually took my breath away. It was only an inconvenience now. That I had to round a corner before I could see her.

Sheets were pulled back from the bed, strewn over the floors. At her feet was their duvet, dyed pink with waters and blood. She stood, though–barely. Bent at her hips wearing only her white cotton sleeping gown, her hands braced on the edge of the bed. In the light of the window, the silhouette of her breasts and belly hung down, moving with her breath.

Hielo was at her side in an instant, putting counterpressure on her back as another contraction hit, and she moaned out a long breath through the pain. When it was done, she turned her sweat-slicked face to me.

"Looks like it's time for you to deliver a baby."

⇔

Nuria and Dion stood guard outside the door. A sound shield had been put up around the tower, so that none might hear the High Lady's cries. Unnecessary, now, to glamour herself any longer. The babe was a bit early for the year-long term of Fae gestation, but for all that time, she'd used her abilities. Not only to block the physical nature of the pregnancy from sight, but to alter the perception of her glamour to each mind, as she had done with Dion when he first arrived. Now, with only the people she trusted most here to witness, she allowed her belly, her fuller breasts, and the scent that came with carrying a child show.

On her knees over the duvet now, Jolie knelt in front of Oksana while Amedeo sat behind her, still trying to brace her hips. Jolie ran a cool cloth over her sister's brow, and talked to her in soothing tones. The females would occasionally smile, as the former would talk about times when they were small, but then Oksana would get another contraction, and those moments felt like hours to those who loved her.

I wondered, sometimes, the reason for it. Why a Fae birth, or even a human birth, was so painful and dangerous. While horses and cows and many beasts of the wild seemed to experience little discomfort as their babies were born, so long as there were not any complications. Why was it that, as animals ourselves, that wasn't the case? Had something gone wrong in our evolution from the beasts we were millenia ago, to what we are now?

Whatever the reason, though human births were surely not easy, birthing a Fae child had proved to be even less so. Both the mother and the child perished more frequently, and, if both survived, it usually was still an unimaginably painful experience.

I knew that some believed the explanation that, because we were immortal beings, the universe had found balance by making it so that we could not have many children. A prevention for overpopulation–both in how difficult it was to get a female with child, and in the exponentially more difficult experience of actually giving birth to that child. A world could not be overpopulated if either the mother or baby died, or the couple could not get pregnant in the first place.

But these were not the thoughts I should be having as I palpated Oksana's belly, as I'd learned to do months ago, when she and Amedeo had first asked me to act as midwife. It would be an honor, they said, if Gabriel Vey's child would bring their own into this world.

"Oksana." She'd instructed me to call her by her name during this process. Turning her face to me, her sienna eyes hardened; enduring, through this pain and this fear. "I need to reach in to feel the baby, and make sure that they're in position." She nodded once, and Amedeo moved from her back to allow me to take his place.

I hiked up her dress a bit, and prepared her as best I could for my hand. She hissed a breath through her teeth as I probed, and thankfully felt the baby's head, not their bottom, or feet.

I told her as much, and she clutched my hand with enough strength that it made me hopeful she would make it through the birth without complication. Jolie took a place at her side, while Amedeo went to her head, putting his brow to hers, and running his fingers through her hair. I stayed behind her, and it all seemed to go—mercifully—very quickly from there. And I wondered if there was something to be said for a female who had already suffered enough.

There was blood, but not too much; not anything alarming. As soon as the babe was in the world, crying its little lungs out, Oksana shimmied the loose-fitting gown down until it hung beneath her breasts, and held her newborn to her chest. The child's cries quieted quickly, but her small breaths and coos could be heard throughout the room, along with her parents' soft sobs of joy and relief. Amedeo kissed his mate gently, and then looked down at their child.

"It seems you were right," he whispered, running a finger so very delicately over the baby's cheek.

"I always am," she responded, and I grinned. The afterbirth was simple for this female after all of that, and she held her baby throughout. I collected all the soiled linen and piled it into the fireplace, lighting it a heartbeat later. When it was blazing, and Amedeo was lying with Oksana and their baby on the bed, staring at the child with so much love, I donned the uniform jacket and sword I'd laid on the credenza close to the exit, and walked quietly to the door with Jolie, my heart filled with joy.

But when I opened the door to give Dion and Nuria the good news, neither of them were there. Jolie stuttered to a halt beside me, and we exchanged a glance. We were only lucky that the couple and their new babe were paying no attention to us. Jolie called back and informed them in a falsely sweet voice that we were going to give them some privacy, and then we stepped out into the hall.

Shadows already swirling around my palms and forearms, I handed Jolie my dagger, and unsheathed my sword from my back. While she might not have nearly as much training as Nuria, she should still be able to defend herself if necessary.

We took the steps in a staggered pattern, rounding each turn with caution. My ears practically rang at the absence of noise, but still I listened. When we got to the base of the steps, though, the scents of our mates went in two separate directions.

My heart pounded as I even so much as contemplated having Jolie follow hers on her own, but she said, "Go. He might need you."

"So might you," I replied, feeling my soul strain and tug me to my left while my heart was split at the fork with the rest of me.

"No one here will harm me. And if someone has come who

might, I can handle them. But I thought about it on the way down those steps; I think the only person who Nuria would have left our Queen for…would be someone else's."

My eyes widened. Something wrong with the human baby– the poor child who I hadn't even thought about since Amedeo and the library. Yes, Nuria would have gone to ensure the health of the babe. And of the alliance between our nations.

"Alright. But sheathe that in your bodice or something, so that if anyone friendly does pass you, they don't know anything *might* be happening. No need to cause a panic."

Jolie nodded, and slid the thin dagger down her dress, its hilt only barely peeking out. "Just don't, I don't know, bend over or something without taking it out."

"Your confidence in me is heartwarming, Ari." And, with that, she set off at a leisurely pace down the hall to my right, following her mate's scent.

I sighed, but took my own advice, sheathing my sword and scattering my shadows before setting off in the opposite direc- tion, following the scent of white oak and amber. It continued down to the ground floor of the castle, and my stride length- ened and quickened the further I got from the tower. Some- thing was definitely wrong. He would never have gone this far from where he was supposed to be, guarding his mate and his rulers, if there was not a danger that was better kept far from them.

I was nearly running, heedless of any watching eyes, by the time I reached the tiled floors of the entryway. His scent trav- eled briefly into the entrance hall, where our High Lord and High Lady had first greeted him when he'd arrived what felt like so long ago. Then, accompanied by a scent that was the same and yet not, he'd gone out the large walnut doors, to the grounds in front of the castle.

I followed, noting that the guards stood by the gates, as

normal. Staff worked, bustling about with crates and horses and each other. Nothing seemed amiss, but I could feel it, like a second heart within myself. Pounding in panic.

I followed all the way along the side of the castle, toward the gardens. Finally, I heard his voice. It was calm, but I still had that feeling in my chest. Putting on a show for somebody.

I slowed my pace, keeping my blade sheathed as I got closer and closer to him. It sounded almost like he was talking to... himself?

I thought I knew who had come, then, and why Dion had needed to ensure that he met him far from where our High Lord and High Lady were. And when I took the first path from the grounds into the gardens, and rounded a large hydrangea bush, I saw that I was right.

Beside Dion was a male with the same complexion, the same slightly curling brown hair. I could only see their backs, their hands folded behind them, but followed on silent feet muffled by shadows. They were no longer talking, only walking side by side through the flowers, beneath the honeysuckle-covered trellises.

Knowing they would see or scent me soon enough, I bent the shadows to my will. As my power grew with age, it showed me new things, new abilities. I hadn't even known that the shadows could take me with them to wherever I casted them until last week. I'd been...*overwhelmed* with Dion, and had somehow ended up in the corner of my bedchamber, legs splayed; he had been stunned, still in position, just inches off the mattress.

As I had been practicing since then, I pictured the shadowy area beneath the willow that was not yet in their sights, and became those shadows. Those that I gathered around me took me with them, and then my feet were on grass instead of cobblestone, the willow's branches hanging around me.

They were near now, their identically measured footsteps sounding down the stone of the path. I took off my uniform jacket, and glamoured my scent to be free of birth and new life. The sword, I kept sheathed at my back.

I stepped out from the willow when their steps sounded close enough to see me, but not so close to startle. I pasted a wide smile on my face, and said, "Lord Dion–"

I cut myself off, smile falling a bit. It was partly an act; my pretending to have not known he would be with someone else. But I had to keep my expression fixed in surprise and confusion as I saw the two of them together for the first time.

If Dion were not my mate, and I didn't know every detail of his face and demeanor, I might not have been able to tell them apart. If I had not seen him this morning, and known that he hadn't cut his hair or beard since then, I still might have taken a moment to tell them apart. Dion had allowed his hair to grow out since his arrival, but Olin's was just long enough to suggest at the curly texture. Dion had facial hair in the form of a well-groomed beard, while Olin was clean shaven.

But their eyes were the same. Green and gold, framed with thick black lashes. The same cheekbones and full lips, their skin that lovely golden-brown. It was the expressions in those faces that separated them. Not merely the immediate fear I watched Dion suppress as I stepped in front of him and his brother. No, it was the coldness of Olin's features–the same face that I knew and loved, and had seen filled with such warmth– that set them apart.

"Ah, Lady Ciaragen," Dion said, his voice bland. "Apologies if we disturbed you during your...relaxation?" His brow rose, and he scanned me, with none of the affection I had come to know. "I was just showing Lord Olin the gardens. Olin, this is Lady Ciaragen Vey."

Olin looked me up and down, and I wished I'd kept my

jacket on. I felt, rather than saw, Dion bristle at the way his brother took me in. Without an ounce of respect or propriety. Purely a male taking account of a female, where the former believed the latter to be utterly at his mercy. For his mercy.

But he bowed low to me, sweeping an arm as though he was the most gallant male alive. When he stood, he smiled. But it wasn't my smile–the smile that Dion gave me, that made me warm inside. This grin seemed to pour ice water in my veins, chilling me to my core so that I had to remember to curtsy back to him.

"A pleasure to meet you, Lord Olin," I said, pulling my lips up at the corners in a courtly smile.

"The pleasure is mine, Lady Ciaragen. Or, is it Lady Vey? Is your mother still living?" he asked, his brow furrowing.

"She is, my Lord."

"Lady Ciaragen, then." That grin came back, as something rotten shone in his eyes. "Can I ask you a question?"

I almost eyed Dion, almost looked to see if he would give me any inclination towards one option or another. But the farce of knowing me little enough to use my title had to continue. So, I answered, as any lady would to a high-standing lord. "Of course, my Lord."

"Why is it that you smell like cunt and blood, my Lady?"

42

THE ONLY KINDNESS

JOLIE - 21 YEARS EARLIER

I WALKED DOWN THE TILED HALLWAY UNHURRIEDLY, ARI'S DAGGER slim and cool against my skin. I kept my breaths shallow as I scented for my mate, striding further towards the east wing, where the visitors chambers were. Grinning happily at the guests I saw, I passed through the common spaces, the remaining nobility of Planici and Grevosch mingling around tables of sparkling wine and fruit juices, and platters of pastries. I spotted Bayani with Annalise at one of the tables, his own smile small and sad.

But I continued on, smelling Nuria's gardenia, orange, and nutmeg scent carry into the halls of the rooms. Not joining another's, which was not so much surprising as it was concerning. Her power of knowing where she was needed most, taking her from our own Queen—our High Lady, our ruler, my sister—to the Queen of the humans. And I knew what that meant. That, although our nation's child had been born well, the mother healthy, the Weaschten babe, or Lydia, was likely not.

I knew Nuria well, even after less than a year mated. I knew that she was intelligent, and kind, and outgoing. That she was fiercely loyal, and protective to those who deserved it. And I knew that she would not have left her Queen, left me, if something had not gone horribly wrong. And so my heart ached for the human Queen and her baby as my steps clicked lightly down the bright halls of the castle.

I reached the chambers given to the Weaschten King and Queen, but wouldn't have known it if I had not brought them here when they'd arrived. No guards stood on duty, and, though my mate's scent disappeared behind that door, I could hear no sound. Not a baby wailing, nor its parents crying. I took a deep breath, and softly called Nuria's name, hopefully quiet enough that she might be the only one to hear inside that room of grief.

I heard no footsteps, but the door opened before me, and Nuria stood there, her golden tattoo looking unusually dull on her paled face. The dark, lovely skin that I'd showered with kisses was gaunt, her black eyes filled with dread and sorrow— and anger.

Gently, she reached through the threshold, and took my hand. She pulled me into the foyer, and, like entering the film of a bubble, I could hear. Soft sobs, and quiet sounds of consolation. Once past the sound shield, Nuria released my hand, and I knew that it was for the sake of the distraught humans. They did not need to see expressions of love, when they had just lost so much of it.

My heart aching, I followed just behind my mate as she led me through the foyer, and into the bedroom. But I smelled it then.

Not the beginnings of rot, and decay, as I was expecting, but the scent of new life. Lydia had her head buried against Aron's chest, and his head was bent as he whispered to her, tears running down his own face.

It was not to them that Nuria took me, but to a bassinet shoved into the far corner of the bedroom. Once there, she folded her hands behind her back, as though restraining herself from making any kind of contact with it, or with what lay inside.

I stepped up to her side, and looked down at the baby.

She was white-haired, small curls already forming atop her pale head; white lashes nearly touched her cheeks as she slept. Skin like fresh cream, small blue veins pulsing in her chubby little legs, beautifully spider-webbing in her temples. But I knew that even these details, however abnormal the humans might have thought them to be, were not why the child lay by herself in a corner.

It was her arm. Gone at the elbow on her right side, slightly narrowed into a stump. Her left arm was whole, all five fingers clenched in a tiny, pale fist by her face.

And I knew immediately what the human King and Queen believed the innocent babe to be.

I had to restrain myself, as Nuria did, from reaching into that bassinet. From stroking a finger gently down that precious cheek, and making sure she knew at least some kind of love in her first hours of life. But I understood why she held back, and why I had to myself.

We could not show affection for a *faerie* child.

Not without seeming as though we were alright with the faeries taking the newest heir to Weaschte, and replacing her with a baby of their own. Not without looking like we were happy to see a child of our land, and cared not for what had happened to theirs.

Without looking at her, I asked Nuria, my voice so low that

the humans would not have a chance of hearing. "What do they want to do with her?"

Nuria's voice was tight as she answered. "Apparently there's a ritual. The babe is left in a natural holy place, and the faeries have until sunrise tomorrow to give them their baby back. If they do not, the *faerie* child is left to die. A kindness, that their souls would still be passed to the gods, even if it is not of their own kind."

I took a deep breath as that processed, and the dagger in my dress sliced into my breast. Thin as a paper cut, but blood beaded from the wound. Nuria's nostrils flared as she scented it, and looked at me with widened eyes. But I saw her gaze move to my chest, finding the hilt of the dagger only just visible over my bodice, and she sighed.

In an ordinary situation, this probably would have been one of the monthly conversations we had about her buying me weapons of my own, or getting me fitted for scabbards and sheaths. But, aside from the fact that I had no interest in such things, this was absolutely not the time for that talk.

"What do we do?" I asked as my skin healed.

"This is their baby. They might not understand it, but she is human. I'm not sure I want to do anything about it, except knock their heads together until they see sense."

I looked up at her from the corners of my eyes, and saw the tightness in her jaw, in her shoulders. She was angry, and rightfully so. But...

"They won't see it that way, my love. They will only hear justifications, and lies. And we need their alliance. We need them to look to *us*, when the time comes."

"You don't have to whisper," Lydia said from behind us, her voice thick. We both turned to her, and I hoped only the sorrow I felt showed in my expression–even if it didn't stem from what hers did. Her blue eyes were red-rimmed, and she still laid in the linens where she birthed her baby. But it was the agony etched into her face that made my heart ache for her. We might know that she was wrong, but to her–to her, she'd lost her baby, before ever meeting her.

"You can talk to me," she went on, Aron putting his arm around her, supporting her as she sat up. "I know things must be different, since she's in Eshelle. But she should still be with her family. And I–" Her face worked as she held back a sob, but a tear escaped down her cheek nonetheless.

But when she spoke again, the queen within shined through, fury mingling with the pain. "I want my baby to be with hers. I want *her*. She's *mine*. So, what will you do to get her back?"

I stepped forward, folding my hands in front of me, so they could see them. I didn't think they feared anything from us, but it couldn't hurt to be as nonthreatening as possible. Though Nuria was bright and kind, and could smooth over situations as well as I could, I thought my particular skills would be better suited in this one.

I reached with my power to feel out the Queen. I felt that fury, that agony, but also the fear. For her baby, whom she thought to be lost. I would not erase those feelings, but I could convey what needed to be known more than words alone could express.

"I am so sorry this is happening to you, and your family, Your Majesties," I said, letting the sincerity I felt little of amplify through my tone, into their minds. "I want to work to get your baby back myself, but I need to ensure that I do right by your ritual. Do you mind telling me more about it?"

The King and Queen looked at each other, but turned back after a moment, and nodded. I took a step closer to them, but Nuria did not follow.

"Nuria, if you would please guard at the foyer, so their

Majesties' privacy can be assured." I looked over at my mate, my face turned away from the couple. She held my gaze, and I hoped that the humans' eyesight wasn't good enough to see the tightness in her usually joyful face.

But she said, "Of course," and gave a–albeit stiff–bow to the King and Queen before walking to the foyer, disappearing from sight around the corner.

I turned back to them then, and Lydia swallowed before speaking, her voice rough from laboring screams and grieving cries. "The baby must be brought to a holy place in nature. From what we know, the faeries will not go to man-made structures to get their young. The holiness of the place is so that, if the child is not claimed, their soul will still be accepted by the gods." The Queen paused before continuing.

"I know what you must think. That we let those babies starve. I've thought it, too." Her eyes darken, but look past me, and I don't think she's seeing the wall behind me. "When I was young, I would sneak out of my parents' manor to look for them. I would venture into the woods, and hear screaming babies, and walk until I found them. And when I looked at them, in their hollows, or tree stumps, or in beds of flowers, I saw what their givers saw. The people that were not their parents, but put them there to give them back to the beings that were.

"I saw their half-purple faces, or their missing limbs, or whatever else there was that had given them away as inhuman. But what I saw most of all, was a baby. Tiny, and helpless, and so, so alone. And I would hold them. I couldn't feed them, having nothing within me to give them. But I held them as they screamed from hunger, and I cried with them as I waited for their parents to get them. Prayed and prayed to the gods to usher them to me, so that they could save their baby. And when it didn't work, when it *never* worked, I held them as they died."

I felt like a weight had been dropped into my gut. How many babies, senselessly dying? How many didn't have a young girl give them the only kindness they would ever know in their too-short lives?

More tears rolled down Lydia's cheeks, and she did not wipe them away. "I buried them. All eight that I found over the years. Right there, in those places where they'd lain. I dug into the earth with my hands, until my fingers were raw, and gave them flowers, or stones, or the cloak from my back. Favors, to take to the gods.

"When I was burying the last one, my mother found me. She'd followed my tracks with a guard, and found me about to place the first smattering of earth over the babe.

"I bore the mark on my face that she gave me, and the bruises she had her guard dole out on my body for weeks. I never went into those woods again." Her blue eyes concentrated on mine once more, lined with tears. I could see, now that I looked for it, a small line across her left cheekbone–probably invisible to the human eye. How hard must she have been hit, to have a scar after all these years?

"So, yes, Lady Jolie. The babies starve. And I cannot save them. I can only save mine. So, if you are going to be the one to go get her, as you said, then please do so. But if I could ask you to do one more thing, then I might be able to rest, as I have not since my labor started."

I had to clear my throat before I could speak, but my voice was still rough when I said, "Of course, Your Majesty."

A single tear trailed down her cheek. "Stay with her. Until they come. Stay with her, and then bring my baby back to me."

And though part of me wanted to scream at her, to grab her by the shoulders, and say *This is your baby!* I knew it would do no good. And I knew the only thing she could offer with the knowledge she had, with the *beliefs* she had, was for this child to experience the kindness that so many had not. She may be angry, and distraught, but she would not let those feelings be taken out on the babe in her bassinet.

I only bowed to her, no promises passing my lips. Instead, I asked as I rose, "Would you like for me to take her now?"

Lydia looked over at the bassinet, but nodded slowly after a moment. I walked over to it, and scooped up the still-sleeping baby with gentle arms. She hardly fussed as I tucked her to me, and wrapped her blanket over her arm, so that their last glimpse of her would not be marred by what they saw as a flaw, as *other*.

"Wait," Lydia said as I began to stride for the door. I turned back to the King and Queen. Aron was looking at his wife with confusion, though grief still lined his young face. "Can I see her, just for a moment?"

I knew it wasn't smart to get hopeful at her question, but my heart had always been more prone to hope than desolation. When I learned that my sister had not been wed by Oleander, and the capital claimed she had left him, my family believed her to be dead. I did not; I had hoped, and fought. When our parents had me under guard at all hours so that I could not go to Oschverre, still I did not stop.

After half a century, my heart had weakened. But I knew that she still lived–in whatever conditions, she was still alive; I could *feel* it. Four decades after that, twenty years since I'd seen the world outside of my home estate, I killed my first male–one of those wretched guards–in one of my many escape attempts. I was caught on the border of Parvata, and I still took pride in how many males it had taken to restrain me, and bring me back.

When I was once more locked away, with less freedom even than I'd had before, my hope was only an ember. Stepped on so many times in an attempt to stifle it. How many times was I told to let go, and live my own life? To stop fighting for hers, when, to everyone else, she had been lost for nearly a century. When, to our mother and father, they were protecting their last living daughter.

I refused. Always. I knew Oksana would *never* have given up if our roles were reversed. If she hadn't been the eldest, that very easily could have been the case. So, I raged and hoped within the walls of my pretty prison until our parents passed seven years later, and could no longer stop me from going to get her.

The day I gained my freedom I rode to the capital with that hope in my heart. And when I met my mate on the Oschverren border, on horseback with my *living* sister seated in front of her, I'd decided that hopeful was the bravest thing a person could be. I knew that, without it, I would have become someone neither Oksana, nor I, recognized after all of those years. And while I would have had my sister back, she would have not had hers. Not as I had been when we were girls.

With that spark still alive inside me, more vibrant for all it had been through, I walked over to Lydia with the white-haired babe in my arms. When I reached her, I held the child slightly away from my body. *Hold her*, I wanted to say. *Just hold her, and you'll feel it. She's yours.*

But she did not. She only reached out, and gently brushed back a wispy curl with her finger. Then she sat back against her husband, and closed her eyes. One last tear trailed down her cheek, but she did not open them again.

I pulled the babe back against my chest, and stepped away from the bed, my heart heavy. There was no sound from the King or Queen as I took their child away, and rounded the corner to the foyer where Nuria waited.

Her own face was lined with the drying streams of tears, shimmering in the dim light. I knew, through the bond we'd made, sealed by each of our claimings, she'd felt all I'd just thought of. Pain for our current situation, for this child, compounded by the ache of my memories, shone in both our faces. She cupped mine for a moment between her hands, and then leaned in to kiss my lips. Soft, warm, and needed. Pulling me into what we had to do, and away from what was done.

I trusted that she had already gotten somebody to organize a distraction to clear the halls of our remaining guests. She opened the door for me, and we strode out into the hallway. As soon as the door was shut, I let out a shuddering breath, and looked down at the baby that seemed a personification of the moon. Lovely, and sweet, her little pulse visible in those cobweb-thin veins at her temples.

I looked up at Nuria to ask her what we might do from here, but the look on her face had the words sticking in my throat. Instead, what came out was, "What's happened?"

43

UNMOVED

I THINK THAT I SCREAM.

As the arrow goes through Adathan's skin, muscle, and bone. There's a ringing in my ears that's horribly familiar, and though I feel my mouth open, feel my chest strain, I hear no sound. I only see, as he crumples like a marionette, blood trickling out of the wound.

It's not the bleeding on the outside that will kill him. His mouth opens to pull in breaths that won't come, and I see blood in the back of his throat, coating his tongue and teeth. Blood that he's drowning in, unable to cough it up. I'm on my knees somehow, and I think I tell Adathan that I'm sorry for the pain before I rip the arrow out of his neck. Because it won't matter if I'm slow and meticulous, to minimize the ripping skin, if he's dead by the time I'm done.

I wrap my hands around his neck, his life's blood flowing hot and thick through my fingers as I throw all of my magic into him. I feel hands on my shoulders, and they try to wrench me away from him. I don't hear their bones break, but the hands are gone a second later.

I feel it when Adathan's spine heals. He coughs, and blood showers my face, coats the bare skin of my wrists. His eyes focus then, registering me, and he must feel my hands on his neck now. But I know he also feels the pain, as I heal the muscle and skin pierced and shredded by the arrow. I siphon some of that pain, and pant through my teeth as I knit the fibers of him back together.

His broad hands rise to cover mine when all that's left to heal is skin, and he gently but effectively removes my hands from his neck. The pain disappears, and I see, through the blood, that only a small wound remains. It leaks crimson, but less and less as the seconds pass, and I know his Fae body is working on the rest. Glamoured amber eyes rove over my face as a breath expands the vast muscles of his chest, and the healed ones in his throat. His hands squeeze mine briefly before he releases me, and the strength in them slows the racing of my heart. His life is no longer in danger. I watch my finger run delicately over his stubbled cheek, feeling separate from it as it leaves a trail of his blood in its wake.

Then, slowly–so slowly, I begin to turn from him, to whoever shot at us. I hike my skirt to my thigh, and I spin on my heels as I rise, unsheathing the dagger from my leg, all in one smooth motion. I stand straight, between them and him, and look up from under my brow as I turn fully.

What I see almost makes me drop the dagger.

Atlas clutches his wrists, his teeth gritted in pain. The bow is slung over his shoulder, along with a quiver of arrows.

Beside him, looking at me with black brows lowered over deep blue eyes, is Ciaragen. Her full mouth is open slightly as she looks at me. Blonde hair, tied back with a prostitute's scarf, blood coating my hands and drying in droplets on my face.

Yesterday, I might have been glad to see them. I remember wondering why they hadn't come for me yet; what could possibly be stalling them with their Fae speed. I remember believing that perhaps they didn't want to find me. Now, Atlas is probably sorry that they have.

So, the first words out of my mouth aren't kind. They aren't grateful, or scared. Because I will not show them what I feel, only for them to tuck tail and go their separate way from me, and the mess I am now. I will not let them make me feel bad about who I have become, and who I've made an ally of, in order to survive.

"What are you doing here?" is what passes my lips. My ears no longer ringing, I hear Adathan stand behind me, and feel a small rush of relief that he's able to do so. I restrain myself from taking a step back, towards him and away from them, unsure of what it means that the impulse even comes to me.

"We came to free you from Olin," Ciaragen responds in her oddly-accented Ceraschen, as Atlas sets the bones in his wrists with a grunt. I pitch forward slightly before righting myself, as if my body has more of an inclination to go heal him than my mind does.

But I hear the female's words. Not rescue me, or save me. But free me. "Well, he's taken care of that bit." I gesture behind me with a thumb.

"Yes, and I'm sure his motives are completely pure." Ciaragen's voice is filled with venom as her eyes rove over the male behind me with loathing and mistrust. Atlas, however, has at last looked up from his hands, and the storm gray eyes I'd come to know so well rest on me now, unreadable.

I sense the hulking male tense slightly behind me at her

words, but say, "If it weren't for him, I'd be on a ship with Olin. And we've already had a chat about his motives, thanks."

"You don't know how deep his betrayal goes, Althea."

And maybe she didn't mean to talk down to me, but that's how it feels. My voice is hard when I reply, "What I know is that he fucked up. But now he's fixing it." *Please, don't make it more complicated than that*, are the words I don't say. *Please, don't make me hate him again.*

"It's not that simple–"

"Well, we don't really have the time to talk about it right now. If you hadn't noticed, we're trying to keep a low profile. And between the running, and the shooting, and you calling me by my name, that's shit now. It should be fun to try and find a captain." I say the last part to Adathan, turning my head from them to glance up at him. But his eyes are on the male and female before us.

"A captain?" Ciaragen asks, and I look back at her to find her brows furrowed, a small line forming between them.

"Yes." I cross my arms, not caring about the bloody hand-prints it makes on the already ruined cotton shirt.

One of those black brows raises now. "To go where?"

I suck on a tooth, but reply, "Ardhavi."

The other brow rises to join its sister. "Ardhavi, *Eshelle*?"

"No, Ardhavi on the moon."

She takes a step toward me, and I can almost *feel* Adathan's jaw feather in response. But she either doesn't see it or doesn't care, because she takes another step before saying, "Why in the world would you want to go to Eshelle?"

"To kill Olin." But when I respond, my voice has an echo. Only a half a beat off from my own alto tones, Atlas's baritone joins in, answering with me. My eyes dart to him, and he's already watching me. I can't hold his eyes long enough to read what he might be thinking as I see the tender way he holds his hands.

But Ciaragen's gaze moves again to the male behind me, incredulity and anger brewing in that look. "And you were just going to take her across the sea to help her do that, were you?"

"Yes," is his only response. Hard, and final, the husky bass of his voice rumbling through the small alley.

"Really?" Ciaragen's voice quiets, and she takes another step towards us, but this time she's not looking at me. Her eyes hold Adathan's, nearly a foot above my head, and a small, cruel smile twists her lips. "Interesting. I wouldn't have pegged you for one to kill your own father."

⊕

I think I'm supposed to feel betrayed. That this revelation is meant to make me see Adathan as 'Olin's son'. Evil incarnate, spawn of murder.

Has he lied to me, though? Perhaps through omission. Not telling me that Olin is his father, when I had no reason to think that anyway. No reason to ask it. He kept the information from me, but what I need to decide is whether I find that suspicious, or in line with our working relationship.

No verbal promises of truth had been made. I'd only assumed a mutual trust. Is that violated now? And, if so, my assumption was mine alone. He had no part in it, other than displaying mannerisms that made me internally agree to it.

So, am I betrayed? I'm not sure. I feel a bit sick, deep in my gut. But not sad, or scared, or angry. Not really.

Still, I turn away from Ciaragen and Atlas, and face Adathan. I look up into the face that I've looked at for four fucking days straight, but I don't say anything. He doesn't either, just watches me think; letting me decide what to do with this knowledge, without providing an explanation, or a story. What do I think of it on its own–a question synonymous, in this case, with what do I think of *him* on *his* own? Purely as I know him–as little as that may be.

Not a fair measure. Impossible, to know a person as well as this question would necessitate, after such a short time. Actions. Actions are evidence. And what that evidence tells me is that he has kept me alive, to his own risk, pain, and wellbeing. Whether for ulterior motives, or for honorable ones, as he's claimed...well, I would have to assume that he's told me the truth in all that he's said outright.

Omission is one thing. I don't like it, and that nausea churning in my stomach puts an exclamation mark on that fact as the seconds pass. But has he lied totally? Attempted to fool me, or just hidden things about himself that he perhaps doesn't want me to know? Maybe, doesn't want *anyone* to know?

These questions flit through my mind, and, if he's to be believed in all he's said, I know he sees them on my face, too. One of the many times he called me out as I am since day one. One of the many times he had the opportunity to lie, to speak words that might bring false comfort, and instead he'd chosen honesty.

I turn away from him, back to Ciaragen and Atlas. "We're going to Ardhavi. Are you two coming, or are you planning on taking a separate ship back home?" I hike up the skirt a bit, and reach further to sheathe the dagger against my thigh once more.

Ciaragen's mouth opens slightly, surprise apparent as she flicks her eyes between the two of us. I hear the all-too-familiar sound of Adathan crossing his arms behind me. Ciaragen's lips press into a tight line then, and she sighs through her nose.

"We have a ship," she tells me, not seeming pleased in the

slightest to concede the information. "I will have the captain reroute to Ardhavi *if* you will listen to what we have to say."

I take a step closer to her, so that we're nearly chest-to-chest. She's only slightly taller than me, her eyes maybe two or three inches above mine. I lift my chin, and say, "I'll listen. But if what you have to say doesn't impact me or my–friend here, then you'll let us go on our way regardless. Deal?" I wipe my hand on my sleeve before holding it out into the small space between us.

Her eyes spark with something like challenge, and her mouth quirks up at a corner. "Deal." Her warm, calloused hand clasps mine.

⁂

Adathan and I, both covered in his blood, walk back through alleys, following Ciaragen and Atlas to their desired location. Neither of them has any water majick, either, and I can't help but think to myself that, despite the immense power they must hold among the three of them, we'd still be screwed on a desert island.

I've yet to really get a concrete answer out of any of them as to what their exact capabilities are. To be fair, the only question I'd asked had been if they had any way to clean us up. Obviously, as I pick at a fleck of dried blood on my good cheek, the answer had been no. Living in a world where not everybody possesses magic, I'd never been one to ask about it before. If someone has magic, they either say something about it, or perform it right in front of you. I know Ciaragen can wield shadows, having seen her do so. I saw Atlas and his lightning-like sparks the other night. But it feels intrusive, in a way, to ask any of them about the particulars of their majick, when they haven't already openly divulged it to me. Particularly in

Adathan's case, when I already asked him once, and he'd been reluctant at best to respond.

Besides, I believe we've developed an unspoken mutual understanding that many things just don't have to be said aloud. Evidenced as recently as five minutes ago, when his blood had coated my hands, and he'd borne my scrutiny with the same steadiness he's brought to my days since we jumped off the Ceraschen cliffs.

A wrench is about to be thrown in that agreement, I think, since the other two seem intent on spilling all of his secrets to me. I have a feeling that, while the objective of this meeting is to give me information I'm missing, not much of it will be about them–even if I know just as little, if not less, about who they are as I do Adathan. As people, and in regards to the key question: why are they here? In Weaschte, in Cerasche, in this small port city in Dahlih.

I'm sure they believe that I won't think about that, and they won't need to answer it, since *they're the good guys*. Surely all of my queries will be reserved for information about the male who's kept me alive the past four days–perhaps longer.

Not fucking likely.

Because if anything is known, if anything is so damn evident, it's that all of this–whatever *this* is–is centered around me. And I'm determined to find out why, the desire far stronger than my curiosity in hearing whatever they have to say about Adathan.

Finally, we find a spigot close to the pub we'd been at earlier. The water is clear, thanks to the nearby sea and the sewage system of Weaschte, and Adathan motions for me to clean up first. Knowing it would do no good to argue, and not wanting to in front of our new companions regardless, I nod in thanks, and get to removing the dried blood from my hands, face, and neck.

The shirt is lost, so once I step aside to let Adathan use the spigot, I get the dagger out again, and hold the hilt out to Ciaragen. "Do you mind? These sleeves are goners, I'm afraid."

She smirks, and takes the blade from me. Without a word, she steps up to my side, grabs the seam of the sleeve at the shoulder, and cuts through the stitching. After replicating her work on the other side, she flips the dagger in her hand, and raises it for me to take.

"Nice blade," she says as I sheathe it.

"Thanks, it's his." I gesture with a jerk of my head towards Adathan, still bent and scrubbing the blood off his neck.

Ciaragen seems to be interested in spite of herself. "Won, or given?"

It's Adathan who answers. "Won." He straightens, and as he faces us, I see that he's missed a small spot high on his cheek. Discreetly, I meet his eye for half a second, scratch that spot on my face, and turn back to the other two.

To find Atlas smiling. Small, and a tad amused. "I would have liked to have seen that."

"It was awesome, complete take down," I respond, unable to keep a corner of my mouth from tipping upwards. Atlas, my... friend. He's still that, at least, even with what I know now. Right?

His own smile softens, a silent affirmation to my internal question. After a beat of hesitation I walk up to him, stopping a bit closer than a casual distance away. "Sorry about your hands," I say quietly.

"You felt threatened, and you defended yourself. Besides, look: they're good as new." He holds them up now, flipping them this way and that.

"If I recall, that nifty healing was nowhere to be found when you burned yourself–how many times in the kitchens?" I raise my brows.

His smile turns chagrined, his high cheekbones darkening. "Appearances and all, you know."

I hum in confirmation, and though my feet carry me a half step closer to him, the slight smirk on my face is smug. This– this normalcy, the easy conversation. I hadn't thought about missing it. For days, it had been one life-threatening event after another, and simple things had stopped feeling, well, simple. But this is easy. Familiar. And—

"If you two are done, we have things to discuss," Ciaragen mutters, but, when I look at her, her eyes sparkle with a bit of happiness.

And, for some reason, it hits me in the gut. The contentment ends just as quickly as it began. My grin, however small, falls. What right do I have to that normalcy, that ease? I *shouldn't* feel the same. My mother is dead, and the events that have been so heavy, have also been distractions from that grief. And somehow, it's alright that those things that have caused me pain provide that escape–but not the things which might give me joy, after what feels like an eternity without it.

Four days. But she's gone forever.

From where he now stands with Ciaragen, Atlas turns, seeming like he expects me to walk by his side. But instead, I draw back to Adathan. Atlas's face falls a bit, but I stare past him, to the street ahead, adding the joy I've leeched from him to my list of sins.

We don't go back into the same pub. Ciaragen and Atlas have glamoured their ears, to remain at least a little inconspicuous, but they don't feel the need to bring me to a dark, loud place, where no one could see or hear us without us returning the favor. Whether that means they're naive or rightfully unconcerned remains to be seen.

Past lunch, now, the dineries closer to the sea have opened up some. And I may have had a full meal not too long ago, but, given my starved state over the past few days, I'm ready for another now.

But Ciaragen and Atlas move to sit at an outside table, where the servers don't tend. I hesitate for the shortest beat before following them to the table, and two things happen at once. Atlas pulls a chair out for me, and, on my other side, Adathan nudges my shoulder with his arm and raises his brows. I give him a grateful close-lipped half smile and nod, before moving to sit in the chair Atlas scoots under me.

"Going somewhere?" Ciaragen asks, raising her brows.

Adathan turns halfway back to us. "I'm getting her some food. Feel free to start talking about me without me." And then he walks through the pine and glass double doors of the restaurant without a second glance.

"Althea, I'm so sorry, I didn't realize you might be hungry," Ciaragen says, her brows scrunching together.

"It's alright, thank you," I respond, and wince internally, straightening my skirt over my lap. Back to being proper regardless of what I actually want to say. Which is, *Yeah, that tends to happen when you have to rough it through the woods for a few days.* That old part of me tells me that making her feel worse for what I've endured won't make me feel any better. The new part tells me the purpose isn't to make her feel badly, but to educate her on the naivety of her statement.

I tell both parts to shut up.

Then sigh. "You wanted to tell me about Adathan." I look up from my lap to her eyes, keeping my expression blank. Atlas, beside me, flits his gaze between us.

"Yes. I believe you should have all the facts before deciding to bring him with us." She waits for a response, so I nod, folding my hands over my stomach. She gives a dip of her chin, and begins.

"You knew Adathan as Artur. Twenty-one years ago, we

knew him as Arthur–not a very creative male, apparently. Not very creative, *but* skilled enough in glamours that we did not see him as he truly was. With us, he was red-haired and blue eyed, as opposed to the blond he had been in your home. He served as a guard to the High Lord and High Lady of Sabrian, a country in Eshelle. Kept to himself, didn't try to make friends, and we just assumed that he was reserved. We were not a quiet court, to be sure." She smirks slightly to herself, but sobers before going on. "What none of us knew, was that he had been *sent* to us from the capital after–after the murder of a very important member of that court. That, once he arrived, he didn't serve our country, or its rulers. He served Olin–the male who committed that murder, at the instruction of his king.

"Oleander Gervan, who claims the throne as High King of Eshelle. For a long time, Olin served Oleander. Thus, *Adathan*, by extension, served him as well. From what I've gathered by peeking through your library at Castle Cerasche, you have no texts on the Fae realm, never mind its histories, so I'll give you a brief rundown of what you need to know for the purposes of these events. Oleander has been king for nearly one hundred and twenty years. High Kings before him ruled for centuries more than that. Some were cruel, some were kind. But Oleander, it seems, is the worst of them all. Not only cruel, but indifferent. He cares nothing for the continent, or its people. Only for his own pleasures.

"There is a story, that is not ours to tell, about some of the things he has done. What I *can* tell you is that, especially as it seems Olin's ambitions have surpassed that of his role as the king's second, any male who serves Olin is no friend. Adathan is a monster, just like his father. He betrayed our court, and he has betrayed yours. Are you truly going to accept his claim of allyship, knowing that you'll just be one more notch on his collar before his job for his sire is done?"

My face is blank for another moment, as I wait for her to ask more of me, or provide further context for Adathan's evil. When none comes, my brows raise. "That's it?"

Her eyes widen, and shift to Atlas, who has his own hands folded on the table. I don't look at him, not wanting to see what emotions might be filling his stormy eyes at my apathy. Ciaragen moves her gaze back to mine, still wide-eyed. "*That's it?*' He is a *liar*, Althea, and he will go on betraying those stupid enough to trust him–"

I smirk, tilting my chin up and to the side, looking down my nose slightly at her as I cut her off. "Stupid, huh?"

She sucks on the inside of her cheek. "I didn't mean you. It was more about me."

"Yeah, I think that's a common theme in this conversation." I lean forward as she seems to struggle for words. From the corner of my eye, I see a familiar figure approaching. "He was in your court, glamoured, and you didn't see it. He was in mine, glamoured, and *still* you were not trained well enough to see past his glamour, even after more than twenty years. I, at least, had the excuse of ignorance to Fae majick. All you've given me so far is reason to trust my own instinct over yours."

"Yes, that instinct seemed to serve you well four nights ago," she snaps, her eyes glinting with anger.

Slowly, gently, a plate of fried fish, greens, and potatoes slides in front of me, a large glass of water joining it. But my gut has turned to lead at what the female has said–has reminded me of. I stare at the fish with disgust, and agony roils in my chest.

"Say that again," Adathan says quietly, the timbre of his voice rumbling through his chest like a growl. The deadly calm in it chills my very bones.

Atlas is silent beside me, and I don't care to look at him to see what he might be thinking. I think he's caught between defending me, and making sure this doesn't escalate further, but he doesn't know the male on my other side like he thinks he does.

"Thank you, Adathan, for the food," I say, my voice whisper-soft, but not weak–thankfully. I look up from my plate at him, and though he takes a moment to tear his falsely amber eyes from the deep blue set diagonally across from me, he does. When his anger-filled gaze meets mine, I say, at the same volume, "Please sit."

The rage subsides by a small margin, and he looks at the chair beside Ciaragen for half a beat before grabbing it, and pulling it to the head of the table, on my left side. He sits, and the woven pine fibers of the seat groan a bit under his weight.

I look back at Ciaragen, who seems to be stuck between incredulity and regret. She turns her gaze to me, and the regret takes the foreground. But before she can open her mouth to attempt to apologize, I say, "Instincts are hard to trust when you're constantly fighting against them to do your duty. Every day for a year, I had to try to convince myself that the fate I was prepared for was what I wanted. Spend that long telling your gut something, when it knows another, and it gets quiet.

"When I woke up in the woods, surrounded by enemies, I began to listen again. And, while my instincts took time to gain their strength, I'm not going to deny them when they do speak to me any longer. So, unless you can tell me a better reason for why I should send him away–other than, from what I under-stand, the things he was forced to do by his father–he stays."

But my brow furrows, and everyone at the table seems to hold their breath. I look over to Adathan. "If you want to, that is."

His own brow scrunches, just a bit, so I continue, while keeping my gaze on him. "You saved me. More than once. The road ahead won't be any easier. And you know what's at the end of it. If any part of you remains only because of that initial desire to do the right thing–to free me…I want you to know, you don't have to."

His eyes are unreadable, but they do not leave mine. A long moment passes where my heart starts to squeeze in my chest slightly, preparing for him to leave, his self-imposed obligation done. This male who was my enemy, turned reluctant ally, has become inextricably tied in my mind to this path I've set myself on. Him being with me, at some indefinable point, started to matter–and then became a want. I want him to stay, and I'm not entirely sure what that means about me.

But, finally, he says, seeming to fight to get the words out, "You don't have the whole story. And I can't tell it to you."

44

IN BEDS OF FLOWERS

THEA - PRESENT

IT'S BEEN TEN MINUTES. I MANAGED TO WORK MY APPETITE BACK up, and have been eating the food Adathan brought me, observing the stare down between him and Ciaragen. He can't tell me the story I'm supposedly missing, and she says that it's not her story to tell.

Adathan's arms have been crossed over his chest ever since she contested his inability to relay the tale. It took about two seconds for me to connect his refusal to a command he is blood-bound to follow. And, while I'm not sure why Olin would have ordered his silence, I know that Ciaragen will have to be the one to break if I'm to know the full history behind why she hates and distrusts him so much.

After another five minutes, my plate is empty, and I take a sip of water as I glance between the male and female, still in a standoff at this little diner off the docks. Their eyes did not move from one another the entire time I ate.

I turn to Atlas, and raise my brows at him, at the situation we're in. He smirks, though not as easy as the expression once was, and shrugs. And I hate this new strangeness between us, that had not been there when he was only a server, and I was not a kidnapped princess. Hate it, while also not feeling entirely inclined to sort through it. Not with the secrets I know he's keeping. Not when he's sitting here, as if only a bystander to everything that's happened this week, and not so obviously just as connected to it all as the two currently battling wills at the table with us.

When I look back at the two in question, I have a feeling that, while his eyes never left Ciaragen's, Adathan had been watching us, too. His jaw is tighter by a fraction, his fingers pressed a bit more firmly into his biceps.

I sigh. "It's really not that important. Whatever it is, I'm sure it can wait until we're on a ship."

"It is important, sweetheart," Adathan says, still not looking away from the female. "I will stay, if you'll have me. But I'm not sure you will once you know. Lady Ciaragen and I have the same goal; to make sure you have all the knowledge necessary to make your decision. And I *can't* tell you. So, she just has to decide if she can get over her pride enough to do it for me."

"It's not *pride*, asshole. It's honor. I have sworn to keep this secret, and breaking that promise is not something to take lightly."

"Well, the day is wasting." I lean back in my chair, and kick my legs out under the table, crossing my ankles. Both Atlas's and Adathan's shins brush my skirts. "Let's be honest. If I get up from this table right now, not one of you will let me get on a ship alone. The way I see it, you all have one minute to start talking, or I'm going, and I'll just see who follows."

That small, almost unnoticeable smirk kicks up one side of Adathan's mouth as Ciaragen stares at me, hard. Weighing if

I'm bluffing or not, probably. I think, if she had to put a name to how I look, it would be: bored.

She sucks on the inside of her cheek. "Fine. Only because, if the person I promised knew the choices I have, they would ask me to tell you now. But, I'll be skipping over some details that you perhaps don't need to know in order to get the full picture. Okay?"

I shrug, but otherwise don't shift my posture or my expression. She sighs, but begins. "Your parents visited Eshelle, once. Twenty-one years ago. Right as your mother was set to give birth." She pauses, letting that sink in, and though my heart strains and my mind whirls at the information, I attempt to keep my face blank. The legs of both males tense a bit around me beneath the table.

"She was lovely. Befriended nearly everyone in our court, and those visiting our castle, despite the prejudices she'd been exposed to here. Your father was kind, a bit quieter than she, but doted on her endlessly. On the day she went into labor, he was in the room with her–which I'm sure is not the typical custom in Weaschte." I nod somewhat absentmindedly at that. It's become slightly more regular over the years, but still is not common practice.

"On that day, we got a visit from Olin. His brother, Dion– who he pretended to be while with you–had been staying at our castle for some weeks, and he played at coming to check in on him. Dion had been sent by Oleander, you see, to spy on our court. On our High Lord. His intentions shifted to our cause quickly, and we thought–we thought we had more time. But then Olin came, and when he did, he spoke with Dion, while I was...otherwise occupied.

"We didn't know we had a spy in our midst. This male that you're so adamant about accompanying you, saw my m–Dion going about business unrelated to the task he was meant to be accomplishing, and saw fit to tell his father, who in turn told Oleander. And, that easily, our court was flipped upside down. Things that were supposed to be joyful, weren't, and things that were supposed to–"

She clenches her jaw, tears shining in her deep blue eyes. Tears of sadness–and of rage, as she turns them to the male to my left.

A muscle in Adathan's jaw feathers, but he doesn't drop his gaze from hers. I ask Ciaragen, "What were you occupied with? While a spy was in your castle, and Olin was endangering your court?"

It takes a moment for those loathful eyes to move from Adathan to me, but when they do, the rage within them quiets. "You must know, Althea, that this story is not...it's not just about *him*. It's about you."

I roll my eyes. "Thanks, I kind of got that. You know, with my mom and dad being there, and having me, and all. So, what? I was supposed to die, and you smuggled me out with my parents? Olin found out, and came here to finish the job?"

Her mouth quirks up at one corner, but it's not a happy expression. It holds the sadness of decades. "In a way, you're right. But not in the way you're thinking about it."

With much more bravado than I feel in my ever-sinking heart, I say, "Enlighten me, then."

"I was occupied with assisting the birth of my High Lord and High Lady's child, while your mother was giving birth in the opposite wing of our castle. When the babe was born, I went to tell Dion the news, only to find that he had intercepted his brother before Olin could get more than a few feet into the castle.

"When I found Dion, I still...I had the scent of the birthing room on me. And as soon as Olin smelled it, he knew what I'd been doing. He knew that my High Lord and High Lady now had an heir. Our court was not in allegiance with his, you see. And an heir…it was the one thing Oleander did not have, that Amedeo would. When Olin made the connection, he would not be stopped from going to meet the child. *We* could not stop him. An attack on him would have meant war with Oschverre, war with *Eshelle*, and we were not yet prepared for that."

Ciaragen's own face pales at the memory, and she takes an extended pause, seeming lost in thought. When her eyes refocus on mine, she goes on, "But when we took Olin to our High Lord and High Lady, he saw a baby that would not be a threat. She'd been born with one arm, and had what they've termed as albinism. She radiated minimal power, and he decreed that his parting gift would be to leave us with the *runt*, as he put it.

"So, they–Olin, and Adathan, and…and Dion–left. We feared that Olin might know of the other babe, but he seemed to have no interest in the humans. Your parents departed later that week, with you in Lydia's arms."

My brows furrow as she finishes her story. Her breaths are too easy, and the males beside me too quiet. "I don't understand," I say.

"Which part?" Ciaragen asks, tilting her head. But something like fear brims in her eyes.

"Your claim is that I shouldn't trust Adathan because he betrayed both our courts. I get that. He spied on you as he did on me, and learned something you didn't want him to learn. But, everything turned out fine, didn't it? I went home with my parents, and the Fae baby was unharmed as well. I don't…" I stop in the middle of repeating my previous statement as her words roll over in my head. *You're right…but not in the way you think.* Right about my life being in danger, but then being sent home with my parents. But not in the way I think?

"What's missing?" I ask in a whisper-soft voice, my eyes

dropping to the table, not seeing the empty plate, or Adathan's fisted hand. I know they all hear, but not one responds.

Missing pieces. *It's about you*, Ciaragen had said. In the story, yes. I'd been there, perhaps been in danger, if Olin had taken an interest in the humans or their child. But, if anything, this is about the other baby, too. Born with one arm, palest skin, and white hair. If she'd been born in Weaschte, she would have been considered a–

A changeling.

A changeling.

The word clangs through me, but every fiber of me denies it. Denies what my mind has drawn up as the only explanation for all this–all this *chaos* that has wrapped itself so thoroughly around my life.

"Who was I born to?" I ask, my voice trembling. In all her story, Ciaragen hadn't said it. Said *the child*, never *you*. I look up from the table, and my vision is blurry, but I force myself to focus on those depthless blue eyes. The fear is gone now, and only pity remains.

"That's the reason, isn't it?" I ask, as tears threaten to spill. Deep fear, and sadness well in my chest at what I'm realizing more and more with each passing second. "That's why he came for me. That's why Adathan was stationed at Castle Cerasche. That's why you and Atlas…"

I gulp down a breath, along with the thickness in my throat, but both seem to stick right above my heart. "That baby. She was born to my–*my* parents, wasn't she? And when they came to the only conclusion they knew, that she couldn't be theirs…it lined up perfectly for you all, didn't it? Take her, unwanted as she was by those who created her, and–and–"

I'm gasping now, and their faces are swirling together. Storm gray and sea blue and false amber bore into me, and I can't take it. I jolt from my chair, overturning it to the alarm of those seated behind us, who act as though they hadn't heard any of what had transpired at our table. But I don't care, don't see them either as I sprint down the street, my skirt blowing behind me.

I don't see the shops, or passersby, or the road beneath my feet. And when the sun glints off the ocean at the docks, I don't see the ships, or sailors, or the wood planks that slap against the soles of my boots. Only when I'm on sand, and water seeps into the leather of my shoes, do I stop, gasping.

Still, I force the tears back, force the scream that begs to be let out back down my throat. I focus on the movement of the world around me, instead of the terror that's lodged itself beneath my diaphragm, making it hard to get a breath down.

The ocean washes out, and my feet sink down into the wet sand before the next gentle wave pushes more of it over my toes. The bottom of my skirt swirls in the current, wet fabric lapping at my knees. My hair blows back in the breeze coming off the sea.

I hear him because he wants to be heard. He comes to stand beside me, feet in the water and all, staring out at the boundless ocean as I do. We stand in silence for long minutes, our feet sinking and sinking into the sand as the waves pull it out from under us, and then bury us with it in the next motion. It feels awfully like a metaphor for how my life is turning out.

When finally I master the nausea in my stomach, and the thickness in my throat, I speak without looking at him, keeping my gaze on the glittering water. "I'm Fae, aren't I?"

Adathan doesn't answer, and that's answer enough. It's too gentle, to say that my heart crumples in my chest. My heart has been a burning coal, embers glowing. What it feels like, to learn this, is as if a fist is reaching around my heart–fragile, but still burning; still with a purpose. But that fist squeezes, heedless of the scalding heat, until the coal shatters, only black and gray ashes remaining.

I think I have questions, but can't find the will to voice them. Even if I could, I'm sure that Adathan wouldn't be able to answer. If Olin ordered his silence on the matter, I doubt the blood oath allowed for any leeway if I knew some of the truth. It makes sense, the order to keep this information from me. Olin hadn't wanted me to understand my true lineage. He probably figured that it's much easier to break someone when you know more about them than they do.

"Do you still want to go to Eshelle?" Adathan asks after several minutes, still looking at the waves cresting in the distance.

I don't believe breaking means what Olin thinks it does. I broke when my mother died, and again with Hanna, again with Ahmad. I broke when he had my bones cracked. And, perhaps he wanted to see me break from this...revelation, but not until *he* decided to do it. Until he could use it to break me enough to abandon hope, and give up entirely.

What I don't think he realized is that broken glass is more dangerous than a shining pane of it. Shattered, there's nothing left to lose. And it is far easier to kill with that razored edge.

So much has changed in just the past few minutes, but I know one thing that hasn't. "I'm not ready to talk about me. Or my...parents. My mother was Lydia Cardenia, and I will kill Olin for taking her life."

From the corner of my eye, I see him nod, seeming to expect my answer. "Where are they?" I ask as I step back from the water, pulling my feet from the soaking sand that has buried them. Our new companions are nowhere to be found.

"At their ship, waiting."

I nod, and turn quickly to face the bushes behind me before

vomiting into them. As I retch, a broad hand wraps around my hair, another lying flat on my back; a warm, heavy weight.

When my stomach is empty, I spit some of the remaining bile out of my mouth, and stand, averting my eyes from Adathan as he removes his hands. I rinse my mouth out with the sea water, even the extreme saltiness better than the acidic taste it replaces.

When I stand again, my skirt is soaked from the ocean, pulling low on my hips. I'm sure I must be pale, and look much worse for wear, but when I finally turn to the male, I make myself level his gaze.

"Will you come with me?" I ask him. The big question before that whole story, before my life got turned upside down–*again*–had been whether I would still want Adathan to accompany me to Eshelle after knowing all that he had done. My trust is not whole–still partially formed by a days-long trek through the woods together, and a mutual interest in his father's death. But it's reinforced by the fact that I know if I told him I no longer wanted him to come with me, he would not argue. He would send me on my way with Atlas and Ciaragen, and find another ship home for himself.

And I hadn't missed the wording of his question: *Do* you *still want to go to Eshelle?* Not: *Are* we *still going to Eshelle?*

Even perhaps thinking that I no longer wanted him to come with me, he had been the one to stand with me in the water. And maybe it's a tactic, to make me trust him, but I don't think it is. I think we're both alone in the world. And alone together feels better than the alternative.

Some emotion flits through his eyes, and his jaw clenches as he swallows–the first sign of doubt I've seen from him. Yes, he definitely thought I no longer wanted him. And, as a fellow person with no one else in the world who knows him and his deeds, and accepts them–maybe he'd been attached to the idea of us journeying together, too.

Adathan replies, "I will."

⇔

I stroll up the gangplank to a ship with the words *Burning Rose* painted in gold on the hull, Adathan a step behind me. I keep my chin high and my shoulders back, the midafternoon sun beating down on my still-blonde head.

The boards of the ship floor creak slightly beneath my boots, though Adathan's own steps are silent. Only his steady heartbeat, and a certainty in him that I can't pinpoint the origin of, tells me he remains at my back. I anchor my own heart to his, trying to allow its thrumming to extend the same calm to me as I take in my surroundings.

The sails are being hoisted, creamy white and absolutely enormous. Males–not men, with their pointed ears, or rain-bowed skin–dart across the deck, shouting commands at one another. As far as I can tell, Ciaragen and I will be the only women on board. The thought has my empty stomach stirring, but I walk through the working–and gawking–sailors with my head held high. By the way that some of them quickly avert their eyes, I can only assume they notice Adathan's massive form following behind me. He removed the glamour from himself at the dock, eyes on mine as they changed from amber to gold, until I nodded, and he gestured for me to lead.

I stride for the captain's quarters, having little doubt that Atlas and Ciaragen will be there, notifying him of the two additional passengers they brought. Without pause, I push open the doors. Indeed, both Fae stand within the quarters–and they are not alone.

A male with slanted dark brown eyes, and long, nearly

black hair pulled back into a knot at the top of his head, stands behind a large mahogany desk. Poking out from that hair is a pair of arched ears. And I'm about to wonder if I'm the only human on this ship when I remember–that I'm not.

Swallowing the emotions that build at the thought, I walk through the finely decorated and cared for space. Golden trinkets glimmer in the thick streams of sunshine that pierce the gabled windows, and fall on the intricately carved desk. A chair of leather and mahogany waits, unused, behind the captain, who watches me advance towards him with an unreadable expression on his handsome face.

"Javi, this is Althea, and–Adathan," Ciaragen introduces us in the Old Language, only stumbling a little bit on Adathan's name. "Althea, this is Javi. Captain of this ship, and High Lord of Obala, Eshelle."

I'm not sure if I'm supposed to bow. I'm a princess–but not to him. Maybe not to anyone, now. And, while Ciaragen had given me his title, she hadn't given him mine. Because they're irrelevant here, or because mine holds no bearing to him, or the Fae?

At the very least, to show respect to the captain who will be sailing me across the sea, I dip my chin, and bring my foot behind the other in a shallow curtsy, standing up straight just as quickly. Adathan, behind me, inclines his head in acknowledgement, but nothing more.

"It's a pleasure to meet you, Althea," Javi says, his small smile kind, but guarded. I don't miss–I'm sure no one does–how he doesn't greet Adathan. "We'll be setting sail in about five minutes. I believe Atlas knows where your quarters are located, as well as your... companion's." Dark eyes move to the male behind me, no kindness at all within them.

But Atlas bows to the High Lord and captain, and opens the door for us to exit. And I realize as I leave that I hadn't said a word. Haven't spoken since I asked Adathan to come with me, back on that beach.

I follow Atlas back across the deck of oiled wood and sparsely placed light green circles of mattified glass. This time, as I pass the sailors, I give some of them terse nods of greeting, which they return. We reach a set of stairs which creak the slightest bit beneath my feet, Adathan silent but solid behind me.

The hall housing the cabins is longer than I would have expected, spots of light shining down onto the floor from the ship deck prisms above. A couple of doors are closed, but I don't quite feel like asking who else will be joining us down here just yet. I can see through the few open doors that in each room, which I would guess are about one hundred and fifty square feet, there's a sheet-covered bed, and a small porthole. If the windows opened, I could have reached out and touched the sea.

"We're all on this level," Atlas says, turning to look at us over his shoulder. "The crew are one deck beneath us. There's another staircase, through a door off the bow, leading to the fo'c'sle, and they use that one when their shifts are through. That's also the way you'd take if you wanted to go to the common area, which I can show you later.

"Mealtimes are at six, twelve, and seven. You can usually find something to pick on if you make friends with the cook– which I highly recommend you do." He smirks, and I blink when he sends the look to Adathan as well.

"This how you got here?" he asks Atlas in Ceraschen, his voice as unfriendly as ever.

The other male makes the same change in language easily. "Yeah. Javi brought me about a month ago."

"What's he been doing all that time?"

Atlas's lips press together, but he does answer. "I'm not sure if you're allowed to know. Ask Ciaragen, next time you see her."

"Don't think I'll do that, but thanks, bud."

And, despite everything, somehow hearing Adathan make 'bud' sound like an insult makes me almost want to smile.

Atlas shrugs, either not caring or not realizing that. He points to a door diagonally across from him. "That's yours, Althea." He moves his finger two doors down. "That's mine." Two more doors, all the way at the end of the hall. "And that's yours...what do you want to be called?" His brows furrow as he looks at Adathan.

Who responds, "I don't give a shit what you call me."

"Well, I Don't Give A Shit What You Call Me, you can call *me* Atlas. If you–" But he's cut off as the ship lurches from the shore, carried on a summer breeze out into the ocean. And, more likely than not, some of those *oh so common* wind powers. We all find our feet, and Atlas continues. "If you're hungry, lunch is past, but I'll take you to–"

He's interrupted again, but this time by a door opening to his left. A woman, paler than the moon, pokes her head out, saying, "Atlas–?"

She turns to look at me and Adathan, and blue eyes clearer than the summer sky framed with long, white lashes take us in openly, without fear or judgment. Her white hair flows in ringlets to her waist, looking like the loveliest of clouds.

She steps out of her cabin, and holds her left hand out to me. Her right hangs at her side, ending just below the elbow in a tapered stump. Her berry-pink lips pull up in a bright smile, and she says in the Old Language, "Hi, I'm Emelina. And, you are?"

EPILOGUE
CONTEMPLATION

OLIN - AFTER

IT IS EASY TO GIVE IN TO CONTEMPLATION WHEN STARING OUT AT A sun-gilded sea. It is, I think, nearly as boundless as my mind. Nearly as vast as my fury. Thus, that is what I do as the males on the deck around me propel us to our new destination.

It would be a simple thing to go back to Oschverre straight away. To gather replacements for those I'd lost in the forsaken human continent, and await my Princess. I've no doubt that she will come to me. She will try to kill me, I'm sure–a thought which thrills me. It is even more exciting to think about the passion that flows so easily from hate. I wonder if, when I take her little flower, she will be as wild in the bedroom as she'd been in the woods.

Adathan's betrayal throws a wrench in my previous plan, yes. At least the bastard boy is too soft-hearted to force anything on the female; she might very well still be ripe for the picking when I get my hands on her. He, on the other hand, will be dead before they can ever reach Eshellen soil. My spies on the Obalan ship will see to that.

I should have killed him the moment I found him in that bloody basement. I knew what it meant, when his wounds were worse than David's, and yet, he lived. The healing ability he'd lost as a boy had returned, and there could only be one reason for it. Still, I'd decided to torment him by swearing to marry, fuck, and hurt the female he loves. Stupid. Occasionally, I've come to realize, my desire for living torture, over death, can be a fault.

Regardless of it all, she will be mine. Because, though nothing has gone to plan, a new one has started to form. One which will bring me all that I desire, while inflicting the most suffering on those who forestalled that accomplishment. To kill them right away, as the recognition of my fault demands, isn't enough. Not poetic, and certainly not satisfying.

My dear brother, lying in his own shit belowdecks will have *everything* to do with that suffering–his own, and others'. The smell in the brig now harkens back to his cell all those years ago. It had been fun tormenting him then, when his pathetic heart had been so open after I'd taken it, along with the rest of him, from that Sabriani court. I think this next part, though, will be even better.

Before, I'd contemplated avoiding the war Oleander sought. I would be High King, and perhaps fewer than a hundred people would have died for it, depending, of course, on their willingness to follow me. I would have left Weaschte alone. I would have given Sabrian to my Queen–a wedding present, though I hadn't yet decided whether or not to put her birth parents' heads on spikes outside of the castle gates for her.

No more. I will bring war to those very gates, with the aid of the king who will be throneless by the time the fighting is done.

He will battle the rebels in his land for his own pride, and mine will be the one to win it. For my pride is hurt, all because of my brother and a bastard. And simply killing them both will not heal it.

Winning a war might. When my Princess rises to her power–the majick of which she knows naught–no force will be able to stop us. We will take Eshelle, and then, both out of anger at her for leaving me, and desire for her to have the grandest of wedding presents: Weaschte. She will hate me as I kill her people, but she will love me as I give her the throne she was once so far from. Else, if she could not be grateful, she might find herself in a cell, same as Dion.

Her hate will be passion, or her blood will be iron; either way, she will be mine. And so shall the world be.

BONUS CHAPTER

Keep reading for a special look inside a moment remembered,
but not told, in the point of view of the memory's bearer.

ALL THE WHILE

I knew I was in for an adventure. Not only because of the voyage across the sea I'd just made, and would make again in five weeks or so, but because of the mission given to me; what I was meant to do now that I'd arrived. *Who* I was meant to meet.

The Lady of my country. The daughter of my High Lord and High Lady. I had no idea what she'd be like. I did have a feeling, though, that I'd like her. Wasn't sure why, or how, but I let it be. I let myself be excited for the task ahead, rather than question why I felt like that in the first place.

It had to be me to do it, in any case. Ciaragen was General of the Sabriani armies, and couldn't just leave her post for several weeks for a nonemergent assignment. It couldn't be Hielo or Hiela, with the amount of pain it would cause them to see their daughter, and be unable to do anything about it. No way to tell her the truth of her blood without scaring the daylights out of her.

It certainly couldn't be Lina. Though it had been almost

twenty-one years since the human royals gave their baby to Nuria and Jolie, believing she wasn't theirs at all, they might recognize her. Most people don't encounter a moon-pale, one-armed woman multiple times in their lives, after all. And that's to say nothing of the impact being around them would have on that woman's heart. How much it would hurt to see the life she might have had, if only her birth parents had been led by *their* hearts, and not their biases.

Since we've done everything together since she could toddle, she came with me to Weaschte. But, given the afore-mentioned items, she chose to remain aboard the *Burning Rose* while I went on to the next phase of my assignment. After approving of the glamour I placed on myself to conceal my ears and canines, she'd only wrapped her arms tight around my waist, and wished me luck before sending me on my way, while she set sail with Javi down the Weaschen coast.

A few days on a purchased horse, the saddlebags packed with food, water, and with the scant belongings I'd elected to bring, and I was approaching the walls of Castle Cerasche. I used the language I'd spent months practicing with my High Lord and High Lady, and, long story short, I had a sort of inter-view scheduled that same day.

"The Princess sits on her mother's left side," Nina, the head chef, said to me within the alcove outside of the Great Hall. I held a saucer of soup in my hand, and had a tea towel folded over that arm for whatever reason. My crisp white shirt was buttoned all the way up and tucked in, and Nina had given me a black tie to wear until I could get one for myself–if I got the job. She'd already ascertained my skills in the kitchen, but this was the final test. I wondered why the position of the Princess's assigned server was so conveniently open, until Nina spoke next.

"She's a sweet girl. Do not be surprised if she requests

seconds of her meals from you. Her Majesty doesn't take kindly to even a sour look over her daughter." The woman says it like a warning–as if it ever would have occurred to me to judge a female based on the amount on her plate. The mere prospect of it–particularly the obviousness that it had been done enough to warrant such a warning–made me angry for my Lady.

I didn't think it would be helpful, though, for me to tell the chef that the Princess could ask me for as many helpings as she liked, and I would only be glad to provide them to her. Though it felt utterly natural, I still recognized how strange it was for me to feel so defensive for a female I'd never met.

So, I only dipped my chin in acknowledgment. Nina returned it, then quickly looked around the corner, into the Hall. She nodded to herself, then turned back to me, and the two other men in the alcove with us. "Go on, then."

I followed the others, knowing the King and Queen were meant to be served first. And tell me why my heart stuttered as I took my first step. I was *nervous*, and I couldn't even convince myself that it was because of the precariousness of the state of my impending employment. Not as I saw the back of a midnight-maned head, and my pulse skipped again.

The slightest portion of her profile was visible to me. I saw long black lashes, and the freckled apex of a cheek. Even in the long-sleeved dress she wore, it was clear she wasn't idle; the muscles in her arms spoke of years of dedicated training.

I was about three feet from her when I took a calming breath. When I accidentally pulled the scent of her into my lungs, and she heard it. When I smelled this combination of sunshine-soaked meadows, and something just as warm but wholly different, and she looked at me.

She looked at me.

And I was hers.

I existed only in green eyes, and in a soft smile that faltered.

I died and was reborn within the infinite span of a single second which began the rest of my forever. I knew only this, knew only *her*, anything and everything else that I had been or would be condensed into whatever *she* needed me to be.

And I would have told her. Would have gotten down on my knees, and professed my commitment to her right then and there.

Well, I did end up on my knees. Because, as the knowledge of who sat before me sank into my very soul, the soup I was holding spilled, and sank just as surely into her dress.

"I–I'm so sorry," I croaked, and those were indeed my knees on the ground then. The same thoughtlessness that would have possessed me to confess my truth to her overcame me again. While I used the gods-damned tea towel to pat her dress dry, my hands pressing into her lap over and *over*–

"*Atlas!*" Nina yelled, and the furious call of my name was what I needed. My face burning, I apologized again and again, this time for touching her so intimately. The chef stormed up, the sound of her steps audible even over my heartbeat pounding in my ears. "Your Highness, I am so–"

But Nina didn't get to finish apologizing for me. Because, before she could, a laugh rang through the hall. Clear and lovely as a bell. Sweet as sugar, and sent a buzz through my blood just the same. I worked up the courage to look at *her* again, and it was the best sort of mistake to do so. Because I was limited to just that–to looking–when her face glowed, and her eyes shone. I couldn't touch the pinkened apples of her cheeks, or taste the sound she gave me with my own lips, as I instantly wished to.

"It's alright," she said in a slightly rasping voice. "It was cold soup, and fabric is washable, and so am I."

Her fostering parents both gave huffed chuckles, seeming used to her easy humor. Completely unperturbed by my fumble, too, only going back to their own meals–though I didn't miss the King's sideways glance in my direction.

I couldn't really look at him, though. I was looking at her, while she smiled kindly up at Nina. After a sigh, the head chef said, "Well, if you're going to spill soup on people, it may as well be one who doesn't mind." She looked down at me, her hands on her hips. "I'll prepare a new bowl of soup, and have it brought out. You stay in the Hall. Fetch Her Highness whatever she might want to eat or drink until Their Majesties and herself depart for the evening."

And, with that, she left me to my new job.

Maybe it would have been smart to retreat. To bow, and wait for the Princess to need something, but otherwise quietly remain; seen but not heard.

I never claimed to be smart, though.

"I am sorry, Your Highness. I promise, I'll be better."

Kinder. Stronger. Braver. I would become a male worthy of her, and if that was impossible, then at least I had a thousand years and more to get damned close.

She, of course, only heard the obvious meaning of my words. That I wouldn't fucking *spill soup* on her like a bloody imbecile at each meal.

Still on my knees as I was, those eyes looked straight into mine, no humor at all within them any longer. They stole my breath as much as her voice did when she replied softly, "It was a pleasure to meet you, Atlas."

My heart actually stopped. A full beat of time, but none in my chest. Had my name ever sounded so important? So precious?

I was named after the bearer of the Heavens. Now, I was sure that the Heavens were right here. In the form of the female whose own heartbeat I could hear, fluttering and stuttering in her chest. Yet, her eyes...steadily, they were losing light. I watched them flit over my face, and I watched them get *sad*. And I wanted to ask her what was wrong, I *needed* to do something to help her, but my position bound me–

My position.

Her position.

Quietly, I responded, "The pleasure was mine, Your Highness." Then, I stood on forcibly solid knees, bowed low to her, then to her parents beside her, and retreated. Most walls had some form of staff at their edges, but at one there was only a sober-looking doorman, ready at his post. He didn't look at me while I walked, and nearly all others did, probably hoping to converse with the newest staff member–or else just watching the idiot who spilled food on our Princess on his very first day. I didn't care. I just wanted to stand in silence, with nothing but my own thoughts. So, I took up residence at the wall a dozen or so feet from the doorman, and did just that.

Because I'd just met my mate. My fated. Yet, fate had decided to take what we might have been, and make it impossible.

I didn't know if she felt anything when she looked at me. She was enveloped in the human world her whole life. If she did feel something, she would have no idea what it was, and if she didn't, well. I couldn't blame her. She had a lifetime of being closed off and closing *herself* off from whatever might have felt unnatural when none of those around her had those feelings or abilities.

And it couldn't matter. Whether she felt something or not, for whatever reason her soul found fit–it couldn't matter. I wasn't here to fall in love with her. I was here, essentially, to spy on her. To see if she was happy, and therefore find out if we could wait until it would become obvious she wasn't aging, or if we needed to give her her truth as soon as Ciaragen could shadowwalk our High Lord and High Lady here.

If she was happy, though, I would leave. I would go back to Sabrian after her birthday, not to see her again for years.

So, no. It couldn't matter. Because, if she did feel something for me, it would only end in me hurting her when I left. And if there was one hope I had in the life that only began as I stared into her eyes, it was that I would never cause her pain.

If she did feel something for me, therefore, I would have to be the one to reject it. Reject *her*. Know, in my mind, that she would eventually fall for someone else, without me there to limit her heart. As long as he made her happy...I could live with that. Love her from whatever distance she needed, even if that distance was right beside her as she loved *him*–whoever he might be.

I could do it, because it would be for her. And, as I'd decided while on my knees before her, I would be anything she needed me to be. If she ever decided she needed to be mine, however long it took, I would only be grateful. I only hoped she wouldn't mind, whenever she might make that choice, that I will have been hers all the while.

CONTINUE THE JOURNEY WITH
THROUGH THE TWISTED VINES

~

Keep reading for a sneak peek of chapter one!

1

SPLINTERED

Thea - Day 1

I wish I had summoning magic.

That's what I think about as I throw the dagger again at the opposite wall of my cabin aboard the *Burning Rose*. With a *thunk*, it sinks half an inch into the moisture-softened wood. And I walk across the small space to retrieve it. Again.

Aside from me and the dagger, the only other things in here are a bed with sheets that smell of saltwater, and a change of clothes. I still wear the skirt I'd swindled from the shopkeeper in Dahlih, the shirt with its cut-off sleeves, and, wrapped around my head, the plum-colored sash that belonged to a woman named Evie.

The dagger flies once more across the room. *Thunk.*

Yes, summoning magic would be helpful.

Or, *majick.*

My jaw clenches as I wrench the blade out of the wall. I don't know what to call myself anymore. What to call these—

these *things* that run through my blood, and give me the abilities to heal, and to break. Because, as I'd found out just about an hour ago, I am not a Mage, as I've believed all my life. I'm not even human.

I'm Fae.

Kind of.

My grip on the hilt tightens as I remember the conversation. How *she* had slunk back into the cabin she'd emerged from, while Atlas eyed me as though I was some beast about to lose control, and tear into him. With words, or with the blade I hold now, I couldn't be certain. I hadn't even been certain at that moment that I *wouldn't* attack him. That he–nor anyone– had thought to warn me that the woman whose life I'd been born to, and she to mine, was *here*. That facing my true heritage was going to be so immediately forced upon me.

Surprisingly, none of the animosity I held was for that woman. Emelina. If anything, I empathized with her; there was no feigning the shock, and wariness in those painfully familiar eyes when Atlas gave her my name. She hadn't known I would be joining them for their journey back to Eshelle anymore than I had.

No, all of my anger was reserved for those who had kept yet another secret *about* me *from* me. They'd tried to talk themselves out of it, of course. Ciaragen miraculously came down the steps mere seconds after Emelina introduced herself to me to help Atlas explain her presence. From there, they'd just dumped information on me, so many nervous words meant to distract me from the secrets they still kept.

And, damn me, but it had worked. I stood there and listened, my one ally a silent, solid force at my side, while they distracted me with selective truths.

What they chose to share, in their frenzy to tame whatever

they thought I might unleash in my anger, had been about the glamour placed upon me. The majick that has suppressed not only my natural appearance, but also the abilities that I'd been born with. *Everything* is dulled. No super hearing, or scenting, or sight. No Fae beauty, or arched ears. And no Fae-level majick.

That's not even the kicker, though.

No, one of the many reasons why I'm alone in my cabin throwing a knife at a wall, is that not only is this glamour on me–but not one of the oh-so-majickal Fae on this ship has the capability to remove it. The only one who can is the person who cast it. And she's not here. But maybe that's good.

Because one of the other–again, of several–reasons I'm in here by myself is that, when I'd been told all of this, I'd responded that I don't even know if I want it removed. I'd walked into the cabin and closed the door amid the stunned silence in the hallway.

I haven't been able to think about it logically yet. I'm sure that's what they hope I'm doing. Sorting it out in my head, as I have with almost every other damn thing that's happened over the past week. But I don't want to. I want to throw this dagger, and *not* think. Because, for the first time in days, I know what's going to happen next.

Nothing.

The *Burning Rose* cuts through the Evredis, the breeze and the wind majick of the Fae on deck carrying the ship across the sea. I can see the sun-gilded water through the porthole to my right. It splashes against the glass, and leaves behind droplets that then cascade in rivulets back whence they came.

Thunk.

Absolutely nothing will happen, for at least a moment. No life-or-death situations will arise. No life-changing secret will be revealed (I mean, what else could there possibly be at this point?). The ship will keep moving, and I will keep throwing, and that can be it. For at least a moment.

I wish that it could be longer. That I could have hours to myself, and do nothing but watch the sun run its golden course over the sea. Maybe I would sleep for some of that time. Maybe I would change into those stranger's clothes, and out of the ones stained with drops of Adathan's blood.

I might even wish not to be totally alone. But the only person I might have sought, the only one I know would give me that company *and* allow me that silence is down the hall, and my way to him is obstructed.

Obstructed by the two people I came in here to avoid. Who don't seem to be inclined to leave, regardless of the blade I've made obvious use of, and the even more obvious amount of time I've left them out there to argue.

I sigh, and throw one last time. *Thunk.* Then, pulling the blade out as I go and creating a splintered notch in the wood, I walk to the cabin door, and open it.

Atlas and Ciaragen stand there, their bodies facing each other while their faces are turned towards me. In the light streaming through the cabin portholes, and down through the ship deck prisms above us, I can see the surprise in their widened eyes. "Just because I don't have Fae hearing doesn't mean I can't hear you two whisper-screaming at each other out here," I tell them in their language.

Atlas composes himself first, moving to fully face me, his high cheekbones darkening. Ciaragen follows, and it's she who replies to me. "We just wanted to see...how you're doing." She softly clears her throat, and this female, who I doubt very much is prone to blushing, or fits of self-consciousness, experiences both now.

I furrow my brow. "Why should I be anything but alright?"

She sucks on the inside of her cheek, unsure of how to continue. Luckily, wonder-boy is on the job.

"You have no reason to be alright," Atlas says. "Everything you knew has changed, in a matter of days. The better question is, what can we do to help you?"

"Nothing." It's not meant to be rude, or stubborn. I'm not withholding a way they could 'help' me. There just isn't one. And I'm done adding frills to my words for the sake of propriety.

"Aly–"

"*Don't.*" I step into the hallway until I'm just a foot away from him. I look up into the face of the male who might still be my friend with my teeth barred. "*Ever.* Call me that."

Hurt flashes across his features, but he masks it in a heartbeat. He opens his mouth to say something else, but when words come, they're not from him.

"Is there a problem out here?" a familiar rumbling voice asks from down the hall. I don't turn, but Atlas and Ciaragen do, to watch as the male approaches, his footsteps silent despite his size.

"There is now," Ciaragen half-grumbles, half-growls at him.

It's quiet for a moment–long enough that I finally turn from Atlas to look at Adathan. I'd thought his eyes would be on Ciaragen, after her comment, but those irises the color of the sun on water rest on me with the same directness they have ever since their natural shade was revealed. In my periphery, I see Ciaragen shift in annoyance.

Then, he says, "I'm going to get some food. Would you like to come with me?"

It's probably the only question I don't have to think about before answering. I nod, and sheathe my dagger back under my skirt at my thigh. He walks through the male and female that stand between him and me, and they have little choice but to make room for him given the sheer size of him, and narrowness of the hall. Adathan gestures for me to go ahead of him, and I turn without a word or a glance at the others, disliking the coldness of the move, but not knowing what else to do.

Something within me just feels...other. Not one of them, but not me either. And maybe they mean well, but I find myself feeling things too similar to what and how I felt about Adathan three days ago. That until they came along, my life was fine. Great, even. And now it's not. In fact, so damn *not*, that the blonde hair still flowing to my waist in place of the black feels somehow comforting.

I'm not me, and I'm not them. My feelings about that make too little sense to even begin to sort through. The one thing I've been able to establish any certainty over is that I resent Ciaragen, and Atlas. They were in my home, and for what? To protect me? No matter how much I hate myself for it–in a long list of things I already hate myself for–I find myself angry at their failure. They were in my home, and *for what*? I still got kidnapped, and beaten. My friends are still dead. My mother is still *dead*.

In the woods of Cerasche I'd had so much time, trekking through the endless pines. So much time to think about what I felt about Adathan's betrayal, and sort out what it really meant to me. From that thinking, I realized that I blamed him, if only to keep some of the burden from myself. I came to know that, regardless of his position, his work, his very existence, Olin would have found me. The only thing that would be different if Adathan did not exist would be that I would now be on a ship with Olin, instead of without him.

Adathan had allowed me silence. That time to think, without being questioned, or consoled, or pitied. And maybe Atlas and Ciaragen believe the hour I had to myself was enough time to do some more thinking. The problem is, as I recognized before, that I don't want to do it anymore. So, where I could make the same conclusions about them as I have about the male striding up the stairs behind me–that I would be in this position regardless of their action or lack thereof–I haven't. And I don't want to put in the work to try just yet.

My hands clench into fists at my sides as I step out into the mid- afternoon sun. I make way for Adathan behind me, and find Atlas, then Ciaragen following him. My jaw tightens, and bright gold eyes lock with mine two steps from the top. I watch his chest rise as he pulls a breath in through his nose, and then his lips part as he breathes out. I almost roll my eyes, but instead I find myself copying him.

When my exhale is finished, I say, "Your breath still stinks."

One corner of his mouth just barely lifts. "Right back at you, sweetheart," he replies, which has a bit of humor relieving the remaining tightness in my chest. Then a throat clears from behind him, and I remember that the other two are trapped in the stairway, Adathan's frame blocking the exit.

He ignores them, holding my gaze until I nod once. He returns it, then steps up and moves aside. Atlas gives me a slightly wider berth than necessary as Ciaragen comes up, deep blue eyes on Adathan. The male moves first, clearly leading us to the mess hall that I'm sure my walking buddy intended to find with only his super-smelling-Fae powers. But the female doesn't budge an inch until Adathan falls into step behind me.

As Atlas moves through the deck and down another set of stairs, I'm intrigued in spite of myself as I watch the crew make way for him–one even jumps back down the stairs when he sees Atlas about to descend. They smile at him, and greet him by name, which he returns, not stumbling over a single male.

As we approach the mess, I hear the sounds of several deep voices, and forks scraping against plates. But when we reach the bottom of the stairs, me behind Atlas, and Adathan behind me–silence.

The part of me that's been trained to be a princess of a continent lifts her chin, and straightens her already-straight shoulders in the face of the judgment she feels weighing on her. But I don't avert my eyes from theirs, as I would have just a week ago. No, I look at each one of them, leveling cool stares and terse nods to males whose irises are brown, and blue, and even eyes that are wholly black. Faeries.

I keep my expression relaxed, but my stupid human-bred heart isn't as easily controlled. It thumps hard in my chest, and I know that all the keen ears in the room can hear it. Still, I don't lower my chin or my eyes, even as I watch some of the expressions in the room turn mocking.

Then growls sound from both in front of and behind me, and the sources of all those gazes become very interested in the table tops. Meanwhile, the sources of the growls continue with me towards the counter. Observing the perhaps two dozen males currently in the room, I'm able to note the difference between the gazes lowered in deference to Atlas, and in fear of Adathan.

The cook is already pouring stew into wooden bowls, and he sets them on the counter with webbed fingers once filled. His skin is the most interesting combination of dark and light blues, and though his irises are overlarge, they're a pretty silver that's bright even in the dim light provided by the portholes in the wall.

But another set of silver eyes flash in my mind when I open my mouth to thank the faerie for the food. Hanna's face, as it had been when I'd seen it last–pale, frightened, and still–clouds my vision. So, my thanks passes my lips in only a whisper. The cook dips his chin in acknowledgement, his throat bobbing as he takes in the male at my back.

Then I hear some muffled chuckles from the others in the mess, because of course they think fear softened my voice, instead of grief. And, that quickly, all other emotion is chased away by anger.

I will *not* be afraid of these males. I will *not* let them stifle me. Instead, I allow a single ember of the burning rage within me to escape as I turn toward the sound, shifting my expression into a mask of boredom.

At one of the several rectangular wooden tables scattered throughout the mess sit a faerie and two Fae males, still grinning, shoulders shaking with their mirth. My bowl of stew in hand, I stride over to them, the heels of my boots clicking with each step. Surprise takes the place of some of the humor in their expressions, and two of them straighten in their seats on the long benches set on either side of the table. I don't stop my approach, my boots scraping and clicking through the lazy steps I take until I'm just a foot from the only male still slouching.

I take a bite of the stew, and suck on the spoon a bit as I pull it from my mouth. It's much better than I'd dared to hope for—hearty, and flavorful. I chew and swallow the bite, and still their eyes don't leave mine until I ask, "Something funny?"

The faerie shakes his bald blue head, and one of the Fae even lowers his eyes to the table after doing the same. But the other, with closely shorn black hair, and blue eyes paler than the early morning sky, looks me up and down. Slowly.

I hear a shuffling from behind me, but don't turn to see its source, and neither does he. I give him a half-grin, and purr, "What are you looking at?"

The room around us is utterly silent. Not my companions, nor the other males in the hall, seem to be so much as breathing too loudly. I set my bowl down, and take another bite. My cut-off shirt shifts around my breasts as I lean down, and even with my nonexistent experience in the area, I know that's desire that begins to brim in the male's otherwise baleful eyes.

Then he finally speaks. "To answer both of your questions: you."

I smile wider, allowing it to appear real; pleased that this oh-so-handsome male is looking at *me*. "Oh, yeah? And what's so funny about me, sailor?"

He turns where he sits at the end of the bench, opening his legs as he does so. "Nothing, anymore," he replies, his voice low.

"And, why is that?" I lean down further, so that my eyes are only slightly above his.

"Well, because now I'm thinking about fucking you until you forget any of the human filth you've had so far."

I give a throaty chuckle, able to guess what the new Divani word means by the sentence surrounding it, and disregard another small sound of movement behind me. The male smirks, happy to be holding my complete attention. "Mmm," I half-sigh, half-say. "There's only one *small* problem there."

"What's that?" he asks, not even attempting to be inconspicuous as those blue eyes take in my chest. While he's otherwise occupied, I knock my remaining stew into his lap.

He shouts, almost moving to stand up. But, faster than I've ever moved, faster even than Adathan had trained me to be yesterday in the woods, I pull my dagger from its sheath, where I'd been reaching for it as I leaned down, and down. At the same time, I flick the blade he'd kept on the hip he'd so willingly exposed to me out of its holster. The former is at his throat, the latter at his balls, before he's able to rise an inch off the bench.

"Hard to fuck if you've got no balls, isn't it?" I ask, giving him a sweeter-than-sugar smile. "Even harder—no pun intended–if your throat's cut open. Wouldn't you say?" I tilt my head, and let the grin fall.

He doesn't nod, doesn't even dare to speak with how close the blade is to his carotid, though his eyes burn with fury. "I thought so." My brow furrows. "Adathan?" I call, not moving my gaze or my blades from the male before me.

The familiar rough bass says from behind me, "Yes?"

"Our rule on winning weapons–does it apply to all Fae?"

"It does." I think I hear humor in that voice.

A corner of my mouth kicks up in the first real show of a positive emotion since this encounter began. "Just checking." I drop my hands, and the weapons in them, to my sides, and back up a step. As anticipated, the male stands quickly–so quickly he rocks the table, and the bench he sat on rolls onto its side–and his own dagger is once again at his groin before the fist he has half-raised can find its mark.

I click my tongue. "Now, let's not get off on the wrong foot. Finish that move, and I believe you wouldn't be able to get off on much of anything anymore." In emphasis, I press the blade in just enough that it knicks his trousers.

Though the loathing and rage in his eyes persists, he pales. His jaw strains, and he stares at me hard for another moment before backing up, and turning to stride quickly through the mess, and up the stairs.

Once he's gone, I look at his two compatriots. Their eyes are wide, but otherwise they give no response to my action against their friend. So I say, "I apologize for disturbing your meal." Then I turn back to my own companions.

Adathan and Atlas are slightly further from the counter than they'd been when I approached the male. Adathan stands in front of Atlas, looking too much like a barrier to reaching me for it to have been anything else. His smirk is subdued, but those golden eyes are far more bright.

In the gray eyes, however, lies disbelief–like he doesn't recognize the person I am now–which does something to my heart. I turn from him before that look can further harm what I might have dared to give him just days ago.

"I hope that wasn't anyone important," I say to them with false bravado, tossing my hair over a shoulder.

And Ciaragen, who's been still this whole time, tips her head back, and laughs.

ACKNOWLEDGMENTS

In Beds of Flowers may have taken the blood, sweat, and tears of my characters to bring to life, but all it took on my end was:

The realization that there's no age limit on when you can start pursuing your dream

A whole lot of patience

Five drafts

Countless meals at my desk

The car rides where I came up with some of my favorite scenes

And the most important people in my life

To Mike, who was this book's first fan. The man who, when I said "I think I'm going to write a book", didn't hesitate to support me, despite the fact that I hadn't written since my creative writing class in ninth grade. The man who then built me a computer, so that I wouldn't have to work on my small MacBook screen anymore. And the man who has supported me in every moment since April 2, 2023, when I first began to put this story in ink.

My love, you are my favorite person. I could not have done this without you, and I am so grateful that I'll never have to.

For a long time, I kept *In Beds of Flowers* a secret from almost everyone else in my life. Not out of embarrassment, or even any kind of desire to avoid the possible judgment. But because I was doing it for me. I was finally reawakening the creative part of myself, after the years of corporate work had largely put it to rest. Truly, that the idea became a draft, and the draft became something I could actually *see* in the hands of readers was a surprise. Now that we're here, though, I wouldn't change a thing.

Know only this: *In Beds of Flowers* wasn't originally born out of a desire to be a best selling author. It was of a soul-deep nourishment that came from doing something I'd forgotten I loved, for only the sake of itself.

I have been privileged enough to be able to dedicate time to such a thing; the making of art for enjoyment, rather than livelihood. I worked full-time throughout, don't get me wrong. That, combined with Mike's consistent, never-fucking-ending work ethic, brought me the ability to write for pleasure, rather than purpose.

The thing is, though, that I couldn't have done any of this if I were not the product of my parents–who are only allowed to read this section of the book. Mike has made me believe in myself for over seven years, and I seriously cannot overstate how much his support has brought about the completion of this book. But, before him, there was them. And there was what they taught me. Which, of course, was many things, but two in particular contributed to where *In Beds of Flowers* is now. Being: the determination it takes to start something, and finish it; and the bravery it takes to pursue that thing, even when it's not easy.

My mom worked two jobs for most of my childhood and adolescence. Things were not easy for a long time, but what should never be mistaken is that difficulty does not detract from abundance. Not here. In our house, there was an abundance of love. Of effort. Of singing silly songs with made up words.

Then, when I was seventeen, she got cancer.

What anyone who's made it this far into the acknowledgements needs to know is that she is now fifty-seven, and annoyingly gorgeous and perky. But that line was not without purpose. Because, after surgeries and complete remission, she started to volunteer at the same hospital in which she was treated. And then, at forty-eight years old, she decided to get her nursing degree.

Mom, I forgive you for using me to practice your blood draws because my "veins are terrible." Because I never get sick of how proud I feel when I tell people how you got into nursing, and how amazing you are at it today.

Then there's my dad, who *also* worked (at least) two jobs for most of my childhood and adolescence. Another house where things were not easy, but that should never be taken to mean that they weren't good. Great. The house that gave me and my brother two of our best friends. The house that, even when it moved to Virginia, was one of my favorite places to be, because of course it was never about the house. But the people I loved within it.

My dad still works two jobs. But, a few years ago, one of those jobs became his own painting business. He claims, in front of family and friends, to be about twenty years younger than he is–and, in the same breath, will say my stepmom is actually from BC times. But what everyone knows, including him, is that he started his own painting business in his fifties.

Dad, you're so fucking cool. And I can say that because I remember how proud you looked when I hit my knee on the truck door and said "Fuck!" in front of you for the first time.

With ALL of that being said, I think the opening is understood. In their own ways, both of my parents showed me what it looked like to do something hard, and finish it anyway. But there is a huge purpose to those stories that I'll conclude with: timelines mean *shit*.

Start nursing school in your forties. Start your own business in your fifties. *Write your first freaking book* at twenty-eight. Do whatever the hell you want *whenever* the hell you want. Because, at the end of it all, you can either be amazed that you did it, or disappointed that you didn't even try. And there is no age limit on being amazed by yourself.

Or by the people around you. Speaking of which, finally, I have to thank just a few more people who encouraged me along the way.

Val, my amazing cover artist. Hannah and Sam, my editors. Thank you for helping me to make this book as beautiful as you all are.

Finally: Jess, Amanda, Erin, Julia, Brittany, and Sarah. Boss bitches all around. Thank you, and I love you.

ABOUT THE AUTHOR

Jess was born and raised on Long Island, NY. She may not live there anymore, but she will always talk with her hands, and drive like a New Yorker because of it.

She has a degree in health sciences, hence the partiality towards using that knowledge in Althea's points of view. She took creative writing in high school, shortly after the Twilight/Hunger Games/ Divergent craze, and even started writing a bit herself in her free time. But, those journals have long since been lost, hidden, or thrown away.

This is her debut novel, which she wrote after her shifts in her corporate job nearly every day, and more on the weekends while her husband played video games beside her. She lives with him, their dog, and their baby boy–who is currently napping on her as she makes this final edit to the final draft of In Beds of Flowers.

For signed copies, custom bookmarks and stickers, and prints of your favorite characters, visit authorjesslayne.com

Find canon and headcanon scenes on Jess's Patreon! Canon scenes include Adathan's and Atlas's POVs of events previously only given in Thea's POV. If you're interested in finding out more about our Hielo and Hiela, and how their relationship progressed, take a look at the mini series "SanaDeo" (SFW and NSFW scenes included).

Get the latest information on TCT and upcoming books on Jess's Instagram, and follow her page on Facebook (Author Jess Layne)!

Be the first to see book covers, learn pub dates, receive ARC applications, etc. by joining Jess's email list. Go to her website, and fill out the quick popup!

Instagram, Pinterest, and Patreon: @ authorjesslayne
    Facebook: Author Jess Layne